"This room must have been your haven," Eleanor said. "After your parents...neither Dorothea nor Lilianna would have dared to redecorate this private sanctuary."

"And somehow they resisted all these years? They must have been tempted—look at all this stuff. And I wonder how they kept Wayne out. I can't believe he would have been able to keep his hands off all these old records and other things. They must be worth something."

"To teenage boys, perhaps. There's not a lot of interest in high school yearbooks, or picture frames engraved with the date of the Eastfield High School Senior Prom. Which, I notice, doesn't contain a picture."

He nodded, and took a few steps closer to her. "That's why I was going through the yearbook. I don't seem to have any other pictures of the old days."

"That may be a good thing. The big hair, the oversized glasses. The years may all be better forgotten," Eleanor said uneasily, and took a step backwards. "We were all so young, so unformed. We scarcely understood what we wanted."

"Oh, I understood what I wanted. I just wasn't sure how to get it." He gazed unblinkingly at her, leaving her with no doubt what he was talking about. "I'm still not sure how to get it, but I've had a lot more practice."

Though he wore his heavy work boots, his steps were light and quick when he finally cornered her, and took her in his arms and kissed her.

Thrifty Means

by

Sharon Sobel

Dear Elinor,
With very best
wishes,
Sharon Sobel

THRIFTY MEANS

Cover Art by Angela Anderson

The Wild Rose Press
PO Box 708
Adams Basin, NY 14410-0706
Visit us at www.thewildrosepress.com

Publishing History
First Last Rose of Summer Edition, 2010
Print ISBN 1-60154-682-3

Published in the United States of America

Dedication

To my nieces and nephews:

Kate Joanna Popa
Jonathan Marshall Popa
Sarah Victoria Kolodny
Justin Brian Kolodny

Though you're still in the early chapters of your books, they're already filled with adventure, discovery, enthusiasm, and the enduring love of friends and family.

Prologue

*"There's history behind every book, every bowl,
every scratch and ink stain on an old desk."*
Lucille Armitage, Antiques Appraiser

When the first killing temperatures of autumn
delivered a layer of delicate ice onto the pumpkins
standing sentry at the front doors of every home in
Eastfield, Connecticut, even the most optimistic
souls finally admitted summer was over. Labor Day
made it official, of course, but lingering glimpses
back to the heady days of July and August remained
tantalizing until the night frost of October. Until
then, woody impatiens still thrived in stone planters,
and overripe tomatoes dropped off their stems onto
the soil, splattering seeds holding the promise for
the following spring. But first winter would come.

"Can you roll up the window?" Ellie asked as she
crossed her aching arms over her worn Fair Isle
sweater. "I'm freezing in here!"

Her companion, a new driver, dared to look
away from the winding road for the briefest moment.

"If you weren't wearing a stupid little skirt,
you'd feel fine," Missy said. "Anyway, you're in my
car and I'm driving, and I like to have the windows
open. The air smells good."

"It smells like smoke. And I'm wearing the
stupid skirt because that's what you wear when you
play field hockey."

Missy slowed nearly to a stop as they rounded a
broad curve in the road. "Oh, like you didn't decide
to play field hockey just so you can wear the skirt."

She tooted the horn, though Ellie didn't see anything moving anywhere near them.

Ellie smiled, and stretched her legs as far as the small car would allow Her shins were bruised and a little scabby, but the hours spent working at a day camp all summer left her with a tan disguising the worst of it. Daily workouts with the team, even one boasting the worst record in southwest Connecticut, gave her lean and smooth muscles. She wondered how they'd look in black tights, and what sort of Halloween costume she could manage to put together, both revealing and acceptable to wear to school.

"A black cat," she said, suddenly.

Missy jammed on the brakes, and Ellie was thrust towards the windshield. The seatbelt dug into her sore shoulder, but held her back from any real harm.

"Where?!" Missy cried. A car approached behind them, slowed and honked its horn, and then went around them.

Ellie blinked at her. "Where, what?"

"The black cat. Oh, God, did I hit her? If she's under the tires, I will never touch this car again. What if she belongs to someone? I'll lose my license. Maybe she ran off? Did you see?"

Ellie was grateful for the fading light. She tucked her shaking hands under her bare thighs, and took several deep breaths. She felt like an idiot.

"I think she ran off," she lied. "Maybe she was heading towards the reservoir."

Ellie looked out the window towards the gentle wooded embankment, and saw the double exposure of her reflection over Missy's in the tinted glass. It was a study of contrasts. Missy's straight hair was cropped short and was so pale as to appear white; her pale blue eyes were often protected behind sunglasses. Ellie's thick brown hair could only be managed if she tied it back, so she grew it long and kept a fine assortment of clips and ribbons in all her pockets. Her eyes were hazel and almond-shaped, and rarely missed a thing. Missy's small frame was perfectly comfortable in her little car, while Ellie felt cramped and stifled.

The girls became friends on their first day of kindergarten, when Missy approached Ellie for help in getting onto the playground swings, thinking the tall girl was an older, worldly first grader.

"Well, that's not good," Missy said, and cautiously continued along the road.

"What?" Ellie asked, startled.

"The cat," Missy said, distracted by the series of sharp curves in the road.

"Because she's going to the reservoir? Maybe she lives there, in one of the old houses," Ellie said, trying to sound very logical. The old houses were the ruins of family estates appropriated by the state many years before, so the land could be flooded and a water source would be available for those without wells. For as long as most people could remember, the stone and brick piles were the places where the kids in the town could hang out, engaging in activities usually illegal. Eastfield didn't have a teen center, but none of the kids in town protested.

"No. It's not good a black cat walked in front of us. It's bad luck, especially before Halloween," Missy said. "I hope it doesn't mean I'll fail my English midterm."

"I hope it doesn't mean I'll fail my road test," Ellie groaned, forgetting for a moment there was no black cat, and the whole thing was a stupid superstition anyway. She had a black cat, for heaven's sake. And Midnight walked in front of her all the time.

"Oh, you'll be just fine." Missy managed to sound very mature, very reassuring. But she had three month's advantage over Ellie, who only just turned sixteen. And she had her own new car, whereas Ellie would have to share an aging Chevy with her older brother. "There's really nothing to it."

They were through the woods and making their slow way through the valley of the Belvedere River. Here, the last shreds of sunlight had already disappeared, and the air felt frigid and the darkness oppressive.

"Should you turn on your headlights?" Ellie asked, realizing she could scarcely see a thing in front of them.

"The manual says headlights go on fifteen minutes before sunset. And sunset is at 5:18. I checked."

Ellie wasn't sure about the rule or the time, but she did know if a real black cat suddenly crossed the path of the Honda, they'd never see her.

"Doesn't it matter if the sun goes down earlier?" she asked. She pulled her hands out from under her, and pressed one palm against the dashboard.

Missy turned towards her and smiled, looking away from the winding road for just a moment too long.

****

Evan Zane slumped down in the back seat of his father's station wagon, and pulled the collar of his varsity jacket up over his ears. He wondered if part of his punishment was to hear his parents arguing incessantly over every possible aspect of their lives. They disagreed about everything, he realized, except for their politics and their son.

On their son, they were in absolute agreement. He failed his history midterm, and they decided to ground him for a month. His new Jeep rotted in the garage, and he couldn't go out on Friday and Saturday nights. He would miss the homecoming dance, a Sweet Sixteen, and a few Halloween parties. He was allowed to play football, for his parents were nothing if not team players. They just couldn't play on the same team.

Though he tried to shut it out, their argument of the day was about putting in a new lawn in place of a meadow at their farm. His mother wanted the meadow to stay, pleading the case of the wildflowers and the small animals living among them. His father wanted grass, perhaps even a putting green. But almost certainly something Evan would have to mow on a Saturday, when his friends were heading to the beach.

"And I called the tutoring center," Marianne Zane said.

Evan shrugged out of his collar, but remained in his dark corner.

"He doesn't need a damn tutoring center, charging us fifty bucks an hour! He needs to study. He's just lazy!" Mark Zane shouted.

"He needs a tutor more than you need an idiotic putting green!" Marianne shouted back. She had turned her head so she could see Evan, which made everything ten times worse.

Evan wasn't sure why he couldn't get a handle in his reading courses, but he knew what he needed. He needed to get away from home, and go to college. He needed to get away.

They passed the shortcut to the reservoir, a long rutted road once serving as the driveway to a grand estate. He thought his great grandfather might have been the gardener on the estate, or one very near. He had loved to listen to the old man's stories about the year the land was flooded, when farms and stone walls were submerged beneath the rushing waters. With a sort of perverse Puritan pride, Graham Zane retold the legend of how his elderly Zane cousins refused to leave their home, and drowned when the waters came. In the spirit of all the best ghost stories, their bodies were never recovered.

Evan nodded, silently vowing that if he ever got out of this place, they wouldn't recover his body either.

"Are you listening to me?" his mother shouted. His father swerved around a corner, kicking up loose gravel. "Evan!"

"What?" Evan said crossly.

"You're starting tutoring next week, every day before school starts."

"Before football practice? When do I have to get there? Five or six?"

"Five thirty," his mother said, with an expression daring him to defy her.

Maybe being grounded wasn't such a bad thing; he hadn't been getting to sleep so early since he was in third grade.

"Who's going to take me?" he asked.

For one blessed moment, there was nothing but silence in the car. Outside, the wind rustled through the brown and gold leaves, and a duet of dogs—or coyotes—were howling. A car honked its horn.

"Mark?" his mother asked.

"Me? I'm not the one who sits around staring at a typewriter all day. Someone's gotta support this family." The car moved faster, almost certainly too fast for a frosty night on a winding road, Evan thought.

"Well, I'm not getting up so early. Why don't you just call Margaret to drive him? She took care of your brother's little problem, maybe she'll take care of yours," Marianne said, under her breath. Evan wasn't sure he heard her, or what it meant, but the air in the car seemed as frigid as the air outside.

"Maybe I should just sleep over at the tutoring place," he suggested, trying to thaw the tension. "You can drop me off the night before and leave me there. You'd save a lot on food. And you can yell at each other all night, and not worry about waking me up."

Evan knew he had gone too far, but when his father cursed and said something about Uncle Pete, he wanted to hear more. He unclipped his seat belt, and leaned forward, his head between the two neck supports of the front seats.

"Whaddya say, Dad?" he asked.

Mark Zane's hand reached up and grabbed Evan by the collar, pulling him even closer. He turned his head, so his mouth was inches away from Evan's ear. Evan understood this only vaguely, for he watched the road, and wondered what blocked the road ahead of them and reflected the beam of their headlights.

Too late, he realized it was another car.

****

Ellie recognized the moment she died and went to heaven, for she was far too cold to be in hell. A whisper of air tickled her ear as she ascended and the faint dripping of water echoed close to her ear. When she tried to raise her arms to see if she already had the wings of an angel, she realized she was stuck and not at all comfortable.

She opened her eyes.

Wherever she was, it was not yet the road to heaven. The air was brutally cold, and she was twisted into a very tight place with scarcely enough air to breath. Her head hurt and something stabbed her just above her knee. Her bare leg ached, covered with something soothing and damp. Everything was over, she considered. Her stupid life was over, and she never even got her drivers' license. Or got to make love.

She sat where she was, waiting to see a bright light beckoning her to wherever.

Someone cried out, in pain and fear.

Missy! She forgot about Missy!

Abandoning her wait for the bright light, which was taking too long anyway, she struggled to move her arms.

Several moments passed before she realized where she was and why she was held captive.

She still sat in her half of the Honda, though her legs were pushed together so tightly her knees were up near her chest. Her left hand should have been resting on the seat beside her, but was dangling in the cold air. There was no seat beside her; there was no other half of the car beside her. Painfully, she turned her head and took in the sight of the wreckage of Missy's side of the car. As certain as Ellie knew she was alive, she knew her best friend was dead.

Ellie twisted and slid down into where the driver's side of the car was only moments ago, and released her seat belt before the nylon band strangled her. She proved to be higher off the ground than she supposed, and would have fallen if she hadn't grasped the wires dangling from the splintered dashboard. She landed unsteadily on her feet, hugged herself for warmth and comfort and courage, and realized she ought to find Missy, just in case.

When she turned, she stumbled and fell onto the road. Broken glass, like a million sharp pebbles, cut into her palms and knees, and she said a word she never would have used at home. Crawling her way through the wreckage, her path lit by a beam almost certainly not illuminating the pathway to heaven, she approached the pile of twisted metal.

Someone cried out again, and Ellie lifted her head, like a dog on the scent. The cold air dried the sweat on her face, and she sniffed the woodsy odor of logs burning in distant homes. Then she smelled something else, acrid and closer. The cry broke through the dark night.

Scrambling to her feet, she looked towards the light and for the first time, realized another car lay upon the road, one headlight aimed towards her, and the other eerily towards the sky. The front of the car was smashed, and the whole thing was on its side. She approached cautiously, slipping in something oily on the road, and the smoke grew thicker here.

In its haze, and with the light flickering on the cracked glass, Ellie had the impression something was moving in the wreck. She glimpsed it again, and realized a face—a familiar one, somehow—pressed against the broken windshield.

She recognized him. And he was alive.

Ignoring her pain and the dangers around her, she climbed onto the car, finding footholds on the fender, the headlight, and grabbing onto the windshield wiper. When the plastic snapped off in her hand, she grasped the door handle, which held her. Soon she was atop the car, balancing as she would on a slippery raft on a lake. She bent down to pull on the handle but could do little. Who ever imagined a car door would be so heavy?

Unexpectedly, the door started to open towards her, and she pulled with every bit of strength she could summon. Two arms emerged, a head, a torso in a tattered shirt.

"Help me," a man said, as Ellie wrestled with the door, and took off her sneaker to prop it open. She caught him under his arms, startled to feel how warm he was against her body. "The car's burning," he said.

"I know," she said, bending as he twisted to pull himself out of the car.

"We've got to get out of here."

He stood beside her, very tall and large. Blood covered his face. As he opened his eyes, he caught hold of her shoulders, peered into her face.

"Oh, you're Evan Zane," Ellie said, dazedly.

"You're not a man."

He shook her, gently. "And if we don't get the hell out of here, I'm never going to be." He dropped his hands to her waist and, without warning, jumped off the car, pulling her along. They fell together onto the pavement, and Ellie wasn't sure if the loud crack was one of her bones or his. "Come, quick."

Evan Zane dragged her to the side of the road, ignoring whatever nonsense she babbled. They slid together into a drainage ditch and fell onto a bed of cold, wet leaves and goodness knows what else. As flames spread across the road, they huddled together, listening to the approach of sirens in the dark night.

Chapter 1

"Just when your stock—and your energy—is completely depleted, a treasure comes through the door."

Miriam Pell, volunteer since 1948

Eleanor Gilmartin held the Betsy Ross cup up to the light, not looking for flaws on the shiny surface, but for a way to get out of an awkward situation. An elderly woman, dressed far too warmly for a late May day, watched her, her hands clasped in expectation.

"What do you think, dear?" the woman asked. "The cup is a family treasure, at least a hundred years. My mother saved it from the floods of '55, and I saved it from the hurricane in '85. My grandmother told us Betsy Ross kept her pins safe within when she made the flag. No tomatoes for her!"

Eleanor glanced at her friend Liza, who could barely smother her laughter.

"It's a lovely little cup, Mrs. Detworth, and has such a wonderful history." Eleanor paused, still searching for the words she must say. "But I'm sure Betsy Ross wasn't lucky enough to ever own it. 'Made in Taiwan' is written on the underside. Do you see, here?"

Maria Detworth snatched the worthless cup from Eleanor's hand.

"What do you girls know, anyway? I should have brought the cup to Wayland Antiques in the first place, instead of wasting my time with you! You're just a bunch of volunteers, after all!" She turned towards the door, but Margaret Brownlee blocked her path, even more imperious than usual.

"I will not have my volunteers insulted, Maria," she said softly. "You can go to any antique shop in New England, and you won't find a more knowledgeable group than the women of The Thrifty Means. Take your cup to Wayland, and if Michael offers to pay as much as for any china cup made in the last twenty-five years, I hope you'll have the sense and decency to hold your tongue. And, for once, admit you're wrong."

Mrs. Brownlee stepped aside, and Maria Detworth pushed her way past her, nearly dropping the cup in the doorway.

"Oh, goodness! If she dropped the damned thing, would she have sued The Thrifty Means for damages?" Liza asked, still laughing.

Mrs. Brownlee shrugged. "I'm sure we could have paid her for the value of the cup from the cash box. Twenty-five cents, perhaps?"

"Thank you for defending us, Mrs. B. Though I'm sure I wouldn't want to challenge any of the local antique dealers to a trivia game," Eleanor said.

Mrs. Brownlee waved her hand dismissively. "Trust me; most of them make it up as they go along. I've seen everything. And I've been around long enough to know Maria Detworth has never been right about anything."

Eleanor lifted a dusty carton from the front desk, and tested the weight on her left knee before she tried to move to the back room. It was a defensive instinct born of habit, the result of many months of physical therapy after an accident suffered when she was just a kid. But the carton wasn't too heavy for her to manage comfortably.

"I'm sorry to hear that, Mrs. B. No one has called me a 'girl' in years, and I kind of liked it. Hanging around with Mrs. Detworth might be good for my ego," she said.

"You're a sorry woman if you need a nutty old bat like Maria Detworth to boost your ego," Liza said, and reached for one end of the carton.

"I'll remind you, girls, she and I were in school together. Our families were among the first settlers in Eastfield." Mrs. B. smiled, and Eleanor guessed she was remembering a time before traffic tied up Norwell Road, before the supermarkets and chain stores distilled the unique character of the town. "But Maria was always a little nutty."

Liza smiled over the carton at Eleanor, as the two of them edged through the narrow main aisle of the shop.

"What did she mean about Betsey Ross' tomatoes?" Liza asked. "I never heard she was a gardener."

"I suppose they all were at the time. But that's not what she meant. In the old days, craftspeople stuck their pins and needles into ripe tomatoes; I think the acid kept the metal from rusting. The most popular design for a pincushion is still a tomato. It's one of those things everyone recognizes, but no one thinks about," Eleanor said.

Over Liza's shoulder, Mrs. B. nodded approvingly, like the proud teacher she trained to be many, many years before. She taught only a few years before she married, but throughout her life managed to maintain both the voice of authority and the manner of a schoolmistress. Her thin gray hair was always neatly tucked into a bun and her posture remained rigid and a bit intimidating. She dressed as if she might go off to High Tea in the afternoon, and not for the work of unpacking dusty cartons and old dishes. But she looked upon her casually dressed and cheerful group of volunteers with a great deal of affection.

"You are the smartest women in the business,"

Mrs. B. said. "If you ever go head to head against any of the professional dealers, my money would be on you."

"I'm glad we saved the twenty-five cents on the cup," Liza said under her breath. "That might be all the risk you'd want to take!"

****

"This is a big collection of garbage," Eleanor said, and tried to brush blue lint off her white sweater. "What is this stuff?"

Liza flicked a speck of blue onto her fingernail. "I don't think anthrax comes in colors. I bet this grit is from the polyester blouse on the counter."

Eleanor lifted the vintage garment and a shower of blue grains hit the tiled surface. "Oh, for goodness sakes! I didn't know polyester biodegrades!"

"Why should cheap fabric be different from anything else? Now I bet you're thinking about going home and cleaning out your closet. In case leisure suits and hot pants ever come back into style, I'm sure I have something in my basement you can borrow."

Eleanor used her hand to sweep the counter, and was rewarded with a blue palm.

"Why would your clothes fare better than mine? And, anyway, there's nothing in my closet older than ten years. When I moved here after my divorce, I wanted to start fresh. I threw out everything reminding me of that sh....of my husband."

"But you kept the kids. Good thinking."

"It wasn't easy. I didn't have a steady income—still don't—and had no idea how everything would work out. But thanks to Harriet Tubman, we were able to buy our house here in town."

"You're going to have to explain yourself, you know. Did she leave you her sewing needles or some other treasure?" Liza rolled her eyes.

"Even better. I was working on a historical novel

based on her life and researching old houses in the area, checking out some of the places with reputed vestiges of the Underground Railroad in their root cellars. I had to move quickly to get into the house on Milkweed Lane because it was for sale, and there were rumors a developer wanted to buy the place as a tear down."

"So what else is new? I hear a developer made an offer to David North, for Shaker Hill Farm."

"He'll probably jump at the offer. I don't see how he can even make enough money to pay his taxes." Eleanor paused, thinking she ought to stop at his farm stand more often. "But I got a decent advance on the Harriet Tubman book, and used it to put a down payment on the house. I used every other penny I made on the book to make the place livable. The hiding place in the root cellar might have been the last improvement made before then."

"But it's a sweet home, Eleanor."

"And dear Harriet Tubman started me on a writing career. Anne Hutchinson, Dolley Madison, and Mary Todd are all members of the club, now."

"But not Betsy Ross. If you had only done your homework on her, you would have appreciated the value of Mrs. Detworth's family heirloom."

Since Eleanor was happy to forget the little scene in the front of the shop, she did no more than shake her head, and concentrate on the contents of the box. The blue shirt was the packing material for several plates, and they proved to be little better in quality. Chips and crazing marred the surface of what had once been fine china, and Eleanor wasn't sure they remained sufficiently waterproof to serve the last possible use of all broken plates: as water trays under flower pots. Beyond such use, there was nothing.

Liza unwrapped a mug, minus a handle. Eleanor retrieved a little ball attached to a wire, and hadn't a clue what it was. A customer walked by the table and, familiar with the casual atmosphere of The Thrifty Means, examined a cracked tray.

"It's all garbage," Eleanor repeated. "Why would someone waste her time putting this stuff away, just for us to unpack?"

"Because she can't bear to throw something away? Because she believes there's always a use for something, even a used teabag?"

"Or a plastic soda cap?" the customer offered. Eleanor and Liza looked at her in disbelief. "Don't laugh, my sister uses them to make jewelry. She does a good business at craft shows."

As she walked away, Liza muttered, "Or crap shows."

Eleanor laughed. "Oh, have a heart! If people didn't like old and slightly useless things, The Thrifty Means wouldn't be in business."

"If we continue to get junk like this, The Thrifty Means won't be in business!" Liza retorted.

"Now, girls, don't argue," Mrs. B. said, as she came up behind them. "I'm sure we're going to get some interesting things soon. The McConnells are moving to Houston and Mary wants to get rid of all her country things so she can redecorate in Southwestern style. The college kids will be coming home soon, and their mothers will make them clean out their rooms. And since we've lost poor Dorothea Zane this spring, I'm going to hope we'll be getting a lot of her things as well."

"But doesn't your cousin still live in the house?" Eleanor asked, hoping she wasn't being too forward about a living arrangement that made some of the old-timers a little uncomfortable.

"Lilianna," Mrs. B. said, frowning. "She does, but the house still belongs to the nephew, who's let his aunt live there all these years. He's been in New York, and has had no interest in the place since that accident killed his parents. People say it was his fault."

"But they don't know, do they?" Eleanor asked. She couldn't imagine why she sprang to his defense, since he had had no interest in her either, but she hated gossip and innuendo.

"It doesn't matter," Mrs. B. said, and was probably right. "What does matter is Garland is still his house, and he probably won't be as generous to Lilianna and Wayne."

"Who's Wayne?" Liza asked. Eleanor looked at her in surprise and then remembered the Silvers only moved to town five years before. In sorting out the affairs of Eastfield, it certainly was an asset to be a townie such as herself.

Mrs. B. frowned. "Wayne Durant grew up in Eastfield, in my own home, with my own kids. He was a difficult boy, so when the nephew went off to college, I was happy to send him over to Lilianna. He's been with her and Dorothea for all these years, working as a handyman. Sometimes, he's hired to clean out a house or help someone move, and brings the things they don't want here, to the shop. You may have seen him."

Eleanor did see Wayne in the shop every once in a while but avoided him. It was an old habit, learned from their days in the school playground. Wayne was the sort of kid who started fires under the bleachers during football games, and blew up mailboxes with firecrackers. Busted in junior high for dealing drugs from his gym locker, he pulled a knife on the principal. To this day, when she saw him walking down the street, she quietly crossed to the other side.

"He lives in a cottage on the farm, no more than a shack, really," Mrs. B. continued. "He deserves better, since he does all the work around the place. But he's a handy fellow, so he'll get another job if the nephew lets him go. I worry about poor Lilianna. She'll be homeless."

Margaret Brownlee managed to convey the sense her cousin would be out along Norwell Road, begging outside the Market and fashioning a tent with rags and her walker.

"I'm sure she'll find a place to live," Liza said comfortingly. "Someplace closer to town, where she can walk to stores and the movies. Maybe we'll be able to recruit her as a volunteer for The Thrifty Means. She can help us sort through the things from the estate."

Mrs. B. drew herself up stiffly and looked down at the array of donations on the counter.

"Who knows what that Zane boy will do? He's not known for his sound judgment, and certainly not for his kindness. But I have already contacted him and made my appeal, so perhaps we'll get poor Dorothea's things soon," she said, and left Eleanor and Liza to haul the junk out to the dumpster.

****

Eleanor had a few hours before she had to pick up her fifteen-year-old twins at Eastfield High School, and decided she could better utilize the time by remaining at the shop than by going home and reworking the last chapter of her current project. Frances Trollope was an unusual subject for her, since Eleanor made her reputation writing histories of American women, but Mrs. Trollope lived for several years in America, and her own journal of those years was enormously successful. Eleanor enjoyed some modest fame, but she would do almost anything to write a bestseller like *The Domestic Manners of the Americans*.

Well, almost anything. She wasn't quite motivated to go home and revise the messy manuscript.

Instead, she walked around the shop with a dust

cloth in hand, and examined some of the merchandise she hadn't noticed before. The two volunteers who were working their shift at the cash box were busy with their own gossip and the occasional customer, and made themselves comfortable in a pair of overstuffed Queen Anne chairs. One of them, June, spilled her latte on the arm of the chair, and asked for Eleanor's dust cloth to soak it up.

Wordlessly, Eleanor handed the cloth over, as she wondered how much the value of the chair would now be diminished. If The Thrifty Means were a privately owned antique shop, the woman might have the amount deducted from her paycheck. But volunteers were even more precious commodities than old chairs, and the shop's volunteers, in particular, more noble than most. The money they raised supported the array of social services in Eastfield.

If Lilianna Durant, Mrs. B.'s cousin, needed assistance, she would find public support and help settling into a new place. If anything, the townspeople would be far more sympathetic to her plight than to Dorothea Zane's successful nephew, who played a part in local history the people of Eastfield would rather forget. Mrs. B. was right in this, as she was in so many things. Eleanor doubted Evan Zane had any need of an old house, in a town he left many years before.

"Well, what have we here?" June's friend, Lynn, whispered, and Eleanor abandoned her musings along with the coffee-stained dust cloth. She looked out the window to see a stack of three cartons neatly supported above a pair of sturdy khaki-clad legs, coming their way across the parking lot. Dark hair curled over the edge of the uppermost box, but the man could not possibly see where he was going, nor be able to manage to open the door.

Eleanor stepped over the legs of the volunteers and went to the door, pushing it wide, and struggling against the resistant wind gusts. The day seemed more like March than May, but the tulips along the nearby Belvedere River were already in bloom, betting against the possibility of more frost.

"Can I help..." Eleanor began, but as the man angled past her, she recognized him, and decided he could help himself.

"I have donations from my aunt, and more in the car," he said in a deep voice, and the boxes shifted precariously.

"We'll help you," Lynn said eagerly, and jumped to her feet.

"Do you want us to come with you to the car?" asked June.

The man leaned slightly forward, and the uppermost carton slipped into Lynn's arms, as her friend took the middle one.

Evan Zane held onto the last, and smiled as if he were posing for a jacket photo for one of his ridiculous books. His dark hair had blown carelessly off his forehead, and he looked as if he either was a regular at a tanning salon, or spent more time in the outdoors than a man who was as prolific a writer as he had any right to do. His eyes were light, pale grey perhaps, and age—or the tanning salon—had given him creases at their corners. His crooked nose had never been fixed, and no doubt people told him it gave him character.

With a sick feeling, Eleanor remembered precisely how the nose came to be broken, and resented the possibility it was probably his own red badge of courage.

"You look very familiar," June murmured.

"Well, I grew up in Eastfield. But you look far too young to have been in my class," Evan Zane said gallantly.

"Oh, no!" She giggled. "I grew up on the West Coast. But I mean, I think I saw you very recently."

"I got into town yesterday, and stopped at the gas station. I've already been to the Market, the hardware store, and now here." He shifted his box again, and Eleanor wondered what he brought in. Bricks, she hoped.

No one spoke for several moments, and Eleanor guessed he waited patiently for one of them to identify him. He smiled again.

"Oh, goodness. You're the guy on the cover of the *EZ Guides*! You were sitting on my dining room table this morning!" Lynn cried out.

"I hope I didn't knock over the centerpiece," he said.

Hardly a joke worth noting, truly witless, the comment nevertheless got the giggles Evan Zane fished for.

"My son wouldn't have passed US History 1 if I didn't buy him the book. I hope you also have one for Asian History. He's taking the class in the fall."

"I do, including individual study guides for each country. There's a new one out for North Korea."

Lynn sighed, and gazed at him as if he just said he negotiated a peace between the Koreas. "You write such wonderful books."

He had the grace to look embarrassed.

"But, you know, Eleanor here writes books also. History books, aren't they, Eleanor?" June asked. "I keep meaning to buy one."

"Historical novels," Eleanor gently corrected. "And we carry them right here in the shop."

Evan Zane apparently considered this information important enough to set his box down on the floor, neatly blocking the entrance. Eleanor watched a customer glance through the door, think better of it, and walk away.

"Eleanor," he said slowly, as if testing the

syllables on his tongue. "Do you write under your own name?"

"I do, though I'm not lucky enough to be able to copyright my initials as a brand name. I'm Eleanor Gilmartin." She politely held out her hand, and waited for his recognition.

If he did recognize her, he said nothing. The moment his palm met hers, the nightmare of what happened one October night returned to her in all its horror. Once again, she smelled the smoke and heard the sirens. And when his warm hand closed over hers, she remembered how he held her as they huddled in the filthy drainage ditch, bleeding and in shock. They shared an extraordinary moment in time, something undiminished in the accusations and recriminations of the following years. There was nothing in his eyes or expression suggesting he had any idea whom she was.

Eleanor pulled her hand away, still studying his face. She was a fool for thinking it mattered. Or for thinking he would wish to reopen any part of an event changing his life so much more horribly than it did her own, and for which he must still have an unspeakable guilt. Perhaps he no longer recognized her name, or saw the girl in the woman she had become.

She only wished he would stop smiling in such a ridiculous manner.

"Well, then, Ms. Gilmartin. Perhaps we'll work together sometime. Appear together on a panel at the library. Collaborate on a book."

"Sort through your aunt's possessions, perhaps?" Eleanor asked, before she realized how insensitive she sounded. "I am sorry for your loss, Mr. Zane. But my only professional collaborations are here at The Thrifty Means. My books are entirely my own. And I think it's fair to say we approach history in entirely different ways; I may be guilty of complicating matters, by adding characters and situations to the events."

"And what do I do, Ms. Gilmartin?" he said softly, asking for punishment.

"You simplify history to the most reductable, obvious, and bare bone parts. 'The war was started, men were killed, and the war ended'," she exaggerated his style, knowing she sounded like a snob.

He stood looking at her, his lips parted as if caught unaware at some act of mischief. Here it comes, she thought.

"Ms. Gilmartin," he said slowly. "Perhaps I can persuade you to write for the *EZ Guides*. You seem to have the knack for simplicity."

"Oh, do it, Ellie!" June said, entirely missing his sarcasm. Eleanor turned; surprised to see her there for she had forgotten they had an audience.

"Ellie," he echoed, and his light eyes widened. No one had called her Ellie for many years, and she had no idea why June chose to do so now. Evan Zane noticed at once. "Ellie. Perhaps we ought to get together for dinner one evening and talk," Evan Zane said. "I'll be in Eastfield at least a few weeks, and know hardly anyone here."

"Perhaps some of your high school friends are still around," Lynn said helpfully, and settled her box on top of his.

"Perhaps they are," he said. "Though I haven't thought about them in years. And I doubt they've thought about me."

How wrong you are, Eleanor realized. Scarcely a day went by when he hadn't returned to haunt her.

June dropped her box onto the pile, and something broke within. "Oh, dear! I hope it wasn't expensive!"

"I'm sure nothing expensive and fragile survived my childhood at Garland ," Evan Zane said. "Just be careful unpacking, so you don't get cut."

"Of course, Mr. Zane. We always empty our bags and cartons very carefully, so we don't handle the occasional mouse or cockroach or broken glass," Eleanor said, and then wished she hadn't. Lynn gasped and looked like she was ready to hand in her resignation.

"A very wise policy." He leaned back against the counter, looking like he'd be comfortable spending the rest of the afternoon wasting their time with small talk. "And what is the most unusual thing you've ever found among your donations?"

Eleanor was surprised by the question, for in ten years of volunteering at The Thrifty Means, she never considered it. "Oh, we get the usual assortment of false teeth, and lost credit cards, and cash. Last year someone brought in a wallet stuffed with outdated European currency. But I think the oddest thing I've seen is a freeze dried cat."

Eleanor was prepared for their sounds of disbelief because, truly, she could scarcely have believed it herself. Indeed, such things were not as rare as she would have imagined even if grotesque. When she first glimpsed the gray and white cat curled in the window, she assumed the poor thing slipped in with a customer, and decided to stay in the warm shop. When Eleanor leaned over to pat its head, she realized the cat was long past needing warmth—or any other creature comforts.

She looked at Evan in surprise. "In fact, your aunt's friend bought it, I believe."

"Lilianna?" he asked, though he must have known his aunt had no other friend in the world. "Are you sure?"

"Oh, yes. She and her cousin seemed very excited."

"Wayne, do you mean? The caretaker? He's not exactly her cousin; he's some sort of …"

"A distant relation," Eleanor finished quickly. "Well, we all should be grateful for small favors. But I don't mean him. I meant Margaret Brownlee. She's the manager of The Thrifty Means."

"Yes. I received an interesting letter from her. She thought I ought to assume my responsibilities at the estate and quickly see to the disposition of the spoils. Though why my personal affairs should matter to a perfect stranger is really beyond me" he said.

"You have been gone from here too long, Evan," Eleanor said softly, speaking as an old acquaintance. "Everything matters. No one's life is private."

Liza had retreated to the back room, and June and Lynn were helping a customer at the front desk. Mrs. B. was on the phone, very loudly.

"I would have thought Dorothea and Lilianna managed better than most," Evan said, and shrugged. He looked at her speculatively.

"But not as well as they might have liked. I assume you understood everything when you had a small funeral service, to keep the gawkers away."

"'Gawkers' sounds like a very Eastfield word," he said.

"Gawkers? Get used to it, Evan Zane," Eleanor said a little rudely. "There will be plenty of people who would like to get a glimpse of you, as well."

"They'll likely be disappointed, then. I don't have half the style of my aunt. She looked better in men's clothes than I do."

Eleanor looked him up and down, and he made her even bolder by studying her as she did so. He had looked good to her in high school and like other well-made things, seemed to have improved with age. He was always tall, but he gained another inch or two in the years after he left town. His body was sturdier, stronger, and he had lost the swagger of a star athlete. He now appeared more confident, as if knowing women would notice him even if he sat still and silent in an audience of a thousand other men.

Eleanor wondered who those women were, and whom among them he had noticed in return.

"Oh, I don't think you have to worry. You'll do. Besides, men's clothes just don't seem to lay right on women," she said, and put a casual hand on her hip before she realized what she was doing. Flirting? Was she actually flirting?

"Perhaps you'll come across the cat and see for yourself," she added quickly.

"Which cat?" he asked gruffly. His voice was deeper than she remembered. "They're all over the place."

"The freeze dried one. You're likely to see only one of those!"

"Are you still talking about a stupid cat?" Liza asked, appearing from behind a cupboard. "Why don't you bring your donation to the back counter for us, Mr. Zane, so we can empty the box and see what broke. June and Lynn could give you the tax receipts, if you'd like." As Liza turned away, Eleanor heard her say, "Or anything else."

He had that effect on most women. In high school he seemed more mature than most of the other boys, and slightly aloof. What was probably shyness was then mistaken for sophistication. Recruited for several varsity teams, he managed to charm his way through most of their honors classes, while the rest of them spent hours in the library or passed up parties to do research projects. His looks were his calling card, his rare combination of dark well-defined features and startling light eyes. His family had been in the theatre for generations, and Dorothea Zane had enjoyed the Broadway spotlight for several years, retiring only to assume the care of her orphaned nephew. She sacrificed so much, everyone said at the time. When Evan went off to college, and she could have returned to the stage, she stayed at Garland, the centuries-old Zane farm in the rocky hills of northern Eastfield.

Eleanor walked to the back of the store, feeling Evan's eyes on her as she moved. She ducked behind the sorting counter, grateful for the barrier between them. He put the ungainly cartons on the empty table and waited as she stripped the tape off the top of the first box.

"Is there anything else I can do for you, Mr. Zane?" she asked a little too sweetly. Her children, hearing such a tone, would have reclused themselves in their rooms for hours, checking periodically to see when the coast was clear.

"Well, you can start by remembering my name is Evan. You're going to be seeing me a lot in here, and it'll be hard to keep up formalities in a place where all our family skeletons are out there for everyone to see. And, for that matter, where you have skeletons hanging from wire hangers on the clothes racks."

For a moment, Eleanor had no idea of what he spoke. She had lived here for years, had an intimate knowledge of every damn bone on those cursed skeletons. He was only just back in Eastfield, and already was ready to put everything out on display? He realized her confusion, and gestured to a clothes rack behind him, where three plastic skeletons hung between the cashmere sweaters.

"Those ridiculous things are Mollie Davidson's idea of a joke," she said, relieved.

"Wouldn't they sell better before Halloween?" he asked, shaking hands with a bony, plastic hand.

"Yes, but someone brought them in after Halloween. That always happens here. We get tons of Christmas stuff during the first week of January." Eleanor shrugged and smiled. "It's hard to say no to any donations, no matter how untimely they might be."

"Oh, no, these guys are always timely. You just need the right customer."

"How about you, Evan?"

He looked at her and smiled. "I have to empty a house of a lifetime of collections, not fill it up." His voice faded as he looked around them, past the skeletons, to the elegant grandmother clock, to the Depression-era glass, to the hobo art sculpture looking like a desperate man's idea of the Eiffel Tower. "I think I have one of those."

"No! It's not possible! Whoever did the tower probably lived on the street, working whatever bits and pieces he found. He would not have considered making a matched set."

"Pun intended?"

It was not, but Eleanor smiled and nodded. At least half the tower was made of burnt wooden matches, as was usually the case with hobo art.

"Well, I think I have something similar. Is it worth anything?"

"Almost certainly, to the right collector."

Evan frowned, and turned away. Thinking he had lost interest in her, Eleanor started to unpack the box, pulling out fine china and a wooden box filled with tiny glass animals. She attempted to look industrious, but it was impossible not to steal a few glances in his direction.

When had he outgrown his teenaged vanity of long hair, falling nearly to his shoulders? She hadn't thought about his hair in years, but remembered just the way it caught the wind, and how it made him easy to identify beneath his lacrosse helmet. He had let his hair grow after the accident, perhaps to distract people from the web of small scars marking his face, and many girls envied it. Eleanor always wondered how the rather formidable Dorothea Zane had allowed his mild rebellion, but perhaps his aunt had every reason to keep an open mind about the unconventional.

Evan Zane reached for an old atlas, and Eleanor watched the muscles in his arm tighten, as the leather-bound book must have been heavier than he imagined. Balancing his find on a tipsy music stand, he scanned the worn pages.

Eleanor pulled a similar atlas from the box and, surprised, looked up at him just as he turned back to her.

"I'm going to need help," he said, quietly. "I don't know what's garbage and what's not."

"Old mattresses, tires, yesterday's newspaper. That's garbage. You can bring the rest here." Eleanor was brusque, finding his plaintive look unsettling. "Or why do anything at all? Just keep the house and everything there."

"Including Lilianna Durant?" he said, without any humor. "No, I prefer to clean out the place, let the sunlight in, and maybe a family will make an offer to buy."

"Eastfield is still a great place for kids. And lots of people come up just for the weekend." When the phone started to ring, Eleanor glanced towards the front of the shop to see if Lynn or June would answer. It didn't look likely. "Excuse me, Evan, I'm expecting a call."

"I'm not married," he said, as if excusing himself from needing a beautiful old farm in the country.

"Neither am I," she returned, and picked up the phone.

Leslie was on the phone, as Eleanor expected, asking for a ride home from soccer practice. Usually Eleanor was quick to respond, and often managed to get to the field even before Leslie could pack up her sports bag. Today, she decided her daughter could wait a few minutes in the sunshine.

"My daughter," Eleanor said when she returned to the desk though she didn't owe him an explanation.

"Your daughter? But you're not married?" Evan asked, without waiting for an answer. "So will you be able to help me figure out what I have in the house?"

Eleanor paused, wondering if he realized how transparent his logic and suppositions were. Maybe he was thinking the same things about hers.

"What else do you have? Anything as interesting as the cat?"

His smile faded, and she could see something bothered him, possibly herself.

"By definition," he said slowly, "nothing could be more interesting than a cat in the house. My aunt detested them."

Eleanor frowned as well. She was rather fond of cats, and her estimation of Dorothea Zane just slipped a notch. "But if she was allergic, perhaps a freeze dried cat wouldn't bother her."

"She wasn't allergic. She just didn't like them. She believed them not much better than mice and rats, and only a slight improvement over dogs. But now she's gone, there are a dozen strays who hang around the place, trying to get in whenever I open the door."

"The poor things. They must be hungry."

"Wayne seems to be feeding them very well. They're very comfortable at Garland. And treated much better than I am."

"Isn't Garland your home? I understood your parents..." Eleanor's voice trailed off once she realized she was revealing more than she ought. She had just cautioned him there was no such thing as one's own business in Eastfield, but she hadn't intended to demonstrate the point by being a busybody.

Evan met her gaze and she realized in that instant he remembered everything, particularly how much more she knew about him—or once knew about him—than anyone else. They almost died on the same road, at the same time. Such a thing would have bound them forever in the memories of Eastfielders. They did not die on an October night, thus binding their living souls together, privately, for the rest of their lives.

"Garland is my house," he said slowly. "But many years have passed since it's been my home."

"Then why have you come back?" Eleanor said, treading foolishly into waters where the swimming was treacherous. "Why not let Lilianna stay at Garland, where she's been for so many years? With your aunt gone, the place must be a comfort to her."

"I'm glad Garland is a comfort to someone. The place brings no joy to me," he said, and stepped back. "But I'm not holding on to it for Lilianna, no matter how comfortable she is. Or how much she likes cats. I've already asked her to find another place to live."

"Perhaps she could move to the cottage with Wayne."

Evan made a sound that pretty much summed up what he thought of the idea, and shrugged his shoulders. Beneath the thin cotton of his tee shirt, his muscles bunched and stretched the fabric.

"So, what do you think?" he asked, catching her off guard.

"Of what?" she asked, too quickly.

The smile reappeared, as did the look of confidence. Evan Zane understood the effect he had on women, and still used it to his advantage.

"Of coming over to help me clean out the place. I'd rather spend an afternoon with you than with Lilianna's snooty cousin."

"Lilianna's cousin happens to be the manager of The Thrifty Means, and a very busy woman. She couldn't possibly accommodate you, Evan. Nor can anyone here, as a matter of fact. We don't usually make house calls." Eleanor started to put away the supplies she used to price items, so the next volunteer in the shop would find them at hand. When she put her red marker into the rubber band box, she realized how distracted she was by Evan Zane's presence.

It was time to head over to the soccer field.

"What about the small town atmosphere, neighbor helping neighbor and everything?" he asked.

He had her there, as he knew he did.

"If you're trying to take advantage of me because I'm a member of the Eastfield Chamber of Commerce, you've succeeded, Mr. Zane. I'll see if I can get someone to come over." She paused, thinking of someone who might make him think better of his plan. "Ah, Miriam Pell, perhaps. Do you remember her? She used to be a fifth grade teacher."

"I remember. Unless she's forgiven me for my science experiment, I'm not sure she'll think me a neighbor worth helping. Are you sure I can't interest you, Ellie?"

I'm sure you interest me much more than you ought "You'll like working with Miriam. And she's very forgiving."

"Thank you. I hope you are as well," he said, and held out his hand. Eleanor hesitated, remembering what his touch did to her minutes before and not wanting to reawaken what was better off buried. He reached across the counter, and caught her hand, sealing some sort of bargain. Still smiling, he let go and finally made his way to the door, stopping only when he saw the display of Eleanor's books. Picking up Louisa May Alcott, he studied Eleanor's photo on the back of the cover.

Somehow knowing she still studied him, he looked across the length of the shop at her.

"Good picture," he said, so softly Eleanor

couldn't be sure those were actually his words.

She was grateful for the distance and the afternoon shadows, because she blushed like the teenager she used to be.

Chapter 2

"People buy souvenirs to remind them of places they've been and people they've seen. Yet twenty years after the fact, they look at one thing or another and have no idea how they got it. And so they bring their junk into the shop, where someone else can buy it and claim it as his memory."

Mindy Dawson, Psychologist
and volunteer since 1995

Eleanor stretched out on her couch with *The Eastfield Edition,* a newspaper offering news mostly to those who wanted to see their kids' names in print, and scanned the pages until she did indeed see their names in print. Leslie received citations for her excellent defensive soccer plays this week, and Lewis prominently figured in an article about students who worked for the Rivershed Association, testing the waters of the Belvedere River for pollutants. Eleanor smiled in some satisfaction, for it was always gratifying to know others recognized the goodness she encouraged in both her children.

It was a pity their father didn't stay around long enough to recognize such rewards.

She closed her eyes, enjoying her solitude as the sounds of the house settled around her. The steady beat of a drum was all she could hear of a CD playing upstairs, and someone was clattering about in the kitchen as corn popped in the microwave. One of the cats was busily scratching away at the arm of the sofa, and an annoyingly long fax was grinding through on the machine in her study. Everything was in its place, but she.

Her business demanded she spend several hours writing each day. On Tuesday and Thursday, when she regularly showed up at The Thrifty Means in the morning, she worked on her computer at night. Here she was, at home with a deadline looming and happy to be anywhere but in her study.

She had many things to think about, and such had to be her excuse. Her children wanted to register for driver's ed, and she already decided she would not have them drive until they were thirty. At least. Until then, she had to be willing to drive them all over town because Eastfield had not yet discovered the advantages of sidewalks or bicycle lanes. There was no public transportation. School bus schedules were inflexible. Every kid in town of legal age owned a car.

What were her choices? For her children to hitch rides with friends, who might speed, take chances or drive drunk? Or for her children to drive their own cars, and be responsible for the consequences?

Did she want to continue to drive them everywhere, all the time, on all their dates, and back and forth for every school function?

What would she spend on two more cars with every safety feature money could buy? What would insurance cost? More than she had, for sure.

Damn! She really had to finish the book.

Then she considered Evan Zane, his books pouring endlessly from an open spigot, and his manner of appearing at home in the world, wherever he was. What she believed was confidence could just as easily be arrogance. When some would consider him a survivor, she judged him superficial and unfeeling. No wonder he had trademarked his initials; they were the very hallmark of his character. Everything was easy for Evan Zane.

Somehow, nothing was easy for her.

He had climbed up out of a wreck that killed his parents and her best friend, sported a few bandages for a week, and was back on the lacrosse field in the spring. His aunt gave up her career on the stage and allowed him to keep the farmhouse in which he had grown up, even when he left town for college and a career. What an absurd, obvious, and ridiculously successful career he had! He wrote books designed to atrophy the minds of high school students throughout the country, and he probably spent about fifteen minutes writing each one. They were banned in the Gilmartin home since Lewis brought home *The EZ Guide to the Battle of Gettysburg*, and Eleanor wanted them banned everywhere.

Eleanor lifted her legs under her, knowing she was psychologically moving further and further away from the work waiting her in her study. She was remembering when she first noticed that damn book, recognizing Evan Zane's face on the cover. His marketing team was very clever, for was there ever a face more likely to inspire confidence? Or a face mothers of a certain age would prefer to have staring up at them from their kitchen tables?

Did no one think about the inappropriateness of the title? Was there anything easy about the Battle of Gettysburg? Could any single part of those dreadful days be reduced to simple terms? What would be next? *The EZ Guide to Auschwitz*? Was the man wholly insensitive to death and suffering?

Of course he was. It was why she resented him all these years, why she felt the nightmares she continued to conjure were her unshared burden, and why she was obliged to visit his parents' graves in Belvedere Cemetery whenever she visited Missy. Someone needed to remember what happened one night, and to mourn those who did not stand up and stumble away from the wreck.

Eleanor took several deep, steadying breaths,

and ran her hand over her damp neck and chest. Even now, she could barely think about that October night without breaking out in a sweat and feeling faint. She unfolded her legs, feeling the familiar stiffness in her left knee, and dropped her head between her knees. Right now, she was angry enough to get some writing done after all.

"Mom?" She looked up a little too quickly and put a hand to her aching head. Lewis stood at the door, popcorn spilling over the stainless steel bowl. "I left my laptop in school. Could I use your computer to check emails?"

Eleanor looked at him, wondering what he thought of her state even as she already guessed the answer. He wouldn't think anything at all. They might as well be researching firsthand the *EZ Guide to a Mother's Hysteria*.

"Can I?" he repeated, though several moments passed before she remembered what he asked.

Did she have any options? She certainly wasn't in the mood to drive him back to school.

"I don't want popcorn all over the place," she said. "And wipe your hands before you touch the keyboard."

He smiled and she reflected—as she often did— she looked in a mirror offering a younger, boyish version of herself. He was nearly sixteen and but for the defection of his father when he was still a baby, he had been protected from pain and heartbreak.

"How long will you need?" she asked.

"A while. We're working on a group project on sustaining life in the river." He walked past her through the room, his bare feet large and sinewy.

Eleanor watched him, wondering when he had grown so tall and if he'd need all new clothes for the summer. Why not? His sister always did.

He paused at the door, and turned to see if she had anything to say. She just waved him in and smoothed down the newspaper in her lap.

She wasn't in the mood for writing, anyway.

****

Nothing was as frustrating as feeling like a stranger in your own home, Evan thought as he opened one cabinet after another, looking for a can of soup. He had been to the market only the day before, and bought enough food to feed a small army. Now, he could only find half of a loaf of bread and a banana.

He glanced out to the den, where Lilianna Durant watched *Jeopardy* and yelled wrong answers at the flickering screen. He must own the last black and white television in Fairfield County, but he doubted the uppity ladies at The Thrifty Means would consider it an antique worth having. For Lilianna, the television might not be worth saving. He could have bought her ten new televisions if she wanted, but she never wanted anything except Aunt Dorothea's attention. She certainly didn't want his.

He opened the refrigerator, and wondered what a bologna banana sandwich on whole wheat would taste like and if cranberry sauce would overpower the other tastes. If he didn't find his food, he'd soon find out, or else drive into town and eat by himself at Ludlum's. He could be both the guest and the host at his own homecoming dinner.

Maybe he could find someone for company. He recalled a few friends he ran into this week, but couldn't imagine spending more than a few minutes of conversation with them at the post office. He didn't want to spend any more time with Lilianna than he had to. Then there was her moronic relative Wayne, freeloading in the guest cottage, probably stoned out of his mind, and belching up the food he stole from the kitchen.

No, he wasn't interested in Wayne or Lilianna, or the guys at the post office, but he wouldn't mind sharing a dinner with Ellie Lambert. Gilfix. Gilmartin. Whatever her married name was, it didn't really matter if she was no longer married. She had changed in more substantial ways, intriguing him more.

He remembered a bright, skinny teenager with braces on her teeth and her dark braided hair that once smacked him in the face when she turned quickly. Everyone liked her and wanted to be on her team; Evan wasn't so old he didn't remember this was the ultimate test of rank in school. She didn't like him and, even after the accident, would have nothing to do with him.

She made it clear she wanted nothing to do with him now. What would she say if he called her and asked her to dinner? Would the good, neighborly spirit she advertised as Eastfield's tradition overcome her standoffishness? Did her dark hair still smell as good as the day it hit him in the nose?

He wasn't in the mood to find out.

"Do you know where the food is, Aunt Lilianna?" he called instead.

"Henry Kissinger!" she yelled with the depth of someone who can barely hear herself, let alone others.

Evan walked to the door, and when she still didn't acknowledge him, stepped in front of the television.

She scowled at him, which was one thing, at least, making him feel right at home.

"Have you seen the food I brought home yesterday?"

"I ate everything. I was hungry," she said tersely, and tried to wave him out of her view. Her arm looked skeletal, which either suggested possibilities about her metabolism, or who really ate the food. "Wayne wasn't even in the house."

Evan nodded and walked away, wondering how

39

quickly he could get the Durants off his property and out of his hair. It was his own fault things had gotten this far, and if his aunt hadn't died, the situation would have continued for years. He never questioned her decisions or her demands for more money, and he trusted her to manage Garland and her life with the same sort of no-nonsense approach she brought to everything else. Somehow, with Lilianna and Wayne, none of the rules applied.

He opened the package of bologna and sniffed it. The meat smelled musty, like everything else at Garland and, suddenly suspicious, he sniffed his sleeve. He hadn't yet become one with the ancient paneling. The bologna probably wouldn't kill him.

Evan knew why the rules didn't apply to Lilianna. He had known why even when he was a small boy, and Dorothea and Lilianna lived in New York, curiously exotic and unconventional. He heard what his parents spoke about in hushed tones even though he didn't understand. Later, when he did, he eyed his "aunts'" relationship with some curiosity but with acceptance. After all, they were all he had.

His mother had no family and his father only had Dorothea, who once was married to his younger brother. He remembered the days of dismal uncertainty after the accident, when she came to Eastfield to take care of the funerals, but was surprised anyone would think she would take care of him. Sensing her dismay, he imagined all sorts of possibilities, from living alone in Garland, to begging for food in a Dickensian orphanage.

He was just a kid then.

And now, begging for food.

"There's potatoes in the root cellar," Lilianna called out. There must be a commercial on.

"Did someone buy them, or are they just growing there?" Evan asked.

"Walden Pond," she yelled.

Dorothea and Lilianna both lived in Eastfield as girls, and Dorothea knew Peter Zane from childhood. When they married, they moved to New York so she could pursue her career on the stage. When he died, Lilianna left Eastfield to move in with Dorothea.

The two women returned after the accident, sold their apartment, and attempted to finish the job his parents started. Neither of them had children of their own; the women's only notion of parenthood possibly came from television sitcoms or more likely, from Dorothea's Broadway stint as Agnes Gooch in *Mame*. The house was always full of guests on the weekend and during the summers, and the two entertained lavishly and well. Evan was free to do whatever he wanted, which is exactly what teenage boys think they want.

Before long, he realized his freedom was the consequence of benign neglect. What he really wanted was someone who worried about whether he got home at night or did well on his SATs.

He left for college, with a few scholarships in hand. He was, after all, the kid everyone pitied, the kid whose parents weren't there for his graduation. The good people of Eastfield, always eager for a cause, lavished generosity upon him. In gratitude, he rarely came back.

He sliced the banana onto the meat and patted down a slice of bread. Then he pushed the whole mess off the edge of the table and into the garbage can.

A cat stared at him accusingly with unblinking green eyes until he fished some of the meat out of the garbage. He didn't know if cats ate luncheon meat, but then he didn't know much about cats. Dorothea hated them, citing some sad event from her childhood. After he read about the same incident in one of her scripts, he doubted both her memory and her truthfulness. Evan put the bologna onto a

41

paper plate and before he could set the meal onto the floor, the cat sprung onto the stool next to him and started to eat.

He walked back into the den, just in time to change the channel for Lilianna. Living in Garland again was a sort of adventure, a return to the days before color television, remote controls, internet access. If Wayne Durant continued to raid his pantry, he would regress further to hunting and fishing for his dinner.

"Whose cat is in the kitchen, Aunt Lilianna?" Evan asked, turning the horizontal focus knob on the set. He looked over his shoulder.

Lilianna sat wrapped in her granny afghan, staring at him accusingly with unblinking green eyes. Maybe the cat was her familiar, which kind of justified what kids always said about her anyway.

"Who owns the cats?" he asked again.

"The marmalade cat? Her name is Ginger."

"How about the grey cat? The one who's eating my dinner?"

"Lincoln? He's Wayne's cat."

" Does he have him trained to steal food from the kitchen? Shouldn't a cat named Lincoln be an honest little guy?"

"Wayne named him Lincoln because he paid five bucks for him at the Grange Fair in August," Lilianna said, though she looked confused about the "honesty" issue.

"What did Dorothea think about having cats around the house?" Evan asked, not for the first time. Lincoln glided through the door and jumped onto Lilianna's lap.

"I don't know," Lilianna said so emphatically, she might have been talking directly to Alex Trebek, who gave her a particularly taxing answer to an unknown question.

Evan understood her frustration. He felt like he

didn't know anything either.

"I'm going out for a while," he said, but he might have been talking to himself. "I may drive into town."

Walking through the kitchen, he picked up his wallet and car keys and pushed against the old farmhouse door. A strong wind blew a storm of sand and dust into his face, and he quickly changed direction, so he walked towards the old barn, rather than to the driveway. Beyond the barn on a small rise was the cottage Wayne Durant had made his nearly twenty years before. Evan wondered how he might extricate him from the place, or if he'd need a bulldozer to push the whole thing—Wayne and all—into the river.

Wayne had shown up at Eastfield High most days like a stray bear in someone's yard, scrounging for food, and something anxiously avoided. It never was clear to whom he belonged and if anyone actually cared. Lilianna was indifferent to his presence. The Brownlees took him in, if as something less than a welcomed relative. He worked for them in exchange for his room and board, and when he bothered to come to class, wore paint stained clothes and a tool belt. No one at school quite understood what to make of him, least of all Evan, who was only grateful he wasn't living at Garland.

When the rest of the class left for college, Wayne stayed behind, and never graduated. He was a guy who needed to "find himself:" the popular moniker for someone who had no ambition, no direction, no future. Wayne managed to find a position anyway, because Dorothea offered him the cottage in exchange for caretaking duties around Garland. After Evan got over his concerns Wayne would steal his record albums and smash his athletic trophies, he admitted the sense of the plan. After all, a man about the place would be able to take care of the chores becoming onerous for two women who could barely change a light bulb. Knowing firsthand the loneliness of being an orphan, he had some sympathy for the guy.

If Wayne merited sympathy, he did not prove himself worthy of trust. He lived on the land, grudgingly mowing the lawn in the summer and plowing the drive in the winter. In the fall and spring, he probably did nothing at all. If he ever changed a light bulb, Evan had no evidence of it. If he contributed at all to the maintenance of a large property, the property wasn't Evan's. In fact, the property value would probably go up significantly with Wayne's removal.

Evan pulled up his collar against the cold and heard a window shutter slam against clapboard. It was a sound familiar to those who grew up in New England, and Evan had a rare moment of feeling at home in his surroundings. Before he could find any comfort there, the feeling was gone.

Something was burning.

His thoughts returned to Ellie Lambert as his heart started racing. One night years ago, he believed he was going to die along with his parents. Desperate to escape the smoke and greasy fumes and locked in his seat, he could do nothing but beat on the door and yell his head off. The acrid smoke got into his lungs and he started to choke. He was going to die.

Then she appeared above him, with a strength he didn't know girls could have. She grabbed him under his arms and pulled him into the painfully cold air of the October night. When he didn't think his legs had the power to move him, she pushed him off the burning car and dragged him to the side of the road.

Did she still have nightmares about that night? Did she realize he would have died if she hadn't shown up when she did?

Something was still burning, close by. It was not the nightmarish smell of spilt oil, and gas, and plastic and rubber tires. Neither was it the odor of pine and cedar logs on fire in a wood stove nor the earthy scent of leaves turning to ash in a metal bin. The old barbecue pit hadn't been used in years. This was something different.

Something popped as the sound of shattered glass splintered the quiet evening. Evan turned towards Wayne's cottage just as a line of fire ran up a wooden beam to the cedar-shingled roof. Damn the man!

Evan ran up the slope, throwing off his jacket. He glimpsed Wayne's silhouette flicker through the window shade and then drop down as a small explosion ignited the back of the cottage. Forgetting any advice about rushing headlong into a fire, Evan opened the unlocked door and stepped into the smoke-filled porch. The place was filthy, though it would hardly matter in the morning. Wayne was filthy too but that was about normal.

Otherwise, he looked fine, or as fine as anyone with a fried brain could look. As Evan grabbed him under his arms, he smelled another sort of odor on Wayne's clothes, more familiar to anyone who has ever lived in a college dorm than to those who lived in Eastfield. Absurdly, Wayne's feet started moving, as he tried to walk up a wall.

"If you're going to walk, stand up, and get the hell out of here," Evan said irritably. He coughed and tried not to breathe.

Wayne scrambled to his feet, swayed, and fell flat on his face.

Evan, thinking his torn socks could not be any more disgusting than the rest of him, started pulling him by his feet, backing towards the open door. Once they were outside, Evan pushed him over, so he was face up, and tried to get him down the stairs without breaking either of their backs. Together they crawled and stumbled to the nearby stone wall.

"I owe you, man," Wayne said.

"Yeah," Evan agreed. "You owe me about twenty years of work."

"I mean my life, man."

Evan had nothing to say Wayne would understand. What happened just now was somehow greater than risking one's own life pulling another out of a building. The moment connected him to his history and to his reasons for returning to Eastfield. He hardly understood it himself.

Now was not the moment for contemplation. He fumbled in his breast pocket for his cell phone, guessing Lilianna was still yelling at the television screen and would have no idea what drama unfolded in her back yard.

"What are you doing?" Wayne said desperately. He pushed up onto his knees and gagged. "You're not calling the police, are you?"

"Your house is on fire," Evan said, realizing Wayne would prefer if the police didn't get too close to his belongings. "This isn't about your stash, or anything else you have in there. It's about the barn, the house, and the sheds. I'm not going to let the whole place blow up just so you don't get busted."

Wayne tipped over and lay on his side on the damp ground. His hand lay limply at his side and Evan imagined it looked eerily like his own, pulling him back to the other time, when flames ignited all around him in a flattened car.

"I'm not the one who's going to be busted. I got friends. They didn't care what happened to your aunt, but they'll care what happens to me." Wayne started shivering and drew his knees up close to his chest.

Evan closed his phone, staring into the night as

he tried to make sense of Wayne's angry words. "My aunt died in her sleep," he said quietly. "I saw her death certificate."

Wayne snorted and wiped his nose on his sleeve.

"You go on believing, man. Yeah, she went to sleep. But I don't think she planned on sleeping so long."

"What did you do? What do you know?" Evan said evenly.

"I know nothing." Wayne shifted onto his back and stared senselessly at the sky.

Even as a kid, Evan recalled Wayne knew nothing at all about anything. But he was wrong. Wayne knew something.

Chapter 3

"Even if the shirt on top of a bag of donations is soiled, the merchandise might get better as you dig deeper into the pile."
Eleanor Gilmartin, volunteer since 1997

Eleanor glanced anxiously at her watch when the phone rang at 7 in the morning. Leslie was already out at the car, loading her soccer equipment into the trunk. Lewis was gulping down some concoction he made for himself each day; one guaranteed to make him grow taller. Eleanor was balancing a package she needed to drop off at the post office and an unwieldy bag of empty soda cans. She pressed her hip against the doorframe, feeling the hard bulk of her keys in her jacket pocket. She really had to get to the high school.

"Just leave it, Lewis. The machine will pick up."

Lewis glanced at the phone's Caller ID, and shook his head.

"Brian's on the phone," he said. "Something must be up."

Brian and Lewis met in kindergarten, and never outgrew their boyhood passion of playing in the mud. Eleanor wasn't sure if that's why their science teacher recommended them for the Rivershed program, or if they actually had real scholastic talents in the field, but was sure the work they did for the organization would look impressive on their college applications. She and Brian's mother drove them up and down the Belvedere River, endured the lingering smell of fish in their cars, and bemoaned the tenacious stains of mud and clay on khakis and tee shirts.

"No kidding! What happened?" Lewis asked excitedly. "Did the grass get into the water?"

He turned to look at Eleanor as he spoke, but ignored her frantic gestures of pointing to the clock and motioning for him to wrap the conversation up. The soda cans crunched together as she shifted the bag, and the parcel nearly slipped out of her grasp.

"He wants us to get up there? We can get out of history? Awesome!" Lewis's enthusiasm wavered when he saw the expression on his mother's face. She wasn't the sort of parent who indulged excuses to get out of class. For her benefit, she was sure, he very clearly added "And Mrs. Elkins is letting us go?"

Eleanor slipped the bag onto the kitchen table. If the principal was giving her blessing for whatever would excuse the boys from class, it must be something important. Leslie wasn't excused and she needed to get to school.

"Okay, I'll be there as soon as I can. The test kits are still in my Mom's car. Yeah." Lewis nodded, and smiled when his sister stamped back into the kitchen behind Eleanor. "I'm cool with it."

"With what?" Leslie demanded as soon as he hung up the phone. "I can't be late."

"I can," Lewis said smugly as he finally picked up his backpack. His empty glass was still on the counter, but Eleanor didn't want to take the time to remind him to wash it. "In fact, I can be so late I don't have to show up at school at all."

Leslie said something, earning her a look from her mother.

"Let's go," Eleanor said. "Tell us what happened when we're in the car. It has to do with a gardener? You said something about grass."

Lewis' mouth twisted, as he tried hard to keep

from laughing. The expression was one he wore whenever he saw his sister punished for something he might very well had had a hand in, and always made Eleanor rethink the situation.

"Not that kind of grass, Mom," he said, and his sister laughed out loud.

"Let's go," Eleanor said again. She never liked a reminder her kids were cooler than she was.

"There was a fire last night, around dinnertime," Lewis said as he walked past her, taking the package from her hands. "I think Garland burned down."

Eleanor's blood left her face and she leaned against the door again, for support. "Garland?" she gasped.

"You know, where those two witches live," Lewis said helpfully.

"They are—were—not witches. They were famous actresses on Broadway."

"Well, they couldn't be too famous, Mom, because no one's ever heard of them. Once Michaela went over to sell them Girl Scout cookies and the crazy man told her to go away," Leslie added.

"The crazy man?" Eleanor asked. Why would anyone think Evan was crazy? Who wouldn't buy cookies from a kid in pigtails and a cute brown uniform? "Oh, you mean Wayne Durant. Well, he's a little different..."

"He's in the hospital," Lewis interrupted.

"Was he hurt?" Eleanor asked, though the answer was too obvious to deserve speech. "Is everyone else okay? Miss Durant? And was Mr. Zane there?"

"Who's Mr. Zane?" Lewis asked.

By now they were in the old car, and Eleanor waited until the engine caught and sputtered until she answered.

"Mr. Zane is the guy who writes those books

everyone has. You know, those *EZ Guides*."

"Everyone has them except us, you mean," Leslie pointed out. "Why we can't have them? Because you hate this guy or something?"

Eleanor backed out of the driveway, pausing as the school bus passed. Damn, now they would be later still, as she'd have to stop at half the driveways on the street.

"I don't hate him. I haven't even seen him since high school. But still, I hope he isn't hurt," she said diplomatically.

"Maybe he's dead. Maybe he burned to death in the fire," Leslie said, seeing no reason to be diplomatic. "Anyway, why do I have to go to school if Lewis doesn't?"

"I don't know if Lewis has to go to school or not," Eleanor said, as she stopped the car. Three little girls ran down a driveway and threw themselves up into the bus.

"I don't," Lewis said. "And, Mom, you should have your blinkers on when you stop in the middle of the street."

"Thank you very much, Lewis," Eleanor said between her teeth, "but I know how to drive."

Lewis nodded, and she could see he was thinking about a day, possibly not too far off, when he would be able to prove how well he could handle a car.

"The Rivershed Association got a call this morning from the EPA. There was a fire last night at Garland, and someone dumped a lot of stuff into the river. The firemen are usually careful about such things, but other people were helping out so the house wouldn't burn down. Mrs. Elkins said Brian and I could work at the site today, and do tests."

In the back seat, Leslie said something very rude.

"Garland is a beautiful house," Eleanor said. "I

51

remember going there many years ago, to a birthday party. There's a little theatre, kind of like an amphitheatre, and I always imagined that's where Miss Durant and Miss Zane entertain their guests. The place is very pretty. It's a pity if it's all gone."

"It's a pity if that Zane guy died, because now half the high school will flunk history," Lewis said.

Eleanor shot him a look. "How are you and Brian getting up there?"

"You're taking us, Mom. Brian's mom dropped him off early because she had to get to work, and he found out about everything. He'll be in front of the school, so when we drop Leslie off, we'll pick him up."

Leslie hit him on the back of the head, but Eleanor was too preoccupied to say anything. While she liked being at home with her kids, she resented the fact no one thought she actually did anything all day, and was therefore free to run children all over town at all hours.

"We have to stop at the Post Office first," she said.

"Oh, Mom! Brian and I want to get up there."

"You will. But when I'm ready to take you," she said firmly. In her heart, she was anxious to get up there as well, to ease her mind about the beautiful home and even, in a very small way, about Evan Zane.

****

Evan found his missing food supplies. Unfortunately, they were spilling out of a charred cabinet in what remained of Wayne Durant's kitchen, their labels burned off. Evan didn't doubt they were his, as they were the only things in the wreckage of the cottage looking like they had any value. He suspected the stash of drugs would have been worth a good deal more, but somehow Wayne managed to get up, run back into the burning building, and dump everything in the river even as the fire trucks sped up the long drive to Garland.

When the rescue workers found Wayne, some time later, he was barely conscious on the riverbank. As they carried him off on a stretcher, with dear Lilianna sobbing as she was helped into the ambulance, one of the EMT crew explained to her Wayne was trying to save himself by going to the water. Evan knew better, but saw no reason to mention anything of Wayne's real motives. The guy's reputation was already tarnished enough.

With any luck, it would end here. Wayne couldn't come back to the cottage and Lilianna might not want to stay on the property without Wayne. In fact, it was so perfect, there might be some who would think Evan purposely planned this fire to get them off his property.

Then he remembered what Wayne had said last night about Dorothea's death, and wondered if someone else had planned this fire for him, or despite him. Why would someone who might have gained from his aunt's death try to get Wayne out of the picture? The property was still Evan's to do with as he pleased.

In fact, despite the drama of the night before, Evan was embarrassingly pleased. Wayne and Lilianna were gone, at least temporarily, and he had Garland to himself. The cool spring breeze brought the first fresh smells of earth and greenery to the place, and he could yet enjoy the broad vistas of the hills and valleys around him. The river was at overflow, as snow melted in the higher elevations. For the first time, he wondered if he was a fool to think about selling this place.

Just as he contemplated doing something foolish, like jumping around in the ruins of the cottage and whooping it up, he noticed two kids coming up the rise. They looked intent on some little gadget they held between them, and didn't notice him at all, even when he kicked around some of the cans.

"Hey, boys," he called.

They looked up, frowned, and quickly put their hands in their pockets.

"Who are you?" one of them asked.

"I own this place," Evan said, "and you're trespassing. Who are you?"

The shorter boy looked behind him, as if expecting someone else, but the taller, leaner boy smiled.

"You're Evan Zane. My mom wondered if you were here. And if you died in the fire."

Who was his mom? Evan wondered. How would she know he was here—or care? He studied the young man for a moment longer and had his answer. The dark glossy hair, the hazel eyes that looked so intently at you until you wondered if you just sprouted a pimple on your nose, the high cheekbones and pointed chin were the more masculine features of someone he once knew, and had seen recently.

"I'm Lewis Gilmartin," he said, though Evan already guessed. "This is Brian Coley."

"Aren't you guys supposed to be in school?"

They laughed and gave each other a high-five. Evan supposed that meant they were supposed to be in school and somehow got out.

"Our science teacher got a call from the Rivershed Association this morning. There's all sorts of stuff washing up downstream, from your house. The one that burned. It's really close to the river and people might have thrown burning things into the water."

"What kind of stuff?"

Brian Coley looked behind him again and this time, Evan saw the approaching figures of a man and a woman.

"Just stuff," he said. "We volunteer for the Rivershed and they want us to fish some things out of the water and take test samples. We're supposed to report if we see any dead fish or other animals. Sometimes ducks and geese eat whatever they can find at this time of year, when they're making their nests."

"Well, I wouldn't want them to eat the stuff. And I certainly don't want them to smoke anything," Evan added quickly as the man and woman came up to them. The two boys snickered.

"Good morning, Mrs. Gilmartin," Evan said politely. "Didn't expect to see you again so soon." He looked questioningly at her companion.

"I'm Mike Longo, the biology teacher at the high school," the man said, sounding like a pompous ass. "The boys and I have a grant to do studies of the river, and what we have right now is one big mess."

The man somehow implied this was Evan's fault. Even if it were, he wouldn't admit it in front of Ellie Gilmartin.

"I don't like the look of things, myself. And it's my house, which, I suppose, makes it worse."

"Not really. The Belvedere River belongs to all of us in the Rivershed, and to everyone who uses Long Island Sound. It's our collective responsibility, and every drop of litter has an impact."

Evan wasn't in the mood for a lecture, and especially not from a teacher who looked younger than himself. Ellie stood there, smiling at his discomfort, and looking very beautiful in an old corduroy jacket and patched jeans.

"What happened to Miss Goldberg?" he asked.

Mike Longo frowned. "Do you mean Betty Goldberg, who used to teach science? She left years before I got to town. I think she died."

"She was a very good teacher. Very patient and kind."

"Before my time," Longo said. "Yours too, Mrs. Gilmartin?"

Good, Evan thought. At least the little snot wasn't calling her Ellie.

Eleanor Gilmartin ignored her companion and looked at Evan as if they shared a private joke. Well, they shared something, though there wasn't anything funny about it.

"No, in fact, it was just my time," she said. "The happiest time of my life. Everything felt like it does today, in the early spring, when everything seems possible."

Evan sensed her lovely eyes pulling him closer, seducing him into believing things he scarcely imagined with her, reminding him of what they had for one brief moment in their history.

"Ahh," Longo sighed on an exaggerated note. "Spoken like a writer, making romance out of the mud." Somehow, he managed to sound both disparaging and dismissive.

"Mom, did you used to know Mr. Zane?" the tall boy, the image of his mother, asked. Evan wondered if the boy caught the same longing in her words as he also imagined.

"Not really," she said, deflating Evan's ego and everything else. "But we were in school at the same time."

"We were both in Miss Goldberg's class," Evan said tersely.

"Oh. I hadn't remembered."

Evan told himself to ignore it, and ignore the looks passing around the circle. This is the Ellie Lambert he remembered: cool, aloof, tantalizing.

"So, what are you hoping to do here today?" he said. "Help me rebuild the cottage?"

"I'm just supervising the boys and helping them get started," Longo said. "I've got classes to teach."

"And I'm just the chauffeur," Ellie said. "I've got

a book to write."

The two boys looked at each other. "We've got nothing to do except this," Brian said, glancing at his science teacher.

Longo didn't notice; instead, he watched Ellie Gilmartin's fingers as she ran them through her hair.

"Same for me, boys," Evan said briskly. "Show me how to work these gadgets and let's get our feet wet."

****

Eleanor stopped at the post office on the way back from Garland, and met two friends from the Eastfield PTA. She decided she needed to pick up a few things from the market, and spent nearly an hour reading the ingredients on the boxes of baked goods. Then, since the market was around the corner from The Thrifty Means, she decided to see if anything new had arrived. A set of pewter sconces were just the thing for her dining room, but before she bought them, she unpacked and sorted three cartons of glassware. She cut her finger on a cracked vase and spent ten minutes looking for a bandage.

Then she went home and stared at her computer screen for an hour.

Honestly, she just wished Evan Zane would get out of town already. She hadn't accomplished a thing since he walked into the shop, except think about him. This wasn't an accomplishment because she had no interest in him anyway.

She pushed her chair back from the desk so suddenly, her collie Sally scampered away in terror. Though redundant, she hit "save" on the screen, and turned off the desk light. With any luck, Lewis would forget his laptop in school again, and she'd be forced to forfeit another night's work.

Lewis. She called him on his cell phone, wondering if he and Brian needed a ride back to school, or any help with their project. Evan wouldn't have spent the whole day with them, and was probably hard at work on his computer, writing one or two or ten books. Damn him.

When Lewis didn't answer, she decided she ought to go up and see what they were doing. After all, they could have fallen in the river, or a spark from last night's fire could have set off an explosion. Brian and Lewis could have told Evan they had their licenses, and borrowed a car to go joyriding.

By the time Eleanor grabbed her keys and her barn jacket and ran down the stone steps to her car, Sally was already waiting at the door, wagging her tail.

"Forgive me, girl?" Eleanor asked, and opened the back door. Of course Sally forgave her; that's why people loved their dogs. Sally drooled all over Eleanor's sleeve as she adjusted the window, and barked to let her know she was ready to go. Sally was always ready to go, anywhere.

Eleanor backed out of her short driveway and onto the road. Her house was an Eastfield antique, but an in-town location meant the rooms proved modestly sized and her lot was small. The original owners of the houses on Milkweed Lane were those who owned businesses and bartered their services and wares for the agricultural products grown elsewhere in town. Her own house had belonged to a shoemaker over a hundred years ago, and his workshop was now her living room.

As she drove through the center of town and into the valley of the Belvedere River, great estates dotted the landscape, many of them built on the sites of the original farmhouses. In most cases, the developers kept the stone walls, and one or two broad-width maples, and put up houses impressive anywhere in the world, but reflected nothing of Eastfield's heritage. However, some of those farmhouses had survived, either because they were on property passed down through generations, or because appreciative owners bought them. The most painful event for the old timers in town was to witness yet another landmark house torn down to make way for "progress."

That was the reason she wasn't the only one in Eastfield who was aware of Evan Zane's return to town. She had her own guess as to why he hadn't returned in all these years, but most people interpreted his absence as indifference. If he was indifferent to the land and buildings in which his family had lived and died for generations, to whom would he sell?

Eleanor rounded a sharp curve a little too quickly, and Sally's weight shifted to the opposite side of the car. They neared a small strip of stores, most of which were closed for the winter. Eleanor noticed trucks were delivering large clay pots to the garden center, and swing sets were already assembled at the business next door. These were signs of spring, as sure and as regular as the crocus in her yard and the barn swallows in her garage.

She turned off the road to follow the path of the river as the water came down from the hills, rushing through flat plateaus of farmland, and tumbling over waterfalls. For the second time this day, she drove between the stone pillars of Garland framing the gravel drive. Some folks believed the place was named for Judy, which seemed consistent with the tastes of the guests who frequented the place after Mark and Marianne Zane were killed. But inasmuch as a long-ago stonecutter chipped away at the hard New England schist to create a design of a flower canopy on each of the pillars, the intent was more likely decorous.

If Evan sold to a developer, would something of the name remain? Garland Acres, perhaps?

Garlandville? EZ City?

Eleanor drove slowly up the drive, noticing each tree and small outbuilding on the land. It was beautiful, truly. The property deserved to belong to someone who appreciated its importance and history.

She turned into the parking area with a small spray of gravel, and startled a lithe black cat. For the first time in years, she recalled her last conversation with Missy, when she thought of what she wanted to dress as for Halloween and Missy believed there was a black cat on the road. Eleanor sat in the car for a few moments, feeling sick.

Sally noticed the cat also, and let her know who was boss—or ought to be.

Eleanor finally stepped out of the car, making sure the cat was out of sight before she opened the door for Sally. She looked around, admiring the lovely property and the indications her child already staked a claim here. Hanging on the split rail fence was Lewis' jacket and a baseball cap. On the damp ground, held down by a rock, was a pile of papers. The air was still thick with the smell of burnt wood and was colder up here in the hills than in town. She wondered why Lewis had discarded his jacket.

Where were they? The windows of the farmhouse looked dark, and there were no sounds of conversation or working crews. Wayne's pickup truck was partly in the garage, but so had it been hours earlier.

Eleanor walked back to the car, and as Sally dashed out the door, Eleanor warned her to behave herself. She walked to the house, thinking she had every excuse to be looking around the property, and might never have another chance. She stepped up onto the wide porch wrapping around three sides of the building, and paused to admire the wooden furniture that probably had weathered more winters than she had. The lace curtains at the windows did little to give privacy to the rooms within, and Eleanor noticed overstuffed chairs and cases of books and pottery. She wondered if Evan Zane had any idea how much all of this was worth.

She turned the corner and walked right into him.

"Oh!" She took a step back, and gaped like an idiot.

"Evan Zane," he said, and smiled. He reached out his arm and caught her before she fell off his porch. Gently, he pulled her close. "I live here. Remember me?"

"Ah, yes. I think I remember you. Didn't you sit in back of me in Miss Goldberg's science class?" she asked, playing along with him, though she didn't know if he meant in the long, or the more recent, past.

"Oh, yeah. I used to pull your ponytail whenever you had a wrong answer."

Eleanor looked into his light eyes, remembering with aching nostalgia how keenly aware she had been when he was so close, able to watch her when she could only sense him behind her. She was fully aware he used to look over her shoulder for test answers, but that never bothered her. Instead, she was more concerned her hair smelled like the expensive herbal shampoo she bought using her allowance money, and her miniskirts didn't ride up too high on her thighs.

"I don't remember," she lied. "Maybe because I never had a wrong answer."

"Neither did I, thanks to you," he admitted. "You must have known I was cheating off of you. I'm surprised you didn't ask to have your seat changed."

No, she didn't. Being near him was what she wanted. In those simpler, sweeter days of high school, that was enough for her.

They stood for several minutes in the warming sun, his hands still holding her close, and she realized this was no longer enough; she wanted much more, and there was nothing sweet or simple about it.

"I guess I owe you," he said, when she didn't answer. "I'll find a way to make it up to you."

Though years had passed since she shared anything other than a simple friendship with a man, she recognized the prelude to something deeper, much more complicated, with Evan's quiet words. Circumstances brought them together for the second time in their lives, and for her, an inner longing rekindled after being banked for so many long years.

"You can start by helping me find Lewis and Brian," she said idiotically. Evan released his hold on her. "I have to take them home. I assume they're still around? I see Lewis' jacket on the fence. They're too young to drive so Brian's mom and I have to take them all over the place." She was babbling, she knew, but all she wanted was to get away before she pulled him into the house and assuaged her curiosity to see if he was a better kisser than he was in the fourth grade.

Evan leaned over and brushed something away from the corner of her mouth, briefly touching her lip. "They're around somewhere. I think they're in the barn looking at the guns."

"Guns?" Eleanor cried, all thoughts of seduction banished.

"Relax, Ellie. I don't think they've been used since the Civil War. If Wayne had gotten hold of them, I'm sure all the windows at Garland would have been shot out years ago." Though his tone was light, she caught an underlying anger in his words.

"Wayne. I forgot about him. He's still in the hospital?"

"And he can stay there, for all I care. He'll live."

He opened his mouth as if to say something else, and then thought better. "Come, walk with me. I need to think things through."

He put her hand between his arm and body, bringing her close again. His worn jacket smelled of smoke and pine and warm soil and Ellie had the feeling she would soon smell of these things too.

"I'm not sure I can help you. Wouldn't you be better on your own, Evie?"

"I haven't heard that one in years. Maybe we shouldn't let anyone else in town hear it either," he said, but didn't appear annoyed at the childish nickname. "And no, I'm beginning to think I'm not better on my own. I'm used to it. But that doesn't make things better." He shrugged, and Eleanor felt his lips on her hair. "Come."

She went, allowing him to lead her around the house and down the back stairs.

"I suppose the wild beast is yours?" he asked. Eleanor looked up in time to see Sally dash by, chasing after some small creature.

"I hope you don't mind? She really likes to come with me in the car, and the place did look pretty deserted when I let her out."

"No, I don't mind. Garland needs some people and pets around the place. Watch here, there's a broken step," he said. "I hope old Wayne doesn't expect a gold watch for his years of service. I'm not sure he ever did anything resembling a day's work."

"Well, some would say the same about you," Eleanor pointed out.

Evan dropped his hand and turned to face her. She noticed, in the unfiltered light of the late afternoon, how weary he looked, as if he had been working the rocky New England farm all these years, instead of living a comfortable life in New York. She knew even as she reflected on this, such a view was a highly romanticized one; these days most

Eastfielders grew a few tomato plants on their patios, and considered them a "crop." To be fair, even for someone as seemingly carefree as Evan Zane, the past few weeks had been pretty rough.

"But you wouldn't," he said, and paused while she remembered what she said to him. "Only someone in the same line of work understands how real a job writing is, with deadlines and contractual agreements and the frequent inability to produce anything at all. My mother was a writer, so I grew up with full disclosure. I knew what I was getting into."

"I forgot she was a writer," Eleanor said gently, and looked away from him. She had never heard him mention his parents after the accident, even when she went to visit him in the hospital. "I wish someone had prepared me for what I was getting into. Writing just seemed like a convenient thing to do for someone who was divorced, with two babies. I'm just lucky things worked out."

"Very well, I guess" he said generously. It was a little like Emeril congratulating the cook at Ludlum's for a well-turned grilled cheese sandwich.

"Not very well. I make enough to live on. I've gotten some nice reviews in The New York Times."

"I know. I've read them."

Eleanor wasn't sure what to make of such information. Of course, almost everyone read the newspaper, but that he should identify the author of the historical novels aimed mostly at a female audience with someone he once knew surprised her. Had he watched her career, as she did his?

"I wish I could return the compliment," she said artlessly. "But I haven't read any of your books. Your guides."

He looked up at a hawk circling the sky over his meadow, and smiled. She noticed a small line of a scar along his jaw and shivered, remembering the night when she had showered for hours and hours, scrubbing her body of her blood and his. "Oh, you misunderstand me I didn't say I read your books, only the reviews."

Eleanor had no reason to be indignant, but she was. It was what this man did to her. She tugged her hand out of the shelter of his body. "Well, maybe you ought to try reading them. You might learn something about history!"

His light eyes settled on her again. "I think I know enough about history. More to the point, I know about the struggle to learn about history if you're a kid with learning disabilities. Being assigned a hundred pages of reading a history text for homework is an impossible task if every word has to be sounded out for meaning."

What did he know about such things, after all? Hadn't he been the smart ass in every class they had, the darling of every teacher in the high school? Eleanor was unsure of memory, of the way things might have been over twenty years before.

"What do you know of my aunt?" he asked.

"Lilianna Durant?" she asked, caught off guard. "I heard she suffered some sort of shock and is with Wayne in the hospital."

Evan made a gesture of impatience and bent to pick up a branch across their path. "Lilianna is not my aunt. Wayne can have her all to himself."

"Oh, you mean Dorothea," Eleanor said, and wondered what she really did know about a woman who was more legend than neighbor in Eastfield. "I know she was very beautiful, and had a career on Broadway before she gave everything up."

"For her poor orphaned nephew, who showed his gratitude by escaping at the first convenient moment. Yes, she was truly a martyr. And reminded me of it at every opportunity. Thank goodness she never caught on to the internet; I would have had daily postings from her on the subject."

"I suppose she could have gone back to New York after you went to college," Eleanor said thoughtfully.

"Or at any other time in the last twenty or so years?"

Eleanor looked at him, wishing she understood what he wanted. The distraction caused her to trip over a piece of charred rubble, and he quickly reached out again. She caught her breath.

"Are you okay?" he asked.

The damn thing was, she was pretty sure she wasn't. The stark teenaged emotions had always run a little wildly when he was near her, had stirred every time he touched her, or even looked her way. It was ridiculous, and a little embarrassing. She was the mother of two teenagers, for goodness sakes.

"I'm okay," she said.

He looked satisfied, and pulled her around a barrel filled with some sodden mess. Sally was sniffing excitedly. "We'd better keep her away from this. It's Wayne's brew."

Eleanor pulled on Sally's collar. "It's disgusting. What is it?"

"I'm not sure. Old underwear, maybe. Nothing this guy does surprises me anymore." He picked up a sheet of jagged metal, dropping it over the barrel to cover the mess. "That's why I'm curious about my aunt."

Eleanor stopped in her tracks. "Surely you don't think...Wayne would not have had the nerve. What would a woman like her have seen in him? He's such a sniveling weasel."

Evan stuffed his hands in his pockets and looked like he was about to laugh. "What are we talking about here, Mrs. Gilmartin?"

"Sex?"

"Sex?" he repeated. "I would love to talk about

sex with you, Ellie Gilmartin, but I think we can forget about it as far as Wayne and Dorothea go. For one, she was old enough to be his mother, but he might have been too stoned to notice. But she also had Lilianna, and one would have to be in a coma not to notice that."

"Oh," Eleanor said softly. Her face was bright red, only partly from recognition of the long-time, slightly scandalous relationship between Lilianna and Dorothea. "So I guess it's true."

"You can't tell me there's a person in this town who didn't know my two aunts were lesbians."

They walked along in silence, Eleanor acutely aware she revealed too much in her confusion. He must think her a prude, or at least, stupidly naïve. What made her burst out with such a blunt guess? Well, if she was honest, it probably had something to do with the fact he was inches away from her, and she could think about nothing else.

As they approached the remains of the little cottage with its picturesque view of the Belvedere, Sally ran past them to the river, pausing only to check out Lewis's and Brian's testing kits and a notebook on the ground. School would have let out an hour or so ago so they no longer needed an excuse to miss their classes. Eleanor wondered if they had even bothered to get the information Mike Longo required.

"But I'm more interested in her other relationships, those she enjoyed in Eastfield these past few years," Evan said, bringing her back to his earlier question.

Eleanor shrugged. "I really don't know. I'm not even sure what circles they traveled in."

"None, I would think. I'm not sure they ever left the place."

They stopped in front of the remains of the cottage. The stone foundation outlined the footprint of a small building set at an angle to the river. Within was charred furniture and house wares, ruined beyond saving.

"Oh, I would see them occasionally in town. They didn't know who I was, but I always said hello, and they were pleasant enough." She paused at his expression of surprise. "They would come into The Thrifty Means and look around. So did Wayne. In fact, his name and number is up on the bulletin board, advertising him as a moving man for any large pieces customers might want delivered. I think he got a few jobs."

"Okay, I take back everything I said. He wasn't a slacker after all."

"Most people would think he was more gainfully employed than we are," Eleanor pointed out.

Evan kneeled down to study a twisted piece of metal. "Well, I think it's a fair guess he ran other businesses on the side. A fairly enterprising guy, all in all."

"I can ask Mrs. B. about him. He lived with her for a while, after all."

"Mrs. B.?" He looked up, shading his eyes against the afternoon sun behind her. She stepped to the right, effectively blocking him, but his hand remained saluting even as he rose. "Who's Mrs. B.?"

"Margaret Brownlee, of course. That's what we all call her down at The Thrifty Means, though I'm not sure she really likes the familiarity. She's so straight-laced, one of the last members of the old school. But she does a wonderful job, and somehow manages to get estate treasures into the shop. And, of course, they're all donations. She's responsible for a lot of our success as a fundraiser."

"I'm surprised she ever admitted to knowing Wayne, let alone trusting him in her home."

Eleanor laughed, and she realized this was the first time she was truly enjoying herself in weeks.

"I suppose every family is allowed a couple of black sheep," she said, and then more seriously, "Some in town would say the same of you, you know."

He dropped his hand, and though the sun highlighted the strong lines of his face, the expression in his light eyes was unreadable.

She took a step back, feeling a discomfort even more acute than when he first walked into The Thrifty Means, and at a loss to understand it. Why had he stayed away all these years? How long would he hold on to Garland?

"This has been very tough winter for the town, you know," Eleanor said, picking a safe topic. "We lost three old timers before your aunt and people started to look for reasons, aside from the obvious: old age. A few people blamed the oil companies for not delivering during the snowstorms, and some had their water tested for toxins. That's how Lewis and Brian got involved in the Rivershed work. But all died a natural death, except, perhaps for Mrs. Bannock, who must have slipped on the ice near her barn. Her dog barked for hours before someone came by to see what the problem was, and there she was, frozen in the snow."

"And you consider this a neighborly town? A dog could bark for hours before someone notices? Or cares?"

Eleanor recoiled as if he slapped her. Why should she have to defend Eastfield from someone who knew the town nearly as well as her?

"I consider Eastfield a town in which neighbors live at least two acres away from each other, maybe more. If something happened here at Garland, who would be close enough to see, or hear?"

"Something did happen here at Garland," he reminded her. "Last night, in fact. But Wayne said something making me think something may have happened before, and it wasn't an accident."

Eleanor wrapped her jacket more tightly against her body. The air was chilly in the shade, a reminder it was too soon to put out the seedlings started on windowsills weeks before.

"Who was with your aunt when she died, Evan?"

He looked at her with the barest glint of a smile, and she realized the answer was a little too obvious. "Lilianna, I suppose. I never asked."

"But you didn't come up until she was already dead." Eleanor realized the words sounded like an indictment. It was a statement of fact. He wasn't here. He never was here.

"She wasn't ill. The last time I spoke to her, she said she was thinking about buying a new patio set for spring. The one we have here is probably thirty years old." He glanced towards the barn, which probably doubled as storage shed, and Eleanor looked to see what interested him there. The boys were just walking out of the old building and trying to figure out how to close the antique sliding doors. "Who else died this winter? Who did you say?"

"I didn't say," she answered. Did he really care about the people of the town, some of whom were already elderly when they were kids?

"Your aunt and Mrs. Bannock. Moira Priestly on Shaker Farm Road. Douglas Alvarado on Mather Street. We also lost Michael Dennis to cancer, but I don't think you would remember him. He was in his forties, an art dealer in New York, and had a beautiful collection here in Eastfield. Mostly American impressionists like J. Alden Weir."

"You seem to know a lot about him."

Eleanor looked at him cautiously, wondering if he might be jealous. How very curious, and how delightful, she thought. "He was a wonderful person, very generous and giving. We spoke about collaborating on a book."

"And with him, you actually meant it? Unlike with me, whose books you think are a joke?"

"Of course I meant my offer," she said, answering his first question.

"So the winter was very sad in Eastfield," Evan said, fishing for more.

Eleanor refused to rise to the bait. "And yet, when Eastfield suffers loss in population, The Thrifty Means has a good season. It sounds very mercenary, but it's true. When houses are cleaned out, we are the beneficiaries." She shrugged. "We just have to set personal matters aside."

"I see. And there are no exceptions."

"Of course there are exceptions. There are as many special cases as there have been people in Eastfield. And yet we seem to endure. The shop's been here sixty years." Something rustled behind them and he turned. "Hi, boys! Did you get everything done?"

Lewis and Brian came up behind them, brushing cobwebs out of their hair. They looked guiltily at each other, which was their way of saying they hadn't.

"Maybe we can get out of school tomorrow?" Brian asked hopefully.

"Maybe not," Eleanor said, with more firmness than the words implied.

"Nice try, though," Evan said. "How about if I pick you guys up on Saturday, and you can do more tests, and we'll pull out the trains?"

"You're going to play with trains?" Eleanor asked, hoping the girls in the high school didn't hear about this.

"They're antiques, Ellie," Evan explained. "You're going to love them."

"You're going to be surprised," Lewis said, looking a bit surprised himself. Eleanor was sure her son never heard anyone call her by the childish diminutive.

"I can hardly wait," she said dryly. Very much aware of the way Evan Zane looked at her, she realized it was true.

Chapter 4

"There is a very small market for used light bulbs."

Margaret Brownlee, volunteer since 1965

"Eleanor, dear, we have a problem." Margaret Brownlee sat behind her large roll-top desk, and peered at Eleanor over the gold rim of her glasses. "Someone just called about a donation, and I tried to discourage her, but she wouldn't listen. Her husband's on the way down to the shop."

"I don't have time to go through her things now, Mrs. B. I have to pick up Lewis and his friend at Evan Zane's house. They're been helping him clean up around the place."

Mrs. B. sucked in her cheeks, though Eleanor wasn't sure if it was because she'd have to take care of the donation herself, or because Eleanor had some indirect access to Dorothea's lifetime of accumulation. As to the former, Mrs. B. had put in many years of her life at The Thrifty Means, but age and, perhaps, a natural weariness for the business had made her impatient with her customers and bored by the donations that never stopped coming through the door. She would do anything to avoid going through a box of donations.

As to the latter, Eleanor couldn't help but wonder if Mrs. B. imagined the treasures Dorothea Zane left behind were simply extraordinary and wanted to peruse them herself.

"I'll be back in a few hours," Eleanor said, and

reached for her sweater on the clothes tree. She waved cheerfully to Mrs. B. and to the other volunteers who busied themselves around the shop, but a wagon suddenly appeared in the aisle and blocked her way out the door. A blanket covered something large and cubic.

"If you're bringing in a refrigerator, one of the college kids will be glad to buy it for a dorm room," she said cheerfully to the man who pulled the wagon, as she walked around him.

"Isn't," he said, and lifted the blanket, to reveal a filthy birdcage. Huddled in a corner on a chewed up perch, scared and hungry, was a blue parakeet.

"I'm sorry; we're not allowed to sell animals. We need to abide by the health code," Eleanor said. She leaned closer and whistled to the bird. He perked up.

"Then take the damned cage, and I'll let the bird fly out the door."

Eleanor looked at him to see if he was kidding, but seeing nothing beneath his grouchy exterior, took him at his word.

"Just leave him here, sir. We'll take care of the bird. Does he have a name?"

The man looked at her as if she offered to fly away herself, and muttered something about his wagon. Eleanor lifted the cage; he pulled the wagon out from under, and still muttering, shuffled out of the shop.

"What a nice guy," Eleanor said, for the benefit of the laughing volunteers. "Why don't I take True Blue home with me, and pick up some bird seed for him?"

"The gentleman said he didn't have a name," Mrs. B. said, coming forward now their unpleasant visitor was gone. "And I understood you were going over to Dorothea's house."

That plan was now somewhat inconvenient. Something in Mrs. B.'s expression made Eleanor perversely determined to carry on.

"He has a name now, and I'll just take him with me. I'll stop off and get some birdseed, and he'll be fine until I get home."

"At least he won't have to worry about the cat getting him!" Miriam Pell said.

"What cat?" Mrs. B. asked sharply. She looked suspiciously around the shop.

Eleanor studied the older woman, wondering if something was troubling her. The women of The Thrifty Means had few secrets from each other, and she was sure she would have heard if Mrs. B. was ill, or had financial difficulties, or if her children were coming for a visit. Mrs. B. greeted carpenter ants with more cheer than she did her relatives.

"The freeze dried cat. I always wondered who bought the poor thing and it turns out Dorothea Zane wanted it."

"Oh, I see," Mrs. B. said, but like any joke needing to be explained, the wind had gone out of the sails. "Your bird doesn't have to fear the cat."

"Not that one. But there seems to be a lot of cats prowling around Garland. I consider it odd, since Dorothea Zane was apparently terrified of them. Did Lilianna ever say anything about her cats, Mrs. B.?" Eleanor asked.

Mrs. B. was already tidying some wax-faced dolls on a shelf, rearranging their hair and smoothing down their yellowing baby gowns.

****

True Blue cheered up as Eleanor drove carefully along the winding hills of northern Eastfield, and after eating enough birdseed to fill his teeny tummy, chirped like his little life depended on it. Eleanor, who had yet to eat lunch, nevertheless shared some of his spirit. The day was beautiful, the sort banishing any lingering reminders of winter. The trees displayed the pale green tips of their first buds and ferns were just beginning to unfurl along the marshy shoulders of the road.

Though Eleanor knew almost every road in the town, only an occasional play date for the children or a meeting of one sort or another ever brought her up this way. Because of Evan Zane, she and Brian's mother were carpooling the boys to Garland, and she came to see the route as one of discovery as she noticed something new almost every day.

The same might be said for Evan Zane. She would have guessed his aversion to Eastfield so enduring he would quickly take care of business, and leave down. But he gave every evidence of taking his responsibilities seriously, and already showed up at some of the town meetings and events. The boys were enjoying their time with him, having little to do with the Rivershed work. The trains were not the small models Eleanor remembered boys her age collecting; they were large enough to hold human passengers and apparently once chugged along on narrow tracks around the estate. She remembered hearing something about them from her childhood; how an accident finally caused the Zanes to dismantle the whole thing. Lewis and Brian were fascinated with the train cars and wanted to help Evan refurbish them. Whatever his plans were for the future, he appeared happy to indulge their enthusiasm now.

Nevertheless, as she came through the old gateposts and started up the long driveway, Garland still looked desolate and neglected. More than the trains needed refurbishing to bring the place back to its storied glory. She understood from Mrs. B. Wayne was out of the hospital, though she had no idea where he lived now, and Lilianna appeared very much put out that the owner of all this claimed a right to live in his own house.

True Blue's chirping had scarcely let up and now

attracted the attention of a cat, who raised his head from where he had been asleep on the stone wall. He blinked and settled back into what only a cat would consider a comfortable resting place. Eleanor drove slowly, fearing the sudden appearance of his companions, and pulled in next to Evan's white Jeep.

Eleanor didn't bother to analyze why she paused to glance at herself in the car mirror, or why she reapplied her dark pink lipstick. The situation was hopeless in any case; her pale skin was sunburned after the gardening she did last weekend, and her nose was peeling. Her dark hair curled around her face and when she plucked at what looked like a spot of dust at her temple, she was horrified to realize it was gray hair. How had she not noticed before? She quickly ran her fingers through her bangs, hoping to cover the evidence.

Stepping out onto the graveled driveway, Eleanor straightened her white shirt into her waistband, and wished she had worn her new black and white capris, instead of her worn jeans.

"No one's going to look at you here, Honey. It ain't a fashion show," came a wavering voice. Since these were pretty much the same words Eleanor's subconscious was whispering at the same time, it was a moment or so before Eleanor realized someone actually said them. She looked around, and there, under an apple tree, glimpsed an elderly woman sitting in a rocker. The pose was so quintessentially New England gothic, Lilianna might have been sitting for a portrait.

"Miss Durant!" Eleanor said, probably too loudly. Somewhere, a screened door closed. "I'm here to pick up the boys. Is Mr. Zane with them?"

"Don't know and don't care. He thinks he can move me out of my home, where I've lived for twenty five years." Lilianna rocked harder, emphasizing her anger.

"Of course, you'd rather stay. Couldn't you pay him rent so you can go on living here?" Another small voice reminded Eleanor it was none of her business, but then, in Eastfield, everything was everyone's business.

"Who wants to live here? No one to talk to, except Wayne. Hate the place. Margaret's already looking for someplace else for me."

Eleanor opened her mouth and closed it again. Lilianna's logic was something she was accustomed to hearing from the mouths of children, and she understood at once that she couldn't win in this conversation.

Heavy footsteps crunched in the gravel, and Eleanor turned—somewhat gratefully—to face Evan Zane.

He looked happy, and far more approachable than he did when she saw him some weeks ago in The Thrifty Means. There was no doubt now his tanned face was the result of working in the sunshine, and his hair was shorter, looking combed with his fingers. There were raw scratches on his forearms, and a greasy stain on his denim shirt suggested he hadn't been sitting at his computer. Eleanor could barely take her eyes off him, even as Lilianna continued to grouse from her rocker.

"I'm glad to see you," Evan said, sounding a little breathless. Eleanor glanced at the way he had come, and realized his state probably had more to do with a rough uphill path than anything like excitement in seeing her did.

"What have you been doing?" she asked.

He hesitated and looked over her shoulder to where Lilianna sat in her chair, still reciting a litany of grievances.

"I've been throwing out stuff," he said defensively. "Wayne is better now, and supposed to be helping me, but he left on a dump run about two hours ago. Isn't the dump still on Fayreweather Road? About five minutes away?"

"He's probably looking through the garbage. Next to The Thrifty Means, the dump is the best place in town to pick up treasures. But do you know what you're doing? You might be throwing out some valuable things!"

"Broken light bulbs? Calendars from 1985? Old medicine bottles? Even I know garbage," he said. "Though Wayne really liked those calendars."

"Were they pin-ups? Never mind, I don't want to know. There's nothing on the list Wayne could be selling to a dealer and making a profit. It's genuine junk, which makes you more discerning than some other people in this town."

"I like to think so," he said, and gave her a frankly appraising look. "But what did you have in mind?"

"Probably not what you did," Eleanor said under her breath. "I was only thinking about the sorts of things people bring through the door of The Thrifty Means. You would be amazed and appalled."

"Right now, I am amazed and appalled at the things Aunt Dorothea didn't take to the dump ten years ago. Do you want to see for yourself?" Evan made a little bow and invited Eleanor to lead the way. Since she had no idea where they were going, she mimicked his gesture, and they walked along side by side.

How familiar it felt, and achingly comfortable, though years passed since Eleanor had felt the presence of a certain kind of man by her side. Since her husband left them and dragged her through a long, protracted divorce, she had mostly sought out the company of women. Most often, she had a small child hanging onto each hand. Michael Dennis, bless his soul, had been an amusing companion. Now, with Evan Zane, something else altogether happened.

She glanced up at him, and squinted against the sun. He smiled back and nodded towards the house, but said nothing as they walked together down the path. They climbed the few steps onto the porch and he wiped his hands on his worn khakis before turning the cut-glass knob on the front door. Eleanor's heart skipped a beat; years passed since she was inside the colonial farmhouse, and knew few people, aside from Mrs. B., who had been recently welcomed here.

The house smelled of summer. Though Lilianna and Dorothea lived here all year round, there was mustiness, an earthiness evocative of a summer cottage near a lake, and tapestries of cobwebs on the window sash. Eleanor blinked as her eyes grew accustomed to the dim light, and the living room came into focus.

"Oh, Evan, it's just wonderful! The place really is filled with treasures!"

She ignored his expression of skepticism as she walked from table to table, and paused to examine old prints and artifacts, and exquisite miniatures framed under glass. There were hand painted plates, and old clocks, and pewter aged to a rich, dark patina. A Tiffany window hung over the fireplace. A jade sculpture rested on a bookcase, surrounded by an array of tiny netsuke. The first thing Eleanor picked up was a hideous wooden box, painted in an array of colors.

"I made that treasure in Boy Scout camp," Evan said, and made a face. "I should have packed it up for the first run to the dump."

Eleanor smiled at him, loving the idea his aunt kept the dreadful thing all these years, and loving his house. "Your aunt was also a person of discernment," she said. "Was she your mother's sister? Or your father's?"

"Neither. She was married to my father's brother."

"Oh!" Eleanor said, revealing more surprise than she intended.

Evan studied her for a moment. "They were married for a very short time. But afterwards, she remained friends with my mother. When my parents died, there really wasn't anyone else to take me in. Or, for me to take in, I should say."

Eleanor reflected on the large network of friends and family she had, who supported her after her divorce, and who could be counted on to step in again for Leslie and Lewis, if anything happened to her.

"Your uncle?"

"My father's brother? He died when I was a baby and he and Dorothea never had kids of their own. That's probably why she and Lilianna scarcely understood where to start when they inherited me. I don't think I made things easy for them, and they certainly didn't have the time to read up on how to handle an angry teenage boy. They pretty much let me do what I wanted, as long as I didn't bother them."

"And I guess you didn't bother them for all these years."

"They preferred it," he said slowly. "And so did I. There wasn't a lot of affection between us."

"Is that why you're making Lilianna leave? She seems very disgruntled."

Evan crossed his arms. "Oh, I'm sure she is. She's disgruntled about everything. For starters, although she and my aunt ought to have expected the outcome, the kid grew into a man, and she's not too crazy about men. She doesn't like the food I eat, the hours I keep, the car I drive. But you're wrong about one thing: she can't wait to leave. She hates this place."

"I don't think so, Evan. She's sitting out there now with the attitude of someone who is willing to shoot the first person who comes near her."

"And I've managed to dodge the bullets so far. I did offer to sell her Garland, at less than market value, but she told me she'd been desperate to escape for years. In fact, I think she sees my aunt's death not as a great tragedy, but as an opportunity."

"An opportunity?" Eleanor was incredulous, though certainly she realized something of the same thing after her divorce.

"Yeah, an opportunity to complain to a whole new community of people. I wish her well, and I wish her gone." His expression hardened, and his fingers began to tap on the table. "But come see the kitchen."

Eleanor followed him into a small room, but one extending beyond the great rectangle of the house so yellow fields of daffodils grew on three sides. Someone had cut a few stalks and set them out in a jar in the center of the table.

Eleanor said nothing, until she looked down at the remnants of breakfast still on the table.

"She may be a malcontent, but Lilianna is right about one thing. If this is the food you eat for breakfast, it's just awful."

"I invited you here to see the stemware, not my sugar crispos. And you're not looking at breakfast but last night's dinner."

Eleanor knew what she wanted to say, but pride and the Women's Movement made her hesitate. Evan Zane might be planning to donate thousands of dollars of merchandise to an organization to which she had a passionate connection. A man who had lived in a household with two brazenly unconventional, controversial, women probably harbored few illusions about the old stereotypes. She sucked in her breath.

He looked at her expectantly.

"Would you like to join us for dinner tomorrow night? We usually eat around 7," she said so quickly, she wasn't sure he understood her. "I'm not cooking anything special, but I would consider it an act of mercy."

"Do you mean, saving me from my own cooking?"

"You really can't call this cooking. This is pouring and spooning."

"I suppose you can do better?"

Here was the arrogant Evan Zane Eleanor remembered, defending a fort made of paper and toothpicks. Could she do better? Her twins could have done better by the time they were eight years old.

"Yes, I can."

"Well, then, you're a woman of many talents. Writer, antiques expert, chef."

"Mother," she added. "Which means among my talents is a capacity for infinite patience. However, in your case, I'm thinking of making an exception. Do you want to come for dinner or not?"

"Let me take you out, instead."

Eleanor's blush spread across her face. She guessed at least fifteen years passed since anyone asked her for a date, but she recognized all the signs. His request, a little tentative. Her pleasure, made too evident by the rush of excitement. His waiting for an answer, immediate and unambiguous. Her desire to give the answer he wanted, but the rule of the game made hedging necessary.

Was she playing a game? Did the old rules still apply? Did any rules apply when you were nearly forty years old?

"There's Lewis and Leslie. And Brian is at my house all the time," she said.

Evan shrugged. "I suppose they have to eat

also?"

"They eat all the time. They barely pause between lunch and dinner."

"Then I better take the checkbook." At her expression of protest, "Or we'll just go to Ludlum's. How's the old joint?"

Eleanor giggled, partly in relief he was making this so easy. "You've been back in town for weeks and haven't been back to Ludlum's yet?"

"Well, you see my whole reason for the offer. I need an excuse to go back."

He meant it as a joke and Eleanor smiled. But the words weren't particularly gracious. Ludlum's was a family restaurant, and she supposed Evan Zane needed a family. The notion reminded her of those who "borrowed" children—nieces and nephews—for a trip to Disney World.

Still, how nice if he had preserved her giddy illusions, and allowed her to continue to think he had asked her for a date.

"Should I pick you up at 7?" he asked. "Where do you live?"

She supposed she ought to be insulted he hadn't wondered where she lived before this; he wasn't curious enough to drive by and see how she managed. He might have said the kids could pick up a pizza, stay at home, and he just wanted to be with her.

"I live on Milkweed," she said. "And seven is fine."

He nodded, and she wondered if her tone signaled a shift in their conversation. His fingers started tapping again, and somehow, Eleanor couldn't bear to watch or hear them. She opened a few more cabinets in the kitchen, noting the pottery storage jars, and painted tole trays.

"I'll let you look around," he said, and disappeared before she could turn around to answer him. When the outside door closed, she realized he really had left her on her own. Perhaps being with Lilianna made him desperate, and he already regretted asking her out.

Eleanor did look around, but even with his permission to do so, she felt like a snoop. She opened drawers and cabinets, revealing the little bits and pieces of a person's life, the things never opened to a stranger.

What would someone find in her own house after she was gone? A fifth grade valentine? A ripped tee shirt she held onto for sentimental reasons? Lewis' and Leslie's baby shoes? How many dumpsters would they have to bring into her driveway?

Eleanor glanced into a bedroom she guessed must have been Dorothea's. A large marmalade cat sprawled across the chenille bedspread, and barely opened his eyes to acknowledge the intrusion. She took a step in, but the presence of the dead woman was too strong, her death too immediate. If Eleanor felt like a snoop in the kitchen, she really wasn't prepared to look through Dorothea's bureau or night tables.

A large brown duffle bag was open on the bed in the next bedroom, the contents spilling out and strewn on the floor. If an invasion of Dorothea's drawers was too intimate, Eleanor was certainly not going to explore a room decorated with men's underwear and socks. She resisted the impulse to start picking up the laundry, and moved on.

This house was working some sort of spell on her. Before long, she would be offering to polish Evan Zane's lacrosse trophies!

Did he have lacrosse trophies?

She opened the door to the corner bedroom. He had some sort of trophy. When she walked across the worn blue carpet, stepping over old books and vinyl records, she took in the memorial to the life of the boy who once lived in this house, preserved just as it was when he left for college.

"Is there much of a market for old pinewood derby cars and outdated textbooks?" Evan Zane said from the doorway. Eleanor jumped about a foot.

"I'm sorry; I didn't hear you come back in," she gasped.

"Don't be sorry, I told you to look around. Though this may be the only place in the house without a single piece of fine china or lace."

"But lots of boy stuff. Everything seems to be blue."

"Well, yeah, for all my parents' liberal views—and behavior—my mother still lived in a pink and blue world." He walked over to the desk and closed a book. Eleanor might not have bothered to notice otherwise, but now she recognized the cover of their high school yearbook. She wondered what he was looking for.

"This room must have been your haven," Eleanor said. "After your parents...neither Dorothea nor Lilianna would have dared to redecorate this private sanctuary."

"And somehow they resisted all these years? They must have been tempted—look at all this stuff. And I wonder how they kept Wayne out. I can't believe he would have been able to keep his hands off all these old records and other things. They must be worth something."

"To teenage boys, perhaps. There's not a lot of interest in high school yearbooks, or picture frames engraved with the date of the Eastfield High School Senior Prom. Which, I notice, doesn't contain a picture."

He nodded, and took a few steps closer to her. "That's why I was going through the yearbook. I don't seem to have any other pictures of the old days."

"That may be a good thing. The big hair, the oversized glasses. The years may all be better forgotten," Eleanor said uneasily, and took a step backwards. "We were all so young, so unformed. We scarcely understood what we wanted."

"Oh, I understood what I wanted. I just wasn't sure how to get it." He gazed unblinkingly at her, leaving her with no doubt what he was talking about. "I'm still not sure how to get it, but I've had a lot more practice."

Though he wore his heavy work boots, his steps were light and quick when he finally cornered her, and took her in his arms and kissed her.

Eleanor closed her eyes, and refused to think about all the complications stemming from this one moment, of how she and Evan Zane were about to start something neither of them might have any desire to finish.

But it wasn't one moment; Eleanor wondered if the boy who had become a man in a household where his presence might have been an inconvenience was making up for years of dreaming. His arms were strong and bracing as he pressed the length of his body against hers. His mouth was warm and tasted of garden mint, and he kissed her as though he was starving. Eleanor's lips were abraded as they met the dark rough beard of his chin as he moved on to her nose, her eyelids, her forehead, but the sensation awakened something in her long asleep.

Her hands went up to clasp his neck and she didn't protest when they circled where they stood and his body arched hers towards the narrow twin bed.

A sharp knock at the door nearly made him drop her, and she struggled for balance. Evan said something rude under his breath.

"None of that in this house, my boy," Lilianna

said with something of the stern schoolmistress in her voice. "Your aunt's dead, but you can't disgrace her memory."

Without waiting for an answer or apology, she moved heavily down the hallway and slammed a door behind her.

"Either she goes or I go," Evan said.

"Or I go," Eleanor said, and reached up to smooth down her hair. She was shaking, she realized, and more than a little embarrassed. "I'm not sure it's such a good idea for me to come here to help you, Evan. This is not the sort of thing the ladies of The Thrifty Means do at all."

"Do you mean, make out with boys in their bedrooms?"

"You're not a boy, and I'm certainly not a girl. And I don't think anyone has used the word for twenty years."

"A pity. What do they say instead?"

"I'm not sure. But I'm sure it's a lot more explicit and leaves a lot less to the imagination." Eleanor ducked under his outstretched arm, and started towards the hall. A cat ran across the foyer.

He caught her with his free hand and pulled her gently back against his chest. "I'm willing to try a more modern approach."

Eleanor sank back against him, sighing as his arms came around her once again. "But I'm not sure I am. I have two children and responsibilities in this town. And I'm hopelessly out of practice."

His chest rattled her as he laughed. "Hopeless? I don't think so. I'd say you don't need any practice at all." Though she still wore her jacket, she could feel the heat of his hands on her arms. "But I'm willing to go slowly, so we can brush up as we go along."

She turned in his arms, no matter how difficult to confront him with any degree of seriousness when his nose was inches away from hers and she could see her own reflection in his bright eyes. "Are you going to stay a while?" she asked. The notion put a whole different cast on this relationship, if, indeed, it was a relationship.

His eyes crossed slightly as he leaned forward and kissed the tip of her nose. "I think I will. There are a few things interesting me here in Eastfield. I wasn't expecting to think it when I came back for the funeral."

"Most people think we're still a little provincial town, but you should have known better."

He nodded. "Things were never so simple. And now, they've gotten complicated."

Eleanor's pride would have insisted he only meant her, since he now had a compelling reason to stay around. Her reason overruled her emotions, reminding her there was a pattern more intricate somewhere, something she did not yet understand.

"I'd like to talk to you about it, but not here and not now," he continued.

"Where?" she asked a little dreamily, mesmerized by the intensity of the look in his eyes.

He grinned, and the look was gone in an instant. "I assume we still have a date tomorrow night?"

"With my two children, and maybe Brian," she reminded him. "A wise man would back out."

"I believe it will be the highlight of my week." Evan paused and looked around at the boy's bedroom once his own. "Well, maybe not."

Eleanor wiggled out of his arms, discouraging his line of thought. She ought to leave. Leslie would already be home, and Eleanor had a birdcage to clean out before the old thing could occupy a place in her kitchen. Evan watched her as she walked into the hallway and he followed her through the living room, where she stopped at the coffee table to examine something she had only briefly noticed before.

It was the *EZ Guide to the Civil War*, a cheerful one-hundred page condensation of the worst war on American soil, during which her citizens endured years of suffering and deprivation. Evan Zane's face was on the cover, looking both professorial and reassuring, but nothing like what she had seen only minutes before. That side of Evan Zane, a little unsure of himself, was a private one, much more appealing.

She turned back to look at him, and wondered what he was thinking. Did he regret what they just shared? Did he see their kiss as the start of a new chapter, requiring some revision before he got it quite right?

Or did he see their mutual longing as she did, as the inevitable outcome of a history started long ago? Was it history if neither of them recognized it, spoke of it, reflected on the horrible events of that icy night? In all these years, did he ever think about Ellie Lambert, the girl he so assiduously avoided until he escaped from the whispered gossiping and pitying glances of Eastfield? She never understood why he shut her out of his shattered life, when she imagined he needed as much as she did to find some comfort in their shared grief.

He went on then without her, as if he scarcely recognized her. In all this time, she hadn't seen him until the day they met in The Thrifty Means.

"Good picture," she said, echoing what he had said about her own book cover recently. She closed the door before he could answer.

****

Evan rubbed the back of his neck, remembering the feel of Eleanor's hands as she trifled with his hair. He had told himself a hundred times, since the moment he recognized her in The Thrifty Means, that their relationship was strictly business and once the old house was cleaned out, he would probably never come through Eastfield again. The town was once his home, but every minute he spent surrounded by his childhood junk only brought back all the depressing memories. Until now.

The vision of Eleanor Gilmartin standing in his damned bedroom, looking far more delectable in her well-fitted jeans than any girl he might have dared to bring to the house and examining his trophies as if they were every bit as interesting as Dorothea's antique silver, filled him with a yearning for something he hadn't even realized he desired.

It wasn't only that she was beautiful, and wore clothes somehow making her appear both casual and seductive. There must be more than the flowery scent of her dark brown hair cascading over her shoulders. Or her hazel eyes, which were bright and inquisitive, letting you know in a moment just how very clever she was. All this would have been enough to ignite his desire.

There was more. She was a woman he would want to come home to. The sense had nothing to do with cooking—though he wouldn't mind some decent dinners—or cleaning, or any of the things his generation had attempted to redefine. His yearning had to do with the comforts of conversation, of sharing the day-to-day minutia of one's life, of reliving memories and making new ones.

Good God! A few weeks back in Eastfield and he was becoming a sentimental idiot! If Eleanor guessed his thoughts, she would laugh in his face.

No, she would not. That's what made her different from other women in his life. She would know exactly what he meant.

Something rubbed up against his leg and he bent to scratch a gray kitten between the ears. Down the hall, he heard Lilianna cackle like a witch. She probably had enough to laugh about: she was still able to interrupt his lovemaking, cats were taking over a house where once they were dreaded, Wayne had probably already emptied out Dorothea's bank account and for all he knew, Lilianna was sprinkling arsenic into his lukewarm iced tea. Garland was a veritable funhouse.

He looked around at the beams and cabinetry so familiar he hardly noticed them. The place wasn't a fun house, and certainly wasn't a place to raise a child. But it could be.

Evan lifted the kitten into his arms, where he promptly curled up and, purring, closed his eyes. Well, one thing was for sure; the little fellow was already quite at home. He couldn't be more than a few months old, and Dorothea was dead nearly as long. Had she been so far gone she couldn't protest the intrusion?

Dr. Stanley told him there had been no warning; no reason to think Dorothea was near the end. She was on medication for a few ailments, but everything seemed under control.

Except her fear of cats. Nothing would ever control such unreasonable terror.

The sound of breaking glass shattered the quiet in the house, and Lilianna laughed again.

Evan looked down at the sleeping kitten, who curled up tighter into the crook of his arm.

Chapter 5

"A little polish can make even the most tarnished teapot respectable."

> *Gail Madison, volunteer since 1996*
> *and unflagging optimist*

Eleanor looked in the mirror and grabbed a washcloth off the towel rack. The Tallulah Bankhead look was out and if she rubbed off her lipstick one more time, there would be blood on her chin. The whole thing really was ridiculous. Okay, so she hadn't had a date in five years. Ten years. This really wasn't going to be a date anyway. Not with her two children talking nonstop and goofy Brian Coley analyzing the protein content of everything on the menu at Ludlum's.

"Mom?" Lewis poked his head through the bathroom door. "Whoa. Did you burn yourself or something?"

"Something." She picked up the lipstick again and decided against it. Her lips were bright red without any added color, and felt as if she had been kissing sandpaper. She reached for the lip-gloss. "Are you almost ready?"

"For what?"

Eleanor closed her eyes. On one hand, her kids complained she reminded them of comings and goings all the time. On the other, they always professed surprise when she dragged them out the door to one place or another.

"We're going out to dinner with Mr. Zane," she said calmly. "Do you remember he invited us?"

"Evan? Yeah, but we told him we have to get the report ready for tomorrow. He's coming to school anyway, and said he'd come by the lab to get the results. Don't worry about Brian and me; we'll order in a pizza."

"When did he become Evan? And why is he coming to school?"

Eleanor studied Lewis' face in the mirror, and recognized his look of amusement before he caught her eye. He shrugged.

"He's not our teacher or anything. And he's coming to school to talk to the history classes."

That got her full attention. She had been living in town for years and no one ever asked her to talk anywhere. Evan Zane comes to Eastfield with no more forethought than if he were stuck on the road with a flat tire, and he's invited to speak to the history classes?

"About what? About how to avoid doing real research?" She pinched her lips together, feeling the sting, and reached for the light switch. Who cared what she looked like? "Let's get out of here. Where's Leslie?"

Lewis backed out of the bathroom. "She's at Jennifer's house. She told you."

The accusation was probably justified. Eleanor did nothing but nod her head in the car this morning; her kids could have been asking her permission to move to the North Pole, for all she knew. She was too busy thinking...about Evan Zane. The man was making an idiot out of her.

She paused as she walked past another mirror, and realized while it really didn't matter what she looked like, she looked good. Her hair fell in graceful curves around her face, and she managed to comb over the most conspicuous areas of gray. Her green sweater made her eyes look brighter, and, of course, her lips were bright enough.

"So, does this mean I'm going out with Mr. Zane myself?" She hoped she sounded sufficiently indignant.

"You guessed it," Lewis said, and shrugged again.

"Your idea or Leslie's?"

"Actually, I think it was Evan's," Lewis said, and for the first time, Eleanor noticed something intriguing and a little disturbing about him. He wasn't speaking as her son, and certainly not as her little boy. He was speaking as a man who colluded with another man about the one thing—aside from the Red Sox - transcending age and status. Tonight, even in the eyes of her son, she was just a woman.

"I suppose you think you're very clever."

"As a matter of fact..." he began, just before the doorbell rang. He didn't finish his sentence. There was no need, after all.

****

Evan drove his car along the narrow road, straining to read the house numbers. Was the town always like this? Did Eastfield residents always profess to welcome newcomers, even as they made it impossible for strangers to find their houses? Didn't anyone in town ever think of streetlights?

A number reflected in his headlights and he realized he had gone too far. Backing into a driveway, praying he wouldn't hit anything that mattered, Evan turned the Jeep around. Coming from this direction gave him a better perspective, and he realized the orientation of the street was towards the park at the corner. Memory returned to him in a flash: swimming in the old quarry there, hiking with friends, bringing in girls who appeared very sweet, but proved to have more sexual experience than he did. He never realized Eleanor Lambert lived here.

But she didn't, then. He finally remembered her

parents' house up on Ridgeford. His Aunt Dorothea brought him there some weeks after the accident, reminding him she had also suffered a great loss; Ellie Lambert saved his life, and he owed her kindness and consideration. They never got past the driveway. Dorothea, reprimanding him for his tears and anxiety, brought him home. He never managed to get back.

He still didn't. This modest bungalow, replete with slate pathway and bird houses in the trees, was nothing like her old home. He need never face that again.

He only needed to face her.

He pulled into her driveway, accompanied by a chorus of barking dogs. A light went off upstairs as he jumped from the car, and a cat appeared in the front window just as he rang the doorbell. And rang again.

Ellie opened the door and looked at him with the general annoyance one reserved for door-to-door salespeople and religious missionaries.

"I'm not trying to sell you anything, ma'am," he said.

Her eyes narrowed and she took a step back, silently bidding him enter.

"I'm not so sure about that," she retorted as he walked past her.

"Hi, Evan!" Brian said, looking up from a magazine. Lewis was on the phone, but waved a hand in greeting. In a cage in the corner of the room, a little blue parakeet squawked his head off.

"I understand it's just the two of us tonight, right?" Ellie asked in the manner of one of their junior high school teachers. He didn't think she was trying for a sort of homage; she was just being severe. Evan turned back to look at her as she leaned against the door, closing behind her, and realized her act just wasn't working. No one who looked and moved liked Ellie Lambert could be so big a pain in the ass.

"Do you have a problem?" he asked, knowing damn well she did. "We're just going to Ludlum's. Unless, of course, you prefer somewhere nicer. Someone told me there's a new French place across from the library."

"L'Avignon," she said. "But I'm not dressed for it."

He gauged the longing in her eyes, the way she closed them for a second as if savoring something delicious and forbidden. Well, if the restaurant was able to come through on the delicious promise, he'd work on the forbidden. He had already started on the latter.

"You look fine," he said, and then when she frowned, "You look great." The boys snickered and Evan could hardly blame them. He hoped they weren't expecting him to be suave. "And this is Eastfield."

She loosened up a bit. "And you expect us to wear flannel shirts and jeans? A lot has changed in twenty years, Evan. We have fancy restaurants, designer shops, gourmet cheeses at the market. The general store was always overrated, I think."

"I always liked the place," he said staunchly and opened his arms. "But what are you saying? This isn't good enough?"

He supposed he asked for it. Her eyes started at his, and then her critical gaze moved slowly down the lines of his body. He tried to steady himself, trying not to give her anything to focus on. If she noticed, she didn't say anything. But then she wouldn't, not with the two boys in the room.

"We don't have reservations," she said, in a low voice. "And don't tell me this is Eastfield and we don't need them."

He didn't say anything at all, but fished in his

pocket for his cell phone. She mouthed the word "L'Avignon" as he called for information, and got through to the restaurant.

"Ten minutes? Yeah, I think we can get there in time," he said into the phone. "We're in luck. Wayne must've cancelled his reservation."

She laughed as she walked over to the coat rack and pulled off a fluffy blue sweater. Evan paused to notice the way her shirt pulled up to reveal a sliver of smooth white skin, and then followed her to take the sweater from her hands. He held it up as she slipped her arms through the sleeves, nearly settling into his embrace, and he looked over her shoulder to see Brian and Lewis give him a thumbs up. Maybe he was more suave than he guessed.

"Don't do anything I wouldn't do, Mom," Lewis said as Evan took her elbow to walk her to the door. She stiffened.

"Well, I know you wouldn't eat cassoulet," she said. "And I just might be tempted."

Evan savored the promise of things to come, but saw no reason to let the boys know that. He opened the door and listened to the sound of tires on wet pavement as a car went by. Rain fell lightly on his face.

They walked quickly down the steps to the driveway. Eleanor looked up at the cloudy sky, squinting into the drizzle as he pulled her around to the passenger side of the car.

"You'll drive carefully, won't you?" she asked.

He recognized the importance of the question. When he slipped through the driver's door and shook his head to shake off the rain on his hair, he answered. "I always drive carefully."

She shot him a look in the darkness, and then pointed out the windshield just as the wipers went on. "You can take Greenwood for a shortcut to the center."

As he edged carefully down the driveway, the rain doing nothing to improve his vision, he said, "I remember Greenwood was a dead end. Doesn't the street go to the quarry?"

"I guess I'm not surprised you remember the quarry," she said, not in a complimentary way. "But it gave up the ghosts a few years ago when a developer flooded the pit and built four luxury homes on what is now beachfront property. Greenwood Avenue skirts the development and intersects with Main Street."

"And the ghosts are gone."

She nodded in the flash of light from an oncoming car. "Of course. They would bring down property values, you know. So, Old Headless Mike is vanquished. The Lady in White probably moved downriver. And all the stray pets who wandered into the quarry and were lost must forever be consigned to memory. Poor little things."

"They weren't the only things lost at the quarry."

She didn't say anything for several minutes as he turned onto Greenwood. In front of them, illuminated like cathedrals, loomed several houses with the requisite four-car garages. The old dead end still appeared incorporated into the roadway, like a bulge in a snake's belly.

"I suppose you mean the virginity of precocious high schoolers?" she said at last, back to her severe tone.

He was surprised she resented it so much. "No, I mean pocket knives and canteens and such," he lied.

"I see," she said, and he had the impression she did.

They rode the rest of the way in silence, as the rain picked up and traffic got marginally heavier as they came into town. A traffic light Evan never noticed before was in place at what was formerly a quiet intersection. The old grange hall was now a teen center. Well, the former team center, the reservoir, proved overrated anyway. Then he noticed the library, which looked bigger than he remembered, and the handsomely painted sign of L'Avignon.

"I guess we're here," he said as they pulled into the last available spot.

"Good," she answered. "I never take anything for granted."

Apparently not, for she pulled an umbrella from her handbag and opened it in his face as he came around to her side of the car. She pulled him under, and they walked closely together across the lot.

"If you think Ludlum's is the standard of excellence, you'll be put off by this place. But if you've done nothing else to distance yourself from Eastfield but develop an enterprising taste, you'll walk out of here satisfied," Ellie said as she shrugged herself out of her damp cardigan and handed it to him to hang in the coat room. The gesture was so familiar, so comfortable, there might not have been twenty years of separation between them.

"Well, I expect to be satisfied in any case," he said softly, as the hostess approached them, smiled, and led them to two seats by the window. On a warm summer day, the location would have been splendid. Tonight the location was a little too drafty and the patter of rain too evident. "And I've never tried to distance myself from Eastfield."

Ellie made a small sound revealing what she thought of his comment statement, and settled herself into her seat. "I think you ran as far and as fast as you could go," she said. "If Dorothea lived forever, as she apparently intended, we might never have seen you again."

"I was never very far," he said defensively. "For

most of the time, I lived in New York. And maybe it wasn't the town I avoided, but Dorothea and Lilianna."

She sighed. "Well, I can understand why," she said, as the waiter lit the candle at their table and handed them their menus.

Evan glanced at the menu, and then closed it on the table. "Order whatever you think I'd like," he said.

She looked at him, startled, and her eyes reminded him of the green waters of the quarry, where better swimmers than he had drowned. She picked up the menu and handed it back to him. "I have no idea what you like."

He opened the printed album again and deciphered something that might have been salmon and string beans. When the waiter came over to take their bar order, Evan happily abandoned the menu again to consider some of the wine selections. He looked across at Ellie to see if she approved, but her focus was on people at a nearby table. She nodded, smiled, and gave them a little wave. A moment later, a couple passing through the aisle stopped at the table and greeted them. The man seated with his back to Ellie pushed back his chair, turned, and said something to her.

"I didn't realize you were planning a club meeting down here tonight," Evan said. "Do you know everyone in this place?"

"No, not everyone. But you should be grateful we're not at Ludlum's. Then I would know everyone." She looked up when the waiter arrived and gave her order. It sounded good, so when the man turned to him, Evan said he'd have the same thing. Ellie looked vaguely suspicious, as she reached for her wineglass. "But you know a lot of these people also. You just don't recognize them."

"Like the grange hall," he muttered. "And the

library."

"Have patience. Within a few weeks, everything will begin to look very, very familiar." She spoke as if nothing could be more boring, and yet Evan imagined there was something pleasant about knowing everyone and every place. "But most of my friends are not from the old days, like you are. They're from The Thrifty Means. If you work there long enough, you get to know everyone in town, and their comings and goings."

Evan filed the social network of the store for later use, and focused on the one thing to really matter.

"Are we friends?" he asked. He realized it did matter, to have someone in whom to confide, someone who understand something of his past, and might consider a future with him. When they were kids, he would have only noticed the way her body moved, or how long her hair was down her back. It would have mattered who her friends were, and what teams they played on. He would have noticed her smile and her body. Now, his earlier lapse in her home notwithstanding, there were other things more important. He still wondered about those things, but they didn't have much to do with who she was now, or the man he had become.

"I think I would like very much to be friends, Evan." She sighed, and he wondered how a little whisper of air could manage to sound so plaintive, filled with such longing. "When we were kids, friendship between us would have led to some good natured teasing, and lots of speculation. But we're too old to cause much of a stir now."

He looked over her shoulder to where two elderly women were sitting, nudging each other, and pointing in their direction. The Eastfield phone lines would probably be humming with gossip in less than an hour.

"Besides, you can never have too many friends," Ellie continued. "Life is fragile; we know better than anyone."

Suddenly, there seemed to be no one else in the restaurant, and all the years of his self-imposed exile from Eastfield were gone in an instant. He was a kid again, arguing with his parents from the back of a car racing along an icy road. Ellie Lambert was waiting for him, not yet aware she would pull him from the wreckage of his life, and forever leave open the question of what would have happened if she had also died in the crash. Looking at her now, seeing the way her swollen lower lip glistening by the candle's glow, and how much more beautiful her face looked in maturity; he realized she had been a part of his life all these years, without either of them knowing.

"Are you trying to get me to do something for you?" she asked, and picked up her wineglass. She didn't wear any rings, he noticed.

He opened his mouth to protest, looking for words to explain she had already done more than anyone ought to do.

She sighed again, but not with longing. Rather, she appeared a little impatient. "And I suppose what you want has to do with The Thrifty Means."

"The Thrifty Means?" What the hell was she talking about?

The waiter brought their soup just then, something smelling like onions, with green weeds sprinkled on top. Ellie smiled contentedly, and stirred. She leaned forward, just slightly, savoring its warmth. Evan didn't recall anything served at Ludlum's invoking this sort of sensuous pleasure. Mostly, everything smelled like yesterday's French fries, and diners scarfed their meals down with a gallon of soda from the fountain. He never heard of anyone actually dying of food poisoning after eating at Ludlum's, but he'd been out of touch a long time.

Through the haze of savory steam, Ellie looked at him across the table. Her eyes were half closed, and he could see the pattern of gentle veins on her eyelids. "I suppose you want me to go through all your things at Garland, and tell you what's valuable? I can, but it would take a lot of time. I can't just poke around in a few drawers like I did the other day. I would need to do some research, and keep a detailed inventory. I would have to separate what should go to the dump, what might go to The Thrifty Means, and what deserves auctioning in Manhattan. It could take months and months, more time than either of us have."

Evan was taken aback. He wasn't quite prepared for this offer, and her almost immediate counter offer. While he was thinking about the past, she moved years ahead of him, into the future. He wasn't even sure what he wanted, but now she put it into words, everything made perfect sense. If her proposal meant they would be spending lots of time together, more than simple logic might be satisfied. What did she mean about not having much time?

He said the first thing coming to mind. "What are you saying? Are you going somewhere?"

Now it was her turn to be startled. He could see her reaction in her wide eyes, in the small O made by her lips. The waiter bent over their table, partially blocking his view of her, but she remained still, the spoon held aloft in one hand.

"Are you leaving town?" he said more pointedly. "Or are you ill? Why won't you have enough time?"

Her shoulders relaxed. "No, I'm perfectly fine. Aren't you leaving as soon as you are able? Aren't you anxious to sell the house?"

Evan shrugged. "I'm not in a hurry."

"But your home is now elsewhere, and Lilianna and Wayne will be moving. And Eastfield must be full of awful memories for you." She sounded a little desperate.

Evan watched her carefully. They shared those memories, but neither could yet come out and speak of them directly. He acknowledged what she meant about the fragility of friendship, and hadn't dismissed her nervousness about riding off in the rain. There were words not yet said aloud. Had she erected emotional barriers, all those years ago, to keep herself sane? Why not? After all, he did something of the sort himself. The two of them, alone in all the world, understood those barriers were made of straw.

"I expected that to be the case," he said honestly, and avoided her eyes by stirring the soup. "And I guess it's one of the reasons why I almost never came home in all these years. But now I'm here, I find I like Eastfield. I can get used to the place again. I like the quiet and the easy pace. I think the people are friendly. And Garland is bringing back only the good memories, somehow. So I'm not in any rush to go anywhere."

"Honestly, Evan, you sound as if you've been reading the glossy magazines put out by developers who try to pretend putting wood shingles on the side of a house is bringing back the good old days. Your aunt just died. You've been left with a pile of old junk Wayne will only haul down to the dump if you pay him enough. His house burned down. The Belvedere River is polluted. And you have an old lady sitting in the garden yelling at anyone who comes up the drive. Eastfield isn't paradise. It's life and very messy. I don't know why you would want to stay."

Evan smiled, and looked up from his soup. "Do you want me to stay?" he asked.

The damned waiter reappeared at their table, full of apologies about a change to the menu. It seemed much ado about nothing, particularly since Evan didn't know the difference between a twice-baked potato and a stuffed potato anyway. He wouldn't even know what he was missing. He only recognized what was before him, and she looked pretty good. Ellie sniffed, and returned her attention to her soup.

"What I want doesn't really matter, does it?" she asked, not meeting his eyes.

"Your wishes may matter more than you know," he said, and waited for her response. When it did not come, he wondered if she understood him. He brazened on anyway, briefly wondering if she believed him a perfect idiot. "The junk will be cleaned up if you will help me. Wayne's cottage didn't burn entirely, and I may have the place fixed up as an office for my work," he said. "I'm going to stay."

He watched her digest this unexpected part of their meal. Hell, he hadn't even realized he ordered it until this very moment.

"Why do you need an office if you have the house to yourself? I mean, if you intend to live here," she asked. She dabbed at some soup in the corner of her mouth, and Evan wished he had been quick enough to do the job for her.

Her question was a good one, and Evan did not yet have an answer for her. He had an idea, unformed and speculative at best, about starting a family, about having a place separate from where the kids would play, about having a wife who might not like the idea of tripping over boxes of books and research materials, the tools of his trade. He imagined an idyllic Eastfield life for himself, the sort of thing out of the developer's brochures Ellie so readily disparaged. Whereas the developers tried to get buyers to imagine a fantasy, his life would be very real.

"Your parents would have been very happy," she said quietly.

He was sorry she said that.

"How so?" he asked tersely. His quickly envisioned dream of a happy family life in Eastfield evaporated in a moment.

She put her spoon down in her empty bowl and sat back in her chair. He glanced down at his own serving, and realized he barely started to eat.

"Why, hasn't your family lived here forever? And your parents were so well known in this town, even before...before..."

"They were killed?" He put his own spoon down, and settled back.

"Yes, of course," she said gently, as if the very words opened a wound. "Everyone liked them and admired them. Even as kids, we believed you had everything."

"Except brothers and sisters, like everyone else."

"But you had more friends than anyone else. Popularity must have been some compensation."

The waiter came over, and Evan had to explain why he didn't finish his soup. Yes, everything was fine. Yes, the soup was hot enough. No, he didn't want the lobster bisque instead. The guy could have been his aunt Dorothea, stopping just short of telling him there were kids starving in Africa. Evan finally waved him off.

"Popularity wasn't compensation. Nothing so complicated. It was just a way of getting out of the house." Evan recognized the confusion on her face. "My parents were always fighting."

"Oh," she said, and he realized he burst several bubbles. "I had no idea."

He shrugged. "How would you? How would anyone? In a place like Eastfield, people can protect their dirty little secrets." Though his hands had been edging towards hers on the table, he withdrew them when the salad came. "Why did you get divorced?" he parried.

He could see he made her uncomfortable, but she didn't retreat into her salad.

"We were always fighting. And we needed money. We had two babies, a little sooner than we expected, and I vowed I could make a career out of my writing."

Evan winced, recalling his parents' last argument.

"You needn't worry about upsetting me, you know. Everything happened so long ago, I hardly remember what he looked like." She smiled wistfully. "Except when I look at Lewis."

"I think Lewis looks just like you; that's how I realized who he was," Evan said. "He's a good kid."

"So is Leslie. They're the best things I've done."

Much more satisfying than writing *The EZ Guide to the Spanish American War*, Evan considered. Yeah, the more he considered things, having a family would be just fine.

"So, back to The Thrifty Means," he said abruptly.

"Yes," she smiled. "Another good thing I do."

"Will you have time to help me go through the house? I can pay you, you know."

She looked at him as if something was unexpectedly distasteful, probably not the cucumber in her salad. "I make a good living from my books, thank you. What I do for The Thrifty Means is purely as a volunteer, what I give back to the community. None of us takes any money for working there, and probably buys more stuff than we should. It's hard to resist some of the things coming through the door, you know. And treasures from your aunt's estate are going to generate a lot of excitement. They've already created quite a buzz."

"Have they?" Evan asked, surprised. "How does

anyone know what's up there? Especially since I hardly know myself?"

He wondered if she might have said something to the others, but her expression suggested she didn't know much more than he did. "Why, I don't really know," she said, clearly puzzled. "I suppose Margaret Brownlee might have said something. She must have stopped by to see Lilianna and Wayne through the years, and probably looked around the house. It's a hobby of hers."

"Visiting boorish and ungrateful cousins?"

"Checking out what people have in their homes. She's befriended so many people in town, and sometimes brings meals to the elderly and sick. I know it must come purely from the goodness of her heart, but somehow she manages to get a piece of their estates before they pass on."

"Do you mean, they write her into their wills?"

Ellie giggled, and Evan remembered the girl she used to be, always cheerful and carefree. Before the accident changed their lives.

"Evan," she said, coming closer again. He could smell something sweet, not strong enough to be cologne but perhaps a skin cream or her shampoo. "She's a volunteer also. The very queen of volunteers. When she walks away from a deathbed carrying a vase or a pair of rusty old andirons, it's for The Thrifty Means."

"Very devoted," he said, a little cynically.

"Yes, she is," Ellie said defensively. "And she's been doing this for a long time. There are some who think it's time for a change, and a younger group of women should lead the board of trustees. But how does one argue with Mrs. B.'s continued success? She's very much admired."

"And you?"

She didn't pretend to misunderstand him. "Oh, I'm not particularly admired. I'm just another volunteer."

He didn't quite believe that either.

****

Eleanor now understood how the man managed to survive on breakfast cereals and a loaf of bread. Though L'Avignon was his idea, and she would have been perfectly happy at Ludlum's, he seemed indifferent to the lovely ambiance of the place, and their wonderful menu. He just put it on the table without bothering to read anything, and relied on her choices. Then when their delicious onion broth came, he would have nothing to do with it.

He would make an excellent husband, she admitted, and was startled such a thing should come to her. Here was a man who would eat anything: burned, undercooked, unimaginative, leftovers, take-out. The prospect was heavenly.

And he wasn't bad to look at, either. She wasn't the only one who noticed, as she was aware of curious glances in their direction. Some of the old timers would remember him, but the old timers typically did not come into this restaurant. What some welcomed as an upscale indulgence, others despaired as unwelcome signs of changing times.

Such sentiments were a little like the dynamic at The Thrifty Means. Some of the older volunteers didn't understand why they would want to computerize their bookkeeping, or spend money on new cabinets. Eleanor spent months convincing the board a water cooler in the shop was not going to corrupt the values of the volunteers, and might just be a pleasant convenience. There were still some who refused to fill a cup from its spigot, claiming to prefer the rusty water flowing from the tap for free.

Mrs. B. was one of those. She wouldn't be caught dead in L'Avignon, or in one of the supermarket chains on the outskirts of town. She didn't like the new clothing stores opening in Eastfield, and complained about the modern conveniences people were installing in their houses. Like dishwashers. And air conditioning. Every summer Eleanor enjoyed the lecture about how the houses of Eastfield were cooled by the fresh, stiff breezes off Long Island Sound, though the Sound was more than ten miles away.

Mrs. B. simply believed that if one made do without such things in, say, 1945, one didn't need them in the present. She didn't like anything that wasn't genuinely antique.

Eleanor wasn't an antique and therefore wasn't altogether sure Mrs. B. liked her either. She merely tolerated her, as she did color television and cars having automatic transmission. If Eleanor managed to bring in some of Dorothea's antiques for the benefit of the shop, the woman would be pleased. Unless she believed she had exclusive access to the estate, and viewed Eleanor as an interloper.

"Why, Eleanor Gilmartin! I don't usually see you here!"

Eleanor was startled out of her musings by Lucille Armitage, an antiques dealer in town. Dressed in a stylish wool suit and silk scarf, she made Eleanor acutely aware of her own casual appearance.

"Hello, Lucy," she said cheerfully. "Perhaps we just come in at different times."

"Yes, of course. You probably have to eat earlier in the evening because of the children," Lucille said, and looked curiously at Evan. "Where are they?"

"They're home. They're not babies anymore, you know. They usually stay up later than I do."

Lucille laughed as if this was some fine witticism, and continued to look at Evan.

"Lucille, let me introduce Evan Zane. He's..."

Under a heavy layer of makeup, Lucille's face blushed. "Of course I know who you are, Evan dear," she said familiarly.

When Evan stood up to shake her hand, she sighed blissfully. "I see your aunt raised you to be a gentleman. So important these days," she said, though Eleanor wasn't sure why. In fact, she was beginning to feel left out of this whole strange scene.

"Now, tell me your name, so I'm not at a disadvantage," Evan said graciously.

"I'm Mrs. Peter Armitage, a very old friend of your late aunt. We had some wonderful times together. I visited her frequently these past few months, and we discussed selling some of the antiques from Garland. I'm a dealer, you understand. But I promised her I'd take only a fifteen percent commission. That's a very good deal, and of course, I'd extend the same courtesy to you. Here's my business card, and please call me any time of the day or night." She glanced down at Eleanor, and added, "I'm always up late."

Eleanor wondered if Evan might consider the offer, as the woman was nearly double his age. She could be his grandmother. But flirtation might be something one never outgrew, nor the sense one remained sexually attractive. She looked up at Lucille, but the woman's attention returned to Evan, assessing him with a keen, appreciative eye. Well, the woman was an appraiser; she just wasn't known to bother evaluating forty-year-old things.

"Would you like to join us for dinner?" Evan asked, and Eleanor looked at him in horror.

Lucille giggled, girlishly. "Oh, dear, how sweet. No, I'm just leaving. And I certainly wouldn't want to ruin your little tête-à-tête."

You already have. Eleanor looked pointedly at Lucille.

"But do remember I am ready to help you with anything at all. You would realize a handsome profit from the antiques in the house," Lucille said. "While

The Thrifty Means can only offer you a tax deduction."

"Oh, I hope The Thrifty Means can offer me a good deal more," Evan said, while Eleanor turned to the window, and noticed a car pull out of the parking lot.

"More than a vintage piece like myself?" Lucille said so low, Eleanor could barely hear her.

"And then, I would also be doing a service to the town. And a tax deduction might be the very thing I need." Evan managed to make this sound provocative. Really, the man was outrageous. "But I will certainly keep you in mind, Mrs. Armitage."

Lucille met Eleanor's eyes in the window with a look of triumph, which convinced Eleanor the woman was delusional. Sweeping her scarf over her shoulder, she sashayed to the lobby.

"What a friendly woman," Evan said, as he sat down again. "Just the sort of person Eastfield is known for."

"Scheming and manipulative? Lucille Armitage shows up at The Thrifty Means every day, and tries to bargain us down on our prices. Then, she proceeds to charge five times as much for those items at shows and auctions. I wonder what, if anything, was promised by your aunt."

"Ouch. This is a side of you I haven't seen, Ellie Lambert."

The waiter, who had been hovering near the kitchen door during the little scene with Lucy Armitage, brought their entrees.

"I'm known to everyone as Eleanor Gilmartin, now," Eleanor explained, wondering if he realized what he said. She picked up her fork. "Almost no one remembers Ellie Lambert anymore." Except you.

"I guess someone working at The Thrifty Means would get to know almost everyone in town, young and old," Evan said. He looked at his plate of sea bass and nicely browned potatoes as if he had no idea how it got there, and speared a piece of the delicate white fish.

"Well, yes, haven't I said as much?" Eleanor asked. He could have no complaint about the meal; everything was delicious. "Don't you remember going there as a kid?"

"I'm not sure," he said, and scratched his chin. Eleanor heard the rasp of his beard, guessing when last she saw him he probably hadn't starting shaving. "You sold books?"

She smiled at him. When you were a kid, I didn't sell anything. I'm younger than you are. But yes, the shop has always sold books. I think we have a few of yours there right now."

"Who comes in to buy them?" he asked, and took a bite of his bass. He looked surprised and pleased.

No one with half a brain, she wanted to say. But a man who would eat anything in front of him should not be insulted. "Everyone and anyone. Now you understand my point."

"How often does Wayne come in?"

"I don't think I recall seeing him, but I know he comes by. He may have stopped in once or twice to speak to Mrs. B. Lilianna came a few times. With and without your aunt."

"I see," he said, and she wondered why this should matter so. Perhaps he was evaluating if The Thrifty Means was really a place dear to his aunt's heart. "Did my aunt have other friends?"

"I wouldn't know," Eleanor said, and didn't.

"Did she have enemies?"

"I certainly wouldn't know!"

Evan nodded and attacked his dinner with what Eleanor hoped was appreciation. Wordlessly, he refilled her wine glass, and earned an exasperated look from their overly solicitous waiter. He didn't say another word until they had both finished.

"Dessert?" he asked.

"Just tea," she answered.

"One coffee and one tea," he told the expectant waiter, who looked pleased.

The poor man did not have an eye to their health, Eleanor realized. They were among the last diners this evening, though the hour wasn't all so very late. This was still Eastfield, after all.

When their check accompanied their drinks, Eleanor reached for her purse. Evan's hand reached across the table and stopped her. His palm was warm and rough, and his fingers curled around her wrist.

"This doesn't have to be your treat, Evan. It's not like a date."

"No? I think it's just like a date. And anyway, if you're going to volunteer your time to help me sort out the mess at Garland, I can show some appreciation. Besides, there's some other things I will ask for your help."

He had said this before, but she could only guess what he meant. The house was sadly in need of paint and some updating. Perhaps he wanted to know whom to hire, and where to shop. He was also showing up at town meetings, and perhaps wanted an introduction to some of the key players on the Zoning Commission. If he stayed in town, he might need a personal reference for one of the country clubs. She had no idea if he played golf or tennis, or liked to sit around playing bridge on a warm summer day.

He took his time enlightening her, and she refused to rise to the bait. If he wanted her help, he would have to be very clear what he wanted, and she probably couldn't help him anyway. Even if she could, how close did she want to get to him? She knew almost nothing about him, as she found out this night she really knew nothing about his family.

He could be planning to bring a girlfriend up from New York. Or a boyfriend. He could be hoping to defy the wetlands restrictions put up a dam where the Belvedere River crossed his property. He could open a hunt club on his property, or do something else she would find equally distasteful.

He took his coffee black, as she did her tea. So they wouldn't have to keep a sugar bowl handy in the kitchen.

Where on earth did such an idea come from? She choked on her tea.

"Steady now," Evan said, looking across the table at her and offering her his napkin. "I'm not going to ask you to arm wrestle Mrs. Armitage for the rights to sort through Garland. Or suggest you try to make Wayne Durant a worthwhile member of society. Nothing so challenging."

"I suppose you need a new handyman or someone to mow the lawn?" Eleanor said, convinced they had settled back to discuss the things that really didn't matter.

"I do, but I had other things in mind." He sipped his coffee, and then decided to add some cream. He stirred for a moment, before reaching into his pocket to pull out his wallet and sort through several large bills. The waiter returned quickly, and did not look at all sorry to be lingering with his last diners when he realized what sort of tip Evan was leaving him.

Eleanor noticed these things, but Evan looked distracted, and returned to stirring his coffee. Finally, when the brew was undoubtedly lukewarm, he looked up at Eleanor, frowning and troubled.

"I need your help to try to figure out who killed my aunt Dorothea," he said.

Chapter 6

*"I really can only afford to be nice to one
customer a day. And I'm certain this isn't your day."*
Gracie Ames, Donations Coordinator
and volunteer since 2001

"Where is that bitch?"

Lucille Armitage, startled, dropped a pressed
glass bowl onto the tiled floor, and it shattered into a
hundred splinters. "Probably a cheap repro," she
said to no one in particular, dismissing the mess
with a wave of her hand, but made no attempt to
look for a broom. Whatever was going on at the door
to the shop had to be of more interest.

"She lied to me!"

Margaret Brownlee had been called a bitch so
many times in her life, the insult probably seemed
as familiar as a 1930's tea cozy quilted with pieces
cut from worn clothing. Still, no one could recall
anything in the past week or so worthy of such anger
and a public display. She carefully shelved a lamp
needing to be rewired, and squinted to see who stood
in the doorway.

"If that bitch sold my fishing rod to a dealer, I'm
going to go after him!"

Gracie Ames sighed as she handed a small box
to Miriam Pell. "These must be the chess pieces
belonging to the wooden board we received
yesterday. Let me see what the trouble is," she said.

She walked down the length of The Thrifty
Means, past the books, the picture frames, the
flowerpots, and the overstuffed chairs, to confront a

117

large woman with astonishing red hair. The intruder was not one of their regular customers; indeed, if Gracie had ever seen her before, she was sure she would have remembered her.

"Which bitch would that be?" she volleyed, knowing the list of possibilities could be very long. Behind her, someone giggled.

The redhead narrowed her eyes, giving her a somewhat constipated look. "The tall one, the brunette who's always walking around like a big shot, like she owns the place."

"No one owns the place," Gracie said clearly. "The Thrifty Means is a nonprofit agency, run entirely by volunteers."

"I don't care if this dump is a palace run by a king. The bitch promised me she'd save a fishing rod for me and now I don't see it. I want it."

"But we don't have it," Gracie said, glancing at the layaway area behind the desk. There was a framed watercolor of a puppy, and a few dusty books. "And I can't sell you what I don't have."

"What are you going to do? The customer is always right," the woman continued, the engine of her belligerence gathering more steam. "I want the bitch fired."

"We don't fire volunteers at The Thrifty Means. In fact, we value our volunteers above everything else. Including customers with bad manners and unreasonable demands." Gracie paused, waiting for the woman's wrath to rain down upon her own head, but somehow, the woman didn't seem to get the insult. And, really, an insult going over the recipient's head is not an insult at all. "When did you put the fishing rod on hold?"

"Two weeks ago," the woman said, lacking any sense of self-awareness.

"Two weeks?" Gracie repeated. She looked at the two volunteers at the front desk. "How long can something remain on hold?"

"Two days," they said in unison.

"So, you see, we had every right to sell a fishing rod to anyone at all," Gracie said. "And now I'm going to ask you to leave The Thrifty Means. I don't like your language and I don't like your attitude."

"I'm a customer," the woman insisted.

"Not anymore," Gracie said, and waved her off in the direction of the door.

Muttering something even ruder under her breath, the woman stormed out, rattling the front windows when she slammed the door.

"Well done, Gracie!" one of the front desk volunteers said.

"Thank heavens you got rid of her!" Margaret Brownlee said, from behind a rack of hideously flowered drapes.

"You can come out now, Eleanor!" Gracie sang out.

Eleanor appeared between two vintage wedding gowns smelling faintly of mothballs and lavender.

"Thanks, Gracie. I owe you big time. Ask me to unpack dishes. Tell me to sweep around the dumpster. I'll do anything." Eleanor took a jaunty feathered hat off her head and replaced it on a rack. "The damn thing is I don't even recognize her. I don't even remember seeing a fishing rod."

"Maybe she saw it in another shop somewhere. And I don't think she's been a redhead very long, so the last time she came in, she could have been a brunette." Gracie said. "Besides, I don't think she recognized you either."

Eleanor glanced at herself in the mirror. There was something different about her appearance, and she refused to think it had anything to do with Evan Zane. "I think she got my description down pat," she said.

"Really? I can't think of anyone who would call

you a bitch. You go out of your way to be nice to people. Which is more than I can say for myself."

Eleanor smiled, acknowledging the truth. One of the reasons Mrs. B. wanted Gracie to work behind the scenes, in the back room, was because she had so little patience towards customers.

"Then we played this wrong," Eleanor said. "I should have been the one to confront her, to explain the rules of the shop. Maybe I could have gotten her to buy something else. Like the purple wall clock hanging there for a year."

"Oh no, my dear. If you handed her the clock, she probably would have used it as a weapon. She looked like she would have liked to kill you," Mrs. B. said, stepping forward. She reached for the wall clock. "But maybe we should throw this out."

"Fine with me. We don't want anyone killed," Gracie said, and the unpleasantness of the episode was forgotten. A moment later, they each returned to whatever they had been doing before the interruption.

Eleanor stood between the overstuffed chairs, wondering who in leafy, genteel Eastfield would want someone killed.

"Mrs. B.? I have a question to ask you."

The older woman turned sharply from the shelves where she was setting out pieces of pink Depression glass. Some dust adorned her tight bun and her glasses slipped to the very tip of her generous nose.

"I confess," she said tightly. "I did it."

Eleanor backed against one of the chairs, feeling the cushion press against her knee, and fell into the seat. A cloud of dust burst around her.

"You...did it?" she gasped in disbelief, and sneezed.

Mrs. B. didn't bother to bless her, so anxious was she to spill out her confession.

"I sold the cursed fishing rod to Mabel Roskin last week. She saw it behind the curtain, gathering dust, and said it was just what she needed."

Gracie sashayed between them, holding a repro desk lamp and tripping over the long electrical wire dragging along the floor. "Needed for what? Mabel doesn't strike me as the type to put on hip boots and stand in the Belvedere River waiting for a fish to bite. And if she did happen to catch something other than a cold, and cooked for John, he'd almost certainly die of mercury poisoning. Is that why she needed the rod, to kill him?"

Eleanor settled back among the cushions, thinking there was far too much talk of death in Eastfield recently.

"Watch your words, young lady," Mrs. B. scolded. Only a venerable old dear like the manager of The Thrifty Means could get away calling a fifty-year-old woman a young lady. "The Roskins have been married for nearly sixty years, and should be an example to everyone who divorces at the first time of trouble."

Eleanor sneezed again, and again, Mrs. B. ignored her.

"Mabel and John are moving to Maine, after all these years. He's always wanted to go, and she resisted until now."

"What does she gain?" Gracie asked and rolled her eyes. "A new car? Something to replace her 1973 Gremlin?"

Mrs. B. shot her a look suggesting there was nothing wrong in driving a thirty-year-old car.

"Something even better," she said. "She gets to throw out all her old things, and completely redecorate the new house. That's why she wanted the fishing rod; one room is going to have a nautical motif. She also bought a lighthouse lamp and a lobster trap."

"If any of those talking bass plaques come in, I'll save them for her," Gracie said. A few years ago, half the households in Eastfield believed the number one item under the Christmas tree ought to be a rubber fish wearing a Santa hat and calling out holiday greetings and by the first week of January, twenty of them showed up in the shop—many of them still unopened. By March, they filled the dumpster. "There must be a few people who haven't gotten around to throwing them out yet."

"So you see why I wanted to be so nice to Mabel, and let her buy that rod," Mrs. B. explained.

Eleanor understood at once. "Do you mean, so we can get the things they're going to get rid of?"

"A woman who dresses like Mabel Roskin can't possibly have anything we want," Gracie said under her breath.

"You'd be surprised, my dear. I know for a fact she has a set of old English china in perfect condition. She has a full size Victor Talking Machine in her living room, and a watercolor by Mac Squires."

Gracie and Eleanor looked at their mentor with unabashed admiration. Did Mrs. B. make it her business to take inventory of every house in Eastfield?

"I must know these things," she said loftily. "And how fortunate for The Thrifty Means in this case we will inherit before the owner actually dies."

She took the desk lamp from Gracie and wrapped the wire around the base, looping in the plug to secure it. Glancing around the crowded shop until she found a spot recently vacated by a McCoy planter, she walked off to set the lamp in a new place.

"How fortunate," Gracie echoed. "And for the Roskins, they have a veritable lease on life. After all, they can donate their crap to the shop, and live to tell the tale."

Eleanor laughed. But there did seem to be a mercenary tone to some of their business.

"You know, I hate to say it, but Mrs. B. should have taken care of that customer," Gracie continued. "What if you or I were out of the shop? Would we have wanted our front desk volunteers to handle such of nastiness? If I were new here and just putting in a few hours of my spare time, I would have reached for my jacket, gotten the hell out, and never come back. Who needs to put up with such abuse?"

"We shouldn't have to tolerate abuse either," Eleanor murmured.

"But we agree to tolerate a great deal by spending as much time here as we do. No one says it's pretty, but the job has to get done by someone who can take charge. Mrs. B. has that responsibility, even though we both were here."

"I suppose you're right. But I'd hate to make her feel bad, or not needed. She lives for this place, Gracie, whereas you and I have other lives."

Gracie's eyes lit up. "Yes, there's a rumor going around about your other life. L'Avignon, with Evan Zane?"

"Is nothing sacred in this town?"

"No, of course not. You sneezed five minutes ago, and they probably know about it up at the reservoir." Gracie plopped down on the opposite chair and reached for a pine box from which the faces of the little queens and kings of a chess set poked. "So, how EZ is he, anyway?"

Eleanor would not give Gracie what she wanted to hear. Besides, there wasn't much to tell. "Well, he seems to like to eat almost anything, and we had a nice conversation. Lewis practically worships him." She looked at the chess pieces, thinking they looked familiar. Then, they were probably sitting here in the shop for months, waiting for someone to notice them.

"Well, no wonder. The man can take twenty years of history and condense things to fit onto a matchbook. He could probably start his own church in every high school in this country and attract converts with each new freshman class."

"And thereby dull the minds of the next generation," Eleanor said grumpily. Honestly, was she the only person who despaired of what the *EZ Guides* were doing to kids?

"He's not half bad, Eleanor," said Gracie. When her friend looked at her in surprise, she added, "Oh, I don't mean the way he looks. From what I see, he's all good. He's kind of gorgeous in a country boy, flannel shirt way. And he's certainly smart. I bet you haven't even read his books. But they're good, they're really good."

"Good for kindling. Anyway, how do you know? Don't tell me you read his books?"

Gracie blushed so deeply, Eleanor wondered, for the first time, what Evan Zane wrote about in his guides.

"Well, you remember your book about Nathan Hale?" Gracie asked.

"I wrote it, Gracie," Eleanor pointed out. "I remember every single damned word on every single one of its five hundred pages."

"Well, there you go. I got a little confused about three hundred pages along. I just forgot the names of some of the revolutionaries, and some of the places. And what was going on," Gracie said.

"Did you remember which war I was writing about?" Eleanor asked, a little more sarcastically than she intended.

"Duh." Gracie said. "Anyway, I bought Evan Zane's book on New England history, and figured out what your book was about."

"Great, Gracie. That's just great." Eleanor leaned back against the cushion and closed her eyes.

"Well, it worked for me. I wondered how he guessed what questions I would have about your book, and decided to explain things to me. You really should think about working together. Or sell the books as a set."

"I'm sure that's not going to happen, so stop dreaming."

"Okay. But you know what I can dream about? I am dreaming of the time when Mrs. B. retires, and you take over the shop. You can do better."

"I don't have the time, Gracie. How about you?"

"Well, one of us should. Otherwise, we'll be stuck in the last century. It's time to modernize, to attract new customers. To start taking credit cards, for goodness sakes! How much more would we be able to sell if people didn't have to pay in cash? Does anyone think customers carry around more than a few dollars anymore?"

"There's an ATM around the corner."

"And if it's raining, or snowing? Or if a customer has a screaming baby? Is she really going to run out and get cash for something she probably doesn't need anyway?"

"We're doing all right."

"But we can do better! If we had someone who looked to the future instead of the past, who..."

Gracie's voice broke off just as Eleanor inhaled the distinctive scent of rosewater cologne. She opened her eyes and watched as Gracie's face turned bright red again.

"Girls?" Mrs. B.'s voice hovered over Eleanor's chair. "If you're not too busy, there's a man unloading some boxes by the back door. He could use some help."

Gracie recovered quickly. "He must be quite a guy if he can't carry a few cartons."

"It's not for us to question a man's virility, my dears. Only what he has to bring into the shop."
****

Eleanor stood at Evan Zane's kitchen sink, washing dishes, hoping he realized she rarely did this in her own home anymore.

"I have a dishwasher, Ellie," he said, coming up behind her. He blew her hair off the back of her neck and kissed her there. She wiggled away, but as she was elbow deep in warm suds, she couldn't go far. "I would have washed everything for you, if you asked."

"Then I'm glad I got here when I did, because you would have ruined everything." She held up a large plate with a pearlized glaze. "Do you see the way that shines? The surface is very beautiful, but very porous. If you put it through the dishwasher, it would look like covered in spider webs, made by water seeping into all the cracks."

"Well, live and learn," Evan said, and returned his attention to her neck.

"Evan!" she said. "You'll make me drop it!"

He reached around her and caught the plate in his hand, certain he had a tight grip before he pulled the plate away. Soap bubbles were on his hand, his sleeve, and—when she glanced down—on her breast. When she flicked them off, a little tuxedo cat batted the weightless ball floating to the ground.

"You know, as long as I'm going to be around, I might as well know this little guy's name. He follows me everywhere. What did your aunt name him?"

"Nothing."

"Nothing? How insulting, especially for something as proud as a cat!"

"No, you misunderstand. She wouldn't have named him because she would not have let a cat anywhere near her. She hated cats."

"But they're all over the place now," Eleanor said. She slipped under Evan's arm, and caught the little creature, which now had the bubble on top of his head. "I guess I never really wondered, though you've mentioned it before. Maybe she had a change of heart late in her life, and decided they weren't so bad, after all."

She looked into the kitten's wide green eyes until he blinked and settled against her elbow. He wasn't the least skittish and acted comfortably in human company. This was more than she could say about her own behavior around Evan Zane.

"Strange, isn't it?" Evan said.

"It certainly is," she said slowly, and looked up at him.

He nodded, and as if he guessed what she was thinking, took a step back. They stood silently for several moments, in the sunny kitchen, while the kitten hummed like a tiny motor in the crook of Eleanor's arm. With her free hand, still wet from the sink, Eleanor made little spikes in the black fur along the kitten's back.

"There's something I think you ought to see," Evan said quietly. "Stay here and I'll bring it to you, so we don't wake the little fellow up."

Eleanor remembered the days when she held two sleeping babies at once, straining her back, but unwilling to disturb their sleep. She leaned against the counter, feeling a ridge of dampness seep through her cotton shirt, but utterly content and at home in Evan Zane's kitchen. She couldn't account for the feeling, not really, but recognized the moment for what it was.

What was Evan bringing her? Some souvenir of their childhood? A rare vase or plate from Dorothea's collection?

A door opened and closed at the far end of the house, and another cat skidded across the wet floor. A moment later Evan reappeared in the kitchen, holding aloft a small rectangular package.

A book. Probably a manuscript or the advance copy of his newest *EZ Guide*. Her idiotic notions dissipated in the glare of the sun; whatever she was thinking, Evan Zane was all business. After all, it's what she preferred. She had two teenagers to raise, and a book of her own to finish, and far too many responsibilities. She might have wasted her time dreaming about him when they were kids, but avoided any romantic entanglements since her divorce, and she didn't have time for it now.

"Do you think he'll let you sit down?" Evan asked and pulled out one of the kitchen chairs. It was an old Hitchcock, weather beaten and worn, but with characteristic hallmark stenciling along the back. Eleanor wiggled around the chair, keeping her upper body as still as possible, and sat down stiffly.

"There we go," she sighed. "And he's still purring."

"You know, Ellie, he's just a cat."

"But he's very, very cute."

"Is that all you need to let a lonely guy curl up in your arms?" he asked.

Eleanor caught her breath and turned to him, but he had not waited for her reaction, and was already pulling a Moroccan leather bound book from a plastic bag no longer clear. Little chips of disintegrating plastic decorated the table like fake snow under a Christmas tree. When Evan dropped the book on the table the flakes went flying about, surely polluting the air they breathed. The cat stirred in her arms.

"You shouldn't use plastic," she said. "It leaves an odor and can stick to the leather. Plastic could ruin the value of the book."

"Oh, I don't really think the book is so very valuable as an artifact. It's not a first edition Dickens or anything. It's just a ledger."

"Like the Domesday book?"

He looked up from the book and she guessed exactly what he was thinking; she caught the hint of both amusement that she would try to test him on an easy question of history, and annoyance she could even think he didn't know the answer.

"I was in Mr. Steig's World History class with you, as I recall," he said, as if explaining everything.

Perhaps so, but she remembered sophomore year of high school as well as he did, or even better.

"The class was last period, and you always got out early because of lacrosse practice. I wondered if you might have missed the lecture," she said. "Since you managed to miss all the others."

"I missed nothing," he said, reminding her of how silly she and her friends had been, flirting with him, teasing him, whispering about him in tones loud enough for him to hear. She considered Leslie's little clique at school, and realized nothing changed in all the years, and probably never would.

She was not a sophomore any more, and he didn't look like a man who liked to be teased. And she certainly had no idea how to go about flirting any more.

"Oh," she said, surprised at the husky sound of her own voice. "I think you may have missed out on a good deal."

He reached out to scratch the head of the kitten still sleeping on her arm, and the back of his hand brushed against her breast.

"On what, do you think? The Battle of Hastings?" His voice was just above a whisper.

Eleanor closed her eyes, as if savoring a dessert. "The War of the Roses?"

"The Storming..." He waited until she opened her eyes. "...of the Bastille."

She sighed, and licked her upper lip. "Waterloo."

"The Industrial Revolution." He raised his eyebrows and grinned, looking very much like the boy of her very youthful dreams. And like that boy, he really knew how to throw a wet blanket over any notions of romance.

Eleanor straightened in her chair, upsetting the kitten. "Okay, enough. Show me your old book."

"As you wish," he said, and winked. Eleanor was startled, remembering the line from a movie she knew well, and came laden with meaning. Evan was already concentrating on extricating the ledger from the fragile overcoat. He set the ledger down on the table in front of her, and when he opened the cover, she heard the cracking of a rotting spine. Though the book itself might have been a hundred years old, the first notations appeared about twenty years ago.

"It's a beautiful hand," Eleanor commented. "And whoever wrote this used a fountain pen, though you hardly see that nowadays. Only calligraphers seem to use them, to write out invitations to a wedding."

"And here I would have bet everything was done on the computer. Well, Dorothea might have missed her calling because she could have made a few extra dollars by addressing envelopes. This is her handwriting, by the way."

"Well, how do you know she didn't? Supplement her income, I mean. Maybe she paid for your college education by writing."

"She didn't. I paid for my college education. And I know she didn't address envelopes for a living because every single penny she ever found between the cushions of the couch, or spent on a pint of milk is recorded here in her beautiful hand. You'll be happy to note she..."and here he paused and flipped through a few pages, "tipped Dan Jones fifty cents when he delivered milk on January 24th. The roads must have been icy, so she was sure to make the long trip worth his while. Or here, she notes she received a $42 refund from Nutmeg Insurance for coverage on a sedan through the end of the year. Well, of course, if the car was crushed like a beer can and covered in blood, there certainly would be no reason to think any more damage would occur if a tree fell on it." His tone was bitter.

"Evan, please stop. Everyone handles grief in her own way. You said she remained friends with your mother. And she did give up her life in New York, and sacrifice a good deal." Eleanor sighed, trying to put herself in Dorothea's place. "Maybe she was just trying to preserve your inheritance."

He looked up from the book, and she glimpsed something—anger, perhaps - beneath the smooth surface.

"There's a perfectly reasonable explanation for all this," Eleanor continued, uneasily. "Your aunt didn't try to hurt you with her scrupulous records, by showing you how frugally she lived. Why would she? This was only her way of keeping track of everything. It's perfectly logical."

"Logical? In the way people count the number of toothpicks in a package to make sure they've gotten their money's worth? Or wash their hands a hundred times after peeling an apple so they don't get germs on anything else they touch? Yeah, that's logical. You think she's logical to account for every single cent passing through her hands so her nephew doesn't come after her for ten bucks."

"Well, why not? And you are looking through the ledger now, as she must have known you would. This is her legacy to you—so you can account for everything through all these years."

He shook his head, clearly frustrated and angry. "No, there's a lot I can't account for. Like why she couldn't bear to be around me. Or why she couldn't manage to come to my graduation. Or why she would never talk about my mother, though she slept in her bed and cooked in her kitchen."

"Evan, it's over," Eleanor said, and reached across the table to take his hands in hers. His were warm and hard, calloused from the work he had been doing around Garland. "Dorothea's dead, and your mother....has been gone these twenty years. Who cares if Dorothea tipped the milkman fifty cents or a dollar? He may be gone also. This book is finished. It's over."

He looked as if he was about to say something, but probably thought better. He set her hands aside and abruptly stood. The chair tipped and would have fallen, but he caught the seat in time and set it rudely in place. He stomped out of the kitchen, through the living room and out into the garden, slamming the screen door behind him.

The cat turned in his sleep, exposing a tiny pink belly, and tempting Eleanor to caress the smooth skin. She did, unwilling to disturb him, and unwilling to sooth Evan Zane, who was a big boy and had to confront his own demons. He hadn't needed her twenty years ago and he surely didn't need her now. So she remained in the kitchen, in the stern backed chair, and stuck her forefinger into a random page in the ledger and opened it.

For all Eleanor had defended her, Dorothea Zane really was a little nutty. On one August 28th, she wrote she had bought five composition books for "the boy" and on August 30th she returned one, as his band teacher gave the class music books to use instead. She recorded the cost of postage for every bill she ever sent out, and even did a little balance sheet when she weighed the price of everything needed to grow a vegetable garden, and what the season's yield would have cost if she had simply bought all her vegetables at the Market.

These were things Evan probably would not mind sharing with Eleanor, but the ledger also included more personal glimpses into family life. As she turned the pages, she noticed repeated entries for the cost of tutoring and medical consultations, for physical therapy, and counseling. Of course, there was nothing remarkable about such things a boy who survived a horrific crash surely needed someone to keep him stable and sane. It was hard, even now, to reconcile the carefree young man who gave all appearances of going right on with his life with an individual who needed as much help as the accounts indicated.

Eleanor, who had resented his attitude all those years ago, did not feel much better now when confronting the truth of his secret self. She only wished she had known at the time, for she might have spoken to him as someone who understood what she had experienced.

There was more. She fingered the fragile pages, noting how the costs for oil fuel and electricity had gone up through the years, and a Ford pickup was bought for Wayne Durant. Dorothea noted receipts of her pension, and monthly supplemental payments from "E. Zane," as if he was a business and not her only relative.

About five years ago, Dorothea appeared to have actually started a small business, as she noted income of another sort.

March 2nd. Eight thous. Received from M for long cloak. repaired case.

March 7th. Twelve thous, five hund. REarle woman in blue dress.

March 15th. Three hund. Vint baby quilt.

The notations went on, but the elegant spidery hand now looked stilted, as if the writer suffered from arthritis or wore a bandage on her hand. Dorothea received payment for goods, mostly textiles. Perhaps she sewed or hand quilted items. Or wove woolen garments—eight thousand dollars for a cloak was an extraordinary expense. "M" must be someone new in town, for none of the old-timers would think of spending more for an item of clothing than they once did for their homes.

A sound like a gunshot pierced the air and the dishes rattled in the sink. The cat dug his claws into her arm, leapt off her lap and skidded into the broom closet. Eleanor rubbed her arm, knowing the scratches would feel a lot worse before they got better, and closed the ledger.

The sound of men's voices, angry and abrupt, greeted her as she came to the door and she supposed she was relieved no one was shot. Wayne's pickup truck, likely the source of the noise, was idling in the drive, its driver's door open. The man himself, looking even more disreputable than usual, was shouting something and waving his arms as he scrambled up the rise to where Evan stood waiting for him.

Evan stood his ground. Perhaps his recent spurt of frustration empowered him, or made him discard the cheerful façade that seemed so natural, but he looked as tough as the man cursing him, and returned a volley of several choice words. Wayne charged him, and Evan pushed him away with enough strength to knock him on his ass.

Eleanor hoped it would be enough to end the quarrel. However, when Evan rolled up his sleeves and pulled the fallen man to his feet, she understood the time had come to intervene. She had too many years of motherhood behind her to hesitate.

"Stop this. Now," she said firmly, and held out a hand to each man. When Evan pushed up against her, she would have pulled away, but instead he held her hand to his racing heart. Wayne grabbed her other hand and used her to leverage himself back up. "Are the two of you crazy?" she asked, but she only looked at Evan.

His face was flushed and his mouth was set in a

grim line. He had every reason to want Wayne off his property, but something else was operating here, something she didn't understand.

"I want something of mine," Wayne said, slurring his words. He didn't smell—at least no worse than usual—so Eleanor didn't know if he was drunk or if he bit his tongue when he fell. "I have stuff in the house."

"There's nothing of yours in the house, except for Lilianna, so get the hell out of here," Evan said. "And let me know when you're ready to move her, so I can see what you're taking."

"The mantle clock is mine!" Wayne protested.

Evan made a sudden move, so he now stood in the middle, and he pulled Eleanor closer to his side. She wasn't sure what he had in mind, though it might have been nothing more than to prevent her from running inside to find what Wayne wanted. He needn't have worried; caught up against Evan's denim shirt, sweetly fragrant with of pine needles and wood chips, she had no intention of running off.

Nor did Evan. He hesitated and then, in a calmer voice asked, "The maple clock in the living room? The one with the carved birds?"

"Yeah," Wayne said, though he looked as if he wasn't sure. "Dorothea gave the clock to me. It's mine."

"My mother's father carved it himself, so I would say Dorothea had no right to give away an heirloom to you or anyone else. What do you have to say now?"

"I want my clock," Wayne said, like a petulant ten year old. Intellectually, that might not have been too far off the mark.

"Yeah, well, you make a pretty good argument. There's stuff I want also, but that doesn't mean I can get it."

Wayne grinned an even more stupid looking grin than usual, and looked from Eleanor to Evan. One didn't have to be a genius to know what he was thinking.

"Let me know when you're moving Lilianna. She's not too happy here," Evan said. "And if my clock somehow disappears, I'm not going to be too happy either. Got that?"

Wayne started to step away, as if he was afraid Evan might shoot him in the back. He stumbled over a log, bringing him within an arm's length of the axe Evan had been using to chop firewood. Evan stiffened as Eleanor gasped, but Wayne apparently lost his taste for violence. He turned towards the pickup and heaved himself heavily into the cab. Accelerating out of the driveway, the truck backfired once, and yet again.

"I didn't even know cars backfired anymore." Evan said. He still held Eleanor around the shoulders, and she could feel his heart still thumping in his chest. Whatever primitive instincts came to the forefront when Wayne threatened him, he was surely a man unaccustomed to such violence and not likely to settle down as quickly as his calming voice suggested.

"Well, the car is very old. Dorothea bought it for him fifteen years ago."

"How do you...oh, you read the ledger." He released her, and she felt cold where his damp shirt pressed against her a moment before. "What other amazing facts did you discover?"

He walked to the log that nearly had been Wayne's undoing, and hefted it onto a nearby pile. He picked up the axe, mercifully unnoticed by his adversary, and ran a rough finger over the blade. Eleanor, watching the way the muscles in his arm flexed as he balanced the weapon, forgot he asked a question until he looked up at her. "Well?"

She blinked, trying to remember anything at all.

"Did my aunt note how much she spent on

magazine subscriptions? Her natural curl shampoo? Allergy medicine for her nephew's hay fever?"

Eleanor waited to see if he would allude to the thousands paid for counseling, but he acted as if his hay fever was enough of a personal confession.

"As a matter of fact, she did. She also indicated how much she paid for your school supplies and for a taxi to take her to the hospital to visit you when you had surgery."

"Oh, yes. She did come once, though I was in the hospital for four days." At Eleanor's questioning look, he added. "A hernia repair. About five years ago."

"She came to take you home?"

"No, as a matter of fact. She came on the second day, when I was pretty high on medication. I seem to remember she told me there were some offers on Garland and someone wanted to build a planned community here. Something along those lines. I was delusional about a lot of things, but boys don't usually have fantasies about property development."

"Unless they want to get rid of unwanted property and have a great offer on the table?"

Evan gave her an odd look. "Maybe. But I guess she didn't get me to sign anything, or we wouldn't be standing here now."

Eleanor decided to change the subject. "Perhaps she was busy with her business. You may have been in the hospital at about the same time she started to sell things. Did she ever have a shop here? Or did she weave fabrics or sew clothing?"

"To the best of my knowledge, my dear Aunt Dorothea couldn't sew a button on a shirt." He glanced down at his own shirt and plucked at the breast pocket. "What was she selling?"

"Well, I'm not sure. She describes a long cloak, and a blue dress. I didn't really study the entries."

"It probably is nothing. But you were already

back in Eastfield five years ago. Did she have a shop?"

"If she did, I knew nothing about it. But I haven't had the budget to pay the kinds of prices she got for the things."

"I understood you did well with your historical stories," he said, and she wondered if he was revealing the slightest bit of professional jealousy.

"I do well. I mean, I make enough to support the kids. But I don't have eight thousand dollars to spend on a cape, no matter how elegant."

Evan held out his arm, making the axe an extension of the long line. She wasn't sure what he was doing, but she saw the blade glitter in the sun, and the muscles in his arm tighten again under the strain. She waited for him to say something about expensive clothes, or elegant woman, but he was interested in other things.

"Doesn't your husband support the kids?"

"He's an ex-husband. And he doesn't support the kids either financially or emotionally."

"So he's out of the picture?"

"He's been out of the picture for many years."

Evan finally relaxed his grip on the axe and set it on the lid of an old cistern. Eleanor studied the rough barrel for a few moments, mentally calculating what an artifact like this would sell for at The Thrifty Means, and then chastised herself. Would she ever again be able to look at something simply for what it was, and not calculate its worth?

"Why did you marry him?" Evan asked. He stood, legs slightly apart, and appeared more interested in rebuttoning the cuffs of his shirt than hearing her answer. The dark hair falling on his brow was damp, and curled in disarray. It suited him. He looked like someone who was very much at home on his farm chopping wood, rebuilding his burned out cottage. Surprised, Eleanor realized she didn't know where he actually worked, where he wrote the books that made the idea of him as an Eastfield farmer simply absurd.

"Well, I loved him. Or believed I did. We met in college, and lived together for a few years before we got married. I worked to put him through law school and then I became pregnant with the twins."

"He didn't want kids?"

Eleanor looked at him in surprise. She had been over the story of her marriage and divorce a million times and somehow it always amazed her strangers sensed this at once, as the most likely reason for Paul Gilmartin's unexpected departure. She wanted kids, and couldn't imagine he didn't feel the same. But he didn't. The reality of two babies, demanding and consuming all of their time, was too much for him. For them.

"No, he didn't. I suppose it's a good thing I did, because they became all mine." She laughed, and preferred to believe there was nothing left of her utter despair and pain of sixteen years ago.

"Would you have had more?" Evan asked, and Eleanor realized he was very close. His skin was flushed and still damp and she could smell the starchy scent of his plaid shirt mixed with the natural pine she sensed before.

"Oh, almost certainly. But it's hard to raise kids by yourself. For that reason, I came back to Eastfield, where I feel I had the support of the whole town. It does take a village, you know."

"I do know. Eastfield helped to raise me also, after. You know."

He didn't wait for her answer, but leaned over and kissed her. Eleanor sighed and opened her lips and savored the taste of him, warm and minty, his tongue gently exploring. Rarely had such a sensation been so intense, for they didn't touch each other elsewhere, standing separate but so intimately connected. The even line of his teeth pressed against her lower lip, and his chin gently scraped hers.

Finally, she stepped back, smiling a little foolishly.

"We shouldn't do this. This is exactly what people think we're doing when I come up here to Garland. You saw the look on Wayne's face."

"I don't think Wayne should be our gauge of what normal, rational people are thinking. The man is stoned or, even on his better days, merely out of his mind. And, anyway, who cares what people are thinking?"

"I do. I live here," Eleanor said. "You'll settle things and go back to New York, and people will only remember you from old high school yearbooks."

"And newspaper articles," he said tersely. "But I live here too. My family has been here for centuries—a lot longer than yours, I bet."

Eleanor stepped back and crossed her arms over her breasts. "Oh, so you're pulling rank on me? What does it take to be an Eastfield townie, anyway? Did my relatives have to sign the Declaration of Independence or something?"

"Mine did," he said, and grinned. "If you're good, maybe you'll find an old copy tucked into the back of a picture frame or in the corn crib."

"So much for your knowledge of history, Mr. Zane. I once read the Eastfield branch of your family were Tories."

He sighed and held out his hands in a gesture of surrender. "I believe they preferred to call themselves Loyalists. But you're quite right; I conveniently forget the fact. If they ever owned a copy of the cursed document, they probably threw it into the fireplace."

"A pity. You'd be a rich man now if they kept one around somewhere."

"I am a rich man. And to hell with history. Just

come here." He smiled and beckoned, and she guessed what he had in mind.

Eleanor shook her head. "No, history is too important to forget."

"All right. You win. Let's say I want to rewrite history, and kiss you now like I always wanted to do in high school. Even junior high. Probably since third grade."

This was too much. Eleanor turned her back on him, and started back towards the house. If she hadn't left her pocketbook sitting on his dining room table, she would have gone straight to the car.

"Ellie! What's wrong! Don't you believe me?"

"No," she said over her shoulder. "I don't."

He caught her arm and turned her around to face him. But she couldn't, not when he had just made light of all her girlhood fantasies about him.

"You could barely manage to speak to me," she said. "You ignored me and walked away as fast as you could go when you saw me coming. If I was on one team, you'd try to get on the other. When Mrs. Glass put us on the Safety Committee, you said you couldn't work with me."

"You remember?" he mused. "Damn. I really wanted to be on the committee, and wear that red sash and everything. And boss everyone around."

"Stop laughing at me! I'm serious."

Evan put his hands on her shoulders and pressed his fingers gently into her skin. "I'm serious too. I wanted to be with you more than anything. But if I let everyone see how I felt, they'd laugh at me. We'd never live it down. It's what you're worried about now."

"No, it's not. Being hall monitors is different from going out to a restaurant together. And besides, I had no idea you even liked me back then. Why didn't you let me know?"

"Because I was an idiot? And ten years old?"

"And why...?" Eleanor needed to know more, to understand what happened when their lives fell apart one night. She considered all those payments for therapists, and deferred the question for another day, another moment, when birds weren't singing in all the ancient trees and the ground was fresh with the first sprouts of spring.

If Evan anticipated what she was about to say, he ignored it. "So I think I've wasted enough time dreaming about what I'd like to do to you, though I have to admit that in third grade I had no idea. I've a little more experience now."

"Really?" Eleanor said, trying to sound indifferent, though her heart was racing like an engine.

"Really," he nodded, and seemed to be searching for the right words, "I'd like to ask you for a real date."

"We already had one," she said, thinking dinner at the nicest restaurant in Eastfield was as good as it could get.

"No, that was different. The kids were supposed to go with us, and the dinner was just serendipitous."

Eleanor's first thought was she hadn't heard that word in years. Her second was she had dressed very, very carefully for something not really a date at all.

"What do you have in mind?" she asked, thinking she would like an excuse to get a new dress.

"The benefit for the Eastfield Historical Association. It's next Saturday night, at someone's house. I'm told to expect a big affair."

"I know," Eleanor said thoughtfully, wondering if he ever noticed where the Hamiltons lived. If he had, he wouldn't call it simply a house. Unless one considered a stone mansion with twenty bedrooms, indoor tennis court and pool and eight-car garage a house. "Everyone's been talking about the event."

For once, Evan looked hesitant, even embarrassed. "Oh, I'm sorry. You're already going?"

"No, Mr. Zane. I don't merit an invitation."

"Do you mean, because your family's only been here since the fifties?"

"More likely because I'm not rich."

"Oh, then it's settled. You'll come with me. I have enough for both of us."

Coming from anyone else, such a statement would have been so boastful as to deserve an immediate put down. Standing at Garland, the exquisite blending of nature and settlement marking the measure of any man's worth, the statement was self-evident. Perhaps more to the point, there was something else in that declaration implying a certain generosity, even a promise.

Eleanor looked at him, liking everything she saw, and knew he knew it too.

Chapter 7

"Books are meant to be read, and read again, and read again."

Galen Lynch, Town Librarian
and volunteer since 1987

Eleanor drove back from the Belvedere View Mall, frustrated with having wasted hours of her precious time and having nothing to show except for a few bags of birdseed. If True Blue suffered from starvation for much of his little birdy life, he was now catching up, growing fat and feathery in his new, clean cage. The day was chilly, and Eleanor was glad she kept him indoors today, instead of on the porch where he liked to chirp in response to his noisy neighbors in the trees.

She slowed as she approached Main Street, made a right into the parking lot of The Thrifty Means, and slipped into a spot along the river. Glancing at her watch, she realized she had less than an hour before she had to pick up Lewis from Garland, where he was building some sort of testing station for his water samples.

Someone had dropped off a huge planter, which the volunteers had wisely left outside the shop. If no one bought it in a week or so, they could plant geraniums for the summer, and leave the planter right outside the door. Of course, even in a town like Eastfield, there were no guarantees someone wouldn't come by during the night, stick the thing in the back of an SUV and just drive off. One never knew where one might see something from the shop—and the volunteers only prayed the new owners came to it by honest means.

Eleanor walked through the door.

"You just can't keep away from here!" Gracie called out.

Eleanor smiled at her. "Well, I try, I really do."

"I heard you were going up to the mall? Don't you need a dress for the benefit? Did you get something?" Galen Lynch asked. Galen was a librarian in town, but only worked part time, and regularly appeared at The Thrifty Means to sort through the array of books and ephemera. She looked up from a box of old colorized postcards, mailed when postage was a penny.

"I did. I do. I didn't," Eleanor said. "Which is to say, I still do."

"Did you try Banenfield's? Andee got a gown there for the senior prom," Gracie said.

"They do have a lot of prom dresses. In fact, I was probably the only one in the store over the age of twenty. You don't really think I can stuff this body into a backless, strapless, bra-less, tush-less gown, do you?" Eleanor said grumpily. "I should probably be looking in mother-of-the-bride shops."

"Or here," Galen suggested.

"Or here," Eleanor repeated, and smiled. "You're right. I can't seem to get away from this place. What do we have right now? Anything other than the Dior monstrosity?"

Mrs. B. stuck her head through the door of the back room. "That's a very valuable dress, I'll have you know! Mrs. Wheeler Carter wore it at a reception for Princess Grace."

"And now they're both dead," Gracie said beneath her breath.

Eleanor put a finger to her lips. "She hears every word we say, you know."

"I don't care. As long as she doesn't dress us,"

Gracie answered.

"Eleanor, if you need a gown, I have something for you that just came in," Mrs. B. said clearly, glaring at Gracie. "It's gorgeous."

Eleanor sighed in resignation, as Gracie and Galen laughed, and walked towards the back of the shop. A stack of old hatboxes sat near the dressing room and a pair of cracked leather boots graced the top, like a bride and groom on a wedding cake. Emerging from the back room as if of its own accord, was a cream silk evening dress, finely beaded, and beautifully draped. Mrs. B. held the gown before her.

"It is gorgeous," Eleanor agreed, already mentally shopping for the cream pumps to match, and a gold pashmina in case the night was cool. "But where did you get it? And will it fit?"

"Someone delivered things from Betty Dandridge's estate," Mrs. B. said, answering two questions at once. Betty died the year before, and her various stepchildren and nieces and nephews angrily contested a will leaving her estate to the local conservation society. She had been a tall woman, probably about Eleanor's size. "It was her wedding dress. I remember the day very well."

"Her wedding dress?" Eleanor asked, surprised.

"Women were married in colors other than white, though they all were virgins, of course." Mrs. B. stated fact, as always.

"Of course," Eleanor whispered, knowing if she wanted the dress this would not be the moment to point out the rather more obvious facts of human nature. "When was she married?"

"I assume the era is obvious, my dear. Nineteen twenty-five. She wore a strand of pearls down to her navel, though no one noticed anything but the diamond on her finger."

Eleanor recalled she had a strand of pearls somewhere at home, a favor from someone's Mardi

Gras party last year. Of course, without a diamond to detract interest, everyone would probably notice it was made of plastic. But she took the dress from Mrs. B. and disappeared into the dressing room, reminding herself if she couldn't stuff her forty year old body into a flapper's wedding gown it wouldn't really matter if she had love beads or Hawai'ian leis to wear as accessories.

Eleanor pulled off her clothes, shivering in the cool air. She slipped the gown off the decaying padded hanger and petals of yellowing satin showered to the linoleum floor. The gown itself was more solid than it looked, and remained whole as she wriggled the fabric over her head and shoulders.

It fit. Even more important, it looked like someone had sewn it onto her, caressing parts of her body she usually preferred to hide from scrutiny. She now realized her mistake. She had forgotten assets, and perhaps this was the time to capitalize on them.

"Oh, my God!" Gracie gasped as Eleanor slipped out of the dressing room. "You've got to stop hiding yourself in turtleneck sweaters. This is gorgeous!"

Eleanor turned in a graceful circle, surrounding herself in a cloud of camphor, and hearing some of the beads ping as they hit the floor. "You aren't suggesting I dress like this to come to work here?"

"Of course not. The gown would be very impractical," Mrs. B. said. Eleanor glanced at her certain she was dead serious. She was. "But it would be a very lovely dress to wear to a special event. Did you say you were invited to a wedding?"

"No. I'm going to the Historical Society Benefit. I think this is just perfect."

Eleanor felt as if a stiff wind swept through the shop. Mrs. B.'s body straightened and she looked as if she just opened a carton of moldy books.

"I had no idea you were invited, Mrs.

Gilmartin," she said.

Her words caught the attention of the other women in the shop; they all recognized that whenever their president used someone's last name, a reprimand would soon follow. Galen came forward and stood close to Eleanor's side.

"I was, Mrs. Brownlee," Eleanor said, answering in kind.

"I was on the invitation committee, Mrs. Gilmartin. Are you doubting my memory?"

"I am not, Mrs. Brownlee. Your memory is excellent." Eleanor paused, wondering if Evan was possibly mistaken in thinking he could bring a guest. "I did not receive an invitation from the committee, but from an invited guest."

Margaret Brownlee's expression changed, and Eleanor saw something there she never noticed before. It was more than resentment, more subtle than snobbery. If she could think of one single reason why it should be so, she would call Mrs. B.'s expression fearful.

"I see you have ingratiated yourself to our Mr. Zane."

"Yes, I suppose I have," Eleanor said, feeling bolder once his name was out in the open. She dared to speak recklessly, defying the old woman, and perhaps be a little disrespectful. "Do you think he'll appreciate this gown on me? He's rather bookish, you know. I'm not sure he'll notice."

Galen laughed, breaking through the inexplicable tension. "Oh, I think he'll notice!"

"Well, then. Please give me a price, Mrs. B.," Eleanor said, realizing even as she spoke the words that she might have been a little foolhardy. It was the custom among the volunteers at The Thrifty Means to give a "break" to each other, even as they tried to realize a fair profit for the shop. But pricing could be used as a weapon.

"I think five hundred dollars would be a fair price," Mrs. B. said, meeting Eleanor's eyes.

Beside her, Gracie gasped.

Eleanor's mental calculator raced through some fierce math problems, including how much remained of her latest book advance, and how much she would likely spend on cars for her twins. Five hundred dollars was about three hundred more than she had to spend, and she would still need to dry clean the gown, and buy shoes, jewelry, and the lovely gold pashmina. But if pricing was a weapon, it could be countered with the bold armor of dignity.

"That sounds just fine," she said calmly. "I'm sure the gown is worth every penny."

After she closed the curtain of the dressing room behind her, she heard the hushed whispers of the volunteers and knew her friends were trying to negotiate a better deal for her. She had considered Mrs. B. a friend as well, until very recently. When had their relationship changed?

She could answer very well, of course. It changed when Evan Zane arrived in town. Mrs. B. had hoped to go through the estate herself, but he asked her instead. Since the shop would benefit in either case, how and why had Evan's decision become such an issue?

Eleanor carefully hung the gown on a different hanger left behind by a previous customer, and waited until she heard footsteps moving away to leave the dressing room. Without saying a word to Mrs. B., she went up to the front desk to pay for her purchase, as would any other customer.

"The price is ridiculous, Eleanor!" Galen said. "No one else would have asked so much."

"But she did, and I do want the gown. Aside from anything else, I don't have another day to waste shopping at the mall. Now I'm all set." Eleanor paused to pull out her checkbook and write out the painfully high number. She would probably regret her bravado within an hour. "Though if Mrs. B. really has her way, I'll have to come to the party through the garage, and sit in the pantry all evening."

"I think it'll be worthwhile as long as you can sit in the pantry with Evan Zane," said Gracie. Eleanor agreed.

****

"Mom, are you sure this place is in Eastfield?" Leslie sat on Eleanor's bed, flipping through the pages of her mother's manuscript. True Blue was perched on her shoulder, nibbling at her long hair. "You're way too dressed up."

Eleanor looked at her daughter's reflection in the mirror and met her eyes. Leslie's expression wasn't merely one of concern, but of horror. To children growing up in their small town, Eastfield seemed like the other side of beyond. Then they grew up, and went to college, and backpacked to beyond - and when they returned to Eastfield, the town was full of pleasures and friendships and great comfort. She understood as well as anyone else.

"This is a pretty posh affair. And you know the Hamilton estate; it's the place you once called a castle."

"Isn't it? Okay, you're right. The castle is in Eastfield. But I bet the people who live there never set foot in the Eastfield Cinema or in Patsy's Pizza. They probably don't even know where The Thrifty Means is."

Eleanor played with her long string of pearls, borrowed from Lucy Armitage. She knotted it below her breast, unknotted, and knotted again. "I bet you're right. They probably have pizza delivered."

"And would never step foot in a thrift shop," Leslie said, with certainty.

"You're probably right again," Eleanor agreed,

and turned around. "So, what do you think?"

"I think you look different, Mom." Leslie looked back down at the manuscript, and seemed to find one passage particularly interesting. Something was up.

"Different good or different bad?"

"Mom?" Leslie said, and Eleanor paused, thinking, Here it comes. "Are you going to marry Evan or something?"

Or something. Eleanor wondered if the something might come as soon as tonight.

"I've only known the guy for a few weeks. And this is only our second date."

"But you're always up there. And Lewis doesn't shut up about him. And he goes to the shop all the time."

"There's a lot of reasons to go to the shop, other than seeing me."

"Yeah, if you like chairs and trays and pictures of people's dogs that have been dead for fifty years. I don't think he goes for old stuff."

"Why not? Some of those dogs are really cute."

Leslie shot her a look. "Because he's cool."

"Do you mean I'm not?"

"Sorry to tell you this, Mom, but you're ineligible. Once you're a mother you can't be cool. But don't feel bad. You can't be cool, but you look great."

"Well, then let's hope Mr. Zane is willing to overlook my shortcomings."

Fifteen minutes later, when he rang the doorbell exactly on time, she couldn't imagine Evan Zane overlooked anything at all. Eleanor glanced over her shoulder to make sure the parakeet was secure in his cage before she opened the door to him and they just stood there for several moments, frankly admiring each other and grinning like idiots. He wore a tuxedo, of course, and it is a costume that virtually guarantees praise for even the humblest of males. Evan looked splendid. Eleanor sent up a silent prayer of thanks her New England stubbornness had made her buy a gown far above her means, for she believed she might be a creditable match for him this night.

"Great dress," he said, as he followed her into the hallway. Lewis looked up from the couch in the living room, and waved, perhaps knowing his buddy wasn't going to be in the mood to discuss mud samples this night.

"This old thing?" she said.

"Yeah. Don't tell me you just had the dress sitting around in your closet since your flapper days."

"Someone else did. I bought it at Eastfield's favorite shop last week."

"Really. I happen to have a few connections there; I could have gotten you a discount."

"So you think. I have a few connections myself, but they seem to have cost me a premium this time." Eleanor picked up her gold pashmina, and held it out so Evan could wrap her around. It was a remarkably intimate suggestion, and he responded as if he had been accustomed to doing such things for her for years. The dress was worth every penny.

"You don't look half bad yourself," she said as he turned her around to face him again. "Did you happen to throw your tux into the Jeep when you packed to come up here?"

He looked at her in surprise. "No, I picked it up at my apartment last week."

Now Eleanor was surprised. "You went back to New York?"

Evan laughed, and pressed his lips to her forehead. "Congratulations! You are an Eastfield townie, after all! Only true Eastfielders think a trip to New York requires a passport and a day's worth of survival gear! I'm sorry to disappoint you, my love, but I've been spending a day or two a week in the city since I came up here. It's only an hour away."

"I know," Eleanor said tightly, wondering why she failed to guess the obvious. And why did it matter? If he continued to go to the city, he really didn't see Garland as a home, and somehow the notion was important to her. She refused to think he might be returning to New York to see a girlfriend or friends he didn't want her to know about. My love? Did he really say that?

They walked out to the car in silence, though Evan was very solicitous while she settled the gown around her on the seat. She understood very well if she moved too suddenly or in the wrong direction, the fabric would wrinkle like an accordion. Maybe the damned dress wasn't worth the cost, after all.

"So, where are we going?" he asked, as he got in beside her.

"What did you have in mind? Ludlum's? The Grange Hall?" Your bedroom?

He studied her in the darkness and she had the oddest feeling he sensed what she was thinking.

He sucked in his breath. "I didn't check the invitation before I left Garland. Do you have directions?"

"You know where the Hamiltons live. The estate is high above the river in North Eastfield."

"We're going to the castle?" He whistled in appreciation. "I always thought that was a seminary, or a mental institution or something."

He turned his head as he backed out of her driveway, and the taillight of a passing car colored his face crimson. A shadow fell across his broken nose. For a moment, she was back with him so long ago, near the wreckage of their cars, wiping the blood off his face as the flashing red lights of approaching police cars appeared to make her task hopeless.

"Are you all right, Ellie? Do you not want to go?"

She shook her head slightly and smoothed down the front of her gown. "Oh, no, I have too much invested in this evening to back off now. I was just thinking of the Hamilton estate as a mental institution, and how the description might be somewhat apt."

"Why? Does old Jeff Hamilton keep his wife in the attic or something?"

"If there's anyone in the attic it's Jeffrey himself. A few years ago, he decided to test the locals by rearranging street signs. Last winter he took his tractor out on the road during a blizzard. He drove two snowplows off the road and chewed up some asphalt near Bluebird Road. Finally, he stalled out at the entrance to the fire station, creating some havoc when they had an emergency call because of power lines down."

Evan laughed. "And they say nothing ever happens in Eastfield!"

"Who says so?" Eleanor asked quickly, though she was as guilty as anyone was. "The Hamiltons always were a little nutty. After all, they named their kid Hamilton Hamilton."

"Hammy? Wasn't he a few years behind us in school? And didn't he..."

His voice trailed off, and Eleanor wondered why he didn't want to speak of something once more commonly known than the answers to the history final.

"Get a girl pregnant?" She finished for him, and a little more crudely than she intended. "You mean Blossom Fortague. They were married at 17."

"Hmmm," he murmured, and glanced briefly at Eleanor. "I'd forgotten."

"You'd think after all these years, everyone would have forgotten."

"How'd it work out?"

"They were divorced when Hamilton Jr. was about three years old. But he's following in his father's footsteps, and there already is a Hamilton Hamilton Hamilton. I think Junior's been married four times."

"And Hammy?"

"Oh, he's still ahead of his son. He's been married five times. Maybe six. I've lost count." Eleanor sighed and looked out the dark window. Instead of seeing her own reflection, she glimpsed Evan's. He stared at the road before him as he drove, his hands high on the wheel. He looked tense, and she wondered what she might have said to bother him so. "But you could ask him yourself, if you'd like. He's our host this evening."

"Hammy and his wife?"

"Call him Hamilton, if you please. If you call him Hammy, he'll throw you out of the house. And where will that leave me? Arguing with Mrs. B. over the last carrot stick on the serving tray? No, you'd better behave yourself." Eleanor paused, thinking he might think she meant something else. "And I think Wife Number Six left a few months ago."

"Well, if Hammy kicks me out, you ought to stay and take a chance. Seven is a lucky number, I hear."

Eleanor turned away from the window and looked down at her hands in her lap.

"Eleanor?"

"Yes, I'm here," she said unnecessarily.

"Do you..." he started to say, but then changed his mind. "I'm glad," he said instead, and that seemed to be enough.

They reached the gatehouse for the Hamilton estate, and the barrier lifted before they identified themselves. As Evan drove past the small stone building, Eleanor glanced within and saw someone who might have been old Jeff Hamilton leaning over the desk with a blonde and scantily dressed woman beneath him. Eleanor blinked.

"That wasn't Margaret Brownlee, was it?" Evan asked softly.

"Where?" Eleanor asked, looking out the window. Surely the elderly woman wasn't walking along the side of the drive?

"In the gatehouse," Evan said smugly. "Isn't she a blonde?"

"Very funny. But I doubt you'll ever find Mrs. B. in a compromising position, let alone with her back pressed against a desk. She's far too dignified, too proper. I think she sees herself as our schoolmistress at The Thrifty Means, ready to rap our knuckles if we speak out of turn, or put a piece of silver-plate among the pewter."

"I see. No wonder the Historical Society hired her as their bouncer."

Eleanor looked ahead to the bright lights of the house and noticed a familiar figure all in black, wearing sensible heels and a boxy blazer. Mrs. B., as usual, was playing the part she created for herself, owning the place, being the hostess though it was not really her place to do so. She stopped the guests at the door, welcoming them and undoubtedly checking their invitations.

"Well, then, I better stay away from the silver." Eleanor whispered.

Evan pulled up in front of the house and put the car in park.

"And I promise I won't speak out of turn," he said slowly and turned towards her. "But I have been thinking about misbehaving."

****

Since Mrs. B. rarely missed a thing, Eleanor was sure she spied the two of them mount the steps of the Hamilton mansion, greeting old friends and neighbors as they did so. Just as they approached the last few steps, the self-styled Eastfield matriarch turned to one of the waiters and made a fuss over something on the tray he was carrying.

"What do you suppose the poor guy did?" Evan asked, as Mrs. B.'s angry voice settled over the crowd on the marble patio. "Eat a spanikopita?"

Eleanor laughed, and moved closer to his side. "My, that's a pretty big word, Mr. Zane. Did you use it in your guide to the Trojan War or something?"

"Hey, a guy's gotta eat. And, as a rule, I never eat anything I can't pronounce."

"I see. I guess that's why you turned the menu over to me at L'Avignon?"

He looked at her blankly, but his hand went up to fidget with his bowtie, and she guessed he knew precisely what she was talking about.

"Oh, no. I just realized since you were familiar with the restaurant, you'd know what their specialties are," he said, completely unconvincingly. Then too quickly, "Here's one of your friends."

"Hello, Miriam," Eleanor said. "Don't we have a wonderful night for this?"

"Oh, no matter if we had an ice storm. This is always a wonderful night," Miriam Pell said. Perhaps remembering Eleanor had never before been invited, she added, "and always made nicer when there are newcomers to the mix."

"How nice of you to say so, Miriam. I would think Mrs. B. would be happy, and not ignore me when I arrive."

"I wouldn't take anything personally. She's very busy with that waiter. I believe he brought out white cocktail napkins instead of beige, and all hell is breaking loose."

"I don't know how the women of the Thrifty Means put up with her," Evan said, and shrugged a little stiffly.

Eleanor resisted the temptation to smooth down

the creased shoulder of his tuxedo, and wondered if he had been working too hard around Garland. It was not her place to touch and not her business to wonder, so she looked away. "I think her attitude has to do with Evan's arrival, don't you, Miriam? Mrs. B. has been edgy since the day he walked into the shop."

Miriam glanced up at Evan, who stood silently. "No, it's not Evan. I don't want to offend you, Evan, but Margaret Brownlee regards men as little more than nuisances. She wouldn't want you just hanging around the shop, but as long as you're either donating items or buying things, she's willing to tolerate you."

"How very flattering."

"By Margaret's standards, it's practically a benediction." Miriam smiled, as if she enjoyed an unspoken joke. "You're not the problem. No, Eleanor is."

"I...no, I'm sure I..." Eleanor finally shut her mouth, feeling a fool. Could her friendship with Evan be so distasteful to Mrs. B.? Did the disposition of the Garland estate matter so much?

"I'm just one of the volunteers," Eleanor said quietly.

"You're the volunteer who will take her place one day. And most of us think the sooner the better."

"Why not yourself? Or Gracie? You'd both be great."

"Great at what, my dears?" Mrs. B.'s voice drove between them like a wedge. "And Mr. Zane is here too. Are you enjoying yourself? It's such a privilege to have someone of your stature back in town. There's so much you've missed through the years, and we've certainly missed you! Eleanor, Miriam, would you mind terribly if I borrow Mr. Zane to show him around the Hamilton home? There are some things of particular value I'm sure will interest him."

"Mr. Zane is a big boy, Mrs. B. He's allowed to go where he wants to go, and with anyone he pleases," Eleanor said.

Evan shot her a look begging for mercy, but said, "Sure, Margaret, I'd love to have a look around. I wonder if they have as much junk here as I do at Garland."

Mrs. B. bristled, probably at the "Margaret," and looked like she might change her mind about her casual invitation, but put her hand under his elbow and pulled him away from Eleanor.

"You really ought to warn him," Miriam said.

"About the fact Mrs. B. is going to give him a history of Eastfield including every sordid detail of the life of everyone who ever lived here?"

"Well, of course," Miriam said. "But I was really thinking someone should tell him calling the lady by her first name is a crime punishable by death."

****

Evan understood when he received the invitation from the Historical Society the event was to be a fundraiser and there were certain inherent obligations. He also understood there would be food and drinks, dancing, and socializing. That is why he asked Ellie Gilmartin to be his guest, thinking she would feel comfortable if half her friends and acquaintances were also there. She probably was feeling very comfortable, enjoying the food and drink, and music.

He, on the other hand, was walking through darkened halls with a tyrannical woman who thought he was interested in the portraits of people he did not know, who did things of little or no importance.

"Well, here's a fine fellow," Mrs. Brownlee said, pausing in front of a fellow who didn't look at all fine. The man, dressed in a dark suit and seated at a hearth, had ears of startlingly uneven size, and an expression suggesting he sucked on too many lemons. "This is Joseph Wadsworth, and of course you know who painted his portrait."

"Of course I do not, Margaret," Evan said, and laughed. "But I'm not so hopeless, you know. I'm sure I would recognize a Rembrandt or a Picasso."

She turned on him, looking up into his face. "But you do not recognize a Ralph Earle?"

Evan's stomach rumbled, reminding him he hadn't eaten since a hurried lunch at the kitchen counter. He considered the platters of hors d'oeuvres passed around downstairs and knew he wouldn't care if his napkin were white or beige—if he could only get his hands on a few franks-in-blankets. He wondered how long this private tour was going to last, and what the woman wanted of him.

"Well, now you've shown the painting to me, I think I'll be able to recognize a Ralph Earle the next time I see one. Thank you for this little lesson." He pulled her gently towards the staircase.

He was surprised she went along readily. "That's exactly my point. You need lessons in art and artifacts of the Colonial period, Mr. Zane. How else will you understand what you've inherited from Dorothea?"

"I don't believe I inherited anything from Dorothea, except twenty years of yellowing, disintegrating New York Times. The rest belonged to my parents, and their parents before them," he said. "But I see your point. I hope you are not insulted when I say I will simply trust others as to the value of stuff I have in my house. That's why I asked Eleanor Gilmartin to come over and help me. She seems to know what she's looking at."

"And I suppose you like looking at her."

They had nearly reached the staircase, and Evan paused. What was this really about? Was this elderly woman jealous of Ellie?

"I can't imagine a man who wouldn't, Margaret. But be reassured it's all business between us, and our discussions are of a professional nature." He didn't sound very convincing, and all the more because his words weren't true, and likely to become even less so. He glanced at his interrogator, and didn't think she found them convincing either. "We're both writers, you know."

"Watch your step here," she said unnecessarily, though she might not have been talking about the carpeted stairs. "And, of course, there was the horrible accident you were in."

Something looming on the landing in front of them distracted him from her pointed words, as sharp as they were. It was a grandfather clock, large and lean, and vaguely familiar.

"You know, the accident in which your parents were..."

"I know which accident you mean, Margaret," Evan said firmly. "You cannot think it's something I might ever forget." He stood for a moment longer, staring at the clock, and would have liked to get a little closer. The necessity of divesting himself from Margaret Brownlee became far more urgent than admiring a fine piece of craftsmanship.

****

"Ah, good," Eleanor said, wiping a smudge of mustard from the corner of her mouth. "Here you are. I was beginning to think you would rather spend time with Ralph Earle than me."

Evan looked around to see if there were any waiters wandering close. None. And then he wondered what Eleanor Gilmartin might taste like. "How did you know?"

"Why, you just had lesson number one in Eastfield history. How the great Ralph Earle passed through town, earning his meals by painting portraits of the eminent citizens, flattering them on canvas."

"Flattering? If the prime bit of manhood upstairs is any example, the people in Eastfield must have been a wretched-looking group."

"You're not very kind. We're their descendants, after all." Eleanor pointed out.

Evan looked her up and down, liking the way she blushed. Was there no one in this town who had done the lady any justice in recent years? She was gorgeous, as stunningly beautiful as she had been when they were in school together. When he was sixteen, he had no idea what to do about it. Now, he had a little more experience, and knew exactly what he wanted to do.

"I guess we've improved over time," he said in a low voice and was surprised to see her frown. "But Ralph Earle probably never improved. I could probably have done better myself."

"You seem to have a lot of talents, Mr. Zane," Eleanor said, leaning forward. He tried to stay focused on her face, and not glance down at the temptation offered him. "Or at least, strong beliefs in those talents. Is there anything you've wanted and couldn't have?"

"As a matter of fact, there is. But I intend to rectify the situation as soon as possible."

Eleanor straightened, her dark eyes troubled. He noticed, for the first time, a certain asymmetry about her face, made more apparent by the uneven parting of her hair. Where the brown curls fell away, he could see a small white scar on her forehead and recognized the mark at once, though he hadn't thought about it in twenty years. On the night of the accident, after she pulled him from the wreck of his car and his life, they huddled together in a ditch at the side of the road while fire spread in the gasoline around them. Her head pressed against his heart, his arm pulled her close. Later, in the stark light of the Belvedere Hospital, the doctors examined a bloody stain on his jacket, not finding the source of the injury. The blood was hers, of course.

"What?" she asked and he realized she had been talking to him.

He took a deep breath, leaned over, and kissed her on the lips. Nearby, someone applauded, and a woman giggled. Eleanor must have been as willing to ignore their audience as was he, and swayed closer to him, opening her lips. He tasted the mustard and the rich spices of seasoned meat, and something minty as well.

Suddenly, she pushed him gently away, stood back, and smiled. Her eyelids lowered, making her look both sleepy and sated. "I didn't realize you meant to start right now."

He blinked, trying to remember about what they had been talking. He only knew he felt the aching bond of that horrible night between them, and was grateful they both survived to this night.

"I've been wanting to kiss you for twenty years," he said, awkwardly. He sensed they had an audience and wasn't sure where to begin.

"Well, you certainly pick your moments," she said, visibly amused. People were streaming towards the large room behind them, moving around them as if they were rocks in a current. "And you might have let me know."

"I don't think I realized it until just now," he said. "I think I was prompted by the scar on your forehead."

Her eyes widened, and she blushed, making the thin white line stand out even more. "Blessed scar," she said, and then she gestured towards the open door. "But you're going to have to wait a little longer, Evan. It's time for dinner."

As he took her hand to lead her to the dining

room, he reflected that if he had half an ounce of romance in him, he would have suggested they blow off the dinner and go straight to his room at Garland. But with her promise of waiting a little longer, and the warmth of her hand in his, he was willing to sacrifice the present for the future. Besides, he was very, very hungry.

The large hall of the Hamilton estate was built to resemble the great hall of medieval castles, though fortunately cows and pigs weren't huddled in the corners. The room's decorations featured spring blossoms and hundreds of votive candles, and Evan looked around quickly to see if the fire marshal was present. He'd have a field day here.

"We're over there, Evan," Eleanor said, urging him towards a darkened corner. "At Table 8." She looked wistfully as they passed tables of people she recognized, even some people he recognized, until they joined a group of older couples whose connection to them was not readily apparent. But the uncertainty was resolved in a moment.

"Why, it's Marianne's and Mark's boy," an elderly man said as he stood up shakily. Evan groaned, wondering who the hell was clever enough to seat him with old friends of his parents. If he hoped to impress Eleanor Gilmartin this evening, this crowd of country club lifers was probably not the place with which to do so.

"Mr. Peters, I believe? How are you, sir?" Evan asked respectfully, as he shook the older man's hand. "And Mrs. Peters? Let me introduce Eleanor Gilmartin."

The white haired woman at the table crossed her hands under her chin and gazed up at them. "I'm sure I recognize you, Eleanor. I think your picture was in *The Edition* recently."

"About a year ago, actually," Eleanor said, sitting down next to Anne May Peters. "I write books."

"Really? Then that's why you must know Evan. He writes books, too, you know."

Evan was aware of Eleanor watching him as he went around the table, introducing himself to the others. He didn't hear any of the names, as he strained to hear what she had to say.

"Oh, I didn't know. Books? I had no idea," she said, and smiled too broadly.

"And yet you seem to know each other very well," the woman said pointedly, and looked up to Evan. "We weren't sure you were going to make it in to dinner."

Evan decided to stop this conversation just where they were. "I wouldn't have missed dinner for anything," he said hurriedly. "I'm ready for a good meal."

"What? Has the little lady not bothered to cook for you?" asked one of the men at the table.

Evan glanced towards Eleanor, and realized she found all of this amusing. And why not, since everything was at his expense? "I don't think he trusts me, Mr. Wilcox. He remembers my mishaps in cooking class in junior high."

"Do you go back so far, then?" another man asked, as his wife elbowed him.

"Let's talk about the auction," Mrs. Peters said, dipping her spoon into some sort of jelly already set down at their table.

"Am I supposed to know about an auction?" Evan asked Eleanor as he dropped down into the last remaining seat.

She didn't answer him at once. Instead, she sampled the jelly, mulled it around for a moment, and put her spoon back on the table. Then she turned to face him, and smiled, and he forgot there was anyone else at the table. "Considering you have the invitation, and I wasn't even important enough to be invited," Ellie reminded him, "you seem to have no idea what we're doing here. The auction will be held over desserts, so save some room and some money. You're expected to spend generously on items removed from the Society's collections. People wait for this event all year, so they can pick up some treasures at a discount."

"If they're treasures, why have they been removed from the museum?"

Eleanor nodded, still smiling. "You know, for a guy who writes books for idiots, you can be incredibly clever. They're not treasures, just stuff the Board of Trustees doesn't want to keep, and won't want to spend the money to store. You'll find paintings of someone's uncle's nephew's cousin donated in 1939. Some rusty nails from a barn. Probably an old harness or two. There's nothing for auction here you don't already have a better, more valuable version of at Garland."

"So what are we doing here?" Evan asked, impatient to leave.

"You tell me, smart boy. You invited me."

"I hoped you wanted to come," he said, defensively.

"I did," she said slowly, and looked away. "I wanted to be with you."

Evan pulled his napkin off his lap and set it down on the table as he started to push his chair back.

She gave him all the invitation he needed to hear, all he needed to know from her.

"You're not going yet, Evan, are you?" Mr. Peters looked across at him. "The evening's just getting started. And we have a lot to talk about."

Evan looked back to Eleanor, just as she picked up her spoon again, looking as if their little exchange hadn't happened.

"No, I'm not going yet. I just needed to stretch

my legs," Evan said.

Everyone at the table, strangers really, studied him as if they understood exactly what he was thinking.

Chapter 8

"Always check a man's pockets. But make sure he's out of his pants before you do so."
Ginny DeLoy, volunteer since 1980

Eleanor remembered dancing with Evan Zane once before in her life, but then she was taller than he was. Like most children in Eastfield, they were tortured in a ballroom once each week at Will Chalk's School for Dance, and were obliged to step on the toes of many, many partners until they learned how to comport themselves with grace and style. Their parents all thought it imperative they learn the steps to formal dance, even though the music at school dances and parties were usually provided by DJs who didn't know a waltz from a tango. Every week, the boys put on little blue sports jackets, and the girls, flowered dresses in a vaguely Victorian style, and they left their sneakers at home. The dancing was made tolerable by the general understanding one did not speak to one's partner, nor look directly at him.

For the first time in her life, Eleanor was grateful for those wretched lessons. Evan Zane had grown a bit since those days, and the top of her head came just to his chin. He had obviously forgotten where his hand was supposed to go, and instead rested it comfortably on her hip, leading her along in a waltz. They had already finished their dinners, and endured several speeches and cold coffee during dessert. At the auction, Evan somehow acquired a dovecote once gracing the Town Green, and bid unsuccessfully on several other items. When the formal program ended, the band started playing, and Evan no longer appeared anxious to leave the party.

Eleanor wondered if he was having second thoughts about starting a relationship so full of complications. Things were hard enough when you were a kid, and had to put up with your friends' teasing and parents' supervision. That was a piece of cake next to your own children's supervision and half the town whispering about what you were doing and with whom.

"So, did you find your murderer?" Eleanor whispered against the lapel of his tuxedo. When he said nothing, she glanced up at the set line of his jaw. "Mr. Wilcox, perhaps? Mr. Peters? Or maybe the little woman herself?"

"I can't imagine any one of them getting angry about anything, except maybe a builder tearing down a plywood shack to build a mansion."

"You're laughing at me," Eleanor sighed.

"No, I'm laughing at them. Spending an evening as part of this gang is like stepping into a time machine."

"But they take the business of preservation very seriously. Anyone who wants to make a change to his house has to be prepared to do battle." Eleanor paused, remembering what she first speculated about Evan, about how he might sell Garland to a developer. He might yet. "Did Dorothea threaten to sell?"

"She might have threatened all she wanted, but there was nothing she could do."

"So you've said, but not everyone would know that. Wayne could say anything he wanted, and who would know better?"

"Anyone with half a brain. Who would trust Wayne?"

"Your aunt, apparently."

They danced for a while without saying anything, Eleanor savoring his touch, his scent, and all the other long-forgotten pleasures of such a moment.

"You know, now I recall Dorothea once asked me if I wanted to sell Garland," Evan said suddenly, instantly banishing any inclination towards romance. "Actually, she asked me twice."

"She must have been tired of keeping up the place," Eleanor said, wishing they could forget about the reasons bringing him to Eastfield, and concentrate on the fact he was here.

"Well, once was right after the accident, when a lot of things were uncertain." He held her a little closer, as he did that dreadful night. "But the other was when she made the journey to visit me in the hospital. That's all she wanted to talk about. She had a canvas bag with her, and I remember thinking she might have brought a box of candy, or a plant. But it was filled with papers and ads from realtors. She wanted me to sign something, but never told me what. Finally, she just left the bag on the food tray, along with the green gelatin and tuna salad."

"I have seen the inside of your refrigerator, Mr. Zane," Eleanor murmured, "and I just want to go on record as saying hospital food looks a lot better than anything you seem to make for yourself."

"Oh, I ate everything gratefully," Evan said, and smacked his lips against her forehead. "But I dumped Dorothea's gift into the garbage can, and haven't wondered about it since."

"For five years," Eleanor amended. "Something happened five years ago. Remember the cloak and the other things she noted in her ledger."

A passing couple stopped to speak to them, right in the middle of the dance floor. Another couple banged into Eleanor's shoulder and joked about needing traffic signals. Evan glanced down at her face and quickly pulled her away to the edge of the floor. She said nothing, but recognized he was perhaps the only person in the world who understood she would never find that funny; joking about car accidents was beyond her own, personal, pale.

She wondered if she ought to thank him, and risk casting a shadow on the lovely night. She wondered what he was thinking.

"You know, that painting looked awfully familiar," he said. Eleanor let out a long breath, glad she hadn't said anything.

Instead, she blinked and glanced at the walls of the room, wondering which, among the Hamilton's awful paintings, he meant.

"The barnyard scene?" she asked.

"No, the still life with the dead fish. The one your friend bought at the auction."

"Miriam? You may have seen it in someone's house when you were a kid. I can't blame anyone for taking a picture of dead fish off his wall."

"Yeah, I think you're right. It was in someone's house." His dancing slowed, and she wondered if he was tired. She noticed he sometimes limped, as if he had a stiff leg, after he had been working around Garland all day. "Ellie, do you mind if we duck out? I want to show you something."

"Then I should get my pashmina. I left it at the table."

"No, I don't mean to leave the house yet, just to show you something upstairs."

They could have just stopped where they were, on the outskirts of the crowded dance floor, and make their departure. Instead, Evan led them towards the opposite wall, where two wide sets of French doors opened out onto a dark hall. Eleanor had a sense he was watching the crowd, ready to seize a moment when no one would notice their escape.

"Here we are," he said, after thrusting her out into the hall. "Are you warm enough?"

She answered by lifting his arm, and slipping beneath it as if he was her cape. "Now I am," she said. "Why do I have the impression you want to do this without attracting an audience?"

"Because I don't." He looked around them, as she waited for him to elaborate. "Damn! How do the Hamiltons find their way around the place? It's a lot easier in an old farmhouse."

"And even easier in a small colonial on Milkweed Lane. But I don't think navigability increases my property values."

"Come," he said, ignoring her feeble attempt at humor. "I think the stairway is this way."

It wasn't. Or, at least, the stairway they saw was not the one he wanted. They walked up, only to come down again, and ventured further down the hall to the next foyer. Since she had no idea what they were looking for, Eleanor wasn't much help. To be perfectly honest, walking along with Evan, nestled against his shoulder, was pretty close to what she had been looking forward to for some time.

"There it is," he said quietly, and pulled her up the stairs. At the first landing, stark against pale plaster, she saw a floor clock. "Look at the grandfather clock."

"It's a floor clock, actually. When they were built there already was an interest in old things and antiques, so the manufacturers believed they were being clever by appealing to the popular market. Grandfather clock just sounded like something old."

"Hmmm...you're a useful person to have around," he said. He followed up his praise by dropping his arm and leaving her standing on the top step while he knelt before the large pine clock. "This one really is old, though."

Old, but otherwise unimpressive. "The handiwork is pretty basic, and even the clock face is crude," Eleanor said, trying to be helpful. She watched him spring the latch on the door and run his long fingers along the rough wood on the inside.

"Watch who you're insulting, lady," Evan said tersely. "My great grandfather made this clock. Here's his signature right here. He was an Evan also."

"Really?" Eleanor asked, excited for him, and surprised he would recognize the handiwork of someone in his family. She was sure her ex-husband couldn't even recognize his parents' handwriting. "He was a clockmaker?"

Evan gently closed the door and patted the clock, as if saying farewell to a much-loved pet. "Not as far as I know. This might be the only one he ever made. His son was more skillful, and had a small business in the thirties. Wayne recently tried to lay claim to one of my grandfather's creations."

"I remember. That is, I remember you telling Wayne the clock at Garland was his. But what of this one? What is the clock doing here? Did you know the Hamiltons had it?"

He stood silently, staring at the clock as if waiting for the thing to speak to him, to explain itself. Below them, many rooms away, the band played something at a faster tempo, probably retiring half the crowd. Somewhere, a spring peeper sang into the darkness. Evan reached out, prodded the cabinet, but it did not budge.

"I don't know why the clock is here. The last time I saw it, was in the living room at Garland."

"Recently?"

"A while ago. I happened to be up in Eastfield the weekend of daylight savings and went around the house changing all the clocks. Of course, I couldn't go into Lilianna's room, but time doesn't seem to mean anything to her. The clock on the stove hadn't been working since I was a kid, so I didn't bother. And then Dorothea told me to leave the grandfather clock alone, since it wasn't working either. I offered to hire a clockmaker, and she said the thing wasn't worth the time or the money."

"It's not my business, but I would say the piece was worth both. An antique for which you know the provenance is worth a good deal." Eleanor looked at the clock with a new appreciation and wondered how much the Hamiltons paid. Did Dorothea think it worthless because it didn't work? Did the Hamiltons simply take advantage of her naiveté?

"It is your business now," Evan said brusquely, "because I'm asking for your help. The thing is, the clock wasn't broken at all. After Dorothea made her pronouncement, she sat at the table watching me, as if daring me to take a closer look. I went out to the porch with the newspaper, but she didn't move from the spot."

"Forgive me for saying this, but she really was a Valkyrie, wasn't she? I mean, Garland is yours, after all."

"She was an original, for sure. Anyway, I told her I was going out at night, and she probably figured I forgot about the clock. She and Lilianna retired early, and I wasn't gone too long, and checked out the clock when I came home." He turned back to the clock, and reopened the door. Inside the case, he found what he was looking for, and pulled out a strip of masking tape. "Someone taped the pendulum to the cabinet, so of course the mechanism couldn't work."

In spite of what she said about his aunt, Eleanor was usually prepared to believe the best of anyone. "Maybe she already tried to have it fixed and the clockmaker disabled it? Maybe she intended to have it moved to another room?"

"Maybe she intended to sell the clock to the Hamiltons, and not bother to tell me?"

Eleanor let out a long breath. "Yes, I suppose that's possible also. I don't want to probe into your private affairs, but do you think she needed the money?"

Evan shook his head.

"Perhaps she donated it to the society for a fundraiser, and the Hamiltons were lucky bidders?"

"Keep going," he said.

"She hated the thing, and hoped you wouldn't notice anyway."

He turned away from the clock, and put the tape into the pocket of his tuxedo. He stood silently in the darkness, his head nearly at the same height as his great grandfather Evan's cabinet.

"Evan? What are you thinking?"

"I'm thinking you are a lot more generous to others than you are to me."

"How could you say such a thing? I'm up at Garland all the time and I've agreed to help you with all your stuff, and I went out to eat with you, and here I am tonight. What more can I give you?"

He didn't say anything, but sucked in his breath, and took a step forward.

"No, Evan. I didn't mean to sound so desperate. We're talking about neighbors and friends, and what I do at The Thrifty Means." Eleanor realized she sounded like an idiot, but she hadn't expected the moment to come now, in an abandoned hallway of someone else's house. And yet, everything about their relationship since the day he walked into the shop behind a shield of cartons—and probably a good deal earlier—was leading them to this, right now and right here. "Evan, please…"

He used his body to push her against the wall, gentle, though insistent. His arms came around her, and she lifted her own in response, circling his neck and drawing him closer. He didn't need an invitation; he already possessed it. His mouth came down on hers; easing her lips apart to open to him, savor him, as he kissed her as if this was their final moment, instead of one of the first. He was warm and hard and the smooth wool of his tuxedo held the scent of the votive candles, spicy and exotic. Around them, everything else passed away, and she was only aware of him, and the wonderful things he was doing to her body.

When he had her breathless, his lips moved down her chin to her neck and collarbone, and then dipped further to taste the salty skin where her silk gown slipped delicately to reveal the line of her cleavage. Her pearls rattled as his hand came up to cup her breast.

"Oh, good God, Evan," she sighed, and felt as if her knees could barely hold her. She dropped one arm and braced herself against the wall. "We have to stop."

He paused, and said without looking up, "Why?"

Why indeed? "What if someone comes along and finds us here?"

He kissed her breast, as if in valediction, and straightened up. He still held her close, but they were much more presentable than they were a moment ago.

"You'll just tell him you've been probing into my private affairs. That's what you said, isn't it? And just in case you're wondering, no I don't mind at all. In fact…"

"Evan!"

He took a step back, and propped one arm against the wall, in the manner of a high school boy standing in front of his girlfriend at her locker. Shielding her, claiming her, making a statement for everyone to see.

"I have a reputation in this town, and so do you.

People will talk. We're not kids anymore."

"Don't remind me. When I think about how many years I've wanted this, wanted you, and was too insecure to do anything."

"You, insecure? Impossible!" Eleanor straightened the bodice of her gown, thinking even if she destroyed it this night, her money was well spent. "And why would you be?"

"Do you mean because of football and lacrosse and everything else?"

Eleanor put her hands on either side of his face and pulled him close again. "You know those things never mattered to me. No, I mean, why would you be insecure about me? You had to know I could barely take my eyes off you. You only had to say the word and I'm sure I would have done something terribly improper with you."

He groaned. "Tell me I'm imagining this. You acted as if you despised me."

"You ignored me. Even after..."

"I was a kid. I just lost my parents. I didn't know what to do or who I was."

"I lost a lot that night, too," she sighed. "Not as much as you of course. But I lost my best friend, and somehow I lost you too. Even though I didn't have you in the first place."

"You did, but I was too stupid to let you know." He gave a little laugh. "What a waste."

"Not all, I think. And here you are and here I am, and we're not kids anymore."

"No, we're not. Is it too late to ask you to do something terribly improper with me?"

"That depends on what you have in mind," Eleanor teased, though she knew exactly what he had in mind. It was in hers, too.

"What time do your kids expect you back home?"

Eleanor stiffened, realizing she hadn't discussed those plans with them. They only expected she would keep her cell phone on most of the evening, and she would come home when the party was done.

And now, somehow the party was just beginning.

"When does Lilianna expect you back home?"

"Lilianna is visiting a friend on Candlewood Lake for the weekend. I delivered her myself, and will pick her up on Monday night. And Wayne has found a cozy trailer for himself, up near the mill. I think he's supposed to be the security guard there but no one asked me for references. Good thing. For him, not the mill."

"So." Eleanor accepted there was no turning back now, not when she had practically thrown herself at him. And Evan, perhaps hoping she would, already cleared a path to the front door at Garland.

"So," he repeated. "Do you want to probe my private affairs? And, if I'm good, perhaps you'll let me probe some of yours, as well?"

Eleanor could barely breathe. "Only if you're good," she said, in a squeaky voice.

"Oh, you can bet on it," he said, and pulled her away from the wall and towards the staircase.
****

Garland was dark, lit only by a few lamps strategically placed throughout the farmhouse. Evan opened the door to Lilianna's room, looking as if he could barely believe his good fortune, and moved quickly through the house, locking doors and checking windows.

Eleanor stood in the center of the living room, flushed and tormented with the some sharp misgivings. What did she know of him, after all? Was he involved with another woman, was he married? What was she hoping for, beyond an evening of pleasure? He turned from the large casement window to face her and pulled at his bow tie until it hung like streamers down his chest. The gesture was so familiar, so intimate; it still managed to catch her off her guard.

"Are you married?" she asked bluntly, though he once denied it.

"Married?" he repeated. "No. Not now. Not ever. Why do you need to know?"

When Eleanor didn't answer, he added. "Aside from the obvious. Don't you think the gossips of Eastfield would have managed to let you know if there was a Mrs. Zane hiding in the barn? Or in a condo in New York?"

"Why would the gossips of Eastfield think they had to let me know anything?" she asked, and brought a hand up protectively in front of her. Her fingers caught her pearls, and she started to twist them in an effort to calm down.

Evan smiled, and rubbed his hand against his chin in a contemplative pose. "Another obvious question, I think. I can't seem to go anywhere in this town without someone asking me how you are, and what we're doing, and if I intend to stay here in town because of you. Miriam Pell warned me the women of The Thrifty Means would do something unspeakably painful to me if I hurt you in any way. And even Lewis let me know you were absolutely available, no matter what you might say."

"Oh, good heavens. What do they know about what I want?" she said lightly, appalled at how transparent her interest in Evan Zane had been. Her earlier doubts were entirely justified.

"They're not only concerned about you, in case you're wondering," he continued, as he shrugged off his jacket and tossed it onto the couch. "Most people have noticed—not without a certain glee—how indifferent you are to my attentions."

"What attentions? We went out to dinner? You asked me to come along to an event you agreed to attend without knowing why you were going?"

"No," he said as he came towards her. "I think they've noticed I can't get my eyes off you. I still can't."

And he didn't. He caught her at her waist, and bent her just slightly, urging her back, as he continued what he had begun at the Hamilton affair. His light eyes stayed open, meeting her gaze, and Eleanor was so mesmerized she scarcely registered what else he was doing to her. When she came to her senses, though just barely, her lovely gown was slipping off her shoulders and the pearl necklace was dangling behind her like a scarf in the wind.

"Come with me, Ellie. You're about to indulge one of my most cherished fantasies."

"I'm not sure I like the sound of that," she said lightly, running her fingers along the line of his chin.

"I just hope you'll like the feel of it. I won't embarrass myself by telling you how many nights I dreamed about having you in my bed."

"Then I hope I won't embarrass myself when you see I'm not a sixteen year old anymore."

"Neither am I. I have scars and bruises, and can't fit into my lacrosse uniform anymore."

Eleanor pulled his head down to hers and kissed the tip of his nose. "I hated that stupid uniform. I bet you look better without it."

Evan groaned. "I can't do these word games anymore. Come. Please come."

She did. He pulled her down the hall to the small bedroom of his childhood, in which he kissed her several weeks before, and they were both startled when a cat leapt off the narrow bed and ran between their legs.

Eleanor clutched her heart and laughed, and Evan muttered something about Dorothea having the right idea as he walked around the bed to turn on a small lamp.

"Evan, perhaps not?" Eleanor asked, a little

helplessly, gesturing towards the lamp. "I'm not sure I could bear it."

"I have to see you, Ellie. I can scarcely believe this is happening as it is."

She stood silently as he unbuttoned his shirt and pulled gold cufflinks from the starched cuffed. He pulled the shirt away stiffly and again, she wondered how many of his injuries on a long-ago night still compromised him today. But those thoughts were forgotten as he turned back to face her. He was right; he no longer was a boy of sixteen. His shoulders were broader and more muscular. Dark curling hair emphasized the lines of his chest and ran down his stomach in a tight line to his navel. The scars were there, to be sure, but the thin wavering lines added distinction to his dark skin.

Eleanor put out her hand, which was all the invitation he needed. He took three steps across the room and had her in his arms again. He kissed her as he tugged the shoulder straps of her gown further down her arms, imprisoning her. Her breasts, only protected by her silk chemise, felt the sting of the cold air and made her nipples grow hard. Evan pulled her arms away from the fabric, freeing her, but she only needed to wiggle her hips once and again before the gown slipped off altogether.

He still held her arms aloft as he stood with his head bent, looking at her.

"Evan, please," she begged, feeling painfully awkward and shy.

"Ellie, you're beautiful. Don't regret the girl who was. You were pretty then. You're gorgeous now."

Not entirely believing him, but taking some courage from his words, she reached for the pearls again and pulled them over her head. If she had any concerns the gesture might be too seductive, it proved entirely redundant, for he was already making his way out of his trousers, until they pooled around his feet. He didn't straighten entirely, but caught her around her waist and urged her to the bed as he flung off the covers in a cloud of cat fur.

"Not exactly romantic," he muttered and he brought her down with him onto the mattress.

"Very romantic," she said, glancing at the shelves over their heads. "I always wanted to make love surrounded by trophies of men carrying big sticks."

"I hope you mean that metaphorically," he said, lifting his hips to pull off his briefs.

He stifled her laugh with his mouth, and knowing she was hopeless to protest, pulled away her chemise and panties. Within moments she was hopeless to do anything but meet the demands of her body and his, as he rose above her and tantalized her with every delicious temptation of lovemaking, satisfied her, and left her sated and breathless beside him in their narrow boy's bed.

****

Dreaming of nonsense, Eleanor listened as the microchippy notes of "Greensleeves" intruded into her subconscious, and realized her cell phone was ringing somewhere in the house. She tried to move, but was paralyzed, weighted down by something warm and firm.

"Do you want me to get the phone?" someone said against her shoulder.

Her eyes opened, startled, and she realized at once where she was, and with whom. She pushed away from Evan Zane and fell off the side of the bed.

"No! It's Leslie or Lewis. What time is it? I've got to answer," she cried, a little hysterically, as she scrambled to her feet. Realizing she was naked, she pulled the blanket off the bed, exposing her lover, and wrapped herself in a cocoon. "Where did I leave my purse?"

By the time she stumbled out of the bedroom

and found her purse in the kitchen, the phone stopped its song, and there were three messages in her inbox. As Eleanor went to her address book, the phone clock read 3:35 AM.

"Mom, are you with Evan?" Leslie asked as she picked up at home. She sounded very clear and awake.

"What are you doing up?" Eleanor asked in return, sounding as motherly as one could while wearing a scratchy wool blanket and nothing else at all. "And yes, I'm with Mr. Zane. We...ah...met some people at the party and have been having some coffee. Is everything all right?"

"Yeah, sure. I just wanted to make sure you're okay."

"I am, Baby. Thank you for worrying. I'm on my way home now." Eleanor looked up as Evan walked into the kitchen and stubbed his toe.

"What was that?" Leslie asked.

"Mr. Zane. I think he spilled some hot coffee or something."

"Good thing I didn't," Evan said as he rubbed his hand over his bare chest. "This affair would have been ended before it even started."

"Is he all right?" Leslie asked.

"Oh, he's definitely all right," Eleanor said, hoping her daughter didn't read anything into the comment. Evan did, however. As he was meant to. He came up behind her, pulled away the blanket, and rubbed hands up and down her hips. "He's going to drive me home. Now."

Leslie murmured her satisfaction, and Evan said something very rude and Eleanor clicked off her phone.

"I've got to go home, Evan. Will you take me, or do you just want to lend me your car keys?"

"We had a date, Mrs. Gilmartin. I've got to get you home safely."

Eleanor turned around, brushing her breasts against his chest. "I think you're several hours too late."

"I wish you could stay," he said.

"But you know I can't. Not this time, at least." Her hand caressed the downy depression at the base of his spine, and she pressed him closer. "But it was a very nice evening."

He grew hard against her stomach. "Nice? Is that the best a writer of historical novels could do? Don't you have a fairly florid vocabulary to apply to present circumstances?"

"I do not," she said, deflating more than his ego. "Haven't you ever opened one of my books?"

"Opened? Yes."

"Read them?" she asked, running her fingers up and down his arms until she felt goose bumps on his skin.

"No," he said, and shivered. He stepped away quickly. "Let's get you home."

"Should we get dressed first?"

"Since your kids, and possibly all their close friends, will probably be waiting in the living room for us, I'd say that's a good idea. The Zane family's reputation probably can't survive any more rumors or slurs against our good name."

"And yet," Eleanor said, backing him against a wall, "your name was good enough to get you an invitation to the Historical Society. My name is just good enough to sign permission slips my kids bring home from school. Oh, and annoy Margaret Brownlee."

"Sounds good enough for me," he said, and kissed her.

****

"I hope you enjoyed yourself on Saturday night," Margaret Brownlee said even before Eleanor slipped off her cardigan after arriving at The Thrifty Means on Monday.

Eleanor turned away from the coat tree, and studied the shop's manager for a moment, saying nothing. The question was simple enough, or ought to be, but there was nothing in the woman's manner or expression to suggest she cared one way or another. If Eleanor said she didn't enjoy herself, Mrs. B. would probably say it wasn't her place to be there anyway. If she said she enjoyed herself, Mrs. B. would probably refuse to speak to her for a week.

If she told Mrs. B. she and Evan Zane left the party, went to Garland, and made love for hours and hours, Mrs. B. would probably ask her to hand over the key to The Thrifty Means and purge the shop of any evidence of her existence.

"The party was lovely," Eleanor finally said, and Mrs. B. nearly smiled. "And I couldn't have had a more thoughtful, handsome escort."

Mrs. B. swept her hand over the counter, brushing loose tags and pins into a basket.

"What did he think of the gown?" Gracie asked, watching the older woman. "You certainly paid enough to make him notice."

"Oh, he noticed. He liked it enough to make sure we were seen by everyone. In fact, after dinner, he took me around for a private tour of the house, to make sure we hadn't missed anyone. Or anything." Eleanor said, a little recklessly.

Gracie looked confused, but the barb hit the intended mark.

"You had no business going around the house unescorted," Mrs. B. said tartly. "The Hamiltons were quite clear about that. No one was supposed to leave the great hall, unless to use the restrooms."

Eleanor was frankly enjoying herself, though why she should get any satisfaction from provoking an elderly woman, a pillar of the community, was not something she wished to examine too closely.

"Oh, I am sorry, Mrs. B. Evan must have misunderstood. He told me he had just walked around the halls with you earlier in the evening."

"But I am on the committee. And Evan Zane was a distinguished guest. And you..."

"Were just the guest of a distinguished guest. I see your point. I could hardly be trusted, I suppose."

"I certainly didn't mean to suggest such a thing," Mrs. B. said quickly. "We trust you here at the shop with all sorts of things, don't we?"

"Yes, we do," Gracie chimed in.

"Well, I suppose that's why Evan really wanted to show me around. He probably didn't care about the dress; he just wanted my expert appraisal about certain things in the Hamilton collection. There was a clock he found especially interesting, for example."

"I think we've wasted enough time talking about the affair, and there's lots of work to be done here," Mrs. B. said brusquely. "Gracie, we just received a box of china from Mrs. Salender. Galen, are you here somewhere? There's silver to be polished. And Eleanor, would you kindly sort through that shopping bag? I believe there's some worthwhile ephemera there. Old greeting cards and post cards." Conversation, over.

An hour later, after Eleanor had sorted through shopping lists, an address book of people long deceased, and clippings from *The Eastfield Edition* from 1942 through 1968, all pertaining to the raising of spaniels, she was pretty sure there was nothing of value in the shopping bag. She was just as sure Mrs. B. intended to punish her for her audacity, real or imagined. Pausing in her task, looking around the shop, she remembered what Miriam said to her at the party, and how unexpected it seemed.

Now, in the light of day and in the dust of the shop, everything made perfect sense. Mrs. B. had set a very high standard for The Thrifty Means, but she wouldn't be around forever. While setting those standards, she managed to trample on anyone who offered a different point of view, or threatened to get too close to any real management of the shop. Margaret Brownlee insisted on recruiting volunteers, yet she had almost no connections to the younger population of the town. She was in charge of all publicity, yet had no idea how to use email, or understood what a website was. She maintained her position as the ultimate authority on all the things coming into the shop, but others—including Lucy Armitage—had discovered errors in dating or attribution.

Now as Eleanor counted off a list of the woman's weaknesses, she admitted something else to be true. Mrs. B. mistreated her most valuable asset in a non-profit organization—her volunteers. She allowed personal grievances to get in the way of efficiency and fair treatment, and ruled everyone by the vagaries of her personality. The Thrifty Means meant far more to the community than Mrs. B.'s vanity, and would survive for many years past the woman's abdication of her role.

On that day, someone else would assume leadership. Miriam Pell's vote was for Eleanor. And the more Eleanor thought about the future, prompted by her own sense of indignation, she might have the support of others, as well.

A gust of wind lifted the papers from the table, and trifled with any organization Eleanor had tentatively provided. Now finished, she realized they would best be filed in a trashcan. She looked up to see who came into the shop and recognized him right away, though he was just a shadow against the light.

She hadn't seen him since he left her in the doorway of her house in the early hours of Sunday morning. It was less than two days ago, and yet an eternity. He called her twice, and wondered if she was up for dinner on Sunday night, but she told him she owed Leslie some time for a project they were doing together, and promised to see him during the week. She wanted to see him on her own terms, but here he was. Since he carried nothing in with him, and didn't seem to be interested in shopping, she knew he was here on his terms.

"Hi, Evan," Emma Grace Liddell called out. She was Gracie's mother and came through the shop every few weeks, looking for old quilts.

"Welcome back, Mr. Zane," Gracie said. "I heard you had a great time at the fundraiser."

"You heard that, did you?" Evan said. "I guess that means Eleanor's about. I was hoping she was."

"No, Mr. Zane, they heard it from me. I told everyone about our discussion about Ralph Earle, and your interest in early American antiques. Well, how can you not be, growing up in such a house as Garland?" Mrs. B. stood and walked over to him, standing in his line of vision of the table where Eleanor worked. If she imagined she was blocking his view, she obviously forgot he was nearly a foot taller than she was.

"But when you grow up in a house surrounded by antiques, you really don't pay much attention to it all," Evan said smoothly. "There are only a few memorable pieces of which you're really appreciative."

Mrs. B.'s back stiffened, and Eleanor guessed she was about to ask which he meant. Evan looked over the woman's shoulder to meet her eyes. She recognized amusement there and something else, both stimulating and a little disturbing.

"Hello, Eleanor!" he said cheerfully. "I hoped to find you here when I didn't get an answer at your house." He stepped around Mrs. B., with no more ceremony than if she was a floor lamp in his path.

"When I'm working in my study, I don't usually

answer the phone."

"No, neither do I," he said. "It's a good thing neither of us has been too diligent about our writing or we'd never get a chance to talk. What are you working on?"

"Here or at home?" she asked, casually.

"Here," he said. "I'm fascinated by..." his voice broke off as he looked down at the array of scraps on the table. "Little pieces of yellowing paper."

Eleanor laughed, realizing how happy he made her. "Well, then, have a look. I think you'll find this fascinating." She handed him a grocery list including the item: "two eggs."

Evan pulled up a chair and studied the paper for a moment before putting it down on the table. He didn't seem to find anything quaint or amusing about the dated reference, and she wondered—not for the first time—if he ever did any food shopping or cooking.

"How long do you have to stay here?" he asked.

"Just as long as it takes to sweep all this into the trash. Why? What do you have in mind?" she asked, and guessed by his expression he had on his mind pretty much what she had on hers. Her heart started to race, and she blushed like a kid.

"I need your help pricing Mason jars, Eleanor," Mrs. B. said.

"You know what I have in mind," Evan said.

"It'll have to wait," Eleanor said, answering both. She stood up to go with Evan, wherever he wanted to take her.

"I'm not happy about this," Mrs. B. grumbled.

"But I am," Eleanor said. "And sometimes there are things more important than working at The Thrifty Means."

Margaret Brownlee gasped, and Eleanor's hand went into her khaki pockets, ready to hand over the key to the front door of the shop.

Gracie started clapping and said, "Hear, hear! She's right, Mrs. B. The rest of us need to get a life!"

Whatever Mrs. B. thought was anyone's guess, for she walked rigidly through the door of the office and closed it just shy of a slam.

"Go. Before she comes out with those damned Mason jars. I'm sure they're worth at least fifty cents each," Gracie said as she reached for Eleanor's cardigan.

"Come," Evan said, in the same tone. "I'm more fun than Mason jars anyway."

"And worth more, no doubt," Gracie said as she accompanied them to the door of the shop.

Evan turned and winked, and pulled Eleanor out into the sunny parking lot.

****

"I guess I'm now responsible for an insurrection," Evan said, as he backed the Jeep out of a spot along the river. "I don't understand how the old battleaxe has such power over all of you, anyway."

"She's old," Eleanor said.

"So's Lilianna. But I wouldn't put her in charge of keeping her place in a book, let alone of a hundred volunteers and thousands of dollars in donations." He pulled out of the parking lot The Thrifty Means shared with a half dozen other shops, and starting heading north, towards Garland.

"What do you have in mind?" Eleanor asked again. He glanced across at her, and noticed her hands twisting nervously in her lap.

"Just lunch, and maybe some other things. What did you mean by 'more important things'?"

"What, when?" She acted ill at ease, and he wondered if she had been in any relationships since her divorce. If not, it seemed such a waste; but then, he could imagine she was waiting just for him.

"Back in the shop? You said you had more

important things to do than price whatever the hell Maggie B. wanted to foist on you."

Ellie giggled, and her hands stopped their twisting to move to her knees. "She better not hear you say such a thing. And as for the important things, I was thinking of this beautiful day, and how I was getting very hungry. And you."

"That sounds good to me. Any sentence including me and "hungry" spoken by a beautiful woman is full of promise."

She laughed out loud. "Are we going to Garland?"

"No, actually," he said, as he turned onto Belvedere Road. "Are you disappointed?"

"That depends."

She couldn't know how important her reservations might prove. On Saturday night, they demonstrated there were very few inhibitions between them. But there was yet something there, something they had lived with for twenty years.

"I'd like to go up to the old reservoir. I picked up some sandwiches at the Market before I came to get you so we can have lunch there."

"You must have been pretty sure of yourself. Or of me," she murmured.

"I'm not," he said, admitting a lot. "But I figured I couldn't lose. If you weren't available, I'd have a terrific lunch."

"And now you won't," she sighed.

"I wouldn't say that," he said quickly, and reached out to take her hand. She caught his and gently replaced his palm on the steering wheel. He glanced at her and nodded, understanding her fears and accepting them as a part of her.

"I already spoke to Hammy about the grandfather clock," he said conversationally. "I didn't have to make a big deal, just explained it must have sold mistakenly because it was made by my grandfather and I wouldn't part with it. I offered to pay whatever he wanted, and he just sort of shrugged and said he didn't like the damned thing anyway. With such tact, it's no wonder he keeps losing his wives."

"I wouldn't complain if things work in your favor," Eleanor said.

"It's going to work in everyone's favor. He suggested I write out a check to the Historical Society. They get the money, I get my clock, and he gets a tax write-off. I'm going to pick it up tomorrow before he changes his mind."

"Did he remember where he bought it?"

"Oh, for sure. He bought the clock at The Thrifty Means a few years ago. He stapled the receipt to the back of the cabinet."

Ellie didn't say anything as he drove to the reservoir, on roads he hadn't traveled in many, many years in anything other than his nightmares. But people lived along these roads, and the school bus ambled down the lanes every morning. Houses were torn down and rebuilt. Gardeners waited for the first bursts of life in the springtime. No one ever thought about how, twenty years ago, two cars were on a fatal collision course, moving to a tragic meeting.

"There's nothing there," Eleanor said at last.

"I wouldn't think so," he answered, knowing what she meant. "After the flowers and the notes and the teddy bears were removed, and the rain had washed away the blood and the broken glass, the scene of an accident would not be the sort of place people would return to."

"I have," Eleanor said. "I go there every year in the fall, just before Halloween. But if I could avoid driving there, and if I can prevent Leslie and Lewis from ever, ever going to the reservoir, I would."

"There's nothing inherently dangerous about the

road, you know. It's no more curved or slick than any other road in this town. Things just happened, that's all. My father was arguing with my mother."

"And Missy took her eyes off the road. To look at me." Eleanor wiped her eyes with her hand. "If I weren't with her, the accident wouldn't have happened."

"If I wasn't with my parents in the car, they probably wouldn't have been fighting."

"You told me they fought all the time." Eleanor sniffed and she looked away from him, out the window.

"Yeah, well, that's true. I just wanted to make you feel better."

Apparently, it worked, but only for a moment. She laughed and hiccoughed, but then grew sober again. "So, you see, I'm to blame. Missy was a new driver. If I weren't with her, she wouldn't have died."

"You know you don't make sense. It's not as if you put your hands over her eyes or something." He realized he sounded callous, even cruel. But he was beginning to understand how she suffered from the accident all these years, in ways somewhat different than he did. "But I guess I see things in a different way. If you weren't with her, I would have died."

He drove along, remembering the chill in the air that night, the blood saturating his clothes, the pain of his injuries. Even then, he recognized the horrifying uncertainty of how his life had changed forever. Today he wanted to exorcise those demons, to see the scene with all the promise of the spring coming to life around them, and with the one person who mattered to him then and mattered to him now.

The Jeep shifted as the road ascended towards the reservoir and he imagined he was sixteen again, gazing out over the familiar fields and stone walls. Then, he would not have been entirely sure what to do with the girl sitting next to him in the car. Now he realized teenage fantasies could come true, he knew exactly what to do.

As if she guessed exactly what he was thinking, Eleanor turned in her seat and smiled. Her eyes were red rimmed and her cheeks were damp, and he was tempted to pull over to the side of the road and kiss her tears away.

"The road to the reservoir is just ahead, to the left. I'm not sure you'd recognize it anymore. The buildings are long gone," she said.

"I'm not sure you'd call them buildings, even in our time," he said. "Do you know, my grandfather was the caretaker on one of those estates. I think he was personally responsible for spreading those rumors about the drowned families and tolling bells, just to keep people off the land. He used to scare me to death."

"Oh, you weren't so scared. I remember hearing stories about girls meeting you at the reservoir. Cathy Reed told me..."

"Locker room talk, that's all," he said quickly, but then reconsidered. He pulled onto the rutted dirt road, and was glad he had a Jeep. "Okay, what did she say?"

He could see she was uncertain how to answer, and was touched by her delicacy. He barely remembered Cathy Reed, but somehow recalled some very helpful learning experiences in a sleeping bag at the edge of the woods. Was that with Cathy Reed? He wasn't sure.

"Nothing I don't already know," Eleanor said, and smiled. "Now."

All right, then the delicacy was just an illusion. This woman knew what she was talking about. At least she didn't hold his old indiscretions against him. But what of her? He tried to remember if she ever was anyone's steady; if, in fact, there was ever any locker room talk about her.

"Let's park here, and walk the rest of the way," she said, with an air of certainty.

"You've been here before," he said, knowing he sounded unreasonable and grumpy.

"Hey, I grew up in this town, too." She leaned over to kiss him on his ear, but was out of the car before he could park it and return the favor.

Together they walked towards the water, as sure of their steps as if they had walked here a hundred times before. The ground was spongy, and here and there in the shade, there were still patches of ice. Like receding glaciers, they left fertile land in their wake, and purple crocus poked through the wet soil. Evan wondered who had lived on this land, taken by the state of Connecticut so many years ago to build a reservoir. Who planted the crocus in what had once been a tended garden? What hopes had lived and died here? He glanced back to the road.

"What are you thinking?" Eleanor asked him.

"I'm thinking poetic things. Not my style at all. I'm thinking about the land and who might have lived here."

"And how would Evan Zane write such thoughts down in an *EZ Guide?*"

He understood just what she thought about his books, his little publishing empire. He doubted he could ever change her mind about their literary merit, so saw no reason to dispute anything now.

"A person was born, lived here, and died."

"That's it?" she asked, and frowned. "Are you getting back at me for what I said all those weeks ago?"

"Maybe. But there's my whole story."

"Well, I guess you are a master of the game," she said and changed the subject. "Here's a good spot. Do you prefer sun?"

He spread out a tarp on the damp soil, and then an old blanket he found in the spare bedroom, and reached for the bag of sandwiches.

"How would a historical novelist write about it?" he asked, unwrapping a turkey club. Between the lettuce and tomatoes was a layer of alfalfa sprouts, nearly translucent in the sunlight. Things really had changed in Eastfield, he realized. He remembered when a sandwich from the Market was typically bologna on white, with some mayo on the side.

Eleanor opened her sandwich, studying it as she might the Rosetta Stone. She rearranged the meat, and he wondered if he presumed too much by ordering a sandwich for her. Maybe she was on a diet and didn't eat bread. Maybe she was allergic to tomatoes. Maybe she already ate at the shop, and was too polite to refuse his offer.

"The two girls left the playing field, the cold October air prickling their slim legs. One, just a few months older than her friend, rummaged in her duffle bag for her car keys, listening for the sound of jingling metal. The taller girl envied her, for there was no grander rite of passage in the rural town of Eastfield than the passing of one's road test," Eleanor said, reciting as if from memory. She took a bite of her turkey lunch, sprouts and all, and Evan made a mental note she apparently preferred her sandwich open-faced. "That's what I would write. That's how I would begin."

Evan swallowed, but the food stuck in his throat. He loosened his collar, and realized Eleanor's eyes were on his hand. "It sounds like you already wrote it. It's a book that's already begun."

She looked away, back towards the road. A delivery truck lumbered along, so slowly a living room set could have been offloaded without the driver hitting the brakes. The man had every right to be careful. This was a road with a history, after all.

"No, I haven't already begun. But I've

considered the story for a very long time. I would write about Missy, about what her life would have been had she lived." Her voice caught, and he accepted how the pain of that night had never really gone away. "That's what we do, we novelists. We fill in all the missing pieces from what poor facts we have."

"Do you and Missy remain friends? Are you college roommates? Do you go into business together?"

"I wouldn't know," Eleanor said. "The book is about Missy. I'm not there."

Evan didn't think he would have gotten angry if he didn't know precisely what she meant.

"Do you mean, you were killed instead of her? Is that what you mean? Why you're out of the picture?" he asked roughly.

She turned back from the road and looked at him curiously. "Yes, very likely. Missy crawls out of the car and tries to extricate her friend from the wreck. Just as she realizes how hopeless it is, she hears a shout. It sounds like a boy or a man. For the first time, she realizes there was another car in the wreck, and someone else might have survived."

Evan returned her gaze, savoring the rich tastes of the sandwich, the warmth of the sun, and was grateful they survived to see this day.

"You shouldn't ever be guilty. I was, for many years, and it kept me away from Garland because I couldn't bear to accept everything my parents had lost was now mine. Later, when I finally came to grips with what happened, I believed I didn't really want those things anyway."

"Do you mean, like Lilianna and Dorothea?" she asked lightly, and he imagined he had pulled her out of a valley. "I'm not sure I would have wanted them either."

Evan smiled and plucked a tomato out of his

sandwich. "Well, sometimes we're just stuck with what we have." He popped the tomato into his mouth.

"And sometimes we just leave everything behind, thinking our luck is going to be better elsewhere, or with someone else."

"You didn't leave your husband, or your family."

"I already told you. He left me. Us. There were three of us, and he told me he couldn't bear the responsibility," she said. He listened to the tone of her voice, expecting to hear the deep breaths that still punctuated her memories of the night of the accident. But they didn't come. Instead, he heard determination and resolution, making clear how much she preferred to forget her life with that other man. It was selfish and probably wrong of him to ask for more, but this new appreciation gave him too much pleasure.

"Everything must have been very difficult for you," he said.

"Yes, of course. Sometimes I believed I couldn't bear the responsibility either. But what choice did I have?" She shrugged her shoulders and then fished around in the shopping bag for the water bottles he bought. "And I returned to Eastfield, admitting to everyone I had made a terrible mistake."

Evan's first thought was he was very glad she made that mistake for otherwise they might not have ever met again. The second was he was starting to think like a character in one of her novels.

"Evan, can I ask you something?" she said suddenly. Her cheeks were bright as she studied the label of the water bottle.

He guessed the time had come for a true confession, for some reckoning of his affairs and relationships of the past twenty years. He dated many wonderful women, and one for five years. But he never seemed settled with any one, and right now he could scarcely remember their names.

"Okay, fair enough," he said.

"If you could...if you did write a novel, what would you have to say about the history of the place?"

He did not expect the question, but it was somehow extraordinary their thoughts seemed to be riding on the same wind. He believed he had finally come home. He put the remains of his sandwich back into the wrapper, and took off his jacket. Bundling the thin fabric into a ball, he positioned it at the edge of the blanket, and lay back, one arm under his head. He closed his eyes.

"The first families who came to Eastfield settled along the Belvedere River, where the fields were fertile, and fish were plentiful. The River was apt to overflow its banks in the spring, and some old farmer nicknamed the area "Little Egypt," which was a bit grandiose for a few acres of farmland in the rugged climate of New England."

"I'd forgotten that," Eleanor murmured.

"No interruptions. The master is creating. Well...the River took its responsibilities very seriously, and in 1955 decided to overrun the land. Homes were washed away and people drowned. People who claimed to know how the River could be tamed decided to dam it in spots, and create a series of reservoirs, like beads on a string. The town bought up the farmers' lands and flooded acres and acres for the public good."

Evan heard a rustling of the tarp under the blanket and opened his eyes. Eleanor was on her hands and knees crawling towards him, dropping down beside him so her head nestled on his shoulder.

"I'm not interrupting," she interrupted.

He shifted his body so his arm went around her

and he pulled her closer.

"Some people said the ghosts of the farmers who refused to leave their land and were drowned haunted the place. But the kids at Eastfield High School knew better. They were a fearless bunch, and used to hang out at the reservoir, among the ruins of old barns and farmhouses. One day, a guy, just a typical jock, dared to meet a girl there. She was beautiful, the girl everyone admired. Her hair was long and curly, and she wore it in a pony tail that swung back and forth as she walked down the hall, or played field hockey."

Eleanor put her finger on his lips. "Now, you've gone from history to fiction. I don't think the girl ever met the boy at the reservoir until this very day. But the story is good. It's very good. Are you sure you haven't been reading historical fiction all this time?"

Evan pulled her closer and settled his cheek against her hair. A curl tickled his nose and he sneezed. "I'm sure. I can't."

She laughed. "It's not likely to corrupt you or anything. Why can't you?"

He sighed deeply, wondering how he had gone from a casual invitation to a picnic to this. But if anyone ought to know, that person should be Ellie Gilmartin.

"Didn't you ever guess, all those years ago? You, who was stuck sitting next to me, and had to do class projects with me?"

"Guess what?" Her muffled voice stirred the short hairs against his neck.

"I can hardly read at all. If I lived here in Little Egypt back in the old days, I probably would have been the village idiot."

Chapter 9

"Never question a person's motives for getting rid of the stuff stored in his attic."
Emma Grace Liddell, Customer
and Quilt Collector

"You're being ridiculous," Eleanor said, pulling herself off him.

"Hey, I don't have leprosy. Come back here," he said, reaching out for her. But she ducked under his arm and sat up on the blanket.

"What are you saying?" She asked, plucking dried grass off her jeans. "What do you mean, you can't read?"

The teasing look was gone, replaced by something more troubling, and darker.

"Well, I'm not illiterate. And it's not something I bragged about in high school. But I've always had trouble reading; it was a problem from the day our third grade teacher dropped Huckleberry Finn down on our desks. I just couldn't read, not then and not now."

"Huckleberry Finn is not for third graders anyway. Mrs. Brand was delusional when she assigned the book. But what of high school, and college? And what now? You write books, for goodness sakes!"

"I'm flattered. You've already told me what you think about the *EZ Guides,* and now you're calling them books. There's an improvement."

Eleanor was furious with him, for the cavalier way in which he described a debilitating handicap.

201

She reached down and tried to shake him by the shoulders; but he was rock solid and she could barely budge him.

"I bet you didn't even write them!" she lashed out at him. "What did you do, franchise out your initials?"

The insult was very well delivered, and very poorly received. He opened his eyes and sat up on his elbows. His hair was tousled and he ran a hand over his brow, blocking the sun.

"I wrote every single word. And I write them for kids like myself, who struggle through school doing what everyone else takes for granted, and nobody knows how to fix."

"There are special education teachers in every school. I'm pretty sure there were then, also," Eleanor said, though she wasn't at all certain. She didn't recall anyone needing special help, or admitting to it. "How could we not have known?"

Evan sat up straighter, retrieving his abandoned sandwich, shredding the bread into pieces, and throwing it out for the animals who roamed the field. He picked up the sandwich wrappers and empty water bottles, and stuffed them into a plastic bag. Then, in one fluid motion, he was on his knees and pushing himself up to a standing position. He frowned.

"I'm sorry I said anything," he said. "I see I made a mistake."

She looked up at him, and realized the only mistake was hers. He brought her here to confront the sadness of their shared history, and was prepared to be honest. He shared a secret he probably never revealed to anyone else, and she did nothing but act like a shrew, demanding proof, over and over again.

"You couldn't read the menu at L'Avignon," she said, thinking aloud. She reached out her hand to him, and he pulled her up.

"I didn't have the patience to decipher it. Figuring things out is sometimes harder in the evening, when I'm tired." He let her hand go, and they stood apart from each other, separated by the blanket on which they shared lunch only minutes before. "I can read, and do read, but there's nothing easy about it."

"I don't understand. You sat next to me in history class. You did okay."

He shrugged. "I cheated off you."

Eleanor wasn't sure if his easy admission made her feel better or worse. "You couldn't cheat on everything. There were essays, analyses. This doesn't make sense."

"That's the point. It took me so long to read the material that by the time I finished, nothing made sense. I did have some extra help, and to make things a little easier."

"But you were on sports teams, and in shows. You were always out with friends," Eleanor protested, still disbelieving. Then she recalled Dorothea's earnest little records of various fees paid to professionals and realized they did not all pertain to the accident. "When did you have the time?"

"You mean, because I was always out with friends? I must have had some reputation." He grinned. "But I found the time. In some things I work very quickly."

Eleanor stepped back, realizing she was making far too much of this. The man managed just fine, for goodness sakes. He was rich, successful. He was a recognized author, and probably saved the skin of thousands of kids who had problems like his. She ought to be admiring, wondering at his great skills to compensate for what he lacked. But she was not yet ready to give back to him.

"Quickly?" she asked huskily. "It's taken you

more than twenty years to get me up here to the reservoir."

He hesitated, and she cringed, thinking the femme fatale bit perhaps too ridiculous for a woman her age.

"I wasn't sure you'd go with me," he admitted.

"All you had to do was ask," she said, and walked over the blanket and back into his arms.

****

Some time later, Eleanor opened her eyes and wondered where she was. She heard a bird chirping, but not in the high, squeaky parakeet voice of True Blue. A dog barked, but not Sally. She was laying on something hard and rough and her hair had fallen over her eyes. She shook her head and realized she was looking at Evan Zane's chin and a pinkish smudge of her own lipstick.

The afternoon sun made long shadows across the field, and the heavy, slow rumble of a school bus echoed off the water of the reservoir.

"Evan, wake up," she said, nudging his shoulder.

He gave a little snore, and rolled over to his side.

"Really, Evan, wake up. The last thing I need is for my kids to show up here and find their mother making out on a blanket with a strange man."

That got him, as she hoped it would.

"I'm not strange," he muttered. "They've seen me hanging around you for weeks."

"Oh, I think you're strange enough. This whole reading thing has me troubled and confused."

"Well, imagine what I've been dealing with all these years." He rubbed his eyes and sat up, looking around as if he had no idea where they were or how they got there. Eleanor, now remembering moments of sudden intimacy shared with her husband, leaned over and started buttoning his shirt.

"Hey. My fine motor skills are just fine. Only

reading is a problem," he said, and put his hands over hers.

"That's okay. I didn't want you to catch a cold," she said. She stole her hands away, and started to busy herself with the leftovers of their lunch, and the various items of clothing they managed to shed.

"You, know, I don't think anyone's worried about my health for many, many years." Evan stood up, grimacing when he put pressure on his left leg. He moved in a little circle, as if testing his balance, and then bent slightly. "I'm not the man I used to be," he said apologetically.

"No. You're better, I hope." Eleanor pulled the blanket away from the tarp, and realized her clothes and hair probably picked up the slightly musty odor. Well, anyone would think she had just stepped out of The Thrifty Means. "But what has no one said to you?"

He paused, thinking through their conversation. "What? What did I say? I'm not what I used to be? Well, it's true. I used to be able to juggle twelve conversations at once, which is why so many people assumed I was a native New Yorker."

"Eastfield is only sixty miles away, Evan. You reminded me yourself. You could pick up a New York accent by listening to drivers yelling at each other while they're speeding down the Merritt."

He nodded, and offered a sampling of the colorful language of the urban native. Then, having made his point: "But I only meant no one has worried about my health in years."

"You look pretty healthy to me," Eleanor said but frowned as he continued to rub his left knee. Her own leg was often painful, and she knew a lot about potential problems.

"I could be better, but it's not my health. I mean no one has cared. Certainly Dorothea wouldn't have noticed if I walked out into a snowstorm wearing shorts and flip flops."

"As I recall, you did in our senior year," Eleanor noted wryly.

"You see? You noticed." He started to fold the tarp in a neat pattern, and then gave up and stuffed the whole thing into his duffle bag. "And you cared."

Eleanor had a feeling things were moving along far too quickly. "Oh, it's just a mother's instincts. While you were dodging outbursts of road rage, and picking up four or five girls at a time in the Big Apple, I was juggling a baby in each arm, and picking up rattles and empty bottles."

He nodded and reached for her hand. "Let's walk up to the road."

"But you left the Jeep along the drive."

"I know. Let's drop off these things near the car and take the path from there. I want to see the road."

Eleanor understood why he had to return there; she had done it herself often enough. Nevertheless, she sensed there was something else bothering him and the revelation about his reading was only a prelude to the real thing.

"What were your parents arguing about, before the accident?" she asked.

He stopped and looked at her, making her feel he was struggling to read her.

"My reading," he said, and she gasped. "Well, not directly. My father couldn't understand why I wasn't doing well in school, and complained about my laziness. My mother wanted me to go to private tutoring, which probably would have been a good idea, but neither of them had the time to drive me there. My father was too busy at work. My mother said she was too busy at hers. That is what really got them going. My father didn't consider writing a real job."

"Is it the reason you became a writer?"

"Smart girl. Yeah, I suppose it is. I guess I started to do what I do to prove my father wrong, and my mother right. Oh, and partly because of my master's thesis on cognition."

Eleanor shook her head. She had so much to learn about this guy. "My, my. You really are full of surprises."

Evan didn't answer. They reached the road, and he looked up and down the street. He climbed the few steps over a makeshift stile, and moved to the side facing traffic. That was the rule kids in Eastfield learned from the time they were little and would have made perfect sense if there were anything ever resembling traffic in the town. One car passed them, swerving far to the left. A large crow targeted something in the middle of the road, something Eleanor chose not to examine too closely.

"Evan, why did you tell me about your reading problems? Was it to make me go easier on your *EZ Guides*?"

He turned and smiled. "No. It does matter to me what you think, and I know you hate them, but my books are really successful. I'm sorry, but the fact you don't let Leslie and Lewis use them probably hasn't made a significant dent in my royalty statements."

"Show-off," Eleanor murmured.

"No, but I really do need your help."

"But I already said I would help. And I have helped. I'm working on the inventory. And I've asked around to see if anyone had a grudge against Dorothea. Isn't that what you wanted? Most people don't even remember her, and some assumed she died years ago. I'm sorry, but it's true."

"Don't be sorry. Dorothea chose the life she led. She could have continued acting, or returned with Lilianna to the social life in the city. But she liked the privacy, the ability to shut herself away from the world. If she could have managed to be entirely self-sufficient, and not have to buy food in a market or clothing in a store, I'm sure she would never have left Garland at all."

"There's something I envy, though I imagine such a degree of solitude could turn to loneliness very quickly. I sometimes wonder what my life will be like when my children are off at college. Perhaps I'll never leave Milkweed Lane, except to see what's new at The Thrifty Means, or buy a quart of milk once a week."

"Perhaps," Evan said, "you won't be alone."

"Perhaps," Eleanor said, trying to imagine Evan meant something other than the obvious. Then, quickly, "But if Dorothea had practically nothing to do with anyone else, why would someone wish her harm? If you keep to yourself, you don't make friends. But you don't make enemies either."

"The motive may not have been personal."

"If someone wanted her dead, wouldn't it have to be personal?"

"I don't know. The historian in me tells me she just may have been in someone's way. He might have had no particular gripe against her, just what she represented."

Eleanor rubbed her forehead, trying to sooth her growing headache. "Do you mean, her death might have been a hate crime? Someone wanted her out of the way because of her sexual preferences? Do you think everyone guessed?"

He nodded, and quickened his pace. "About Dorothea and Lilianna? Of course."

"Then that's personal, Evan. No one would gain anything by exacting such punishment. And why not go after Lilianna also? Dorothea, at least, was always mildly likeable. Lilianna is a bitch."

"'Mildly likeable?' Talk about being damned by faint praise. But maybe the words are the best we can muster up for her gravestone."

"She was your aunt. You're a popular writer. You should come up with something," Eleanor said, already regretting her saying such things out loud.

"No, really. That's about as good as it gets. She wouldn't even welcome me into my own home."

"Then I suppose of all people, you had the most to gain by seeing her dead. At least you would be able to get Garland back. And sell the property, if you choose."

"I don't so choose."

Eleanor paused, not caring to examine the prospect at the moment, either. "Because you want to solve a mystery which may not be a mystery at all? After all, didn't she just die in her sleep?"

"I think she was a little young, especially since nothing was really wrong with her. And there are just too many things wrong about all this."

"Like the cats."

"Like the cats. And the clock at the Hamilton estate. And I've been looking for her old chess set, one belonging to my uncle. She let me play a few times, and insisted I wear gloves, so I wouldn't ruin the ivory. The last time I saw it was about three years ago, on the coffee table in the den. But I think the set is gone."

From some mysterious and dark corner of her memory, Eleanor glimpsed old chess pieces, though she could not explain why or how.

"Did it look like the Lewis set, from England? Like the one in the British Museum?" she asked.

Evan nodded. "Yeah, I think so. You must have seen it when you came over to my house years ago."

Eleanor didn't point out she had only been there once since his third birthday party, because the distinctive kings and queens must have made an impression on her. How else would she have envisioned those chunky ivory pieces with their frowning faces lined up on a pine coffee table?

"So what do you want me to do, Mr. Holmes? Be your Dr. Watson? Should I follow you around from party to party, checking out the antiques? Or finding out whose cat had a litter of kittens last year?"

"I was thinking you might be my secretary," he said. They came across a downed tree on the path and, rather than walk around into the high grass, or climb over, Evan started to pull the branches out of their way. This was how he tackled all his problems, Eleanor reflected. Don't avoid them, or ignore them. Just pluck away at them until they were gone. She watched him, not offering to help. Not sure she wanted to, after what he just said.

"Your secretary?" she asked in a low voice when nothing remained in the path but a few whitened twigs. "You must realize I have not worked all these years to be someone's secretary."

"Oh," he said, in his ridiculously disarming way. "You misunderstand me. I don't need someone to type or answer my phone calls."

"Good, because that's not something I would do for you or anyone else."

"I hoped you might read to me. I think I could listen to your voice for hours."

Faint praise, indeed. Easily tossed out, like those branches on the path. Why then, did it seem to have her whole body humming?

"Aside from reading at an occasional book signing, I haven't read aloud since Lewis and Leslie were old enough to read their books themselves. By then, I had practically memorized every book we had, so I'm not sure it counted as reading. What did you have in mind? *The Cat in the Hat* or something?

They were nearly at the road, and the soft grassy earth was now speckled with bits of asphalt and gravel. A buried hubcap poked through the mud and a Styrofoam cup was crushed into the ground, where the fast food restaurant whose name it bore would be advertised for all eternity.

"Oh, I think I could blunder through Dr. Seuss by myself. I was thinking of all the notebooks Dorothea left around, all the journals she had stacked in her room. I might find something helpful there. But if I started to read through them all, I might not live to finish them."

Eleanor groaned. "I have a life, you know. I have kids, my books, and my volunteer work at The Thrifty Means. I have my garden to clean up for spring. Why me? You could get anyone to read to you."

"Yeah. But not necessarily someone I trust."

A school bus approached and they sidestepped into a driveway, allowing a wide berth. The young children at the windows screamed, waved, and jumped around in their seats as much as their seatbelts would allow. Someone threw a sneaker out an open window and it landed near them, in the drainage ditch.

"We were right here, I think," Evan said. "I remember looking at the moon through the tree."

Eleanor looked at the gnarled trunk of the maple, dark against the grasses sprouting around. Soon after the accident, neighbors and friends made a makeshift shrine, delivering flowers and trinkets, memorializing the lives of three people who never expected their stories to end in the twilight along a road as familiar to them as their own driveways. She glanced up at Evan, wondering what he was thinking. A chapter of his story ended that night also, but after the first month or so, everyone expected him to get on with his story.

Remembering the last two years of school, when he had been a star athlete and one of the most popular guys at Eastfield High, she believed he had indeed gotten on with his story. Now, she was not at all sure.

"If you hadn't been there..." he began.

"I know, Evan," Eleanor said quietly. "But we were just lucky I was able to get to you first. The police came so quickly, you would have been just fine without me."

"No, not that. I mean, I'm not sure I would have made it, after all. But I think if I had been able to get out of the crash, I would have just walked away, as if nothing had happened."

Eleanor rushed to anger. "How could you say such a thing? Your parents were in the burning car, and Missy and I..." She choked, not sure she could go on. "You couldn't walk away. It would have been impossible."

He pulled her over to a stone wall, directly opposite the tree. They leaned against the irregular cold rocks, uncomfortable and uncompromising. "Yes, impossible in any real sense. I was dazed and I had spent my whole life walking away from my parents whenever they fought. I would just find a safe place to go, a quiet one, and try to shut everything out. I think if you hadn't found me, I might have done the same thing after the crash."

"But I did find you, and we did find a safe place." She remembered lying against him, bleeding and cold, believing she was going to die and her last moments on earth would be with Evan Zane. Her world had just blown apart, but somehow, absurdly, there was comfort in his presence. Her dazed, teenaged mind even thought it romantic.

"Yeah," he said distractedly, and she realized he was back there with her, huddled together, but thinking very different things. "Yeah, I should have appreciated things then. But nothing was really safe to me and I understood I was going to have to start my life over."

Eleanor didn't know how to answer. She, bloody

and sobbing to her parents and brother that night, recognized her life would be different, but she would recover over time. Who had come to the hospital for Evan Zane? How well did he know his aunt, who now was responsible for him?

"You understood so much, in the ditch?" she asked, genuinely curious.

"I did; looking up at the tree and sky, smelling the gasoline and smoke, tasting blood. My knee hurt like hell." He raised his face to the sky and looked like he was facing an army of his enemies. His breathing sounded labored and a twitching muscle in the corner of his eye distracted her. "It still does."

"Please, let's go away from here," she said abruptly. What was a sad and nightmarish scene for her was morbid for him, sucking him into a deeper, darker, scarcely recognizable place. "This isn't healthy for either of us. Let's get out of here."

She pulled away from the stone wall, feeling a rush of warm air at her back. Evan reached for her, but she jumped the ditch and found sure footing on the road. She paused as another school bus passed, and then realized, just a moment too late, another vehicle was bearing down on her, skirting the very edge of the road.

The driver blared the horn, though there were no opposing cars to prevent him from moving over the yellow line in the road's center. A spray of gravel splattered against the stone wall as the small truck veered slightly off the road. Eleanor jumped back, hitting something hard and warm. Evan put his arms around her waist and used some of his colorful curses as the truck roared down the road after the school bus.

"That was Wayne, wasn't it?" she said, without moving. Another car passed, slowly and carefully, but Eleanor didn't care who observed them embracing on the road. "You told me he was gone."

"Gone from Garland, but still in town. Eastfield is very forgiving of its jackasses. I should know." Evan released her, but must have realized she was still shaking, and put his arm around her again.

"I'm not sure they would have been so forgiving if he killed us in a drunken driving accident," she said bitterly. She considered the children who rode their bikes along the road, the dogs and cats who roamed out of their yards, chasing squirrels and field mice. "And an accident here, in this place? *The Eastfield Edition* would have been all over the ironies of the story!"

"I'm not sure he was drunk," Evan said tightly.

Eleanor pulled away from him, and dusted herself off, willing herself to stop shaking. "I understood he was always drunk."

"No, he's always a jackass. And usually drunk. There's a difference."

They crossed the road cautiously, as if another crazy driver might materialize along this stretch of pavement. Evan helped her over the stile, pulling her up and then catching her on the bottom step, and they started towards the car.

"It was Wayne," Eleanor said slowly.

Not surprisingly, Evan looked at her curiously, as if she might be concussed. "Yeah, sweetheart, we already established his identity. Everything points to his truck, his style, his face, looking like he understood just what he was doing."

She looked up at him, realizing he was concerned for her. He was shaken nearly as badly as she. She had a better idea of what he meant when he spoke of starting his life anew all those years ago. She was by no means alone, having her children, her parents, her siblings, and her very good friends. In his expression, she recognized someone who was concerned about her in a very different way, as if she were precious and fragile. She never saw that in her

husband and didn't know such a thing existed—
except in fairy tales - until a moment ago

"I know it was Wayne; he came about as close to
me as you are now," she said slowly. "I meant it
surely was Wayne who wanted Dorothea dead."

When he didn't say anything, Eleanor wondered
if she had astonished him with her sudden insight.
Why would he be astonished? He had already given
her all the clues. Dorothea was a very private
person, living in relative obscurity with her longtime
companion and her companion's relative. When she
came into town, she did what she had to, and left.
She didn't show up at community events. She didn't
accept invitations. She didn't appear in a booth at
Ludlum's, where everyone knew everyone else's
name. Her world was Garland, and whatever
happened there could stay there. If Wayne was
sober, and clean, and had the vaguest semblance of
manners, he could have been Dorothea's butler.
Eleanor wasn't a big fan of detective fiction, but she
believed the butler always did it.

She didn't say anything more of her theory, nor
did he respond. They walked across the soft earth of
the field, absorbed in their separate reveries. The
Jeep was as they left it, but with a thin coating of
white pollen blown from the trees. Evan opened the
door for her, disturbing the sugary surface, and
promptly sneezed.

"Not very gallant, I guess," he said, wiping his
nose on a sharply pressed handkerchief.

"Not very practical either," she said, "for a man
who's thinking of staying around in Eastfield. If the
pollen of late spring bothers you, the summer will
probably kill you."

"Unless Wayne can't wait so long."

"Evan!" Eleanor cried, just at the moment he
slammed the door closed. She waited an eternity
until he came around to the driver's side of the Jeep,

threw the tarp and duffle into the back seat, and ducked in beside her. "So you do think it's Wayne? I'm right, aren't I? Why didn't I think of him before? When did you figure everything out?"

He sighed deeply, though she wasn't sure if his response had to do with her question, or the fact the Jeep didn't turn over on the first try. Then the engine caught, and idled for a few moments before he spoke.

"I didn't. I mean, I don't. I guess he's more likely a suspect as anyone else, but it's hard to imagine him plotting through anything. He barely has enough concentration to tie his shoelaces. And what would he gain, that he didn't already have? You can argue his life has gotten harder since I arrived and threw him off the property."

Eleanor opened her mouth and nearly bit her tongue as the Jeep went into a rut and bumped its way out. Evan moved a little more cautiously over the driveway until he reached the road. Though they would have heard a car approaching from fifty yards away, he paused, looking up and down the road. Perhaps, like Eleanor, he didn't quite trust Wayne wouldn't come barreling down upon them again.

He made a left turn, back towards the Center and The Thrifty Means.

"But he's not as likely as anyone else. He lived at Garland, close to her. He could have had a million reasons to wish her dead, or any number of desires to get something she owned. Like the Lewis chess set, for one thing."

Evan reached across her, into the glove box, and pulled out a small case. Without taking his eyes from the road, he opened it, unfolded a pair of sunglasses, and put them on. Eleanor frowned when she realized the bridge was not quite on his nose, and he looked slightly tipsy with his glasses askew. She reached up, and balanced them neatly on his tanned cheekbones.

"I'm not sure you need a secretary," she murmured.

"What do I need, then?" he asked.

A wife, but she didn't say the thought out loud. Her generation had rebelled at the old stereotypes, scorning the rituals of tradition. Yet how many times had she wished she had a husband with her to share both the pleasures and burdens of raising children? Why had her heart lurched when Evan suggested she might not find herself all alone when the kids went off to college?

"Hmmm?" he asked, smiling.

It was always Evan. When he scarcely spoke to her in elementary school, she dreamed about Evan. When he was—apparently—cheating off her tests, she imagined herself with him. On the night she believed she would die, she wondered if their families would bury them in the same grave in Belvedere Cemetery. Now here they were, traveling the same old road, and he waited to hear her answer to what he needed and all she wanted to say was "me!"

"You need Dr. Watson, Mr. Holmes. You need someone to ask all the right questions, so you could prove your prowess at solving your great mystery," Eleanor said, sensibly.

"Isn't that what you're already doing?"

"I'm asking questions. But I'm not sure there's a great mystery." Eleanor said. "And none of this is really my business, anyway."

Evan slowed the car as they came up behind a tractor. There were just a few real working farms left in Eastfield, and the townspeople treated the aging farmers as if they were royalty. Even an ambulance, rushing away from an accident, sirens blaring, would wait patiently until a tractor got off the road. Evan strummed his fingers on the leather steering wheel, and kept at a safe distance so the enormous tires in front of him wouldn't kick up muck on the hood of the Jeep.

"I've made my business your business, haven't I?" he asked, still looking ahead. "I pulled you in from the moment I walked into The Thrifty Means, looking for you. When you came to Garland after the fire, and went through the house. When we..."

Eleanor knew what he was about to say, and wasn't sure she wanted to listen. What they shared was in the pleasure of the moment, and had no strings attached.

"What do you mean you were looking for me at The Thrifty Means? You acted as if you didn't even remember me. You waited for an introduction."

He gave a grunt of satisfaction, though she wasn't sure if it was because the tractor finally turned off the road, or because he had managed to trick her.

"You may not want to give me credit for anything, but you have to admit I've always been a good actor. Of course I guessed you were there, and recognized your voice right away. You haven't changed very much, Ellie."

"I'm pretty sure that's not a compliment," she said. "And I was pretty rude to you then, wasn't I?"

"Yeah, like I said. You haven't changed very much."

"You really are a masochist. You could have had any of those women fawning over you, perfectly willing to be your secretary. Or anything else, for that matter."

"But I didn't want them. I want you."

"Oh."

The afternoon sun gilded the palette of the landscape, making even the dry, dead grass sparkle. They drove past a seasonal lake, and several pairs of Canada geese who adopted the wetlands as their breeding grounds. Soon there would be goslings, making a terrible mess of the place, but too cute not to be forgiven. They were like her own children, though Leslie and Lewis' cute phase was nearly over.

"What are you thinking about?" Evan asked.

My two children, driving on this deadly road.

"About children," Eleanor said honestly, and then realized how he might misunderstand her. No, she was not quite right. He would not misunderstand her at all. She was young, younger than some women were when they had their first babies. She could have more, especially if she made a better choice for the baby's father. This had nothing to do with Evan Zane. "Actually, I was thinking about the baby geese, and what a mess they'll make."

"They're all over my property right now. The cats do a good job of chasing them around."

"But a dog, like Sally, will keep them away. If you let them take over Garland, you won't be able to walk into the house with your shoes on."

He laughed. "That bad, huh? I don't remember this problem twenty years ago."

"You've been living in the big city. Years ago, decoy geese joined the native bird population in the Northeast, to keep other species away. But the decoys decided they liked to live here—and stayed and stayed. The problem is now worse."

"So maybe I need Sally as much as I need you?"

Now Eleanor laughed, grateful the moment of tension was past. "Why, that's the most charming thing a man has said to me in years."

"And I have a reputation as a charmer, I guess."

"So you do. And I'm just helpless to resist you. I have no choice, then. I'll bring Sally up to Garland to terrify the geese, and I'll read to you from your aunt's journals. And together we'll consider her cryptic shopping lists, or mysterious receipts for oil changes for the car, or coded appointments to play bridge or go to the doctor. The experience should be just fascinating."

Evan came to a stop at the bottom of the long hill, and waited to make his turn into traffic. This was the busiest time in Eastfield, when school let out and many mothers decided to pick up their kids to speed them to tennis or karate or ballet lessons. Huge backups began behind stopped school buses, and drivers became irritable. Evan, however, remained calm at the wheel, as accepting of this inconvenience as he was of the much more engaging tractor moments before. She admired his patience.

"I'll drop you off at The Thrifty Means," he said.

"I think you have to, since my car is there. I'll stop in to see if anything new came in, or if anyone needs help."

"You do that a lot?"

"Most of the volunteers come in pretty regularly. Part of the reason is purely personal—women like Lucy Armitage are always on the lookout for treasures to resell in their own shops. Some just like to collect things. I enjoy the social life. After all, I spend hours and hours on the computer, writing about things that happened centuries ago, and know I can escape everything at The Thrifty Means."

"Dealing with junk that's been gathering dust for centuries?"

"If I'm lucky," she said, and gathered up her pocketbook as they neared the Center. "But mostly, it's just to see everyone, and share gossip, and have a good time. And we do our work in the name of philanthropy...we donate lots of money to the community."

"And Margaret Brownlee?"

"She signs the checks."

"I mean, does she have a good time also?"

Eleanor sighed, knowing things had changed there, and wasn't sure why. "In her fashion."

"I have the impression she's a little like Sally, scattering the geese as they settle, and making sure no one lays an egg."

"What a charming metaphor. Maybe you should save your lyricism for the *EZ Guide to Poetry.*" Eleanor preferred to give him the impression she was fuming, but actually considered his comparison rather apt. Threatened by her team of volunteers, Mrs. B. made life uncomfortable for them while they were in the shop. Miriam was right; the time was right for Mrs. B. to step down. As Evan turned into the parking lot of The Thrifty Means, Eleanor noticed her car lined up along with others she recognized as belonging to her friends.

"Is that...is that Wayne's truck?" she asked, startled to see the vehicle here so soon after her near miss on the road. He was in a hurry then, but she couldn't imagine he was in a rush to get to The Thrifty Means, of all places. He didn't seem the type to appreciate fine porcelain or gently tarnished pewter. But perhaps he was still in a hurry when he arrived.

"He's lucky he didn't drive the truck up the tree. It looks like he hit the trunk when he pulled in."

The front of the truck was slightly elevated, as the weight balanced precariously on a birch tree. The white bark looked mutilated and a few branches brushed across the windshield. As Evan drove past the truck, Eleanor also noticed large black garbage bags in the back seat. They could be filled with garbage. Or antiques. Or anything at all.

"Evan, I had a lovely afternoon; somewhere between an adventure and a vacation. I..." she stopped when he pulled into the next available space and turned off the ignition.

"I'm coming in with you."

"Evan, don't. It's not necessary."

"Are you afraid your friends will see you with me, and start rumors?" He pulled off his sunglasses and tossed them on the dashboard.

"No, I don't care what they think," she said, realizing she did. Her friends probably already started those rumors. "I just don't want you to get in a fight if Wayne is in there."

"A fight?" he said, as he opened the Jeep door. "No, I don't think I'm up to a fight today. Not now. Garland seems to bring out all my immature passions. But The Thrifty Means makes me think I'm in my grandmother's living room."

"Thank you very much," Eleanor said indignantly.

"You're welcome. But maybe Wayne gets all territorial and angry when he's repressed. Don't worry about us; if we manage to smash all your china and break the glasses, I promise I'll pay for the whole thing."

"So you are looking for a fight!" Eleanor accused him, as she climbed down from the high seat.

He closed the door behind her. "No, I'm just a customer looking for fine porcelain or gently tarnished pewter. I hope your friends didn't sell the whole lot while you were gone."

Chapter 10

"A man who enters the shop wearing a torn sweatshirt and walks out the door in a cashmere coat merits some attention."
Nancy McBride, volunteer since 2001
and security expert

"What the hell are you doing here?" Wayne Durant nearly knocked over a shelf of music boxes as he turned towards Evan.

Evan shrugged, noticing Wayne's high color and unbuttoned shirt. He might have been drunk, as they suspected earlier, but right now, he looked fiercely sober and very, very angry. Evan, even without Ellie's warning, had no desire to provoke him but it was almost impossible to resist the impulse to do so.

"It's a free country." The words were the first stupid thing coming to mind, kindergarten talk, really. But that was a language Wayne could understand.

"What the hell does that mean?" Wayne was consistent; you had to give him some credit.

"It means I can come and go as I please. I'm here to buy some old records. Aunt Dorothea had a Victor Talking Machine somewhere I'd like to check out. You don't happen to know where she stored the thing, do you?"

"Why..." Wayne began, and then stopped.

"Why the hell should you know?" Evan asked. "How did I know you were going to say that?"

"No," Wayne smirked. "Why the hell should I

223

care?"

"Hmmm. I take your point. I guess I could say you were the caretaker at Garland for years, and Dorothea paid you for your trouble, what little there was. But if you were the caretaker, you should know where things are. If things are missing or broken, then that should have been your responsibility, right? I'd hate to send you a bill for the things I can't find."

Wayne looked like he was passing a kidney stone. Evan had no sympathy for him if he was.

"How do you know I did anything wrong?"

"Who else do I have to blame?" Evan joked, but even as he said the words, he realized he wasn't funny. He only had himself to blame, for running away, for avoiding confrontation with Dorothea, for returning to Garland only when strictly necessary.

"Ask your girlfriend. I bet she knows something."

Evan frowned, not only wondering how Wayne made the association, but also if Eleanor might know more about the situation than she let on.

"My girlfriend?" he asked. He wasn't sure he used those words since he was in college, and now they didn't seem appropriate to describe his relationship to Eleanor Gilmartin. He didn't know what might be appropriate, however.

"Yeah, Miss Doll-eyes over there. Has she let you find out if she's a natural red head?"

That did it. Evan's face grew warm and tightened his hands into fists. Wayne managed to get under his skin like a tick, and irritate him with an infection as debilitating as Lyme disease. He couldn't explain things, except perhaps to say Wayne was such a moron it was impossible to argue rationally with him.

"Wayne, I'll have to give you a check. Do you want me to write it out to..." Margaret Brownlee came through the door, not looking up until she walked right into Evan. She stopped and blinked up at him, looking as surprised as if he had shown up in her bedroom closet.

Wayne reached across Evan and grabbed a slip of green paper out of Margaret's hand.

"Whatever," he said quickly.

"Why, how nice to see you again, Mr. Zane," Margaret said, ignoring the other man, in favor of insipid conversation. "I never asked you how you enjoyed the fundraiser at the Hamilton estate. They live in a wonderful house, don't they?"

"I suppose so, but I enjoyed the company even more," Evan said, glancing at Wayne. It didn't hurt to let the guy know there were places to take one's girlfriend other than the reservoir

"Of course! How could you not? Everyone of importance in Eastfield was there!" She looked at Wayne, as if she'd forgotten he was there. "Is there anything else I could do for you, Mr. Durant?"

Evan laughed. Margaret Brownlee might be a stuck-up, pretentious snob, but calling her relative by his last name was a bit much. Especially as he had been Wayne only a few minutes before.

"No, not you," Wayne said as he glared at Evan.

Evan recognized his cue, practically rejoicing. "Is there anything else I could do for you, Mr. Durant?" he echoed.

"Yeah. Let me have your girlfriend for the night. Maybe I'll tell her where your goddamned record player is. Did she tell you I talk in my sleep?"

Evan looked past Wayne, to the front of the store where Ellie examined a large bowl. Hearing something, she glanced up and met his eyes. He caught a glimpse of the girl with the long ponytail and freckles, the one he fell for twenty years ago and never had the guts to approach.

"No, but she told me you can't get it…"

"Gentlemen!" Margaret Brownlee made a great show of cupping her ears, though she took care not to crush her permed curls. "Please take your argument outside!"

"I still have business here," Wayne said, glowering at Margaret.

"So do I," Evan said, and walked towards Ellie and the light of the front windows. She studied him as he approached, and the bowl caught the sun and reflected on her chin. She looked like a renaissance angel.

"This bowl was made in Germany," she said, as if nothing had happened of any interest but a delivery of ornately painted china. "I think it would be worth thousands if in perfect condition."

"What's wrong with it?" Evan was now weary, worn out by too many questions and no answers.

"See the crazing, here?" Ellie dipped the bowl towards him, and showed him something looking like fine webbing. "If you put water in the bowl, it'll probably stain. The glaze is damaged."

"What if I just break it over Wayne's head instead? How much would the thing be worth then?"

She put the bowl down, very carefully.

"You know, for a bookish kind of guy, you have a very violent streak," she said. "I'm not very happy about that."

"Well, you know, we bookish guys just write about stuff, but we never really do anything."

"I think I have evidence to the contrary." She looked at him as if there was nothing or no one else in the shop.

He shifted position, now uncomfortable. "Do you think I'm violent? I would never, ever..."

"No, I mean you can really do something, when you set your mind to it."

Behind him, Evan heard heavy footsteps and the squeaky sound of a clothes rack pushed aside. He turned and looked down at an elderly man, roughly dressed and a little too well seasoned. He took a step back, slightly overpowered by the smell.

"Can I help you, sir?" he asked, as if he had been volunteering at the shop for years. Of course, whatever the man wanted, he realized he wouldn't have the answer.

"I'm looking for my bird. My wife wants him back. I brought him in a few weeks ago and a lady took him."

Evan had the answer, but didn't want to give it.

"I think the bird you mean—a blue parakeet—was bought by one of our customers. We don't keep track of who buys what around here, you understand," he said easily. Perhaps he had the makings of a novelist, after all.

The man grumbled and reached into his pocket. Evan stiffened, but the disgruntled customer only pulled out a filthy handkerchief, and loudly blew his nose. Vowing some sort of revenge, he turned and walked out the door, but not before grabbing a handful of candy from a bowl on the front desk.

"Thank you, Evan," Eleanor said, at his side. "True Blue couldn't ever go back to him."

The thrill of triumph was greatly disproportionate to the act of defending a little blue parakeet. Evan turned to get his just reward, when he realized Wayne still stood only a few feet away from them and overheard it all.

"So you got the man's little birdie, Babe? Do you want to see my little birdie also? What do you say? Do we have a date for tonight? Can you get rid of your kids?" Wayne asked. He stepped too close to Ellie and stared down the V of her sweater.

"I have a date with my kids, as a matter of fact," Ellie said calmly, and took a step back.

"So why don't I stop by for a while? We don't need much time."

Evan studied her face and caught the very moment she understood Wayne's vulgar implication.

"No time would suit me best," she said, her voice scarcely rising. "I think my calendar's full for the next twenty or thirty years."

"You're going to spend all your time with him?" Wayne turned his thumb, as if he was hitching a ride.

"I just might," Ellie said.

Wayne picked up the bowl and studied it as if he knew what he was looking at. He glanced at Eleanor and then made a big show of dropping it and then catching the bowl before it hit the floor.

"Maybe I'll buy this as a wedding present. Or maybe you aren't getting married." He repeated his game and this time almost missed when he tried to catch the bowl. "Maybe he's just telling you so you'll help him clean out the place."

"And maybe I'm bored with this discussion, Mr. Durant. I think it's time you put down the bowl and left the shop," Eleanor said. "Maybe you've overstayed your welcome."

"You can't tell me what to do. Margaret Brownlee is the boss here."

Eleanor took a deep breath, knowing everyone wanted to hear what she would say.

"We're all volunteers here, Mr. Durant. I have just as much right to ask you to leave as anyone else. Or to call the police."

Wayne pondered this, seemingly weighing her comments as he weighed the bowl still in his hands. Finally, shrugging as if nothing made sense to him, he lifted his shoulders and dropped the bowl.

With a cry, Eleanor rushed forward to catch it, just as Evan caught her by her waist to pull her back. Wayne backed away quickly, into a bookcase. The bowl shattered on the tiled floor, and shards rained down on everything, pinging on glass and thumping on cushions. Eleanor gasped as several pieces stung her cheeks and dropped onto her head. She sighed, and put a shaking hand up to her forehead.

"Are you hurt?" Evan asked.

"I don't think so. Nothing to worry about. But I don't think I've made a friend." Eleanor looked around, but Wayne vanished.

"Well, you lost him when you stopped him looking down your cleavage. Wayne wouldn't be looking for good conversation or a shopping companion." Evan turned her around and started to pluck pieces of broken glass off her shoulders, her hair, her sleeves. "But I wouldn't discount the possibility of a business partner."

"What do you mean?" Eleanor asked, standing obedient and still as he examined her. Around them, the other Thrifty Means volunteers scurried around, reaching for whiskbrooms and damp rags.

"If he gets you on his side, perhaps you'll help him steal things out of Garland. As he's been doing for five years. I have no doubt that's what's been going on. I guessed as much from the start, but I tried to be fair. Now I'm back there, and the only way he can get to everything is through you."

"But that's ridiculous. He has to know I find him repellent."

"Well, I wouldn't overestimate Wayne's intelligence. But maybe he sees reason for hope. I have the feeling when I first walked into The Thrifty Means, you considered me repellent as well."

Eleanor looked up at him, entirely aware of his hands exploring her body. Before she could say anything, Mrs. B. pushed right between them and surveyed the damage.

"Well, we had a little accident, didn't we? Eleanor, would you get the vacuum? I trust you to clean this up nicely."

"I think you should call back your cousin, Mr. Durant," Eleanor said sweetly. "He's not a customer, he's not a volunteer. Since he was your guest here, I think you're responsible for him, Mrs. Brownlee."

Around them, everyone stopped. Evan said something under his breath and behind the desk, Grace clicked her teeth in anticipation. Eleanor was wrong to think Evan fighting with Wayne in The Thrifty Means would be the biggest battle of the day; they were in women's territory here. Emboldened by the suggestions of her friends and by Wayne's sheer repugnancy, Eleanor was the first to challenge Margaret Brownlee's rule of law.

"This is a place of business, my dear. Wayne Durant is free to come and go as he pleases."

"What sort of business does your cousin have with the rest of us? He stood here, made sexually explicit comments to me, and then took an item we had for sale and deliberately smashed it on the floor. That was no accident."

"I don't believe you," Mrs. B. said. She was the sort of woman who would wait until the water was lapping her chin before she'd admit the basement was flooded.

"I wouldn't make such things up," Eleanor insisted and leaned back, expecting to feel Evan behind her. When she nearly fell over, she turned around, indignant.

He appeared to have forgotten her, her cuts and scratches, and the righteousness of her stand against Margaret Brownlee.

Instead, he stood over a small pine box, and held a small figurine in his hand. Eleanor recognized the stark features of the little king, and realized he found his missing chess set, a copy of the one from the Island of Lewis.

****

The evening was warm enough for the first

barbeque of the year. Eleanor scraped the cooling grill and gazed at the evening sky, still reddened by the setting sun. There were times in her busy life when she made herself stop, walk away from the computer or out of the shop, and pause to reflect on the beauty around her. Tonight, she needed no reminder; she was in no hurry, no one called to her, no one needed her. And that was a good thing.

Inside her house, Evan and Lewis sat over the chess set, murmuring over moves and strategy. The chess set, though Evan's, had been duly purchased from The Thrifty Means, though it was immediately apparent a rook was missing. Any other customer would have complained and demanded a refund, but Evan was so pleased to have his property back, he did nothing more than post a note to ask the finder of the rook return his property to him. For tonight, a glass pony from Leslie's childhood collection took its place.

Leslie cleared the table, without Eleanor asking her to do so. Evan was a good influence on her children, Eleanor realized, though she believed she understood what motivated them. They liked him and some small part of their collective psyche yearned to have him a more permanent part of their lives. If they behaved themselves, perhaps he would be willing to take them on, as well as their mother who up to now showed very little interest in any man. In fact, perhaps he would be willing to just sort of adopt the two of them, and Eleanor could come and visit once in a while.

Eleanor liked him too, and wondered if her feelings went a good deal deeper. She didn't know. She understood love for her children and for her family. She loved her home and Eastfield, Connecticut. She was passionate about her books. But so many years passed since she fancied herself in love with a man she wasn't sure she could still recognize what she felt. She was altogether wrong the first time around and made a bad choice.

Overhead, a flock of geese flew against the darkening sky, reminding her of the enigmatic Escher print in which geese transform into negatives of themselves. The image was somehow apt. Having Evan back in town and near her had a good influence on her, as well. She had become bolder, a little bit more daring, and for the first time in many years enjoyed the complement of another person. Was it love? If not, did it really matter?

Evan groaned, and Eleanor glanced through the screen door to the man and boy hovering over the coffee table. Lewis looked pleased with himself, and was old enough to appreciate Evan would not have purposely let him win. For his part, Evan looked well and truly humbled, which was a rare moment for him. Leslie came into the room, studied the board for a moment, and patted her brother on the shoulder. Here was a rare moment as well. Sally looked up from her place on the braided rug and if it was possible for a dog to smile, she did so then. The scene was a cliché of domesticity and lacked for only one thing.

Eleanor leveraged the cover of the grill so the rusty hinges just aligned, and glancing once more at the night sky, went into the house.

"Mom!" Lewis said, sounding surprised she was there at all. "Am I named for the Island of Lewis?"

Eleanor wondered what nonsense he had been imagining. "You're named for your great grandfather; you heard the story."

"Well, I just wondered. And I just beat Evan."

Eleanor hesitated, thinking 'Evan' might be just too familiar, but the man himself leaned back against the couch, and stretched as if he had been living in her house for years. He yawned, which Eleanor guessed was his signal to leave. He straightened up and started to replace the discarded chess pieces on the board.

"But as the loser, I get to challenge you to the next match," he said. "You ready for me?"

"Now?" Lewis asked, his pleasure visible in every line of his young body.

"I'm ready if you are," Evan said, leaning towards him.

"Don't you have homework?" Eleanor said at the same time, but Evan heard her.

"No," he said, and Leslie giggled. "Unless you have something for me to do for you around here? Do you need help cleaning up?"

Eleanor exchanged a look with her daughter. "No, the clean up somehow managed to get done while the two of you boys were playing."

Evan looked chagrined, while Lewis did not. "I'll remember for next time," he said. "I promise."

There was something in his words to make Eleanor think he wasn't playing a game at all.
****

About an hour later, he found her out on her small porch, wrapped in a fleece blanket and drifting in and out of sleep. She opened her eyes briefly and smiled, and held out her arm so he might come under the blanket with her.

He hesitated. "I'm not sure there's enough room for me."

"We'll make room," she said, and before he could correct her on her pronoun, he realized what she meant. With a little growl, Sally tumbled off the bench. Evan sat down in her place, and wrapped the blanket around himself, and himself around Ellie. She smelled like smoke, mustard, and something indefinable but sweet. Sighing, she turned towards him and lifted her legs over his thighs. He noticed she carefully avoided his bad knee.

"We'd have more room at Garland," he said

against her hair. "You and the kids could move in and we'd have enough space for each of us to have our own study, and for them to have friends over whenever they'd want. The house is like a tomb, too quiet, too stuffy."

"Your aunt died in the house."

"Am I supposed to keep the place as a shrine to her blessed memory? I didn't bury her there, you know."

Eleanor laughed. "I know. I understand she's buried back in New York, nowhere near your parents."

"And someday, me. That suits me fine."

"I bet the day will come you'll realize what a darling she truly was, and how very much she cared for you."

"I have my doubts. But if the time comes, I promise I'll build a monument to her honor in the living room. For now, I'd like to bring some life back to the place. Right now those cats and me are the only breathing things."

"Do you remember I told you about a freeze dried cat sold at The Thrifty Means? It's pretty much a legend there."

"I'm not sure I remember."

"Well, you asked me about the weirdest thing ever sold, and I told you about the cat. And then I remembered it was bought for your aunt."

"For my aunt? Someone was playing a joke because, you know, she was terrified of cats, freeze dried or not. I don't understand how they've overrun the place now."

"Maybe she was converted? One hears of such things, sometimes."

"Or maybe someone was trying to scare her? Or threaten her? Or drive her crazy?"

"It sounds so sordid. Things like that don't happen in Eastfield."

Sitting beside her, on this quiet night, Evan could believe she was right. With one foot, he gently rocked them back and forth, and looked up into the dark sky, trying to recognize the constellations.

"It's too soon, Evan," Ellie said.

"My aunt's been dead for months."

Eleanor's fingers walked up his stomach and chest and started trifling with his shirt buttons. He closed his eyes and leaned back against the cushions.

"I don't mean Dorothea. I mean us," she said, and released the top button. "You can't really be asking us to move in with you."

"Why not? Don't pretend you don't know where this might be heading."

"Might be heading, Evan. I know where we're heading right now," she said, and slipped her hand through the opening of his shirt. "And I could make a guess about tomorrow or the day after. But I can't afford to be wrong anymore. I had my chance and lost the gamble. I married someone, thinking I understood precisely where we were heading: to a life together and kids and a comfortable existence."

He caught her hand and kissed her fingers. "Well, I think you got everything, except him. That's a lucky break for me. Your fingers smell like sauerkraut."

"You really are so romantic," Eleanor said, whisking her hand away. "I'm just not ready for this, Evan. I hardly even know you."

"You've known me longer than any woman I ever dated."

"I know, and there's my problem." She tried to untangle her arms and legs from their little cocoon, but he held her tightly. "I don't know whom you've dated, what you've been doing in all this time."

He sighed and shifted her onto his lap. "What do you want to do? Check my references? My credit report? The doorman in my building could give you an earful, but I gave him a generous Christmas present last year, so he'll probably keep mum."

"I'm serious, Evan."

"So am I. You've known me forever. You knew me when I was shorter than you were, when I broke my leg falling off a trampoline, when I wore braces on my teeth. You knew me when I ran for class president, when I wore bell bottoms, when I wanted to be a major league pitcher."

"You broke your right leg, I think?" she interrupted, gently touching the muscle above his knee. "I had forgotten the story, about the trampoline."

"I hardly remember the time myself. Old war wounds became irrelevant after the accident, since I had a whole new set of injuries to worry about."

"I know. I notice you limp sometimes." Eleanor sighed and continued to caress his leg.

"I had surgery on the knee a few years ago. Eventually I'll wind up like Humpty Dumpty and no one will be able to put me back together again."

"We've been hurt too many times, Evan. That's why I'm not sure this could work. I'm not sure I can stand any more pain."

"Does this hurt?" he asked, kissing her on the forehead. "How about this?" He trailed a line of kisses down her face, along her neck, to her breasts. With her free hand, she lifted the fleece over their heads and giggled.

"I didn't know you were ticklish," he said, and then tested other parts of her body. She squirmed beneath him.

"I am, a bit. But I'm laughing because of what we must look like, making out under a blanket on the porch. This is so sophomore year."

"You were doing this sophomore year? With whom?"

"Am I not entitled to any secrets at all?" she asked. She found his face with her fingers and kissed him. "Especially since you haven't answered any of my questions?"

"Okay," he said, pulling down the blanket. "I'm suffocating, anyway. What do you want to know?"

"What you've been doing for twenty years."

He didn't answer for so long, Eleanor wondered if he might have gone to sleep. She sat patiently, warm and contented, relishing the closeness of his body against her, and her absolute inability to do anything other than respond to him.

"I think...I guess what I've been doing is taking every single weakness and making it into a strength. I studied learning disabilities and special education teaching strategies. I wrote books to deliver information to children who suffered as I once suffered, and help them make sense of what was almost impossible for them to comprehend. I broke away from the place holding family for so many years and traveled around the world. And I remained aloof from any close relationships, knowing what happens when connections are broken."

"So you know just what I'm talking about. It's dangerous to be so close to someone again."

"Not dangerous. Just risky." He rose to his feet, carrying her up with him, still tangled in the blanket. The leg, twice broken, didn't hinder him. "But I'm beginning to think I made a mistake about the last part. If you're not willing to take a risk on anything, you could wind up with nothing."

The blanket slipped away as Eleanor slipped her arms around his neck. "Where are we going?"

"I'm freezing, though the last time I checked the calendar, the month was June. And since you won't come up to Garland, I guess we're staying right here."

"You can't stay here, Evan. Not while my kids are in the house."

"I have no designs against your good character, at least not tonight. But what about a game of chess?"

Chapter 11

"Please don't bring us your old skis, car seats, and baby cribs. I'm willing to risk pricing an item too high or too low, but I won't risk anyone's safety."
Eleanor Gilmartin, volunteer and
Very Cautious Mother

Eleanor faced the direction of her bathroom mirror, but she did not yet have the courage to open her eyes. Even at her age—or especially at her age—there was something mildly boastful when one confessed to being up the whole night engaged in certain activities. Partying was enviable. Working on a deadline was respectable. Spending the night with a man was shameless, but divine.

But being unable to sleep because one's children were about to turn sixteen was borderline pathetic and possibly full blown hysteria.

Eleanor placed her dry, feverish fingers on her throbbing forehead and opened one eye.

Dear heavens. Her hair stuck out in spikes around her head and her eyes had more baggage than an airport carousel. Shoulders slumped; nightgown straps tangled and—was it even possible?—a blemish appeared on her chin. Could she have changed places with her children overnight? Could this be Freaky Wednesday? Would she be able to pass their math tests this morning?

Once upon a time, not so many years ago, twenty-five or thirty children bearing gifts would invade her little home one day in June. There would be pizza and ice cream and a clown making balloon animals. The biggest problem might be a kid getting a blue pencil instead of a red one in his goody bag. Sometimes soda would spill, or a mother would show up fifteen minutes after the party to claim her child.

Today was not about goody bags or clowns. In fact, there was nothing fun at all.

Her babies were going to get their driving permits at the earliest moment it was legal in the State of Connecticut. And she, who had spent the last sixteen years protecting them from every harm was going to drive them over to the Department of Motor Vehicles and let them.

Eleanor staggered into the shower, stubbing her toe on the doorframe.

****

"They're just getting their permits, Ellie," Evan said, staring out the kitchen window. Sally had given up chasing Lilianna's cats and was sniffing around Wayne's burned out cottage. Evan had hoped to tear the place down weeks ago, but the fire marshal and police chief insisted the wreckage remain as evidence. For what, Evan was not entirely certain, though they vaguely suggested he might not have been particularly upset to see Wayne depart Garland. They were very perceptive he wryly considered. However, there was a big leap from disliking a guy and trying to kill him.

But this was Eastfield, after all, and the police had to get paid for something other than harassing high school kids. Of course, that was a time honored Eastfield tradition; a cop once stopped him for "failing to look frequently enough in the rear view mirror."

"I'm not worried about the permit, Evan. You know I'm not. I'm worried about everything to follow. Driving at night, in snowstorms, with too many kids in the car. Deer stand in the middle of the road, waiting to be hit. And there are oncoming drivers..."

He turned from the window and looked at her steadily. Ellie sat at the table, with boxes of Dorothea's papers spread out around her. He realized she was distracted and upset as soon as he opened the door to her an hour or so before and he understood why. She had let just a few words slip out over the past few weeks, like rough cracks in her otherwise smooth veneer. A few days ago, when he and Lewis played chess, the boy begged for his help. He doubted anything he said could make a difference, but that didn't stop him from trying.

"There will always be oncoming drivers, Ellie," he said reasonably. "There will also always be floods and hurricanes. Those are the risks we take just for living."

She made a dismissive gesture, not accepting any platitudes. "We can minimize our risks. I don't live in a place where there are earthquakes or where tsunamis wash away homes and people. I came back to Eastfield, to raise my kids."

Her voice trailed off, and he understood she would not say what everyone else said about Eastfield: "Where no one locks their doors, and people walk outside at night, and nothing exciting ever happens." They two, better than anyone, understood bad things could and do happen.

But this was not the moment to accede to fatalism, no matter how close it lapped at their shore.

"And you are minimizing your risks," he said logically, agreeably. Evan sat down on one of the antique ladder-back chairs, which creaked ominously under his weight. "Look at things this way: you're minimizing those risks when your kids get drivers' permits, and take lessons, and pass a road test. It's not as if you're sending them out this afternoon with your car keys and a road map. They have to earn the right to drive. You and I did. We all do."

"Missy did," she said softly.

He recognized what this was all about, of course, though this is the first time Missy's name came into the conversation. For twenty years, Ellie could not allow herself to forget what happened one miserable October night. For all she did in her life, all her accomplishments, and diversions, she could never move past it. The accident was like a scar never healing properly, not when she picked at it and made the injury bleed over and over again.

"Let her rest in peace, Ellie. The accident wasn't her fault, and it wasn't yours. My dad was angry with me and distracted and should have seen her headlights. So I'm to blame. And don't think you're the only one to relive the night a thousand times and wish everything turned out differently. If I only got a ride from someone else...if I only did better in school...if only we hadn't stopped at the Market to pick up dinner. We play a game with ourselves. As a historian, you already know how everything works."

Eleanor pushed aside one of Dorothea's journals and groped blindly at a box of tissues. Evan had never seen her so distraught and confused.

"You know what I mean. If only Lincoln hadn't been shot. If only Hitler had success as a painter. If only Henry VIII had a dozen sons with his first wife."

Eleanor wiped her eyes and noisily blew her nose. "Of course I know what you mean. I may be crazy, but I'm not stupid."

Evan took a deep breath. "I never said you..."

"Missy didn't have the headlights on."

"...were stupid or crazy. I just...what?"

"The accident wasn't your father's fault. The evening was getting dark and Missy didn't have the headlights on. We were in the shadows of the trees. He couldn't see us. I told her to put them on, and she wouldn't listen to me. I didn't even have my license yet." She broke down again, wrapped in her own cocoon of grief and remembrance, her own private despair.

Evan didn't know what to do.

"And now this," she cried.

Their relationship? Was he making her miserable just by being with her, and scraping away at the damned scab every time they were together?

"I worry about the children. For sixteen years I've worried about keeping them safe...and alive. For sixteen years, I've had nightmares about losing them, imagining what life has been for Missy's parents. Knowing no matter what I do, no matter what protection I offer, it may never be enough. You can't know how I feel." She reached for another tissue, but picked up one of Dorothea's tax bills instead. She sobered up enough to look at the paper as if puzzled how she came to have it. "You don't have kids."

Selfish though he was, Evan felt the smallest sense of relief. This was not about them. Her issue was still about driving, risk, and trusting whoever was sharing the road with you was not going to slam into your car.

A moment later, he realized it was about him after all. Even in her darkest moment, Ellie hit on the most basic of truths. Evan didn't have kids, didn't have a wife, and didn't have brothers and sisters. He didn't even have a home he cared enough about, until Dorothea's death opened the gate for Garland for him. He was nearly forty years old, and he had book contracts.

He realized now there was more; he had Eleanor Gilmartin and her two children. Of driving age.

"Why not?" Ellie asked, and he looked at her in surprise. Somehow, through no help from him, the storm had blown over. She looked at him over the stacks of paper, as stern as a high school teacher hassling him over his lousy grades. Except her nose was red and her tears left dark puddles under her eyes. Though his thoughts had little to do with anything, Evan realized for the first time she wore makeup. That she did, and he never knew it was somehow endearing. That she did, and might have done so for him, was seductive.

"Why not?" she demanded. "Why don't you have children?"

He returned to the bargaining table, the stacks of useless information, and his stern inquisitor; he sensed whatever they established in the next minutes was going to be the business of the rest of their lives. Over the last several days, he admitted he might very well be ready and able to accept this woman into his life, but now he realized he had not given very much consideration to the things she carried.

"I never married," he said a little stupidly.

She sniffed and made a gesture of impatience. "That is not what I asked. Though you can answer both together, I suppose."

Could he? He contemplated things for a few moments, and realized how poorly he understood himself. There were things he carried, and never bothered to consider before.

"What you just told me, about Missy, is some very small consolation I suppose," he began. "But it doesn't really change anything. Somehow, you think I just picked myself up from the accident and stumbled away with scarcely a scratch. But I think...I know I have been stumbling since that time. Through the rest of high school, and college, and in my life since then. Do you think you have an exclusive right to grief? I lost my parents in a moment. I was a kid without parents. And all the kind people of Eastfield, Connecticut couldn't do a damn thing about it. How many mothers baked me cupcakes for my birthday? When all the time I was missing my own mother who would have gone to the Market, bought a box of cookies, and stuck a candle through a chocolate chip."

He caught her look of horror, but wasn't sure the expression was prompted by him spilling out his confession, or just the fact his mother didn't bake him cupcakes.

"You tell me I can't know what it's like, but I do. I know the accident veered me onto a different road, one I stayed on because I couldn't bear to think about getting back onto the other. I became independent, and learned not to rely on anyone else being there for me. I know what it is to be a son without a father. I couldn't punish another kid."

Eleanor's eyes widened, and she drew a deep breath. Her nose was still red, but she regained her composure. Though he didn't know anything about the makeup she wore, Evan realized he now understood deeper and darker things about Eleanor Gilmartin and himself, the things that really mattered. He shocked her; he was certain. He shocked himself as well. Somehow, he took her argument and flipped her words head over heels.

"You were afraid?" she asked at last, just above a whisper.

Evan twisted in his seat, not even sure he wanted to admit this to himself. He was never one to attempt to analyze his own dreams, or second-guess his motives. Now this revelation escaped from where it had been hiding for so many years, and everything somehow rang true.

"I suppose I have been. I don't think fear crippled me, but I think it's always been there." He drummed his fingers on one of the piles of papers. "Look at yourself."

She looked startled, and brushed her fingers

across her cheeks. She turned towards the smoky glass door of the wall oven, searching for her reflection.

"I don't mean you should be critical. You look beautiful," he said, surely risking her wrath. "You haven't been crippled either. You worry about Lewis and Leslie every minute of the day, and they seem normal, good kids. If you made them into basket cases, they'd never think about driving now."

"Or they would drive away so far I would never find them again," she said, but she nodded.

"There you go," he said, encouragingly. He guessed his words sounded false; and if he imagined so, Eleanor would be certain.

"So where does this leave us?" she asked.

Damned if he knew. There were things he would like to say, but wasn't sure she was ready to hear those words. He didn't think he was prepared to probe any deeper into his motivations and limitations of the past twenty years. At least, not yet.

"Right here," he said.

"With me terrified about the kids getting their permits. So we're back to where we started, after all this. I'm sorry, Evan, but the *EZ Guide* doesn't seem to be making things any simpler. I know it's not rational. I know you think I'm nutty. And I know you have every right to be just as nutty. But I've been dreading this day for years and years." She ran her fingers through her hair, and looked back at the oven door. "I survived head lice and Lyme disease and broken bones. I'm not sure I can survive Leslie and Lewis driving. I'm not kidding."

He understood her fear, and he wished he understood what to do. He loved her, after all. She must know, whatever her feelings for him, he would do anything in the world for her. Even if he felt anything less, even indifference, she was doing him a huge favor, one she was originally reluctant to take on. He had some obligation to her, even though she invested time at Garland in the name of her volunteerism at The Thrifty Means. He owed her something.

"Why don't you let me teach the kids to drive?" he asked impulsively.

"Are you out of your mind?"

He shrugged and smiled at her. "Well, yeah. I think we just established as much."

Eleanor pushed away her chair and stood up. Evan responded by remaining firmly in his seat, if settling back on the two back legs could be considered at all firm. As he looked up at her, his eyes caught the glare of the sun, and he squinted.

"You know what I mean. And if anything, we just established you're normal. I'm sorry to disappoint you, but that's the way it looks from up here." She circled the table until she was close enough for him to catch her, and pull her down onto him. Instead, he linked his hands together into his lap. "But do you think you can sit calmly in the passenger seat when a new driver is at the wheel?"

"Yeah. I was a kid once. I seem to remember leaving some rubber on the road, while my mother... Anyway, I remember." Her body shielded him from the glare, and he looked up at her face. Whatever he expected to see, it was not her expression of relief. "Let's look at the facts. You're a mother who dreads the idea of kids driving—and driving with them when they learn. I'm a guy who has missed out on being a father. Somehow, this seems like a fatherly thing to do. I have a couple of extra cars in the garage worth nothing but for their spare parts. A few dings won't matter at all. If Lewis and Leslie don't mind lurching around Eastfield in Dorothea's old Buick, I don't mind lurching with them."

"You're serious?"

"Not only serious, but looking forward to the adventure. Do you think the kids would go for it?"

"Why wouldn't they?" Ellie leaned one hip on the table, looking relaxed for the first time all day.

"Well, for one, will they resent the fact this fatherly thing is not being shared with their father?"

"They might, but if they are interested in learning how to drive, they know not to wait around for him. He might show up by the time they're finished with college." She paused. "Which now I think about it, may not be a bad thing. They could start driving then."

"Forget about the plan, Ellie. This is Eastfield. There are no buses or taxis. They're either going to drive or depend on friends to drive them around."

"You're right. Well, what's the other thing?"

He looked at her blankly for a moment. "Oh, yes. Well, they may prefer to drive with a shrieking mother in the passenger seat, slamming her right floor into the floor whenever she thinks they should brake and pointing out stop signs two blocks away."

She took several deep breaths, and he guessed he might have started her crying again.

"You're not funny, Evan," she said.

"I'm sorry you feel that way because after all this, I really am in the mood for fun." Finally, he gave himself up to temptation and reached for her. As he brought her down onto his lap, the chair cracked and teetered, and crashed with the two of them onto the hard quarry tile surface of the kitchen floor.

****

A few hours later, Eleanor walked through the door of The Thrifty Means with a stack of wooden chair parts in her arms.

Miriam looked up from a carton of what appeared to be rags, and straightened her glasses.

"The dumpster's in the rear, lady," she said.

Eleanor laughed aloud. "But you don't understand, Mrs. Pell. This is very valuable garbage. The very best garbage, straight from Garland and Dorothea's treasure trove of antiques."

Mrs. B. stepped out from behind the bookcase, and Eleanor's good mood dissipated. How had things come to be so? Only a few months ago, the time spent in their little antique shop had been an adventure, an escape from work and boredom, and a community experience with women she had come to love. Now, she wondered when Mrs. B. would be out of the shop and who spied upon whom. Eleanor realized she was not the only one to feel like this. Working at The Thrifty Means was supposed to be fun.

Instead, Margaret Brownlee glowered at her, and made her feel fully aware of her messed hair, red nose, and dusty flannel shirt—not to mention the broken chair in her arms.

"If that's all you can get out of Evan Zane, I suspect you're not trying hard enough. There's the mirror. See what you look like," she said and Eleanor wondered if she possibly understood her correctly.

"Would you like to send in a professional, Mrs. B.?" Eleanor said pointedly. "Or would just a younger, prettier woman do as well?"

"What a disgusting thing to say. And from you of all people, Eleanor Lambert Gilmartin. You were raised in this town, taught values here, learned some hard lessons."

Eleanor's blood rushed to her face, and she set the wood down on the floor, mostly to compose herself. A little flare of anger caught fire, and burned. She straightened up, and gave the elderly woman a moment to retract her hateful words.

"I learned enough not to say hurtful things to people who generously give of their time and energy.

I learned not to insult those who do me no harm." She had an audience now, but could only guess she also had their support. Margaret Brownlee was president of The Thrifty Means for so long she had a coterie of long-standing, loyal friends. "And I know we don't try to get anything out of anyone. What people donate to the shop, they do so out of goodness and the spirit of community. Sometimes we win, and sometimes we lose, but we respect everyone's decisions."

Mrs. B stood stone faced, almost as if the words meant nothing to her. Something flickered across her face, something truly frightening. She raised her chin and closed her eyes, as if the sight of her recalcitrant volunteer was too much to bear.

"I do not need a young upstart like you to lecture me about our values and our community. I have dedicated my life to this shop." She walked to the front desk, reached for her purse, and marched out the front door.

The shop was absolutely still. Customers, consigners, volunteers, all stopped whatever they were doing to witness the show. Everyone's eyes watched the scene in the parking lot, where Margaret Brownlee stopped to talk to an elderly man, and then got into her ancient Ford. The man shrugged and continued to walk towards The Thrifty Means. From the general area of the linens, someone's cell phone went off.

"Well, at least she called me 'young'," Eleanor said, and a few people laughed.

"And she left. Maybe for good," Liza Silver added.

Eleanor sighed. "Liza. I didn't realize you were here."

"We're all here," Liza said firmly. "Miriam, Lucy, Galen, Mindy, Ginny, Grace. And a good thing, too. No one would have wanted to miss the show."

Eleanor leaned back until her back rested against a pine armoire. "So you say but the show was pretty nasty. I'm not sure what's made Mrs. B. resent me so much. Could it just be the Zane estate? Did she expect to sell the whole thing out from under him?"

Miriam cocked her head, and Eleanor realized she had a wider audience than she first imagined. She recognized several of the customers, and word of the conversation would soon spread.

"Eleanor," Galen said a little too loudly. "Come to the back room. You'll never guess what we found in the pocket of an old sweater!"

This interested the customers a good deal more than the rather mundane accusation of one volunteer to another that she was whoring for merchandise, but the small group of Eleanor's co-workers clustered around her and they moved like a swarm to the back room.

"She resents you for having a relationship with him," Mindy said. "Because you're young and he'd rather spend time with you than the old timers."

"Some of us old timers are very attractive," Lucille Armitage pointed out. Eleanor remembered her blatant flirting with Evan all those weeks ago in L'Avignon, and wondered if Lucy resented her as well.

"Please, Lucy," Miriam said. "Evan Zane is not even forty. He's probably dating girls of twenty back in New York."

"Thanks for reminding me," Eleanor said. She picked up a polished silver charger and glanced at her reflection before Ginny took it out of her hands.

"I just polished the silver, and don't want your middle-aged fingerprints smudging the surface," she said wryly. "Besides, the curve of the charger distorts."

"Just like Mrs. B. distorts. I don't see why she

thinks my spending time with Evan Zane is going to make a difference in what comes into the shop. She doesn't think I'm going to steal anything, does she?"

None of the women answered, and none would meet her eyes.

"Does she?" Eleanor asked in disbelief. "After all this time—ten years!—she thinks I'm going to steal stuff from The Thrifty Means?"

"No, you're mistaken," Galen said quietly. "But don't you see what's happening? When Evan Zane showed up in town in early May, we all believed he was going to settle the estate and leave. When he brought us boxes of his aunt's things, we guessed he might sell out to a developer. He hadn't been to Eastfield in twenty years and we had no reason to believe he'd be staying now."

"I don't think he's made a decision," Eleanor said, though she guessed he had. It involved her, and she was not yet clear how everything was all going to turn out.

"But he has, at least in the short run," Miriam said.

Eleanor looked at her friend, wondering what Miriam knew that she did not.

Miriam chucked her under the chin. "Well, it's obvious to the rest of us. We know the two of you are an item. Oh, please, don't give me that look. Someone who looks like you do can't spend so much time in a man's house and do nothing but check the hallmarks on his mother's old china. And it really doesn't matter, does it? Even if you tell us the arrangement is strictly business, no one's gonna believe you."

"Okay, then, I won't tell you."

"Good. Because we weren't born yesterday," Lucy said.

"But Evan Zane is also showing up at town meetings, and is working with the Rivershed

Association, and spoke at the high school, and came to the event at the Hamilton estate. The point is, he may have returned to town after Dorothea died with the intention of selling out as quickly as possible. Something has made him stay, at least for a while longer. And I don't think it's the Historical Society's exhibit on red ware plates."

"They have a very lovely exhibit," Galen murmured.

"Oh, hush," Grace said. "This is about Eleanor."

Eleanor looked around at her friends, the women she worked with for ten years, who gave willingly of their time with no reward but the satisfaction of turning a tidy profit for the charities of Eastfield. Yet there was much more, for most of them could have just written a check to support those agencies.

They were a sisterhood brought together by an essential goodness in their nature, and by the satisfaction of working in a community of other women. She, who was a member of school and religious and other civic organizations, belonged to nothing else quite the same.

"So even if you're right—and I'm not saying you are—aren't I letting the shop down? Mrs. B is right. If he hadn't asked me to give him a hand, if I hadn't said yes, if I hadn't agreed to go on a few dates with him, if I hadn't..." she paused as they all leaned forward. "...invited him to Ludlum's with the kids and me, then he would let us take what we wanted from Garland. We could have given a bigger donation to the old play shop. We could have bought a few more morphine pumps for Eastfield Hospice. Instead, I'm keeping him here, and his stuff in the old house."

"Well, considering The Thrifty Means has been around for sixty years, I think we can deal with a slight delay. We can wait another fifty years or so, can't we?" Gail asked.

Eleanor tried to keep from laughing out loud.

"You think I'm only going to live to be ninety?"

"Or so," Gail reminded her.

Lucille Armitage nodded sagely. "You know, I read a report about people who have good sex living longer."

"Lucy!" Eleanor guessed her cheeks must be as red as her nose. "I'm not sure I can handle this."

"Then handle this," Galen said quickly, and reaching for Eleanor's hand, put something in her palm.

Eleanor looked down at a ring, lovely and quite old. No longer a circlet, the band was flattened into an oval, reflecting many years of wear. Two sparkling baguettes framed a large faceted stone.

"A cubic zirconia?" Eleanor asked. Their jewelry always sold well and attracted many customers to the shop.

"We don't think so, Eleanor," Liza said. "We think it's real."

Eleanor took a deep breath. "A diamond? Is this what you found in the pocket of the sweater? We have to return this. Do we know who brought in the donation?"

"No idea. Someone left a couple of garbage bags at the front door last night and the girls pulled them in this morning. We almost threw them into the dumpster because of the rain last night, and we figured the clothing might be ruined," Miriam said.

"They were ruined. Well, they were rags to begin with. But of course, we checked through everything, just in case." Liza took the ring from Eleanor's palm and held it up to the naked light bulb on the desk lamp. The stone caught the light and cast a rainbow on the plain concrete wall of their workroom.

"In case you might find a diamond?" Eleanor asked, laughing.

"Well, we did, didn't we?"

"What does Mrs. B. have to say about this? I'm sure this find doesn't atone for my sin of seducing Mr. Zane. I doubt anything can make up for such a misdeed." Eleanor realized she just admitted everything, though she didn't think she surprised anyone.

Liza and Miriam spoke at once: "She doesn't know."

"We're going to handle this, and if we get to the point where we can put the ring up for sale, then we'll bring her in to the business. First, Galen's going to go over to Town Jewelers to have it appraised. If the ring turns out to be worth fifty cents, we'll price it for the jewelry case. If real, we'll run some articles in the paper, though not identifying it of course and we'll try to find the owner. We could use the publicity. Mrs. B. thinks we can go forever on a reputation established in the 1940s, but we need to draw in the newcomers to town. They may not even know about this place," Ginny said.

"Mrs. B. hates newcomers. She thinks they're ruining the town by building new houses and paving the roads," Eleanor reminded them.

"And they have to furnish those big homes, don't they? Mrs. B.—Margaret—may prefer a log cabin, but most of the rest of us like running water and toilets." Galen crossed her arms over her breast.

"M-m-margaret?" Eleanor stuttered.

Galen uncrossed her arms and leaned against the table. "Or how about Maggie? Margie? How about Peg?"

"Oh dear heavens," Eleanor said as the others laughed. "This is pure anarchy, isn't it? What has been going on while I've been..."

"...seducing Mr. Zane?" Liza finished for her. "We are rebelling. And you're coming along."

Eleanor glanced at Miriam, who nodded just perceptibly. She understood what was going on, why the women were so frustrated and ready for a change, and whom they recognized as Mrs. B's logical successor. Her own resume was quite adequate, and she would happily step aside if someone else would take on the responsibility, but, if asked, she would come forward as she always had.

They had her, and they knew it. Just as she opened her lips to make some noncommittal statement, one of the front desk volunteers rushed into the back room.

"Some lady just flushed the bathroom key down the toilet!"

Miriam Pell uttered a few words Eleanor didn't even realize someone of her generation might know, reached for a long hook someone had once made out of a wire hanger, and led the band of sisters to the scene of the crime.

****

Two hours later, after calling a plumber to take care of the mess and dislodge the key and the five inch keychain from the toilet trap, Eleanor drove over to the high school to pick up her twins. Sixteen years ago she was somewhat overwhelmed, though not as much, as things turned out, as her husband. Today, a day she dreaded for so long, might also have been overwhelming, but for two things.

First, there was The Thrifty Means, where she managed to forget her problems, and focus on things that didn't really matter.

And then there was Evan, who somehow promised to share some of her problems and cares with her. She didn't know where their lives would all lead, but for now, she was satisfied.

Leslie and Lewis were waiting in front of the field house, surrounded by cheering friends and a lot of well-meaning advice about answers to the permit exam. Her children looked serious, no doubt concerned about failing the simple test and being bested by his or her twin.

They jumped into her car, and said almost nothing in the ten minutes drive to the DMV. Eleanor saw no reason to distract them with conversation about Evan Zane, or broken chairs, or diamond rings or stuffed toilets. They had enough on their mind.

An hour later, having run the slalom though five lines of red tape and general confusion, they had their permits in hand, and legal permission to give their mother a heart attack.

As they walked out the door, their neighbor Mrs. Winthrop, came through. Eleanor hadn't seen her in weeks, but in a place like Eastfield time didn't seem to matter.

"I heard you had quite a cut up with Margaret Brownlee," Mrs. Winthrop said, leaning close. "Over Dorothea Zane's boy, I understand."

Eleanor only nodded, knowing it was just as she predicted.

Chapter 12

"Here's one thought to keep to yourself: Who would be stupid enough to buy this?"
Ginny DeLoy, volunteer since 1980

Eleanor looked up from Dorothea's journals to see Evan's Jeep coming up his driveway at about 2 miles an hour. One of the cats sat in the road, carefully licked her paws, and sauntered off towards the barn with more than enough time to get out of the way. Sally, who ran to meet the returning drivers, slowed to a virtual standstill to keep pace.

The Jeep veered to the right, to the left, and then missed a tree by a few inches before coming to a stop in the middle of the driveway, effectively blocking her own car.

Two doors opened, and Lewis and Leslie shouted greetings to where she sat on Evan's porch. They raised their hands in a sign of victory, and ran off with Sally towards the river. The third door opened and Evan staggered out, as if in pain. He bent over, his hands on his knees, and then stretched and straightened.

"How'd everything go, Evan?" Eleanor asked sweetly as he came towards the porch. She promised him she would be cheerful and calm, and not let the children see how she really felt about it all. Her skin nearly cracked as she smiled at him.

He didn't say anything, but walked stiffly up the wooden steps, avoided her eyes as he passed the table, and collapsed on the garden swing. Eleanor was glad she replaced the worn cushions the week before.

"I must be out of my mind," he said into the pillow.

"You poor man," she murmured, not entirely sympathetically. "Didn't the drive go well?"

"We were passed by a tractor on Norwell Road. A tractor! There was a line of about twenty cars, all honking at us, and letting loose a string of curses as they passed us. What happened to the good old days in Eastfield?"

Eleanor stood and walked over to the swing. Evan shifted his legs and she sat down next to him.

"You're beginning to sound like Margaret Brownlee. The twenty-first century happened. Margaret's about a hundred years behind the rest of us."

"Ah, yes. The age of innocence." He threw one arm over his head and beckoned her to lie down beside him.

"The children, Evan," she said, though she was sorely tempted.

"They're not so innocent, Ellie. I think they know a lot more of the world than we did at their age."

"But things changed pretty quickly for us."

Neither of them spoke, and a sign of the growing ease with each other was that the silence was not fraught with pain. Instead, there was comfort in companionship, in shared experience, in having survived. Eleanor noticed Sally come over the rise, her fur plastered to her wet body, and a clump of grass spilling over her ears. Lewis and Leslie followed, screaming in protest when she paused, vigorously shaking her body. Then they ran off to the barn, with Sally barking after them.

The age of innocence. They might have the sophistication of precocious sixteen year olds, but Eleanor was allowing them this one last summer to be children. She didn't insist they get jobs, didn't make them go to summer school. Leslie had a casual babysitting schedule, and Lewis continued to volunteer time with the Rivershed; they were learning to drive. There would be time enough for adult sized responsibilities next year. The year after they would be going off to college.

And that would pretty much take care of any remnants of innocence.

She glanced down at Evan and wondered if he might have fallen asleep.

"Margaret Brownlee might still be living in the last century, but she's not so innocent," Eleanor said, possibly to herself.

Evan opened one eye and looked up at her.

"So, it's time to be honest?" he said wryly. "I've felt a little like the old tractor on Norwell Road, trying to pull ahead, but nervous about taking the lead at ten miles per hour. But after the incident last week, I guess it's safer to pull out into traffic."

Eleanor patted him on the thigh, and leaned back against the cushions.

"I know I told you she and I had words, and she walked out in a huff, but I don't think you know what started the argument," she said. She looked down at him, wondering if he realized what they had between them was already the subject of a great deal of local speculation.

"I assume it's because things are missing from my house, and they somehow appear at The Thrifty Means and elsewhere in this town. At the same time, your beloved Mrs. B. is handing over checks to Wayne for something. Of course, judging by the way he smells, she may just be paying him off to stay away from the shop and her genteel customers."

Eleanor glanced at him. "They're not so very genteel. But there are other things smelling funny."

Evan pulled up his legs, and shifted around her

on the cushions, sitting upright. For a big man, he was very agile; but then, he already demonstrated his skills in other ways. Now he contented himself with moving closer, and stretching his arm on the cushions behind her.

"Good. I'm glad to hear you say it. I wasn't going to say anything against everyone's darling Maggie B. What? What's so funny?"

"Never mind. I just realized how well you would fit in with the crew at The Thrifty Means."

He squeezed her shoulders. "Yeah, I'm sure we'd have a blast."

"Watch what you're saying. You're already so popular there you may find yourself the next shop manager."

Evan said nothing, and Eleanor hoped he understood she was kidding.

"If you're thinking about the next shop manager, then I'm right. It is time to talk. About the little business Mrs. Brownlee is running on the side."

Eleanor sighed. She guessed the truth and the evidence demanded she believe what was right before her eyes, but reality dealt the final blow to the inspiring image of the woman.

"I don't know what's going on. I really don't," she admitted. "Wayne is doing something for her, but I don't know if the checks are from her personal account, or if he's picking up a few extra dollars by delivering furniture for people. I asked our bookkeeper a few casual questions, and she didn't seem to think there was anything out of the ordinary."

"Maybe this has become the ordinary. Maybe this has been going on for so long, the bookkeeper no longer notices what's going on? My chess set might have come in at any time before I arrived in Eastfield. Didn't you tell me you found the board before the rest of the set? Things disappeared from

Dorothea for months or years. How would I have known?"

Eleanor didn't state the obvious; if he had come regularly for visits, he might well have known. He might well have been a part of her life for years before this.

She sighed, thinking how different things might have been. They already had that discussion, didn't they?

"What?' he asked impatiently.

"I don't understand what's going on either, because nothing makes sense. If Margaret is doing something on the sly, I'm not sure she's running a business. I don't see how she would make money. Merchandise arrives in the shop, by honest means. I hope. We see things come through the door, and we have a team of women who unpack, price, and put the good stuff out on the floor. All sales go through the volunteers working at the front desk, even those things purchased by other volunteers."

"Maybe your Mrs. B. is buying up things and reselling them at a higher price," Evan speculated.

"I'm sure it happens, and our customers shop at The Thrifty Means looking for a bargain. But why would Margaret do that? After all, we know all the antique dealers in the area, and they go to all the antique shows. The community networks all the time; Lucy would tell us if stuff from the shop turned up in Massachusetts or in New York. As far as selling things on auction online, it wouldn't be Margaret's doing. She doesn't even have an email address. The rest of us find out who's sick, when the shop will close because of a snowstorm, and any other news via email. Whoever draws the short straw has to call Margaret."

He laughed.

"Evan, did Wayne have a computer in his cottage?"

"Do you mean, is Wayne selling things online for her?" Evan stopped laughing. "I didn't see anything under the ground cover of empty beer bottles and supermarket circulars. But that doesn't mean he isn't using a computer. Can't he just use one of the terminals in the library?"

"If Wayne Durant stepped into the library, word of the happening would be all over town in an hour. But really, I suppose anything is possible."

"And if the checks are going to Margaret Brownlee, then she could be giving him a cut of the action."

Eleanor doubted Margaret Brownlee would use those words, but they made some sense. And Wayne, anxious for some cash, might have hastened Dorothea's end so he could get his hands on more merchandise, though he might not use those words either.

He killed her. She suspected Wayne from the moment Evan asked for her help.

"He didn't kill her," Evan said, and brushed her hair away from her cheek.

"What do you mean?" Eleanor said, pushing herself off him. "I thought that's what this was all about."

Evan gave an exasperated sigh. "I thought this was about Margaret Brownlee. I spoke to a few people around town, and they tell me Wayne was up in Hartford when my aunt died. Lilianna was alone with her."

Lilianna killed her?

Eleanor decided to keep the idea to herself, as she struggled to her feet. "And you didn't think you should tell me? All along I've been thinking Wayne is guilty, and have been asking questions about him and avoiding him…"

"And you didn't think to tell me? No, never mind. But wouldn't you avoid him anyway?"

"That's beside the point. And I can hardly avoid him when he tries to hit me with his car. And when he's smashing bowls at The Thrifty Means!"

Evan reached up and pulled her down beside him again. Eleanor glanced over at the barn, and did not see her children. Whatever they were doing, they were quite at home at Garland.

"I didn't say Wayne is innocent. He's too close to the fire not to get his nose singed."

"I wouldn't use the metaphor, considering he almost was burned to death."

"And here I guessed you'd like it, being a writer and all. I never have metaphors in the *EZ Guides*, you know. History is complicated enough without them."

"This mystery is also complicated enough without them," Eleanor grumbled. "So far we have Wayne, who looks guilty of something, and probably is. And we have Lilianna, who's crazy as a loon. That's a simile, by the way."

"I'd call it a cliché. We writers try to avoid those, you know."

"I'm not writing right now, in case you hadn't noticed."

Evan put his arms around her and settled her against his chest. Eleanor closed her eyes as his breath blew against her damp hair. She couldn't remember the first time she was so much at peace. And she certainly didn't imagine she could ever feel at peace while discussing a murder and the probable theft of property. And, yes, while her children were learning to drive.

But Evan had such an effect on her.

"It isn't Margaret. For all her faults, she has no motive, does she? She has money enough. If Wayne is her relative, she could be giving him odd jobs, and even helping him with his expenses. She's a volunteer at The Thrifty Means, just like the rest of us, so couldn't get a percentage of anything sold through the shop. In fact, she actively appeals to her friends, particularly her elderly friends, to remember The Thrifty Means when they...when they..."

"Move on to greener pastures?" Evan asked helpfully. He started to kiss her ear, which wasn't helpful at all.

Eleanor sighed and gave herself up to his caress. Her eyes were open, though, and she looked out towards the acres and acres of meadow, lawn, and wetlands still a part of Garland, one of the great Eastfield estates left from the old days. She now knew Evan well enough to appreciate he would never break this up and certainly never hand the land over to developers so sixty modern colonial style homes could appear on the property. Though he stayed away for so long, he had reasons for doing so. And his history and that of Garland was still was a treasured part of Eastfield.

"Margaret isn't guilty," she repeated. "She has no motive."

Evan was a good deal more interested in the curl of her ear, and Eleanor didn't feel inclined to divert his attention. He must have heard her, for after a while he said, "You told me she wasn't innocent."

When? Why?

"Oh yes," she remembered. In fact, what she had to say on the subject was not likely to divert him, but encourage this interlude of summer lovemaking.

"She accused me of not trying hard enough to get the good stuff from you," Eleanor said.

"Babe, I'm nearly forty years old. This is as good as I'm going to get."

His laugh rumbled through the wall of his chest. "She means Victorian sideboards and depression glass. That's the good stuff. But you're on the right track. She suggested I'm not seductive enough to get her the things she wants."

"So, the estimable Maggie B. is willing to prostitute her volunteers to ensure the bottom line on the shop accounts? Damn—what a noble endeavor! Does Galen Lynch know about this? The thought would shock the bifocals right off her forehead."

"Evan, what an awful thing to say!" Eleanor's first response was rightful indignation. As his words sank in, and his lovemaking became a little more direct, she realized that was exactly was Margaret Brownlee was expecting of her. "But I think you're right."

****

"Evan?"

The soft voice intruded on his dreams, pulling him off an oar-less rowboat washing out into the green sea. He opened his eyes to gaze out on the wide lawn he mowed yesterday, and the sun slipping lower into the afternoon sky. Something tickled his nose, and he glanced down to see the top of Ellie's head just beneath his chin.

"Evan?"

He straightened very slowly so as not disturb her, and looked up at the grinning faces of her two children.

"What's up?" he asked hoarsely.

"Lewis wants to go out driving again," Leslie said, and Evan jerked forward.

"Just kidding!" she said. "We'll give you a break."

"Thanks. But I think you woke your mother."

Ellie murmured something in her sleep, and pressed closer into the crook of his shoulder. He looked up at Leslie, mildly apologetic and a little embarrassed but she just shrugged.

"You'll have to get used to it," she said matter of

factly.

He realized he would have to get used to a few things, and quickly, if he was going to become a member of the Gilmartin family. Or were they going to become members of the Zane family? Except he wasn't much of a family unless he had them, was he? He shook the cobwebs out of his brain, and finally managed to wake Ellie up.

"What's the matter?" she said as she opened her eyes. "Lewis! Leslie! What happened?"

She jumped up, ready to do battle or fight fires or whatever she imagined they needed. Yes, there were definitely a few things he'd need to get used to.

"We want to show you something," Lewis said a little impatiently.

"Good or bad?" Ellie asked quickly.

"Cute," Leslie said smugly.

Evan rose stiffly, wondering what it might be like to sleep with Ellie in a comfortable bed, and tried to imagine what her kids could have found in the barn to fit the description. Not Wayne, for sure. Could they mean the kitchen furniture from the 1940's or the railroad trains? But perhaps Margaret Brownlee managed to steal them away in the night. As the four of them walked up the graveled path into the cool shade of the barn, observed by an array of curious cats who lined the way like bridesmaids and ushers at a wedding, Evan had a premonition of what awaited them.

"This way," Lewis said, and led them to the darkest corner. There in the faint light something rustled and squeaked in a pile of rags.

"Oh, no!" Ellie cried out and sank down onto her knees. "But how adorable!"

Lewis and Leslie scrambled to sit beside her, and shot questions so quickly, Evan could scarcely keep track of them.

"How old do you think they are? How many are

there? Do they look healthy? Can we keep them all? Can we keep one?" The questions went on and on.

Evan's thoughts echoed Ellie's "Oh, no," and not in a good way. The last thing he needed at Garland was more cats. He stood over them all, praying they would take them all.

"Evan," Ellie said, holding two kittens to her neck like a furry muffler. Their eyes weren't even open yet, and their ears curled close to their heads. Okay, they really were kind of cute. "You've got to do something about this."

What was she talking about?

"Do you mean bring them into the house?" he asked. "Should I go down to the Market to pick up some food for them?"

She squinted up at him in disbelief.

"Well? What do they need?"

Ellie stood up and handed him one of the kittens. The little thing fit in the palm of his hand, and purred happily. The little guy wanted for nothing.

"They only need their mother," she said, and her eyes darted to her own children. "But Evan, you're going to have to do something about this cat colony. Within a year, each of these babies will reproduce and you'll have cats all over the place, and the coyotes will have a feast. You'll have to do something."

"They're not my cats!" he protested in a low voice, so to not wake the little guy in his palm. Maybe he'd keep just this one. "I don't know whose they are."

Ellie moved closer, so the two kittens they held were side by side. "I don't know whose they were, but I know whose they are now. When they're older, they'll have to be spayed and neutered."

Evan shuddered. "Poor little guy," he said, and held him up, trying to see what equipment he was wearing.

"They are adorable. But you don't want this to get out of hand."

Evan looked down at the kittens, and at Ellie's stern face, and at the two teenagers on the barn floor, telling the mother cat what a good girl she was. He remembered his dream of the rowboat and realized he was indeed heading out to sea without an oar, but what an adventure was in store.

"We'll do whatever you think we should," he said, knowing he was well on his way to giving up his freedom. So be it.

Ellie looked at him in the dim light, and he knew she knew what he was thinking. How could she not? This was Eastfield, where everyone heard you were thinking before you reached a conclusion.

"Well, let's leave them for now. Leslie? Lewis? They're not going anywhere for a while, if their mother has anything to say. We should give her back her babies so she can enjoy them while she can." Ellie took Evan's kitten and settled the two babies next to their drowsy mother. Leslie and Lewis delivered theirs as well. The four of them stood there, admiring the litter, and grinning like fools.

"Mom, can I drive home?" Lewis asked, and the moment was broken.

"I suppose so," Ellie said dreamily, and Evan wondered if she was truly awake.

"Great! Can I have the car keys? Evan, can I drive the car around in the driveway? I'm allowed without my license. It's private property…"

"Just don't roll the car into the river. I'm not sure how I would explain the accident to the Rivershed and I'm in enough trouble already," Evan interrupted.

"That's not fair! Why does he get to drive twice in a day?" Leslie protested.

Eleanor grabbed Evan's arm and pulled him out

of the barn ahead of her children. Behind them, the argument escalated.

"Welcome to my life," she said, smiling. She reached into her pocket and wiggled until the car keys came out. Then with a gesture so easy, Evan imagined he most certainly was still dreaming, she tossed them over her shoulder.

The kids fought over who had possession.

"You might as well tell me right now if you don't want this to go any further," Ellie said. "Because things are not going to get any better. Fighting, demands, constant interruptions, you name it."

"To which I can only add murder, mayhem, and millions of cats. I guess every family has ups and downs."

Lewis ran past them, having somehow gotten the keys, and stopped at the hood of the car while he fidgeted with the remote controls. The headlights blinked, went off, and the horn beeped.

"I guess he didn't realize I leave the car unlocked around here."

"You idiot," Leslie yelled behind them. "It was unlocked!"

Ellie turned around, but Evan held her back by reaching for her arm.

"If you're patient with him, he'll be patient with you. You've both got a lot to learn," he said to Leslie.

Her glee turned almost immediately to contriteness, and she nodded. As she walked around them and headed down the hill, Ellie sighed.

"Are you outlining the *EZ Guide to Driving*?"

"Maybe," he said. "You see how simple it is to write these things? We can make a bundle."

"I wish everything was so easy. You see how family life is, Evan," she said.

"It's as nutty as everything else. Think of some of the products of Eastfield's families. Hamilton Hamilton. Lucille Armitage. Wayne Durant."

They walked down the slope of the hill, opting to remain on the far side of the stone wall from the driveway, where Lewis was already maneuvering the car around at an excruciatingly slow pace.

"Evan?" Ellie asked, her voice drifting off. He wondered what she saw he did not.

"Ellie?" he countered, and she gave him an unreadable look.

"Who are Wayne's parents?" she asked.

****

Eleanor stood at the front desk of The Thrifty Means, working her monthly shift at the checkout. For all they endeavored to bring the shop into the twenty first century, there was no cash register, no printed sales receipts, no scanner. Instead, the front desk operated a bit like a tag sale, the bill added up with a calculator or in one's head, and customers using the desk as their last opportunity to strike a bargain before paying for what they wanted. Bargaining was discouraged at The Thrifty Means, but some of the volunteers who opted to do all the addition on a piece of scrap paper inadvertently granted one. The simple cash box often had more or less money than was reported on the sales log, but the bookkeeper took it all in stride.

They were all volunteers, after all. From Margaret Brownlee and the deference afforded her due to her seniority, to the newcomers, who were warmly welcomed and treated gently.

Eleanor's partner at the front desk called in sick not an hour before they were scheduled to begin their shift together. Usually Eleanor didn't mind working by herself, for there were always other women to help in case of an emergency.

However, as customers piled their finds around her, asking that she look after them until they finished shopping, and by the tenth time she recited the business hours to a telephone caller, she longed for a respite. Though she smiled and obliged each customer, she continually looked to the office door, where Mrs. Brownlee had holed up since Eleanor walked into the shop.

After their well-publicized spat the other day, she could hardly expect a warm welcome from the woman. Though Eleanor did not intend to apologize, she did intend to be cordial. After all, they would be likely to work together for at least another ten years. For all the recent losses in Eastfield, the most stubborn of the Connecticut Yankees managed to live well into their nineties, and she guessed Mrs. B. would remain on duty until the last day of her life. If she proved really stubborn, she might go on even longer...

She was being darn stubborn right now. Eleanor appreciated the only reason the woman stayed in the back room was to avoid her, and she surely must have run out of things to do by now. She must be straining to get out of there, probably having her eye at the keyhole, waiting for Eleanor to go home. Or hand in her resignation.

Eleanor was well and truly stuck. Customers kept coming and the piles of merchandise continued to grow on the front desk.

"Do you need a break?" Liza Silver asked, as she delivered a pile of leather-bound books to the front window display. "The bathroom or something?"

Or something. Eleanor wanted to start a conversation with Mrs. B. about Wayne Durant, and then—oh, so casually—find out who his parents were. She wasn't sure it had anything to do with what was going on in the shop or at Garland, but she was curious. Evan was no help, as he had only vague guesses and small scraps of information he gathered through the years. Wayne's parents had died, though no one confessed to know how or when, and somehow he came to live with the Brownlees, and raised with their own kids. When Evan went off to college, and Wayne did not, Lilianna decided to take some responsibility as well, and he joined her at Garland.

How and why Dorothea agreed to have him leech on her kindness was just another mystery.

"I'm okay," Eleanor answered. "Maybe a little later, when I start to lose my patience with customers, or something." Or when Margaret finally comes out of her prison, so I can corner her in the pottery department.

Liza fingered some of the treasures adorning the desk. "I don't know how you do this. I don't know how any of us keep our patience."

She looked out the open door towards the parking lot and said something rude under her breath.

Eleanor echoed something of her sentiments. A small pickup truck, piled high with black garbage bags, pulled into the nearest parking spot.

The Thrifty Means depended on donations, requesting them and graciously thanking the community for them. Receiving items stuffed into garbage bags was a little like eating mystery meat. The things could be great, rare, and wonderful, or everything could just smell bad and go directly into the dumpster. Even when donations looked like they came off the floor of someone's garage, contributors were greeted with a smile and a blank receipt for tax purposes. Eleanor signed her name to one as other volunteers came forward to help unload the truck.

"I'm staying right here," Liza said. "I'm too tired and too hot to do anything more strenuous than stand here and talk to you."

"Well, that could get very strenuous, I'll have you know. Look what happened to Wayne Durant the other day. I had him so unnerved with my pithy comments he shattered china."

"You wouldn't have to be overly pithy to unnerve an idiot," Liza said, "though sometimes I feel a little sorry for him."

Eleanor looked at her friend, wondering if people besides Margaret Brownlee knew anything about Wayne. Though people preferred to ignore him, and she doubted he had any friends, surely someone remembered the circumstances bringing him to Eastfield in the first place.

"Do you mean, because he's homeless?" Eleanor said casually.

Liza laughed. "Yeah, I can understand why you and Evan Zane don't want him at Garland, looking in the windows and helping himself from your refrigerator."

"Liza, I'm not..."

"I know," Liza said, still grinning. "But who knows what the future will bring? And I assume you don't want to bring him back."

"You know it." Eleanor put her signature to a few of the tax receipts, before attempting to bring the conversation around to what she wanted to know. "But that's why you feel sorry for him."

"Oh, I suppose. But he's so odd; a part of Eastfield, and yet somehow never a part of what's going on."

"Yes, I know what you mean. I guess he wasn't born here, but he's been around forever."

"He once told me he was born in New York," Liza said, and helped someone with a bulky package get through the door.

"You spoke to him about his background?" Eleanor asked, a little louder than she intended.

Liza narrowed her eyes. "It's not like some deep, dark secret. I mean, I was born in Massachusetts. You're beginning to sound like the old-timers, distrusting anyone who wasn't lucky enough to be born in Norwell Hospital."

"No, you misunderstand me," Eleanor said, carefully backtracking. "I am just surprised his background came up in conversation. Did he...does he remember his parents?"

Liza took so long to answer, Eleanor wondered if she heard her. Meanwhile, the last of the bags arrived in the sorting area, and the donor looked uncommonly satisfied. The women of The Thrifty Means believed the more cheerful the donor, the more worthless the stuff.

"Liza? Did he..."

"I hear you," Liza said, a little impatiently. "But I'm just thinking. Isn't Lilianna Durant his mother?"

"Lilianna?" Eleanor said wonderingly. "But he grew up here in town before she ever came here."

Liza put her hands flat on the counter and pushed down, so she was poised a little above Eleanor's height. "What's that got to do with anything? They have the same last name."

"So do two famous historians, Will and Ariel Durant. So what?"

Liza lowered herself. "And really, he looks just like her."

Eleanor was ready again with a retort of "So what?" but the words died on her lips. So what, indeed.

But wouldn't Evan know if Wayne was Lilianna's son?

"Excuse me?" someone said, and Eleanor returned to the present. The happy donor, her pickup now empty, and the good women of The Thrifty Means having saved her the trouble of unloading the car herself, stood at the counter with her palm open and waiting. "May I have a tax receipt?"

"Of course, and thank you," Eleanor said automatically. "You may list everything you brought in, here in this column. I hope you remember what was in those bags!"

"Oh, I've donated things before, so I know the routine," the woman said. "Look what I do to keep track of everything."

She reached into her large tote bag and pulled out page after page of photographs. Eleanor glanced at them and noticed coats, shoes, and a couple of wedding gowns.

"You take pictures of everything?"

"Yeah, just to keep a record. Everything is on digital, but I print out a copy for our taxes."

"How clever," Eleanor said, truly impressed. The woman took the receipt, and reached for the stapler on the desk, to put everything together. With a satisfied wave, she walked out the door.

"Isn't she clever?" Eleanor asked Liza.

Liza was more cynical. "Clever or obsessive, I'm not sure which."

"But I never heard of anyone doing such a thing before."

Liza shrugged her shoulders. "Mrs. B. does."

Eleanor blinked as she mulled over the words. Surely, she did not hear them correctly.

"Mrs. B. takes pictures of everything coming through the shop?" she asked incredulously.

"Well, she'd never have a digital camera, so she uses an old Polaroid someone donated about twenty years ago. I don't know where she still gets the film, unless someone donated that also. While it's a little nutty, her behavior is not so obsessive. She only keeps a file of the very good things, and their provenance."

"Where they were made?"

"No, I mean, who owned them. Like the chess set we had a few weeks ago? That was Wayne Durant's."

"That was...no, never mind. How do you know about this book?" Eleanor asked.

"She leaves it lying around on her desk sometimes. A brown leather book, smaller than a ledger, but the pages have lines and columns. Everyone's seen it."

I haven't. Eleanor felt a little stupid.

"Well, I'm glad you told me, she said instead. "I mean, if she's ever out of the shop and we have to look up something."

"You're right. Just in case we have to look up who donated a kitchen table in 1952, and how much The Thrifty Means charged."

Eleanor smiled, but the gesture was entirely automatic. "Well," she said. "You never know."

"No, you don't," Lisa said.

A customer stepped up to the desk with eleven goblets—most sets of glasses brought into The Thrifty Means came with an uneven number of pieces—and Lisa looked relieved for the diversion. She joined Eleanor in wrapping the goblets in old newspaper, and finding a box to set them all in. The customer asked for their advice about putting the old crystal in her dishwasher, and then couldn't find her checkbook to pay. She kept them so busy, thieves could have made off with a sofa, right out the door, in front of them.

All that managed to get past them was Margaret Brownlee.

"Good bye girls," she said brusquely, pushing past the customer, and marching out the front door. "I have important matters to take care of and will be out for the rest of the afternoon. Remember to lock up when you leave."

"Like we ever forget," Liza said, shaking her head. "I wonder where she's running off to. You'd think someone was dying, or something."

Maybe someone was dying...or something.

Eleanor said nothing. Instead, she observed Margaret walk across the parking lot, wearing an old-fashioned sheath dress that must have fit well ten or fifteen years ago. Now, the linen creation was a bit snug and certainly too short. Margaret was holding nothing but her keys, and probably kept her purse in her car.

Certainly, she didn't pack away anything else on her person, and definitely not a book of photos and records.

"If you don't mind, I'm going to leave soon as well. It's a gorgeous day, and my mother would like me to stop over to help her with the tomatoes," Liza said.

Eleanor realized she still had her seedling beds on her patio, and hadn't checked them in days. This was Evan's doing. And the children's, who wanted to spend every waking hour driving around, making U-turns, and practicing turning on the hazard lights. Just in case.

After all, they might have to drive to the Market to buy produce, because it didn't look like they would be growing any this summer.

"No, I don't mind. I'll be fine here," Eleanor said.

And she was for the rest of the afternoon. When the last customer finally left, Eleanor locked the front door and counted out her cash box. For all the donations and browsers, this had been a quiet afternoon. Everything was quiet now. Eleanor listened to the steady clicking of a few clock pendulums, and a phone ringing in the shop next door.

Her footsteps, as she walked to the back office, were loud enough to wake whatever might be sleeping in locked trunks and unopened bags. Eleanor pressed against the door, which creaked open to reveal the usual disarray of papers and curiosities and yellowing newspapers. Though the large roll top desk surely once had a key, it was long gone. The volunteers often came back here to find staples, and paper clips and other office supplies in the large drawer on the left. Therefore, Eleanor opened the drawer on the right, and lifted out the leather-bound book she sought.

As she thumbed through the pages, she realized she had seen the book lying about, but never bothered to ask what records were kept within. The contents were exactly what Liza described—pages and pages of grainy photos accompanied by lines of descriptive text and date. The volume looked like a high school yearbook for antiques.

Eleanor placed it in her tote bag, turned out the lights, and left the shop. Having spent the greater part of the afternoon anticipating this moment, she had a plan already in place. Although she was sure she was being far more cautious than necessary, she drove up Norwell Road to Rosemont, three towns and forty five minutes away. Along Main Street, she found a large office supply and business center, and brought in Mrs. B.'s book.

Perhaps she was as obsessive as Margaret was, but she would not take chances in a town where everyone knew everyone's business. In Rosemont, she recognized no one, they did not ask what she was doing, and no one cared she was making a copy of someone's private journal.

Chapter 13

"Rustic is a look. Not a smell."
Gail Madison, volunteer since 1996

Eleanor looked up from her laptop and mentally reviewed the prospect for the next chapter of her book. Frances Trollope, her nineteenth century adventuress, was bankrupt and in debt, and about to return to England with nothing more than a journal remarking on her several disastrous years of life in America. And like many women of Eleanor's personal acquaintance, she was about to reinvent herself in whole new guise, abandoning her career as a tradeswoman, and picking up her pen to stake her reputation as a writer.

"Don't worry. I'm sure they're fine. Didn't they say they were going to a barbecue?" Evan asked, his eyes still focused on his own laptop.

Having him around, nearly all the time, was reason enough for Eleanor to reinvent herself. She started where Frances Trollope left off, taking up the business of history and writing about it. Now another writer joined her for the long hot summer afternoons, breaking into her solitude, sharing her space, but encouraging her to keep on task, and Eleanor believed she was way ahead of the Victorian entrepreneur.

"They're going over to the Roberts' house, and told me they'll just walk home. But I wasn't thinking about the kids. I'm thinking about my next chapter. Mrs. Trollope returns to the family home in England, and finds everything in disrepair, including the family finances."

"You're back in England already?" Evan asked, still looking down at his screen. "You wrote a lot today."

"Twenty pages or so. Not bad. I'm still two months away from deadline on the book."

"Well, you did a hell of a lot better than I did."

She looked at him in surprise. His dark lashes cast a shadow across his cheekbone and made him look very young. "Do you need my help?" She felt a little guilty. After all, he asked her to read aloud to him, but they always managed to get distracted when she did so. She never imagined reading old shopping lists could be so sexy.

He straightened his back and grinned at her. "I think I've already deciphered the important stuff. I've been checking my emails."

Eleanor clicked "save" and lowered the cover of her small, efficient machine. "I believe the first rule of writing is to not be distracted by anything. Didn't they teach you Lesson One at the Hack Writers' School?"

"I was their worst student. But if they did, I must have been dosing off that day. Or checking out the legs of the cute woman across the room." He checked out her bare, tanned legs, and Eleanor was glad she took the time to get a pedicure this morning. "Anyway, if I didn't want to be distracted, I wouldn't spend my afternoon sitting three feet away from you."

Evan leaned over and ran a cool finger under the arch of her knee. "Case in point: I've wanted to tickle you for hours."

"Then, my dear, you should have just tickled me, and not waste your whole afternoon thinking about it." Eleanor tried to sound very proper, but with Evan, a stiff manner was almost impossible. She giggled, and not just because she was ticklish.

Evan teased her for a few more minutes, and then returned to his keyboard. He looked intently at one email message, and was distracted when he spoke. "Oh, I didn't waste my afternoon. I learned lots of things. Did you know some people sleep in their clothes to save time in getting dressed in the morning?"

"Fascinating. And they must look great in their wrinkled shirts and twisted socks," Eleanor answered, wondering what really riveted his interest.

"Boy, you're hard to impress. What if I were to tell you I've apparently won the Nigerian state lottery? They want to transfer a few zillion dollars to my Visa Card account."

"A few zillion?"

Evan gestured to his laptop. "I think that's what the guy says. I just have to give him my account number, so he can transfer the money. Sounds reasonable enough. What do you think?"

"I think you were just looking for a way to get out of writing your book. Although now I think you're trying to get out of telling me something. Is it about Wayne, or Margaret?"

Evan frowned. "I'm not quite sure. I just opened an email from Mitch Ellison, who graduated a year ahead of us. Do you remember him?"

Eleanor not only remembered him, but also dated him briefly, when they were to be the only two divorced people of a certain age in Eastfield. They met at barbecues, dinner parties, holiday services, town meetings. However, Mitch didn't share her politics, which was as lethal to a relationship as chronic bad breath.

She now realized she never asked Evan for whom he voted in the last presidential election, and then considered she could deal with his answer, whatever he said.

"Mitch Ellison?" he repeated, a trifle impatiently.

"I remember him. How's he doing?" she asked casually.

"Better than his grandmother, I guess. She died last night. He's coming down for the funeral tomorrow and wants to know if I can put him up here at Garland. Muriel died in the old house, and he can't stay there."

"Is he afraid of her ghost? Tell him not to worry; she looked pretty frail the last time she came into town." Eleanor conjured up a picture of the cheerful old lady, who rarely appeared without her two aged beagles. Yet, just now, the picture didn't include the dogs. "Didn't you meet at the Historical Society ball? She was sitting at Margaret's table. I think I introduced you."

"How many elderly ladies did I meet that night? It was bad enough all of them remembered when I was a baby—but some of them even remembered when my father was a baby."

Eleanor laughed. "Well, Muriel was over ninety. For all we know, she may remember when Lincoln was born."

Evan shrugged his shoulders. "Mitch says she was a hundred and two."

"I hope when I'm her age, I'll have the strength to stay out late. But she wasn't very strong, so I think Mitch could protect himself from her ghost."

"He could, but he has another problem." Evan's voice trailed off as he leaned closer to the screen, and then gave up and pulled a pair of glasses from his shirt pocket. "The house is a crime scene, and is closed off. Mitch won't even be able to get through the door."

"A crime scene." Eleanor said the bitter words slowly. She had only heard these words spoken on television. "A crime scene. Was there a robbery? Was

Muriel murdered?"

Evan looked up from the keyboard, but she couldn't see his eyes as his glasses reflected the shadows of the porch.

"Mitch doesn't know. The police aren't telling him anything. He only knows something was suspicious."

"Do they know where Wayne was?" Eleanor asked quickly.

"Do they know where Margaret Brownlee was yesterday?" he countered.

"She was at the shop, of course," Eleanor said quickly. "As she is every day."

"All day?"

"Of course," she said instinctively, and the stopped herself cold. "No. She left the shop in a big hurry mid-afternoon, not stopping to talk. She said she had to go see someone."

Evan rocked back and forth on two legs of his chair, his mouth tightly closed. He hadn't trusted Margaret from the start, and Eleanor had tried to dissuade him from a theory that was truly preposterous. Now she wasn't quite sure and was coming to believe nothing was preposterous, no matter how unlikely.

"Did anyone else see her leave?" Evan asked.

"I was with Liza. And there was a customer with us at the time. But Margaret might have been going anywhere. She didn't make it clear whether she was off to the Market or the library, or to kill an old lady."

Evan didn't smile, and she realized he was thinking about Dorothea. She'd also been thinking about Dorothea lately: how a woman who hated cats somehow had cats all over her property, how things rightfully belonging to Evan turned up at the Hamilton house and at The Thrifty Means, but mostly how a woman who lived for many years in

Eastfield could die with scarcely a regret from anyone. Her nephew, remembering years of indifference, didn't mourn her. The man to whom she gave a home and means of support spoke of her with derision. Her closest companion, the woman with whom she risked censure from the community, didn't speak of her at all. Dorothea had no children. She had almost nothing of her own, but a few reviews from her days on the stage, and miscellaneous mentions on official records.

"Evan, I have a book," Eleanor said. She nearly forgot about it, though she read the pages over twice when she brought home the pages she reproduced last night. On her way back from Rosemont, she stopped off at the shop and replaced the original in the drawer where Margaret had left it. Though she feared Margaret would come back to the shop, she now suspected the woman was preoccupied with other things.

Eleanor was preoccupied, as well. When she arrived a few hours ago, Evan was already at work—or so she guessed—on his laptop—and greeted her with a gesture to sit down at the table. His was not exactly the welcome one would hope to receive from a lover, but his manner was so companionable, so familiar, Eleanor took heart. She completely forgot about the book.

"I know you do," he said. "You've been plugging away all afternoon, while I've been playing solitaire and checking emails. I've been watching you."

There was something in the way he spoke that made her want to forget about the book, her aunt, and poor Muriel Ellison. She tried to ignore her immediate response to him.

"It's a book Margaret Brownlee keeps, recording transactions and sources of merchandise. I didn't even know the thing existed until yesterday. But I copied the whole thing up in Rosemont, and replaced the original back in the shop." She pushed aside her studious papers on Frances Trollope, and found a manila envelope, thick with records. "I think I found some of the things you've been wondering about."

"Like my hiking boots? No, you don't have to look at me like that. I know you're serious."

"You'd better believe it." She fingered a page she had already marked with notepaper. "Here's your grandfather's grandfather clock. And don't bother to correct me; I couldn't resist playing with the words. Though I don't remember seeing the clock before the night of the ball, it seems to have come to The Thrifty Means about five years ago, and sold almost immediately to Ham Hamilton. I don't know if anyone took a cut, but The Thrifty Means made about $1500 on the sale. You realize, of course, that's an extraordinary amount of money for us, though a good buy for the Hamilton's. I would have priced the piece for over twenty, even five years ago."

"How do we know the clock is the same?" Evan sounded aloof, even indifferent.

"I have the picture. Mrs. B. is very scrupulous about everything, you know." He only glanced at the photo as she turned it towards him.

"Apparently not so scrupulous at all. We're looking at my clock."

"You're sure?" Eleanor sounded more doubtful than she really was, because she had to wonder how such a piece could have come through The Thrifty Means without her knowing.

Evan finally smiled. "Do you think there could be two of them?"

Eleanor pulled the printout back onto her lap and studied the fine lines of the plain clock. "And it sold five years ago, which seems to be a significant time."

Evan just nodded, and looked more interested in whatever was coming up on his laptop screen.

Eleanor felt a spurt of indignation, of frustration since they were somehow so close to a conclusion and Evan didn't seem to care at all. She guessed it wasn't true. She had daily evidence he cared, and deeply, about a good many things and had a generous nature. Why would the loss of his family's legacy not seem to bother him at all?

He already lost so much.

The answer came to her now, as if the answer hadn't been obvious all this time. What would a clock or a chess set matter to someone who was orphaned at sixteen, and turned out of his own home? Why would someone like Evan remain unattached, unless he feared losing everything all over again? Yet here she was, close enough to try to understand him, and loving him enough to spend the rest of her life reassuring him she would not leave. The realization was a little frightening.

"What are you thinking about?" he asked, roughly, still looking at the screen.

She had no intention of telling him. Not yet, at least.

"I'm just thinking about five years ago, when the kids were eleven," she easily lied. "I was already volunteering at The Thrifty Means and...oh!"

"Did you just remember lugging the clock out to someone's truck?"

"No...but I just remembered something I was reading aloud to you weeks ago. Do you recall I asked if Dorothea did weaving? Or sewed clothing?"

"I think so," he said, but she realized he really had no idea what she meant.

"In the household record, one of the ones you gave me. Dorothea noted a long cloak sold for $8000, to M. That's an extraordinary price for something long and wooly, unless Mary Todd Lincoln wore it. Now I think the notation may not have been for a cloak at all but was a clock. And M might be

Margaret. Everything now makes perfect sense. I just couldn't read the writing."

"But my aunt had beautiful handwriting. Her script was like the model you'd see posted in a classroom." Evan sounded a little defensive, making Eleanor think he might have feelings for Dorothea, after all.

"The handwriting changed at that point, as if the writer developed arthritis. Maybe the bookkeeping was taken over by someone else."

Now she had his attention.

"No, we're wrong," he said, shaking his head. "I have other things she wrote down, much more recently, and they're definitely in her old, reliable, picture-perfect handwriting. She wouldn't let someone else handle her books."

"What if she didn't have a choice? Or what if she just abandoned the project and someone else picked it up?" Eleanor checked Margaret's file again. If Dorothea's handwriting was excellent, Mrs. B's was quite at the opposite end of the spectrum. Eleanor squinted at the tiny scribbles on the page. "I'm not sure I can read this."

"Then we're both in trouble," Evan said.

"Maybe not. The word looks like 'Ilya.' Is that your uncle's name?"

"My uncle?" He abandoned the screen and looked at her in amazement.

"Didn't you tell me Dorothea was your father's brother's wife? Isn't Ilya a man's name?"

"It is, but my uncle's name was Peter." Evan swallowed, as if a pill became stuck in his throat. "Ilya is Lilianna; Dorothea called her by that nickname. In turn, Lilianna called her Theo. I don't think I have to go into details?"

"No, of course not." Eleanor said. "I understand."

"Which is more than I can say. What does Margaret Brownlee have to say about dear Ilya?"

"She's listed as the seller of various items. We don't usually take merchandise on consignment at the shop, but occasionally make exceptions for particularly valuable or rare pieces,"

"That weren't hers to sell. But there's nothing new, except The Thrifty Means made some money off the sale. I'm glad someone profited from the sale of my property, because I didn't." He slapped down the cover of his laptop, and she realized here was something new. He was always so calm when she was agitated. Reasonable when she vented her doubts. Cheerful when she was inclined to be moody. Now he was genuinely angry, and it was a glorious thing to see.

"You can get everything back, Evan. You'll soon have the clock, and here are the records of the rest. We can track it all down, through the past five years. Five years is not so long a time, especially not in Eastfield." Eleanor paused, quite at the end of her logic. "But why five years? What happened then that changed everything?"

"I was still supporting everyone here at Garland. Nothing changed."

"How do you know?" Eleanor asked, quietly. "I mean, you were hardly ever here. What do you know of their life style? After all, you believed Dorothea hated cats, and yet they're all over the place." She paused to pluck a white kitten off the wicker table. "How do you know they didn't need money? For drugs or gambling debts or blackmail?"

Evan sucked in his breath. "Wow. You have a vivid imagination, lady."

"I'm a writer," she said tartly. "It's what we do."

"Blackmail? Drinking? I wouldn't think those things would come up in your line of work."

"You'd be surprised. The old ladies of the republic were not as virtuous as textbooks lead us to believe. Remember that when you're writing your

EZ Guides. Things were often more complicated than they seem. Hawthorne made the point in *The Scarlet Letter,* didn't he?"

"Do you mean even Puritan ministers had illegitimate children? So what do you think? Should we just look around town to see who's wearing the letter 'A' on her chest? Or just check for illegitimate children? We may come up with quite a list." Evan pushed back from the table, nearly catching Sally's tail. He patted her head reassuringly, and Sally stared into his eyes, mesmerized. The dog would be very happy at Garland. They all would.

"Why don't we start with Wayne?" Eleanor said.

"I'd rather finish with Wayne," Evan answered. "But he can't be Dorothea's love child. How could she have pawned him off on the Brownlees? And who would have taken him unless they had to?"

"Lilianna and Dorothea took him in."

"Not in, really." He waved in the direction of the burned cottage. "They took him on, rather. Bad enough as it is."

"Maybe he was drinking too much? Maybe he was ill?"

"He was always drinking too much," Evan said, shaking his head. Then he froze. "I was ill. I was in the hospital at the time, when Dorothea bothered enough to visit. When she rambled on about getting signatures and selling Garland."

Eleanor struggled to remember what he already said on the subject, and could only recall he was dismissive about the surgery. Perhaps to Dorothea, someone so aloof from the modern world, any surgery would carry enormous risks.

"If something happened to you, if you died, who would inherit Garland?"

"I have no family. Dorothea doesn't really count. Right now everything goes to the Eastfield Conservancy, as long as Dorothea could live out her life here."

He stuffed his hands in the pockets of his khakis, and his tee shirt stretched across his back. He looked tense and uncompromising; not at all like the man she was coming to know very well.

As Eleanor reached out and touched his shoulder, gently massaging the tight muscles, she said, "I've never seen you so frustrated about anything before."

He straightened, but didn't pull away. Glancing over his shoulder, he caught her concerned look and smiled.

"Then you didn't know me well enough in high school, when all I wanted was to kiss you behind the lockers." They were at an impasse in understanding the drama playing out around them, but otherwise in perfect, splendid accord.

"Why don't you try my lips, instead?" she asked, and he did.

****

The next day, they waited together at the Eastfield Station for Mitch Ellison's train. The heat radiated off the metal rails, and the humidity was oppressive. The threat of thunderstorms had been forecast for nearly every afternoon for a week, but had yet to materialize. Instead, the air was pregnant with the storm, weighing them all down.

Eleanor turned her head sharply, alert for sounds of change. Her hair was damp and curling around a silver barrette, and if Evan weren't so damned hot, he would have liked to tickle her on the back of her bare neck. Instead, they stood side by side, unable to touch, or talk very much. Speaking required too much effort.

"The sound is coming from the lumberyard. I think they're off-loading some logs," he said.

"Oh, I thought it was thunder," she said, and glanced up at the sky.

Sharon Sobel

Evan studied the line of her jaw, and noticed a
little smudge of ink under her chin. She wore dangly
pearl earrings instead of her usual gold studs and
her silky tank top revealed a little more cleavage
than was usual for her. She had denied any
particular relationship with Mitch, but the guy had
been single for a few years, and lived in town after
his divorce.

"The thunder will wait," Evan said as if he
knew. But the only thing he knew was he didn't
want Eleanor greeting Mitch while she wore a rain-
soaked, revealing tank top. "The storm will hit when
we're standing out in Belvedere Cemetery, with no
shelter but the old oak trees."

"The worst place to stand in a thunder storm,"
she said. "Unless you're knee deep in the reservoir."

"Has anyone ever been struck by lightning in
this town?" he asked.

She turned to face him. "I guess you never heard
about Lenny Parker. He stayed out on the golf
course, telling his buddies they were chicken
because they ran off at the first sound of thunder.
Chicken they were, but they weren't crazy."

"What an idiot. I guess we can't blame Wayne
Durant for one murder."

"No we can't. Especially since Lenny is still
alive." She reached into the straw bag containing
more stuff than he took for a week's journey, and
pulled out a washcloth. She dabbed the pink square
over her eyelids, her forehead, her cheeks. "When is
the train due?"

"In three minutes." In the still, heavy air, the
warning bells echoed at a grade crossing. "Where is
he?"

"On the train, I hope. I can't take this much
longer."

"I mean, Lenny Parker."

"He waits tables at Ludlum's. You've probably

292

seen him: tall, bald, a little strange."

"Sounds like he's right at home in Eastfield," Evan said tersely.

Eleanor stopped dabbing at her collarbone. "Well, so are we, aren't we?" she said cheerfully.

He would have liked to come up with some rejoinder, something clever, and even superior. He guessed he appeared to be as strange as anyone else was, and his neighbors probably spoke about him when they gathered around picnic tables and over poker games. Besides, the Metro North train was already in sight, sending birds out of leafy trees and fields alongside the track.

"There he is," Eleanor said, recognizing Mitch before Evan did. Only a handful of people alighted from the train. Otherwise, he was not sure he would have recognized this tall, distinguished man in his fine tailored suit. He glanced at Eleanor and wished she wasn't so damned happy to see the new arrival.

"Mitch!" she called, and started to walk towards him.

"Ellie! I understood Evan was supposed to be here. Does he have...Evan, there you are!"

"A little formal for the farm, aren't you?" Evan asked by way of greeting, and out of the corner of his eye, watched Eleanor scowl. He shook Mitch's hand.

"I'm coming straight from the office and didn't have time to change. Anyway, I'm planning to wear the suit to the funeral. If that's still acceptable up here? I forgot my overalls."

Eleanor laughed, and he hugged her, suitcase and all.

"How long can you stay?" she asked.

"As long as I'm needed. My cousins and my brother are pretty far away, and my father isn't well. My mother doesn't want to leave him, and of course, my grandmother was his mother, not hers. They never got on very well, anyway. My grandmother once hoped my father would marry someone else, a girl in town, and she never let my mother forget it."

"Yeah, you can never trust anyone from out of town. If someone from Rosemont showed up at a party, the scene might be the Capulets and Montagues all over again." Evan, already tiring of the reunion, started walking towards the parking lot.

"Wait up!" Eleanor said. Her sandals clicked on the concrete platform. "And yet your parents lived here in town. Did your father's old flame remain as well?"

Evan paused, just a little curious to hear Mitch's answer. "She left, but came back when my parents were married for years. She was Lilianna Durant. You know her..."

Evan picked up his pace again. Lilianna? Why would anyone want her son to marry Lilianna? Then reason reasserted itself, and he recalled photos he had seen of her, when she was young and pretty. But Lilianna, and Mitch's father?

How was everyone in Eastfield related to each other?

He turned around went he came to the car. The windows were open and the doors were unlocked. One might fear murder in the town, plots and collusions, but never simple burglary.

"Consider yourself lucky. Lilianna would have made a lousy mother." Evan stood at the driver's door while Eleanor walked around to the passenger side. Mitch threw his suitcase in, and ducked down into the back seat.

"Yeah, I know," he said. "Look at the head job she did on Wayne."

Eleanor's eyes met Evan's over the roof of the car. She made a gesture, as to smack the side of her head, but he felt as if the pile of logs from the lumberyard just offloaded on his brain. She mouthed something, but he was too distracted to read her lips. The first drops of rain started to fall on his face, and he sat down heavily in the car.

Mitch was already on to other things.

"My grandmother had a woman who checked on her every day, but she herself was in her seventies and not feeling well on Tuesday and went home early. My grandmother was still pretty active, still gardening, still crocheting ugly blankets for everyone's birthday. I'm going to miss her, but not those damned blankets. When everyone else was getting a check from their grandparents for birthdays and holidays, I was amassing a collection of things for my hope chest. What do you call that kind of thing for men?"

After a few minutes, Eleanor said, "Are you asking me?" Evan realized she was as distracted as he was, thinking through all the possibilities. "I don't know what you'd call it. A messy closet? Stuff under the bed?"

Mitch laughed as if she was the greatest wit, and not some woman whom he used to know in high school and had nothing in common with any more, and in whom he wasn't interested. As Evan looked over his shoulder to back out of the parking space, he watched Mitch's hand tug playfully at Eleanor's ponytail. He wondered if he was too late to tell him there was no room at Garland, after all.

Eleanor would probably suggest he stay at her house, which really would defeat any purpose he had in getting Mitch away from her.

"How did she die?" Evan asked bluntly.

"At the kitchen table, sitting upright in her chair. When my mother couldn't get her on the phone, she asked a neighbor to check in, Mrs. Palliser, from the bookstore. She walked over to the house and looked in. My grandmother was sitting at the table, with a cup of tea, and her cat sleeping on the rug at her feet. Mrs. Palliser didn't think anything amiss, until she went back an hour later, and nothing had changed. She called the police, and then my mother, who called me."

"I know the police have to come in when there's a death in a home, but why would they consider the kitchen a crime scene? Your grandmother was very, very old," Eleanor asked.

And who would want to kill her? She didn't have to say the words, but Evan realized what she was thinking. The same person who killed Dorothea and other elderly people in town killed her.

"There were two cups of tea on the table, her fancy Limoges stuff, and a paper on the floor under the table," Mitch said. "Mrs. Palliser believed the cat was sleeping on the paper, so my grandmother's guest might not have realized he dropped anything."

"He?" Eleanor asked quickly, and glanced at Evan. "And how do the police know it was his?"

"I don't know. I don't even know who her friends were." Evan studied Mitch in the rear view mirror and considered he looked reasonably unconcerned, perhaps only inconvenienced because he couldn't stay in the family home. Evan could hardly hold that against him, for he himself had been somewhat indifferent to Dorothea's loss. Whatever he was supposed to feel just never awoke from hibernation, making him realize any warm feelings he ever had were long dead.

"I guess I just automatically think a murderer must be a man. It's wrong of me, I suppose. And probably wrong here too; I guess a man wouldn't sit down with some Earl Gray and a chat before killing someone," Mitch continued. "But wouldn't the scene work into a good plot for a book?"

"No," replied Eleanor and Evan at the same time. He caught her smiling at her reflection in the window, and reached across the seat to cover her hand.

"No, really, I mean it," Mitch insisted. "You can have a guy who is a tea salesman, and he goes from door to door selling teas and then he…"

"Mitch, no one goes door to door anymore. No one has the time, and people don't let strangers into their houses," Eleanor said patiently.

Though she spoke nothing more than the literal truth, the implication of her words hit home even in the back seat. Mrs. Ellison would only have admitted someone she recognized, and would not have put out her Limoges for anyone who didn't matter. For her gardener, or a neighbor, or a visitor from the Nursing Association, ordinary mugs from the gas station would have served the purpose.

They rode along in silence, passing the usual sights of Eastfield: the antique shops, the roadside snack bars, the makeshift lemonade stands. Ancient trees made a leafy canopy over the river and the old road encroached a little too closely on the banks. Here and there, fishermen, half-asleep in the shade, had their lines in the water, their backs to the road. Evan envied anyone with so much time on his hands.

"That reminds me," Mitch said, and Evan jumped, nearly forgetting he was there. "I've started a book, and I wonder if either of you would look what I wrote over and tell me what you think. If you like it, we could write the book together or something."

"Or something," Evan muttered under his breath, as Eleanor said, "Of course, I'd be happy to."

"Do you have the manuscript with you?" Evan asked.

"Er, no," Mitch said, sounding off guard. "I only just started it and only have a page or two. I figure I'll email everything to you."

"Good," Evan said and meant what he said, because if Mitch had brought up a manuscript for

Evan to read, he definitely wouldn't be staying at Garland this or any night soon.

"Just send your book to me," Eleanor said sweetly, and glared at Evan. "Though there's not very much anyone can tell from a page or two."

"So what have you decided to do with your grandmother's house?" Evan said. "I know it's soon, and you may not be able to touch anything until the investigation is over, but you must have been thinking about this for a while. The market is very strong right now, particularly for houses with a lot of land."

"Well, my grandmother's house is not exactly Garland, you know. There's only about six acres, and the house is very dated."

"No one's buying the property for the house, Mitch. There's the sad part of it. Developers have every inch of Eastfield mapped out and just wait 'til the properties they want turn up on the market. Sometimes they're a little aggressive. One builder sold off an old stone wall, which wasn't even on the property he bought."

"Well, maybe you're right. We've often estimated the things inside the house were worth more than the house itself." Mitch gave a low whistle. "Look what they did with the high school! Is that a new field house?"

"What kind of things are in the house, Mitch?" Eleanor asked quietly. Mitch probably heard nothing in her inflection to give him pause, but Evan understood precisely what she was asking. His hand still covered hers, and he gently squeezed.

"Mostly a lot of old junk, but there are paintings worth something. My grandmother liked the Meirs, the family whose farm became a museum. They were impressionists, and she has a lot of their work, especially John's. In fact, I think there's a painting John Meir did of Garland."

"I think my father once told me that," Evan mused. He remembered his father's anger when an Ellison outbid him for the painting at an auction. Then again, his father was always angry about something. "If you decide to sell the painting, will you let me have first dibs?"

"Sure, if no one in the family wants it. Not sure why they would, since Garland is your house. Do you plan to hang it up in your apartment and always remember the place?"

"No, I want the painting so I can hang it in the living room at Garland, where I can always see what is mine." Evan realized he had Eleanor's full attention, and he might have come up with a more gracious way of announcing his intention to stay in Eastfield. "He painted a winter scene, as I remember. And winters in Eastfield are best appreciated from indoors, with a fire in the hearth, and a comfortable room with pictures hanging on the wall."

"Well, if that's the case, maybe I'll stay also. If the two of you are here, there probably are a few old timers like us around. Everything will be fun, like the good old days," Mitch said cheerfully.

Evan, with only one hand on the wheel, swerved onto the shoulder.

"Evan!" Eleanor yelled, pulling her hand out from beneath his, and bracing herself against the dashboard. From where she sat, the river must have been nearly beneath the side of the car.

"Sorry," he said sheepishly. "There was a squirrel on the road."

There wasn't, but no matter. If he wanted Garland, Eleanor, and her kids and Mitch's painting as part of his future, he also would need to accept her terror of the road. Or always let her drive, for when she was in control, she appeared confident and cool.

Mitch ducked down beneath Evan's line of vision, and retrieved something on the floor. "If no one wants the painting, you can have it. I'm not going to sell what's rightfully yours to you. I owe you for helping me out here."

"You'll want to reconsider your offer when you find out how much the painting's worth, my friend. You can stay at a very nice hotel instead of the spare room at Garland, and probably still have twenty thousand dollars to spare."

"I'm going to need more than a room," Mitch said. "I need help with the funeral, and whatever is going to happen with the police. I haven't been here in a while. Since..."

"Since you came back here after your divorce," Eleanor answered quickly.

Evan, out of practice with the nuances of dating and more specifically with something reminding him of high school jealousy, now understood what he was missing. They already had a relationship, and nothing came of it. If the spark of something remained, Mitch would have called Eleanor for help, not a guy he hadn't seen in years. His hands were steadier on the steering wheel as he made the wide turn off Norwell Road, towards Garland. "You remarried, didn't you?"

"I wanted to, but things didn't work out."

"Too bad," Evan said, sincerely. He stared straight ahead at the road, thinking his deep concentration would make Eleanor very happy, but instead she glared at him all the way up to the farm.
****

Hours later, tired but still humming with the events of the long day, Eleanor pulled into her driveway on Milkweed Lane. She did not intend to stay at Garland while Mitch was in the next room and just as compelling was the rare opportunity of having her home to herself. Lewis and Leslie were up at Candlewood Lake for a few days, hanging out with friends while under plenty of parental supervision. She had a reprieve from cooking, driving, laundry.

And now there was still at least a half-hour before sunset, and she wavered between taking Sally for a long walk to the quarry, or just letting her run around while she pulled weeds in the garden.

Eleanor paused on the walkway, thinking something was wrong. Nothing was obvious, certainly nothing a passing neighbor would notice from the sidewalk, but the curtains were somewhat askew and the kitchen light was on. From above, a steady, excited chirping caught her attention, and she saw a glimpse of blue between the dark green leaves of the maple tree.

"Blue?" she answered, and puckered her lips to make a strange little sound guaranteed to make True Blue a very happy little bird. From above came the rustling of wings, and the parakeet landed on the top of her head.

"What are you doing out here?" she asked, both suspicious and worried. She cupped her hands over her head and caught the bird before he could fly away again; he must have been altogether exhausted and made no protest. Awkwardly containing him in one hand and reaching for her cell phone with the other, she ran to the back of the house, where she hoped Sally was still safe in their fenced-in yard. She was, and nothing looked out of place in the garden.

While her dog ran around her in circles of joy, and her bird squirmed to get out of her hand, Eleanor called the Eastfield police.

Chapter 14

"People don't buy tee shirts that still bear the evidence of what someone else has eaten."

Gail Madison, volunteer since 1996

"What are you doing here?"

Eleanor looked up, thinking she imagined the words. In fact, what was she doing here? This was her fourth funeral in five months, and though her dark, conservative dress—her funeral outfit—was freshly dry-cleaned, the fabric was sticky and scratchy against her skin. The thunderstorms expected the day Mitch Ellison arrived from Boston still loomed, and the air was thick with threat. Inside the small, modest, un-air conditioned meetinghouse people gasped for breath. Eleanor, younger than most of the mourners, finally decided to sit down on the hard bench, and when she heard a little skirmish behind her assumed others had done the same.

"What business is this of yours? You didn't even know her," the voice repeated, and Eleanor looked over her shoulder, acknowledging her inquisitor.

"I know her family," Eleanor whispered, wondering why she even bothered to explain. Weren't funerals open to the community? Wasn't that, in fact, the point?

"Muriel Ellison was my dear, beloved friend," Margaret Brownlee said, choking on something resembling a sob. Or a laugh. Eleanor wasn't sure, which was a very fine measure of her fully developed cynicism where Mrs. B. was concerned.

"And Mitch Ellison is mine," she said. "My friend."

"You'd better not tell your boyfriend."

Eleanor sat back in her seat, steadying herself by looking at the fine lines of the nineteenth century church, but wondering if the heat had made her delusional. Three months ago, Margaret Brownlee had been her mentor, her coworker, her confidante, and her friend. They once stood shoulder to shoulder examining old china and pieces of unmatched cutlery. The Thrifty Means emerged from the Christmas season with the highest net profit in shop history, and gave away an unprecedented amount of money to its designated charities. Eleanor, with her connections at school and on sports teams, continued to bring new volunteers into the shop, and Mrs. B., grateful, continued to train them with her keen sense of organization and responsibility.

What happened?

All these dreadful funerals happened. The old timers of Eastfield were all nearing their time, and perhaps Mrs. B. feared her own mortality. Such reckonings could make her grouchy and disagreeable.

Then Evan Zane came to town and stayed, to the surprise of just about everyone. Eleanor couldn't help but smile, miserable as she was with Mrs. B. at her back and a coffin at the front. Goodness, but she loved Evan Zane. For so many years, she was fully prepared to ignore the fact of his existence, resenting his escape and his success. Unexpectedly, he returned to Eastfield, and slowly worked his way back into her system, making her as self-conscious as a high school kid, and increasingly reliant on his supporting arm. Still smiling in a manner entirely inappropriate to a solemn occasion, she leaned slightly to the left, so she could see up the aisle to where he stood with Mitch. She loved the way he looked, the way his hair fell over his forehead and the way his eyes squinted when he was amused.

He turned and noticed her right away, though the small church was packed. He mouthed a few words, making Eleanor blush, and hope no one was paying much attention.

Someone was. "What did he say to you? Is he saying something about me?" the voice behind her hissed.

Eleanor counted to ten, very slowly, and then turned in her seat.

"Margaret, dear," she began, so sweetly, her intent was clearly provocative. This edge of sarcasm, of faintly mocking humor, was Evan's influence, as well. "Shall we take this outside?"

Eleanor stood without waiting for an answer, and tried to smooth down the wrinkles in her linen skirt. The darn thing would be back at the drycleaners tomorrow, so she'd have the uniform ready for the next funeral. At the rate they were going, she might have to go out of town to locate next-day cleaners.

For now, she walked through the crowd, slightly sickened by the smell of sweat and burning wax and the anticipation of a confrontation with Mrs. B. Overdue, and overdone.

Outside the meetinghouse, there was no reprieve from the heat. Dust hung in the air, the cars racing past on Norwell Road stirring grit into eddies settling on her hair and clothes. Inside, the congregation of mourners rumbled in a familiar hymn, the sound getting a bit louder as the door opened and closed. Eleanor walked to the gate of the graveyard, fingering the rusty latch before pushing the gate open.

"I don't take orders from you, young woman," Mrs. B. began, poking her finger into Eleanor's shoulder.

"And yet here you are walking out of the funeral of your dear, beloved friend, and for no reason other than I asked you to. Why on earth would you listen to me, unless you think I have something you want?" Eleanor pushed open the creaky gate and walked into the shade of the old graveyard. Here, where some stones were so old their legends were unreadable, trees pushed their way through family plots up to a verdant canopy. She looked around for a place to sit, and settled herself comfortably on a mossy tomb, partially settled into the earth. Her hand, pressed against the granite, rested on the outline of a 7, or perhaps a Z.

Mrs. B. remained where she was, looking very superior, though her height standing was about the same as Eleanor perched on her tomb.

"You have done enough damage. I won't have you talk Mitchell Ellison out of giving Muriel's legacy to The Thrifty Means, like you did with Dorothea's."

"I had nothing to do with Evan's decision..."

"Of course you did! I had Dorothea's promise to give everything over to the shop!"

"The Thrifty Means got everything of Dorothea's, and a lot more besides!"

Margaret Brownlee brushed the comment off like a hovering gnat. "Oh, certainly. Old dresses and ashtrays and a few theatre programs. Nothing of value."

"Perhaps that's because Dorothea was a failed actress who lived off the largess of her brother-in-law, and then her nephew. She owned nothing of value." Eleanor looked down at the letters at hand, and realized she sat on the grave of a long-departed Zane. "If she promised you antiques and treasures, they weren't hers to give away."

"But her nephew had no interest in any of those things. You know that, and everyone else knows it.

He was going to bring everything to the shop and then sell Garland. He already had a plan and everyone knew it." Mrs. B. sounded so desperate; Eleanor wondered how much she had come to believe her own fantasy.

"I realize everyone in Eastfield is obligated by some sort of law to mind everyone else's business, but apparently Evan was out of town when you all came to this decision. Everyone might have known his business, but I didn't. And neither did he. If he decided to stay at Garland and sell neither the land nor the antiques, I respect his decision. None of this has anything to do with me."

Mrs. B. wavered and Eleanor feared she might faint in the heat. "You seduced him."

Eleanor stared her down, knowing this was a theme Mrs. B. had sung before. Even so, her words were no less insulting.

"I'm the middle-aged mother of two children. I haven't been on a date in years. My daughter trims my hair. My clothes are covered in dog and cat fur which may disguise the fact they're a few years out of style." Eleanor realized the picture she painted was pretty grim. "I'm not exactly a femme fatale, Mrs. B."

"That's not what he sees," the old lady insisted. "The minute he walked through the door with those boxes, all those weeks ago, he couldn't get his eyes off you."

Eleanor leaned back on the tomb, supported by both arms, and looked up at the arches made by the leafy boughs. The graveyard was a lovely place, or would be if Margaret Brownlee would just remove herself from the premises. Nevertheless, the woman, in a moment of anger, just made her heart sing.

"He was rude and acted as if he didn't know me."

"He recognized you at once, and couldn't

understand why you were ignoring him."

"He flirted with June and Lynn."

"He tried to make you jealous."

Eleanor stopped, refusing to continue this nonsense. But if she were honest, she'd have to believe the words weren't exactly nonsense. He did make her jealous and resentful. She did vow to ignore him. Circumstances and his own disarming manner somehow turned her towards him. As circumstances, so many years ago, somehow turned him away.

"Evan Zane and I have a relationship; I won't deny that," she admitted. "But I did not set out to snare him or make him stay in Eastfield, and especially not so he could deny the shop the things you were falsely promised. If you listen to what you've said, you'll realize how ridiculous they sound."

Mrs. B.'s expression changed and Eleanor realized she said precisely the wrong thing. Whatever else the woman would tolerate—which was less and less—she could not abide being called ridiculous by Eleanor or anyone else. But the words could not be recalled, and Eleanor was certainly not in the mood to be gracious.

Over Mrs. B.'s well-padded shoulder, Eleanor saw the doors to the church swing open, and two young boys came out to stand sentry. Someone she didn't recognize, from the funeral home no doubt, walked out into the sunshine, frantically gesturing to someone just out of Eleanor's range of vision. She listened to the back-up beeps of a vehicle and hoped it was a hearse and not Paddy's Environmental Refuse Service. Or Wayne Durant, attempting to steal the pews from the hall.

"Did you seduce him for the antiques? For the treasures at Garland? You must answer me."

"Must I?" Eleanor said wearily. "You can think

whatever you want. I don't care anymore."

The simple pine casket came slowly through the door, carried by Mitch, Evan, and a few men she vaguely recognized. She shuddered in spite of the heat, remembering the awful day of Missy's funeral, when Missy's mother, in her grief, railed about the unfairness of life, why Eleanor should live and her daughter died. Eleanor remembered her own mother's arms gently coming around her and pulling her out and away.

So many years passed since someone sheltered her from insult and injury, protecting her. Perhaps her isolation was her own fault, for after the accident she grew up quickly, trusted less to good fortune, and turned inward. To her parents and brother, she probably appeared confident and successful, and for her children, she was always available. She couldn't now remember when anyone last held her as her mother did that day.

Until Evan came back to Eastfield, and her life changed. She saw him blink as he looked around for her, standing a little straighter than the other men, waiting patiently to deliver the casket into the hearse. Now that she knew and understood the man he had become, she could appreciate how the accident had worked a lingering stain on his psyche, as well. Something—guilt, perhaps, but more likely simple gratitude for survival—made him someone who wrapped his arms around others. He used his own handicaps to understand ways to help others. He more or less adopted her two children and some of their friends. He supported local charities and agencies. He answered Mitch's call for help.

And he embraced her, for all her faults. Not just in love and affection, but to offer her a refuge from her cares and troubles, and provide a haven of rest. She didn't know she longed for sanctuary until Evan offered her himself.

Evan finally found her, sitting in the graveyard, and motioned for her to join him. The procession to the cemetery would only take a few moments through town, scarcely enough time for the cars to cool down.

"I must go," Eleanor said. "It's been lovely chatting with you. We ought to do this more often."

Mrs. B. was not yet finished with her. "You've changed, Eleanor. You used to be so respectful of your elders. And now look at you, running after a man. And showing no respect to his family, either. You're sitting on one of the Zane tombs."

"I'm sure they'll forgive me. The man will probably forgive me as well." She slid off the cool stone of the tomb.

Mrs. B. finally took off her black straw hat, and her grey hair stuck up around her ears. She looked slightly deranged, and Eleanor spared a moment of pity for her. But just a moment.

"It's too bad there's no more room in this graveyard, and families now have to be separated in death," Mrs. B. said reverently. "Here are the Zanes, and there are the Hamiltons. Mr. Brownlee came to Eastfield when we married so there are no Brownlees here, but I was a Durant before I was married. We're in the eastern section of the graveyard, the most desirable spot of course."

"Yes, I suppose the sun always rises on the Durants." Eleanor paused, though Evan was giving her semaphore signs to get moving. "Is Wayne's father there as well? His mother?"

"Wayne?"

Eleanor stared at her for a moment. "Do you know many Waynes? I am speaking of your cousin."

"No. You won't find them there."

"Where would I find them? If I should happen to be interested?"

"Closer to home," Mrs. B. said cryptically. "Or a

home you apparently covet."

Eleanor needed a moment to make sense of this, and realized Mrs. B. apparently confirmed Mitch's carelessly tossed-out words. But Lilianna was no longer at Garland, the home Mrs. B. surely meant. Could she possibly believe Wayne's father was there?

"Just tell me, do you want the treasures of Garland for yourself or for The Thrifty Means?" Mrs. B. asked, answering one of Eleanor's questions.

"I haven't given any consideration at all to the contents of Garland. There's only one thing I desire there, and he has nothing to do with The Thrifty Means." Eleanor spoke quickly, because Evan was coming through the gate, looking tired and impatient. But no matter, he was the thing she wanted, after all.

"You need say no more," Mrs. B. said imperiously. "I now know where your priorities are, though I've suspected it for some time. I believe I think I speak for all of us when I say your services are no longer required at the shop. Please return your key by tomorrow morning."

Margaret Brownlee smiled broadly, a little madly, and backed away, right into Evan.

"Steady there, Mrs. Brownlee," he said. "Mrs. Pell is waiting for you, to drive you to the cemetery."

"I've had enough of cemeteries for one day. I think I'll just return to my shop," she said, and stumbled on a gravestone as she left them in the shaded grove.

****

"Her shop?" Evan asked. "Don't you have a stake in The Thrifty Means anymore?"

"No. I've just been fired," Eleanor said, and walked into his arms. He rested his chin on the top of her head, settling into her warmth and the smell of her fruity shampoo. He would have been happy to stay like this forever, but for the heat, and his sticky suit, and the dust, and the fact everyone was waiting for them.

"We've got to stop meeting like this," Eleanor said, and pushed back a bit. He looked down at her face and realized she looked weary and in pain.

"In a cemetery? I think this is something new for us. But I see your point. Come." He reluctantly separated himself from her, and reached for her hand. "We do need a change, something like dinner back at L'Avignon. Or a weekend in New York or Boston."

"I'm happy to take downtown Hartford." Eleanor bent her knee and slipped off her shoe to remove a pebble. "I would love to get away, but I'm not sure we ought to right now. Things seem to be happening right now."

"Because Mitch Ellison is here?" he asked, before he could stop himself.

"Mitch Ellison?" she asked and tossed the pebble towards the road. "I'm not sure I know what you mean."

He shrugged, feeling too stupid for words. "Come with me."

Eleanor remained where she was, one shoeless foot elevated behind her, and balanced on the other. "Tell me the truth. You don't actually think Mitch and I are...you're not jealous, are you?"

"Should I be?" he countered, knowing how obnoxious he sounded.

"You tell me. You could only be jealous if our future really matters to you," she said, dropping the shoe onto a bed of moss. Her foot wiggled it around to stand upright, and then she slipped the dark pump on, Cinderella without the prince.

Here he was, not much of a prince and not particularly charming, but if he waited for the perfect fairy tale moment, he might be single for another twenty years.

"Of course our future matters," he said, taking her hand, and weaving her damp fingers through his. "You matter. You're the reason why I'm here, why I'm going to stay. We'll find out what happened to my aunt, and why my things are showing up at The Thrifty Means, but nothing really matters to me except you. Really. We could be in a cemetery, at Ludlum's, or in a car with your kids and Sally barking her head off. It's where I want to be, as long as I'm with you." He cleared his throat, wondering if he dared to continue. What was she thinking? Why didn't she say anything? "I thought you knew that."

"How would I?" she asked, very quietly. He leaned closer, so his lips might have touched her forehead.

"Because I love you."

She stood very still, very pale, her lips slightly parted, her eyes not focused on anything. Had he ruined everything? Did she just want friendship when he wanted—needed—more? Did she only want to revisit their past, and put everything behind her at last? Was her interest, after all, only about The Thrifty Means?

Their lives were everything but a fairy tale, and yet the princess looked like she waited for release from her trance. He dared to move the last inch, and kissed her damp forehead.

"I love you too," she said, and it was an awful lot better than her coughing up a piece of undigested poison apple. "I love you too. I have for so many years."

"So what are we going to do?" he asked.

He heard the smile in her voice. "Nothing at the moment. This doesn't quite seem the place."

"You're right," he said. "But cemeteries have an effect on us, don't they? They make you realize every moment is precious and fleeting, and you've got to seize the day."

She leaned her head back, so her lips touched his. "Resorting to clichés, are you?"

He kissed her, long and hard. "No, just resolving to tell the truth."

Horns interrupted the sweet solitude of the cemetery, and Evan realized he already missed his place in the line of funeral cars. The hearse must be breaking into the stream of traffic, sobering the moods of drivers up and down Norwell Road.

"We better go," Eleanor said against his mouth.

He pulled back, and his eyes settled on his own name carved on a lichen-encrusted stone. Yes, the time had come to seize the day.

So he seized Eleanor, reaching for her hand still settled on his shoulder and pulling her from this place as much about life as about death.

"We'll take my car," she said, gesturing towards the far side of the lot. Wayne was standing beneath a tree in the woods abutting the parking area, looking like he hadn't a care in the world. He probably didn't.

"I wonder what he's doing here," Evan said.

"Well, as I told Mrs. B., funerals are open to the public. He may have known Muriel Ellison," Eleanor reasoned, as she pulled out her keys.

"I'm sure he did," Evan said, unpleasantly. He remembered their absurd wrestling match back at Garland, and was confident and almost eager to take him on again.

"No fighting," Eleanor said gently, as she ducked into the car.

How did she always seem to know what he was thinking? And yet a few minutes ago, he genuinely managed to surprise her. In fact, he surprised himself a little too. He got into the passenger side after glancing towards his Jeep. Of course, the car was unlocked but with Wayne standing around, perhaps the old rules didn't apply.

"He wouldn't dare steal your car. Everyone recognizes it," she said, proving his point once again.

"No, I was thinking about something else," he lied. "This might have been a good time to corner him and ask him a few questions."

Eleanor carefully backed out of the space, though his car was the only other one in the parking lot. She paused to adjust her seat belt, and then opened the windows. He studied her movements, far more interested in her than in Wayne, and appreciated how methodical she was, leaving nothing to chance. She waited an overlong time to merge into traffic, but he would not rush her. If he missed seeing Muriel Ellison delivered to her final rest, Mitch would just have to forgive him.

Eleanor finally edged out when a truck down the road stopped to make a turn, and she sighed, as if acknowledging a triumph of some sort.

"Is there a cemetery at Garland?" she asked.

"Not that I know of, aside from the place in the rose garden where we buried dogs, a few hamsters, and countless goldfish. You know the place. I suppose we'll need a section for cats now?"

"But nothing for people? Not even a few graves near a stone wall? Under the barn boards? Scattered in the woods?" Her eyes never left the road, even though they were at a stop light.

"Do you suspect my ancestors of something? Have you seen ghosts prowling the hillside?"

"I have ghosts enough," she said grimly, and he guessed he would recognize them. "But this is about something Margaret Brownlee said. I asked her who were Wayne's parents and she told me to look close to home. I think she meant to look close to your home."

He turned his head to look at her, and her face burn bright red. He wondered if the slip was hers, or

Mrs. Brownlee's.

"I don't know of any graves. She must mean Lilianna."

"But she was the one who arranged for Lilianna's move, so she knows she isn't there. Maybe she left behind some papers about his father? Maybe…"

"What?" Evan said impatiently. Somehow, spending even a minute talking about Wayne was a minute wasted.

"He's your father's son?"

"That's the meanest thing anyone's ever said to…"

"I'm so sorry. Really, Evan. I didn't mean to say anything bad about your father. The idea just came to me. I'm probably thinking too much like a novelist."

"I'm not thinking about the offense to my father. I'm thinking about the offense to me. If you think I'd be willing to claim Wayne Durant in any part as my brother, you don't know me very well."

"Any part?" she asked.

"Not a single hair on his brainless head," Evan said, with more bravado than he actually felt. What if she was right? His parents were always at odds with each other, and who knows what currents pulled them apart? His father never had the slightest interest in Wayne, who lived in Eastfield all the time. Why would Lilianna stay silent, if Wayne was a Zane relative?

"Then what could Mrs. B. mean? Do you have uncles, cousins, long lost nephews?"

"No one," Evan said. For once, the admission proved unaccompanied by the usual pang of loneliness. There was no one remaining in his history, but perhaps there would be Zanes in the future. "My mother had no one. And my father only had his brother who was married very, very briefly to Dorothea."

"He couldn't take it?"

"I guess not. He died."

For just a second, she allowed her eyes to stray from the road, as she turned to him and smiled. He wasn't sure whether he should be glad he had such ability, or sad because he just corrupted the safest driver in the state of Connecticut. One glance could lead to another and then before long, she would be talking on the cell phone, putting on makeup, reading a book. Just like everyone else on the road.

"Here we are," she said, and carefully pulled into the new cemetery with wider paths and younger trees. A cluster of cars lined the road high on the hill, and the voices of the mourners droned in chorus with the bees and other flying insects. "I hope we're not too late."

"Mitch will understand," Evan said. "So will Muriel, for that matter."

Eleanor pulled in behind a red convertible and turned off her car. "You didn't think so a few moments ago. I can't believe you believed Mitch and me..."

"Why not? You're both single. You greeted him at the train station like he was returning from war."

Eleanor gave him a look he didn't even know was in her vocabulary of body language. "I greeted him like an old friend, Evan."

"Which is more generous than the way you greeted me."

She flashed him a smile that more than made up for their rough beginning. "Mrs. B. insists she recognized what was between us from the moment you walked into The Thrifty Means. Could you imagine? But she always tells us she has a very good eye."

They sat silently for several moments in the hot car while the other mourners were consigning

Muriel Ellison to the rocky New England soil.

"I guess we should join them?" Evan asked, though he hoped she might say it wasn't necessary at all. Instead, she nodded and sighed, and pushed open the door. He met her at the front of the car, where the heat radiated off the hood and would incinerate them where they stood if they didn't get away quickly. He took her hand, and led her up the packed dirt road.

"When I came to the shop months ago, you looked like you didn't even know me," he mused.

"I wasn't sure I did." He hoped she had more to say, but they approached the party of mourners, and there was no time for anything else. Mrs. B. watched them approach and moved to the opposite side of the open grave. Mitch nodded in welcome. Miriam Pell rolled her eyes, and Evan wondered what Eleanor meant when she said Mrs. B. fired her.

They stood for another ten minutes, while some people sniffed and blew loudly into handkerchiefs and others secretly checked their watches. Mitch looked suitably grief stricken behind his large aviator sunglasses and edged closer and closer to a young woman with very large breasts. Evan glanced down at Eleanor, but she stood wrapped in her own musings, and noticed neither Mitch nor himself.

Finally, the burial was over, with a collective sigh of relief sounding like air escaping from a large balloon. Everyone converged on Mitch, even as he was inviting the group down to Ludlum's for lunch. Perhaps a few people—mostly the elderly ladies - would join him, but most were ready to get on with their day.

"We'll go, of course," Eleanor said.

"I was hoping you would say we could skip Ludlum's," Evan said almost at once, and she looked at him with an odd expression on her face. He realized what it was, and what she meant, of course.

Without any words spoken about their future, they already behaved like a married couple, looking for guidance in the other, doing things as one. Theirs was an unexpected revelation to share in a cemetery, but perhaps a shared tragic history made it less so. "Okay, you win. I'm hungry, anyway. But before we go, why don't we say hello to some old friends here."

She realized he didn't mean those clustered around the grave, and so she led him further up the hill to a small grove of pine trees, and to Missy's grave. What was once fresh and raw, now looked comfortably weathered in this idyllic spot. Someone had left white roses, now dried and scattered on the long grass. Something like a small teddy bear was as dark as the earth and barely distinguishable from the soil. Whatever remained of poor Missy was here, and would be here long after those who remembered her were gone.

"I think of her all the time. I just can't help myself," Eleanor said.

Evan didn't know what to say, or how to give comfort for someone so long grieved and events so long regretted. So he said nothing at all, and somehow provided just what Eleanor needed.

"Would you like to go to your parents?" she asked.

"How did you know they were here?" He supposed it really wasn't much of a question. Most of Eastfield's burials were in this large nonsectarian place, close to the river that attracted the first settlers in the area.

She glanced at him, her expression unreadable. "I've been here to see them."

"Thank you," he said.

"Unless you'd rather go by yourself?"

"I'd like you to join me, if you don't mind. You're a part of this too." This time he led the way, knowing the spot, though he was still in the hospital when his parents were buried all those years ago. He supposed Eleanor believed he meant she was part of the events that took their lives, but he actually wanted to stand with her at his parents' grave and somehow ask for their approval.

"Here they are," he said tightly, and pulled her down onto the marble bench he had erected when he finished his Masters degree. While most of his friends received gifts from their parents, he was obliged to give back to them.

Eleanor dropped his hand and pressed her palms behind her on the bench. Her stance gave him a very fine view of certain parts of her anatomy, but even he understood this was not the place and not the time to do anything about it.

"They have a lovely stone, very romantic," she said.

He supposed so. Dorothea insisted on a double stone, with the two names connected by a wreath of ivy. "I guess there's irony that two people who turned from each other in every way should be intertwined for all time. No one would ever guess they hadn't a thing in common."

"They had you," she reminded him. "You should have been enough."

Her belief was more than enough. He hugged her a little awkwardly, and looked around at the surrounding graves. Uncle Peter was a few plots over, quite alone, and now truly remembered by no one.

"I would like to have children," Evan said, without really thinking how Eleanor would respond.

She hesitated, just perceptibly, and said, "They change your perspective on everything. Your life is never entirely the same, and never entirely yours again. It's a very fine thing, really. Whatever your parents said, whatever they argued about, please be certain having you made all the difference to them."

He had nothing to say, but to think back once again to his parents' last fight, which was somehow about him but also about so much else His father resented his mother's writing, she resented the time he spent playing golf. Money was never tight, but somehow always an issue. Neither of them wanted the responsibility of dealing with their son's handicap. They would either give up on him, or pass him off to someone else.

Evan looked up at the sky, his eyes protected by his sunglasses. A hawk glided above them, probably looking for any tiny things displaced by the digging of the grave. Down the hill, on Norwell Road, a car horn sounded, insistent and rude.

"I know who Wayne's father is," he said. Eleanor stirred beside him and her thigh brushed against his for one electric moment. "It's Peter, my uncle."

"Are you saying this to startle me? You have a habit of doing this, and I'm not sure I appreciate it." Eleanor turned to face him, her nose practically touching his. "What makes you think about him, and now of all times?"

"I'm just remembering something my mother said, in the minute before...it's just something my mother once said. And when you asked me if Wayne was my father's son, you got me thinking. After all, we look a little alike."

"Oh, good heavens," she protested. "Wayne is disgusting. And you're..."

She broke off as he gave her a quick kiss, the barest touch, nothing more.

"Not," she finished.

"I accept the compliment. But really, we have the same coloring, are about the same height. The day I pulled him out of the fire, I looked at his hand, and for a weird moment, I believed it was my hand. His is just the same shape as mine."

"You're delusional, Mr. Zane. We have to get you

out of the heat. Let's go have lunch."

"No, wait. My mother said something about Margaret taking care of Peter's problem, and maybe she'd take care of my father's problem as well."

Eleanor stood, and looked warily down at him. "Why Margaret? What would she have to do with Peter and Dorothea and Lilianna?"

"Why Dorothea?" he countered. "She was practically a stranger, and she wasn't actually my aunt. What had she to do with any of this?"

Eleanor gave a gesture of impatience, one he'd seen her use on her kids. "Mitch must be wrong about Lilianna. Dorothea was married to your uncle. If Wayne's a year older than we are, and Peter died when you were little, then Wayne is also Dorothea's."

"Sweet, innocent Ellie Gilmartin," Evan said, standing and giving her the kiss she really deserved. "Sometimes men have children with women who aren't their wives. I know such things are unheard of in Eastfield, but it's not so unusual in the Big Bad Apple. Come to think of it, Dorothea and Peter were living in Manhattan at the time."

"I'm not so innocent," she said, her response to his kiss giving him proof. "And I don't know anyone who would say I'm sweet. But what you're describing is such a betrayal."

Not for the first time, Evan wondered what happened between her and the lout she married.

"How about someone marries a woman, and finds out she prefers other women? Would that also count as a betrayal?"

"Maybe even a more unsettling one. The truth shifts the foundation of everything you believed about another person. I would imagine it's devastating." Eleanor gave him a sharp look, and frowned. "But you're supposing your uncle also had a relationship with Lilianna?"

He shook his head, not in denial but in ignorance. How would he ever have guessed any of this would be even mildly important in the years to come? When he was a kid, he was happy to spend his days playing in the woods and fields at Garland, creating a universe in which he didn't have to read, or worry about his next test. He didn't remember his uncle, and scarcely recalled Dorothea when she arrived in Eastfield the day after his parents were killed, grimly prepared to do her duty. Before then, he saw them only on some faded photographs.

"Yes," he said. "I think there's a picture of my uncle standing between Lilianna and Dorothea, hugging them both. I never really considered the meaning of that before."

"So, what is the meaning?"

"I have no idea. I'll show you the picture when we go back to Garland, and you can figure everything out. Maybe there's a secret message folded into the frame, or a family genealogy printed on the cardboard. Or do such things only happen in books?"

"I'm not sure. They happen all the time at The Thrifty Means. They just don't seem to happen when you really need it."

She gave him an unreadable look, and then looked down into her handbag to pull out a water bottle. Not for the first time, he wondered how much weight she typically carried around in the quilted thing, because she always had what was needed for any occasion. As she sipped, he studied the pale line of her neck and the sprinkling of freckles across her collarbone, tempting him to forget about lunch and feast right here in the cemetery instead. She finished and licked her lips as she offered him the bottle, looking like she understood just what he was thinking.

"My house was broken into yesterday," she said,

as if the news hardly mattered.

"Broken into? Why didn't you call me? What's missing? What..."

She held up a hand and then flattened her palm against his shirt, over his heart.

"I'm not sure it counts as a break-in if the house is not locked to begin with. I never lock my door. But when I came home, I saw something was wrong. The curtains in the front window were drawn a little carelessly, and a light was on in the kitchen. I called the police."

"Was anything missing?" he asked, and put his hand over hers.

"Nothing, which is why the police are unconcerned. Even when I told them about the curtains and the light and True Blue."

"The bird? Is he..."

"Fine. Just fine. But when I came home, he was up in a tree. I don't see how he would have gotten out of his cage and out of the house when all the windows are closed. And why let him out, anyway?"

"Maybe it was the old geezer who was looking for him."

"Wouldn't he have just taken him? Assuming he even knew where the bird was?"

Evan remembered the unpleasant conversation with the man back at The Thrifty Means, and who might have been listening.

"Wayne?" he said.

Eleanor nodded. "I think so, too. But I can hardly say as much to the police, can I? I mean, I can't accuse a guy just because he says disgusting things and always seems to be connected to some sort of trouble. Everything is just circumstantial."

"It's a little too much of a coincidence, even for the Eastfield police. But at the moment, they may be thinking the same thing about me. I told them I had suspicions about Dorothea's death. And then

Wayne's cottage burned. And when Mitch's grandmother dies, he stays with me. And now your house is broken into—or, at least, entered—and you and I are an item. The Eastfield police may be feeling a little disgruntled if they might actually have to do something."

"What will happen if they never find the answers?" she asked. "Not every mystery is solved. They can't seem to find any evidence of anything."

Evan just shook his head, not knowing where the story would all end. He realized he was still holding her water bottle and raised it high to take a long drink, more than was probably fair. "There. This is will be lighter for you to carry," he said.

"Keep it," she said, turning her back. She squinted into the sun, where a farm meadow met the old stone wall of the cemetery. They listened to the growl of a car engine starting up, stalling, and starting again. "I'll buy another bottle at Ludlum's."

Somehow, she made him feel like he owed her more than a bottle of spring water. "Even if we don't find the answer, I'd like you to stay at Garland for a while. Bring up Sally and the bird, at least until Lewis and Leslie get home. I don't like the idea of you being alone on Milkweed Lane. Besides, there's still lots of work to do at Garland."

"Yes, there is," she answered, over her shoulder. She started down towards the car, the only one left on the narrow road. "But that won't last forever. And when we finish going over Dorothea's notes and ledgers, and poke in every one of her drawers and coat pockets and have thrown out all the junk, we'll be finished. And old ladies will still be dying in this town, and Wayne will still be bringing rare and lovely things to The Thrifty Means. And Margaret can boast about how successful she is as our shop manager."

Evan paused, as the oddest notion tickled his

imagination. He dismissed the idea quickly, for there were more important things to be said.

"Dorothea's notes won't last forever, but we will," he said. She turned to face him, and he realized this was as good a time as any. He might have planned a candlelit dinner at L'Avignon. He might have put an engagement ring between the pages of the ledger. He might have taken out an ad in *The Eastfield Edition*. He might have done any of the million things he imagined in the last few weeks, creative and irresistible ways to get a woman he loved to marry him.

But he'd never get a better time than this. He glanced down at the rich earth, and decided to forgo the bended knee deal.

"Ellie," he began, and cleared his throat. "Ellie, I want to make what we have last forever. This affair never had anything to do with Dorothea's old clothes and chipped pots. It was always about you. When I saw you in The Thrifty Means, I was ready to drop everything, and do what I've wanted to do since we were kids in high school."

"You always say that," she said gently. "But all you had to do then was ask me for a date. It might have solved all your problems. And mine."

He laughed, wondering why he imagined he needed a special moment. Every moment with Eleanor Gilmartin was special.

"I guess you don't know as much as you think about high school boys."

"I have a son," she reminded him.

"And sons don't tell their mothers everything." Evan paused, thinking of his own mother, and realizing how very much he missed her all these years. "What I wanted in high school was to have sex. The dates are just the excuse to get to the point."

"And that's why you're asking me to..."

"Marry me? No, because I'm not a teenage boy anymore. The movies and the popcorn and the dinners together are all part of the deal. So are family vacations and figuring out our taxes. Hell, I'll even throw in some driving lessons for your kids and helping them through college. I want the whole damned thing."

"You really are so romantic, you know," she said dryly.

She stood studying him for several moments, looking as if this was something she somehow never considered, as if he hadn't made everything clear in a hundred ways how he loved her. Now he was so close, he was impatient, as if the weight of all these years held him captive.

"I love you," he said, a little desperately.

She nodded, just perceptibly, and he realized he ought to have no doubts she already understood perfectly. "I want the whole damned thing also."

And so it was done, in an instant, without fireworks or French food. The ring could wait. The crowd at Ludlum's could wait. She dropped her bag, came into his arms, and kissed him.

"I love you too," she said, when she came up for air.

"Do you think the kids will be surprised?"

"Do you think anyone will be surprised?" she asked. "My friends are already looking for wedding gowns to come into The Thrifty Means. Gail told me she has someone already in my little house."

Evan leaned down to kiss her again, when the sound of a car horn blasted through the silence.

"I guess those are our fireworks," he said.

"What?"

"Never mind. Let's wait 'til the kids are back this weekend and talk to them before we say anything to anyone else. Is there any chance they'll be unhappy about this?"

"I think they're quite ready to move in with you whether I come or not. So the answer is no. There's no chance. But we should let them know first." She stopped to pick up a pebble and placed it on top of a grave out of alignment with the rest. Before Evan could ask her why, she went on. "Of course, this means there's the possibility Mitch or Wayne could make a move before it's public knowledge. You're taking a big chance, Mister."

He laughed as they walked together down the hill, knowing he had no competition. Though the thought was absurd, and wholly conceited, he somehow imagined she had been waiting for him, all these years, while he was wandering about without realizing his home was in Eastfield. Now, he had arrived. When he and Ellie were ready, when the children he already considered his own were ready, they would share the news with everyone else in town.

Nearly everyone would be excited about their news, and wish them well.

But a small, nagging, insistent voice spoke up from the edges of his imagination and reminded him once this news was out, whoever was responsible for Dorothea's and Muriel's death, whoever had been selling off pieces of his estate for years, whoever entered Ellie's house, might make a move even more quickly than the news would spread around Eastfield.

Chapter 15

"The trick to shopping at antique shops is patience. When something sells, you can be sure it will return to the market twenty years later, and twenty years after that. You just have to wait and watch and seize your opportunity. And live a long time."

Eleanor Gilmartin, the only volunteer ever fired from The Thrifty Means

Evan might have regretted the lack of fireworks going off above their heads, when in fact fireworks were going off in her head. As Eleanor walked alongside him to the car, reliving the bold and passionate scene between them, she could barely contain her happiness.

Why should she? She married once for what she imagined was love, and spent years recovering from the bruising of the relationship. While she healed, she devoted herself to her children and to her career, and volunteered in the community that always gave her so much support. Now here was the man she wanted from the time he was a boy, willing to share her troubles and pleasures with her, and offering her a joyful future. She was a strong and independent woman, who had no idea she needed rescuing. Fully confident, she realized she could not resent anything at all.

"Do you want me to drive?" Evan asked, and raised his hand to catch her car keys.

"Are you afraid to ride with me?" she asked,

playfully, and walked to the driver's side of her car.

"Considering you let me ride with your kids all over town, you must know I've developed nerves of steel." He met her eyes over the roof of the car. "No, I just wondered of you were a little...distracted."

Eleanor smiled at his choice of words, loving him even more. Distracted? She most certainly was distracted. Surely he understood her well enough to know once she got behind the wheel, she was assiduously focused on the road ahead of her.

"No, I'm okay. I was just wondering if I should take Beecher Road or Langhorne Court."

"How could you take Langhorne? Isn't the street a dead end?"

"You really have been out of town, Mister. They extended the road years ago, and built another ten houses." She ducked into the car and its wretched heat, though the windows were open and she parked in the shade.

Evan slipped in beside her. "They could probably build fifty at Garland. I have nearly a hundred acres."

"I know," she said as she started the engine. She waited a few moments, and then turned on the air conditioning. "There was a lot of speculation you'd sell after Dorothea died. The land is worth a lot of money, you know."

He grinned at her. "I may have been out of town, but not out of touch. We could sell the old place and buy anything we wanted, anywhere. But you don't want to leave Eastfield, do you?"

She heard the slight unease in his voice, and reassured him immediately. "Eastfield is home to both of us, Evan. Garland is a big home, to be sure, but I can't think of anywhere I'd rather be."

"Maybe we can start to fill it up. Sally probably needs a room to herself, just for all the tennis balls she gathers. And then we'll need a place for True

Blue, away from the cats. We can get him a few friends, so he's not the only one around with feathers."

Eleanor looked over her shoulder, and backed her car down to the narrow strip of pavement passing for a road in a cemetery. She caught the flash of reflected metal moving through the field on the other side of the stone wall, and wondered if David North was out on his tractor. Perhaps the tractor made the sound they heard a few moments ago. Then she noticed a white hearse come through the cemetery gate and considered perhaps one of the mourners had taken a wrong turn.

"Perhaps there's another funeral," Evan said. "A child's, with a white hearse."

Eleanor nodded. "Someone told me the story the other day. The family just moved to town, and their baby was very sick from the time he was born. They realized he didn't have much time, but this is where they wanted him to be buried, so they could visit him. Nothing could be sadder." She drove down the slope of the hill, waited for the brief funeral procession to pass, and edged out onto Norwell Road.

"So, which way should I go, do you think?"

"I think you should go past the reservoir and take the shortcut onto Charter Oak Road," Evan said. Eleanor refused to give in to her feelings of dread about the street. Every time she drove there, she had to confront her nightmare all over again. "What are their names?"

"Whose?" she asked.

"The couple whose baby died," he said slowly, enunciating every syllable.

"I don't know," Eleanor said, but knew she would eventually find out, for they would inevitably meet. "But I do know she's pregnant again."

Evan banged gently on the window. "You know everything about a couple's private life, but don't know their names? Doesn't that seem a little odd to you?"

Eleanor bristled. "No. It's not odd if you're in Eastfield. And especially not if you're a volunteer at The Thrifty Means. The shop is not only a clearinghouse for antiques and clothes, but the switchboard for all gossip."

She made a right turn onto Reservoir Drive and waited for him to say something about her choice. Instead, he stared out the window at the gardens and pools and elegant colonial homes, and then he spoke about something else.

"What do you mean, she fired you? Can you fire a volunteer?"

Eleanor laughed, though she was miserable about the whole business. "It might be unprecedented, but I suppose stranger things have happened. Margaret Brownlee runs the shop. She could do anything she wants."

"But she's a volunteer too, isn't she?"

"Yes, of course. She's affluent, and certainly doesn't need the money. But she's been doing her job for years." Eleanor paused, thinking about the discussion in recent weeks, as more and more of her co-workers expressed their disenchantment with Mrs. B. What would happen if she left? What would happen if someone asked her to leave?

"What would happen if someone asked her to leave?" Evan said, precisely echoing her thoughts.

Though Eleanor had asked the same question, she hadn't yet come up with an answer. She studied the road as she considered the situation.

"We would probably repaint the back room, and make the work area brighter. Perhaps carry toys and children's furniture, to appeal to a younger crowd."

Evan tapped the window again, but Eleanor's eyes didn't leave the road. "I don't mean what would happen to The Thrifty Means. What would happen to Margaret?"

Eleanor knew the answer; they all did. "She would be absolutely devastated. The shop means everything to her. She once said the only way she would leave would be flat on her back. I think she means what she says, because she repeats, 'Over my dead body' often enough."

"And what's the greatest threat to her job security? Aside from you, that is. She probably thinks she was saving herself by letting you go. But I bet when Miriam and Lisa and the gang find out, there's going to be trouble."

"I hadn't gotten so far, but you're probably right. Margaret does very well for the shop, and it's hard to argue with success." Eleanor glanced in the rearview mirror, though she believed there was no one around her, and slowed to let a squirrel decide whether to cross the road.

"And if she started to slip? If business was down? If people stopped bringing in donations?"

What would happen? If The Thrifty Means, a successful business on the Eastfield landscape for nearly sixty years, started to fail, wouldn't the board look to replace the president?

As she followed the road to the left, she came into brilliant sunshine, where trees were sacrificed for new housing construction. Just a few remained, at well-spaced intervals and a few yards in from the road. There were many reasons to regret the loss of hundred-year-old oaks and maples, but at the moment, Eleanor felt nothing but annoyance at the loss of the leafy canopy. Even wearing her sunglasses, she could barely see the road. Again, she slowed, and noticed the flash of a car coming towards her. She honked her horn, though she guessed the other driver, with the sun behind him, had better vision.

"What if people stopped giving donations?" Eleanor repeated. "Well, I suppose Margaret Brownlee would do almost anything at all to bring them in. Put ads in *The Eastfield Edition*. Speak to the Chamber of Commerce. Beg at people's doors. Anything."

As the implication of her words hit her, she felt the closeness of the air, the heat beating down on the roof of the car, the blinding pain of the sun. This was the answer then. Margaret embarked on a campaign to save her reputation and her position. Was murdering her old friends in their beds part of her mission?

Eleanor dared to glance away from the road, wondering if Evan was thinking what she was.

"Ellie!" he yelled.

A car, a pick-up truck, was coming at them on the same side of the road. Evan lunged across the seat to grab the wheel, but she was already in control. She swerved off the road, just as the pick-up passed them, nicking the headlight but otherwise missing them. They tumbled along the grassy embankment for some yards before coming to a stop, and she managed to avoid fresh tree stumps and downed branches, hitting nothing that could really matter.

Her heart, however, thumped on the outer wall of her chest, and she closed her eyes, thinking her way out of a panic attack. She did well, she told herself. They were in danger, but she did well. They were unharmed and would be just fine once the moments of sheer terror and relief abated.

Next to her, Evan cursed like a Brooklynite and struggled with his seatbelt.

Was she wrong? Were they in danger? She opened her eyes, and realized he was half out of the car.

"Where are you going?" she said, in a hoarse

voice. Her throat hurt, and she realized she might have been screaming from the moment they left the road. "Don't leave me!"

"Stay here," he said tersely, ducking his head back into the car. "Just stay right here."

"I will..." Eleanor had no idea what was about to pop out of her mouth, but her words scarcely mattered because Evan was gone. She looked in her rear view mirror and saw cars stopped on the road, and people running around. On the pavement, surrounded by waves of radiating heat, a large tire was spiraling very slowly until coming to a stop.

How had she been able to steer the car without a tire?

Eleanor was chilled, as if she was once again living a long ago autumn night before Halloween, as gas and oil and blood seeped through the jagged remains of two cars. She crawled out of the wreck then, and saved Evan Zane. And now he abandoned her.

But Lewis and Leslie needed her, and Sally and the cats and True Blue needed her, and she had a book to finish. She was not going to stay here and die. With determined, shaking fingers, she released her seat belt.

And opened her car door with no more drama than if she had just stepped out into the parking lot of the Village Market.

She was not going to die. Not today, anyway.

She looked over the roof of her car and realized why everyone was yelling. If she hadn't been in a slightly deranged state, she might have remembered there was another car, the one that came right at her and pushed her off the road.

Surely the tire, finally come to rest, belonged to the other car. And there was the hood, crushed on the side of the road. A twisted frame of metal looked like it was climbing up the side of one of the last remaining oaks.

And there was Wayne Durant, lying in a pool of blood, as his fellow travelers in the town of Eastfield shed every spare item of clothing they wore on this uncommonly hot day to cover him and keep him warm. From a distance came the wail of sirens.

Evan, still dressed for the funeral, shrugged off his suit jacket, and dropped it over Wayne's unmoving body, into the blood and dirt. He raised his hand to his forehead, where Eleanor noticed a stream of blood. Evan looked around for a moment or two before his eyes settled on her.

And, absurdly, he smiled.

****

"Is that all you have to tell us?" Leslie asked in disbelief. The twins and Evan sat at the kitchen table while Sally accompanied Eleanor back and forth from the stove. If you were a dog, you lived in eternal hope a chicken wing or meatball might tumble off the serving tray and become fair game.

"What more would you like to hear?" Eleanor asked, settling the tray on the table. Sally walked back to the stove and waited. "I mean, Evan and I are in a car accident in almost the same spot where we were nearly killed years ago, and you're waiting to hear the punch line?"

Leslie glanced at Lewis. "But you're okay, right? And Wayne is going to be all right?"

"He'll be recovering for a while. I don't think he'll be hauling around other people's furniture anytime soon," Evan said as he helped himself to chicken. He preferred white meat, Eleanor noted, which would be very convenient in this dark-meat only family. "But what news were you expecting?"

Eleanor sat down and gave him a look of warning. Such things needed gradual introduction, with lots of preparation.

"Oh, just something more important than a car

accident. Mom tells us about car accidents all the time," Leslie said.

"And there's a reason she does," Evan said in a serious tone. The twins looked at him warily. "You see how dangerous it is to be on the road, driving. You never can trust other drivers. You never know when a deer is going to dash across the road. You have to watch for ice and flooding and oil slicks."

The twins looked down at their plates and no one said a word. In the living room, True Blue chirped happily. Two of the new kittens were staring up at his cage, possibly gauging the odds of getting the door open.

"Well, I have other news," Eleanor said cheerfully, realizing she probably sounded a bit like Blue. "Margaret Brownlee has retired from The Thrifty Means, under some duress. And I've been nominated to replace her as shop manager."

"Don't you have enough to do, Mom?" Lewis said grumpily.

"Well, I figured with the two of you driving soon, you won't need me to do all your errands. And in a couple of years when you go off to college, I'll be..."

In unison, as they did all their lives, her twins opened their mouths and turned to Evan.

Evan dropped his fork and started to raise his hands in a gesture of surrender.

"Look, Mom," Lewis said, finally joining the conversation. "I'm sorry to hear about that guy, and I'm happy you're going to be manager of The Thrifty Means so you can boss everyone else around when we're in college, but we really expected some other news."

"Muriel Ellison died," Eleanor said.

Lewis made a gesture of impatience with his fork. As a piece of chicken flew off, Sally positioned herself, open-mouthed.

"Look you two. Why don't you just come out and

ask?" Evan said, and waited a split second before continuing. "Your mother and I have come to an...understanding...and we want to discuss this with you. The truth is..."

"Can I be your maid-of-honor, Mom?" Leslie asked.

"Can I borrow your Jeep, Evan?" Lewis asked at the same moment.

Eleanor acted as if she didn't hear them. "Evan and I have been thinking of getting married and we won't do anything until we're sure you're both happy with the new arrangement. This is a big change for our family, a big adjustment, and we have to move slowly, so there are no surprises. We'll have to figure out where to live."

"Garland!" the twins said as one.

Eleanor felt a little pang of regret, along with the realization her children might have felt somewhat deprived living in their little house and modest property. "You didn't like growing up here?"

Leslie made a typical teenage gesture to suggest the idea was absurd. "We love Milkweed Lane, Mom. We'll miss being so close to town and able to walk everywhere. But soon we'll be able to drive. We wondered if maybe you'd just rent this house when we move to Garland and then when Lewis or I come back to town after college, we could live here."

The twins looked at Evan, and Eleanor had a suspicion the three of them discussed this before. If so, she was letting herself in for some conspiracies in her own home—wherever they lived.

"I see everything's all decided," she said tersely.

"Except for one thing," Evan said, and reached into his pocket. Sally stood at his side, perhaps expecting him to pull out a brisket.

Eleanor was no less anxious, even after guessing what he held, but still wasn't fully prepared for the rush of pleasure.

"I bought it at The Thrifty Means," Evan said, and slipped the antique ring on her finger, over the plate of the grilled chicken. "Your good friends there tipped me off when it was appraised and became available. Somehow, they figured I would find some use for it. And by the way, as the new manager, you'll be happy to know this purchase should pay for the paint job you were talking about. Liza and Miriam were going to pick out the color this afternoon."

"Aside from my parents and brother, is there anyone left to tell?" Eleanor murmured.

"Probably not," Evan and Leslie and Lewis said at once.

****

The night would have been special in any case, but the twins offering to do the dishes made it extraordinary. Evan suggested some romantic spots around town where they could be alone for a while, but Eleanor decided there was no place lovelier than Garland itself. They picked up flashlights in his house, and set off for the path along the banks of the river. The night was cool, and Evan easily slipped his arm over her shoulders. For a moment, the light reflected off the brilliant facets of the diamond on her finger.

"Do you really think we can be happy?" she asked. "We've been surrounded by so much tragedy and sadness. Car accidents and death and..."

"And madness?"

"Madness?" Eleanor asked. "Or just being resentful? I think Wayne was always angry and cruel. But now I wonder if his misdeeds are the result of his upbringing, unwanted and alone. You could have become that way also, after the accident. After all, Dorothea resented her own sense of duty and took her feelings out on you."

"Dorothea's sense of duty was nothing to

Lilianna's belated maternal instincts, such as they were. I went to see her yesterday, hoping I would catch her at a lucid moment If I could believe what she told me, it all makes sense. In a strange and weird way." He paused and snapped off a twig blocking their path.

"Well, aren't you going to tell me?" Eleanor asked impatiently.

"Didn't we just agree we have the rest of our lives?" Evan asked, and she elbowed him in the ribs.

"Not yet. I need all the facts before I can decide whether I even want to marry into this family."

"Well, what I'm going to tell you isn't going to alleviate your doubts. Lilianna told me she and Dorothea were friends as girls, often hanging out with Lilianna's older cousin."

"Margaret."

"And my Uncle Peter. He had a crush on Lilianna, but she wasn't interested in him. I know exactly how he felt."

"Oh please. You're not going to bring this up all the time, are you? I mean, you hardly spoke to me in high school. How was I supposed to know you even liked me?"

"Well, at least I didn't marry your best friend. No, sorry I said anything. But Peter married Dorothea and they moved to New York. And Lilianna followed them, and got an apartment in the same building." Evan coughed, a little too obviously. "Should I go on? You'll never marry me after hearing this story."

"But I think I know everything already. Lilianna became pregnant, and Peter died after the baby— Wayne—was born. The two women were on their own again, and at the start of a career on the stage, and the baby was just in the way. So they sent him up to Lilianna's cousin to raise. Poor Wayne."

"What about poor Peter? I wonder if those two

witches killed him."

"And why not? Murder seems to be the family business."

"But not my side of the family. I wouldn't be surprised if Lilianna and Margaret were tempted to get rid of me. After all, Wayne is the only blood relative left and with DNA tests and all, could probably make a claim on Garland. He would empty the house, bring everything of value to The Thrifty Means, and sell the property to a developer. Margaret would get the prestige, the shop would have a banner year, Wayne and his mother would get the money, and everyone would be happy."

"But Dorothea wasn't, I think."

"The old girl had a conscience, as it turns out. When I was in the hospital, Lilianna and Wayne must have realized how close they were to getting what they wanted. They sent Dorothea down to see me, to get me to sign over everything to her. Instead, for whatever reasons, she just left everything there. Maybe she just couldn't go through with it."

"But if Wayne is really your cousin, then she didn't really stand in his way, did she?"

"I didn't have a will in those days. Her claim was probably as strong, and Wayne must have realized that. So they started to wear down her resistance, her health, her sanity. The cats were only the first step."

"Why didn't she ask for your help?" Eleanor asked, sickened to believe such a thing could happen in their town. "Why didn't you come?"

"I'm not going to make excuses, and now I have something else to feel guilty about. But she didn't want me. She never did." He tightened his hold on her, and his flashlight skimmed a little wildly over the running water. "She loved Lilianna. And I guess love makes you do irrational things."

"I know, dear. After all, I'm willing to marry

you, crazy family and all," Eleanor said. It was a sign of their almost perfect understanding when he took such a comment for an endearment, and kissed her forehead.

"And I'm willing to marry you, The Thrifty Means, and all," he said. "I hope you figure out a better method of getting donations than killing off the elderly and infirm."

"I already have. Our plan is to marry guys who own houses full of antiques. What do you think? It could be pretty effective."

"Who do you have in mind for Mitch? Liza?"

Eleanor realized he couldn't see her smile in the dark, but the match had already crossed her mind.

"Do we know it was Margaret?" she asked instead.

"I only have Wayne's word, which I guess is about as reliable as his old truck. He says Margaret went into Dorothea's room, and left few minutes later. That's all he'll tell me. I tried to get more out of him, but then the police made me leave. They probably suspected I was going to pull a few of his plugs."

"The police?"

"He ran us off the road, and was stupid enough to do the deed with witnesses. They claimed he did not accidentally lose control of the car, and now the police think so too."

"He would have killed us." Eleanor stopped walking, too weary to continue. It was all too much, too unbearable.

Evan urged her forward, pulling on her arm. He was right, of course. They had to move beyond this, as they had done before.

"But he didn't kill us," Evan said, all of the humor gone from his voice. "You were driving, and you saved our lives. You did, Ellie."

They left the footpath along the river, and

turned towards the broad meadows once farmed by so many generations of Zanes. Who could guess what jealousies and frustrations framed their stories? The simple beauty of the land belied the ugliness of human relations, the messiness of life. Here she was with Evan, feeling a joy much belated but sweeter than she could have ever imagined.

"Mitch told me Margaret Brownlee had tea with his grandmother on the day she died. But the police could find nothing, other than her fingerprints on the teacup, to suggest she was guilty of anything. I guess she just happened to be in the right place at the wrong time."

"Eastfield's very own Angel of Death. I hope she stays away from Garland." Eleanor spoke sincerely, but really preferred Margaret Brownlee to stay away from The Thrifty Means. "I wonder what she's going to do in her retirement? Other than complain to anyone who'll listen about what a lousy job I'm doing at the shop."

"Maybe she'll write a book about all this. She doesn't have a high opinion of either of us, so she probably thinks she can do one better," Evan said cheerfully. "You never know. We could all find ourselves doing a book signing together some day."

"There's a scary thought. But you forget I'll be very busy at The Thrifty Means. I don't know when I'll find the time to write." Eleanor was thinking a writer always finds time to write, even with two babies in the house, or while taking on other responsibilities, or while spending time with a new lover. "After all, the shop is one of the great traditions of Eastfield."

Evan turned off his flashlight and looked up at the dark sky. Somewhere, perhaps in Rosemont, a shaft of light etched the night, calling attention to a new car dealership or supermarket. Together, she and Evan might hold off the encroaching development into the lovely Connecticut woods and meadows. They would have to meet this challenge as well as so many others in their future.

"I hope we might consider starting a few of our own," he said, still intent on the sky. "I have the feeling there are many people here who have been watching us and waiting; who expect great things of us, apart and together. I wouldn't want to disappoint them."

Eleanor laughed, because she understood exactly what he meant. For all that, the story wasn't about anyone else but them, their family, and the home they would make together. She turned off her flashlight and pulled his arm around her shoulders, like a familiar and much loved shawl. To the north, along the river valley, the distant sparks of fireworks punctuated the night.

About the Author

A writer for most of her life, Sharon Sobel is the author of several published novels, short stories, and many essays. She earned a PhD in English and American Literature from Brandeis University and is currently a professor of English at Norwalk Community College in Connecticut, where she actively tutors aspiring student writers and has chaired the annual Writers' Conference. She is a member of the Board of Directors of Romance Writers of America, a founding member of its Connecticut and Lower New York chapter, and is a past president of The Beau Monde, the national chapter devoted to the interests of writers of the Regency period.

A native New Yorker, Sharon also lived in Boston and The Hague before moving to an eighteenth-century farm in Connecticut with her husband and family.

Thrifty Means is very loosely based on some of her experiences as a long-time volunteer and president of The Turnover Shop of Wilton, Connecticut. It is not a place where one is likely to find murder, mayhem, or romance, but it enjoys an excellent reputation as a place to find a great bargain. In its sixty-year history, the wonderful women of the Turnover Shop have contributed over a million dollars to local charities and remain committed volunteers and good friends.

Breinigsville, PA USA
07 November 2010
248818BV00006B/1/P